Another Sunset

Jason Zandri

This book is dedicated to my kids:

Andrew, Angela, Adam, and Alex.

Four amazing children who completed my life by making every day a living adventure and enriched my own experiences in ways I never imagined possible.

I can't wait to see what they do tomorrow.

I also want to dedicate this book to my high school creative writing teacher **Nicholas Vamvakis** who used to give me a generous supply of rope. Not because he figured I'd hang myself with it, but because he was curious what I would do with all of it.

Chapter One

The warm morning sun came through the passenger window of the Peterbilt 379 as it made its way up Route 385.

Peter Dempsey glanced at the clock on the dashboard as it rolled to 7:00 and then looked at his passenger as he began to slow up his speed just a bit as the western route took a turn back to true west and the morning sun moved back to the rear of the big rig.

"Are you awake?" he asked with a voice that was just slightly louder than the din of the engine and the roar of the tires on the road. "We're just about here," he added as he rubbed the week old brown and gray stubble on his face.

David Stephenson opened his eyes and peered from his position out the dusty passenger window to the open fields of dirt and scrub brush alongside the state road as the truck pulled into the small township.

The four-lane State Route 385 that went through the town dropped down to a two-lane road as they entered the town center.

David straightened his five foot eight frame up a bit in his seat and looked over to the man that had been giving him a ride for the better part of the last day, and then looked back out the windows of the truck.

"Well, it does look from here to be exactly the way you described it," David said as he scratched his short brown hair.

David saw a number of small storefronts with residential dwellings above on the south side of the road. A few small storefronts dotted the northern side of the road, but they were mostly small single, and a few double and triple, family homes on the main route.

To the south there were no road spurs, just dusty open land that slowly sloped upwards toward a small hill range.

On the north side there were roads that went north and out of view of the slowing rig with small single family homes spread out more and more sparsely as the road moved away from the main route.

"It's a nice little place," Peter replied as he gazed around slightly as well. "I always thought it would be a nice place for me to stay for a spell when I'm not driving the rig. I make it a point to stop here when my route puts me through the area."

Peter sighed a little as he brought the truck slowly into the large parking lot left off the route next to a small three family dwelling with a storefront where a connecting street on the right named Packer came down and dead ended onto the route. "Aw, hell, who am I kidding? I make it a point to come through here when it's miles out of my way. Texas is full of neighborly folk, but I'll tell you what," he said as he applied the parking brake. "You'll never find sixteen hundred more neighborly folk on the planet than the ones you'll find here," he finished as his southern accent thickened up just a bit.

"So you really think this is the place for me to be?" David asked as he peered out across the driver side window.

"Son," the older man said as his eyes crinkled up just a bit, "if just a fraction of what you've gone and shared with me is gospel, and I reckon it is, and more from what I've seen with my own eyes, then you need to be here and this place needs you here."

"I'm an easy sell. I'll do what I can." David smirked as he opened the passenger door to the rig and began to climb out. "Shall we have breakfast?" David asked as he looked across the main route to the buildings on the opposite corners of Packer Road. One was a hardware/general purpose store. The name on the sign above the windows read *Davenport's General Store* and the sign on the store on the opposite corner read *McNally's Grill and Pub.* Next to the pub was another store called *Barker's,* but from the lot it was a little difficult for David to make out exactly what was inside the store through the front windows.

"Only if you let me buy breakfast," Peter replied loudly as he shut the engine to the rig down.

David replied while he circled around the front of the truck. "I can't let you do that. You just drove me seven hundred some odd miles. I have to at least buy you breakfast."

Peter hopped down and closed the driver's door of the truck.

"Son, I don't have much. I could have a million dollars and it wouldn't be enough to square up with you for what you've done for me."

"I don't need anyone to be squared up with me, and remember what I said. There are a thousand ways to be far richer than the sum of any money you might have," David replied as he looked to Peter and then turned, squinting his brown eyes a bit when he looked in the direction of the morning sun coming up over the eastern plain and the hills in the direction from where they came.

David turned in the opposite direction quickly to get a view of the western horizon.

"I know and I know that's an honest answer, too. Makes it all the harder ..." Peter choked out the last word but then firmed up his voice. "I insist and I won't take no for an answer. Breakfast on me and I'll talk to Miss Charlotte. She'll have some work for you and a room, I'm almost certain."

"Okay, old timer, I know better at this point than to try to win this argument with you," David said with a little smirk.

"Old timer?" Peter said. "Hell, I can't be more than fifteen years older than you. That's your Yankee wise ass seeping in a bit."

David flinched just a little and then composed himself a bit and responded. "Remember now, I offered up a little bit ..."

Peter stopped in front of him, turned to face him, and cut him off.

"Like I said, I don't have much. My word is one of the things I have. I gave it to you. Your secrets, the ones you shared, are safe. I won't talk about them."

"Perfect," David replied and without skipping a beat continued "So let's go see about that breakfast you raved about for two hundred miles."

The pair headed past a couple of parked cars and into the storefront. David looked up at the sign over the front of the building—*Charlotte's Place*.

Peter walked in ahead of David and past the racks and shelves of everyday items that were stocked.

David stopped to look around the small store. Having traveled extensively for some time, he looked around at the store with a certain amount of inquisitiveness. The place was reminiscent of a neighborhood corner store back east. Here, he thought, it was more likely a necessity store so everyday items could be bought without having to drive fifty miles or further to a larger town to stock up.

At first glance, the store didn't look huge. Looking around one more time David assumed it couldn't be more than three thousand square feet in size, but as he looked at all of the items for sale, he was pretty sure the little store had everything you might need for just about anything.

A young girl approached David from the direction of the counter area where Peter had gone and where a couple of older men were drinking coffee.

"Hi, mister, you're new here. Can I help you find something?"

David snapped out of his thoughts and turned his attention to the girl.

"Well, hello," he replied as he looked at her and smiled. "And how are you so sure I'm new here?" he asked in a friendly voice.

"Well," the girl in the yellow top and blue denim skirt responded with a smile that lit up her tanned complexion. "The town, for the most part, isn't getting any larger with the people that keep moving out, and I know I've never seen you before, so I am figuring you're new."

"Well, that's a very good guess, miss. I am new. I traveled in with Mr. Dempsey," David replied, widening his smile a bit and leaning down slightly toward her while pointing over at Peter.

"Mr. Dempsey is a very nice man. You must be a nice man, too 'cause Mr. Dempsey never gives anyone a ride in his truck," the girl replied as she moved her long black hair from in front of her shoulder to the back.

"Well, you're very observant for an eight year old." David guessed her age while looking past her, watching Peter talking with an old, graying woman at the counter and gesturing back in his direction.

"I'll be nine in a couple of months," the girl responded proudly. "My mama said I'm pre ... pro ..."

"Precocious?" David asked.

"Yes, that's it," she responded as she untangled some of her hair from her shirt straps.

"So does the pretty precocious girl with the long black hair have a name for the new customer? Mine is David."

A voice called out from behind David. "Her name is Caroline and I am sorry she is bothering you."

David turned around in the direction of the voice that came in through the doorway to the storefront.

A woman that positively resembled the young girl approached them, dressed neatly in a light blue-checkered dress outfit.

"I am Maria, and again I am very sorry she is bothering you."

"Oh, your sister isn't bothering me," David replied quickly in an honest tone, looking over the slender woman. "As a matter of fact, she was asking me if I needed any help with anything."

"Daughter," Maria responded with a slight sound of disapproval in her voice. She put her arm around Caroline who stood at about four feet tall and just a foot shorter than her mother.

Realizing his mistake, and what it must have sounded like to her, David quickly replied. "Daughter, I am so sorry. Well, she certainly is well mannered for an up and coming nine year old."

David quickly turned his attention to Caroline and said, "Thank you for asking me if I needed any help. I am going to go have some breakfast with Mr. Dempsey." David smiled and then addressed the two of them together. "It was nice meeting you both."

David turned, walked away, and headed over to the breakfast counter next to where Peter was still engaged in conversation with the woman. He stared at them quickly for a moment and then took a seat on the stool a little away from them.

As he sat, he took a menu and looked it over briefly as someone walked toward him.

A familiar voice asked, "Good morning, would you like some coffee?"

Slightly startled, David looked up from the menu. It was Maria who was finishing putting on her apron.

"Coffee? Sure," David replied quickly. "So you're a mom and a waitress. All learned in the same five minutes. I wonder what the next surprise is going to be."

"I am not sure you will be around long enough to uncover any other surprises," Maria quipped with just a touch of her Mexican accent coming through as she filled David's coffee.

"What makes you so sure about that?" David asked.

"Well, it sounded as if you came in with Mr. Dempsey and he generally comes through but will not stay." There was a slight shift in Maria's tone. "It is a shame. People come and go, but they do not stay. Some of us that have been here a while also leave, never to return."

Before David had a chance to ask her what she meant by that Peter approached with Charlotte Cassidy.

Charlotte was grandmotherly in her looks, but her step and stance was as solid as someone half her age. She leaned over the counter a bit from the serving side and looked David right in the eye.

"So young man," she said as she leaned a little closer and stiffened up her tone a bit. "Peter here says you came in on a ride in his truck. Says you're looking for a place to stay and some work to do."

David glanced up to see the reaction to the comments on Maria's face and then looked back to Charlotte as Caroline came over and sat one stool over at the counter.

"Yes, that is the case," David answered. "I am passing through, but I thought I might like to stay a little while and in order to do that I'd need a place to sleep and some work if you have one or both."

"I might have a room and a little bit of work around here. The room ain't the greatest, but it ain't the worst and the work is pretty much the same. It's one hundred dollars a week, but I hate to lock up the room for short periods of time. I'm not looking for a lease or anything from you, but it's a little into the summer. Do you figure you'll make it through the end of the year?"

"If it'll put your mind a little more at ease, I would be willing to pay for the room to the end of the year," David replied, smiling slightly as he sipped at his coffee and slipped his right hand into his pocket.

"The room is on the third floor. It's really just one big room and a bathroom. There's a sleeper sofa up there already, but you'll need to run down to Jim Davenport's for some linens and towels and such."

"I'll take it," David replied without missing a beat.

Charlotte squinted a bit and looked at David a little more closely. "So why is a strapping young lad like yourself coming to hang around our little dust bowl to the end of the year?" she asked.

"Well, I'm not one hundred percent certain how long I am going to stay. I am figuring at least two months, but as I mentioned I'd be willing to pay to the end of the year."

David looked around and noticed that everyone was listening to the conversation, including the two older men at the far end of the counter.

"Why would you want to pay for the months you might not stay?" Caroline asked.

David turned to look at her before her mother could correct her. "Well, I need a place to stay. I might stay that long and I might not, but Miss Charlotte needs to make sense of locking up the room with someone like myself."

"So why are you staying?" Caroline asked.

"Carolena!" Maria scolded in a hushed tone.

"It's okay, I don't mind the questions. It's refreshing to have an honest conversation with someone that has no motive other than to know an answer to a question," David replied turning slightly to Maria and then turning his attention back to her daughter.

"Well, Caroline, everyone needs to be somewhere. Mr. Dempsey talks often and kindly about this little place and I thought to myself now that is a place I want to stay for a while so here I am."

Caroline smiled widely and she looked up at Charlotte who smiled a bit herself. "I like him. Can he stay?"

"That's about the only seal of approval I need. The room is yours," Charlotte quipped as she turned and walked around the counter and headed in the direction of the other two men in the store. "If you want to rest up a bit and come down later, you can start working today. We open at six in the morning and close between six and seven p.m. during the week, depending on who's coming in and what I feel like.... Lots to do," she said as her voice trailed off.

"Is there a key for the door?" David asked.

Charlotte stopped for a moment, looked up at the ceiling and then turned around and smiled with a grandmotherly smile. "I am sure when the door was put in a key came with it. Haven't seen it since. Welcome to our little town."

David smiled widely.

"Caroline, your school bus is coming down the street," Maria said as she pointed out the windows at the front of the store.

David said aloud to himself, "School bus? In the summer?" as he turned in his chair to see an older passenger bus coming down the main route toward the store, stopping at the corner of Packer Road.

"That's the school bus?" David asked Maria as she came around the counter to help Caroline gather her things.

"Yes. It is the bus that takes her to the County school for a summer program she is in," Maria replied as she hustled her daughter off the stool and toward the door.

Peter came up to David and sat next to him. Maria kissed Caroline who headed out the door and onto the bus.

"So, I'll be heading out soon. You can finish the coffee and I gave Miss Charlotte a few bucks. Make sure you eat something. I'll bring in your duffle bag before I go."

"I'd appreciate that. I'd hate to have to buy new clothes, too," David said with a half-smile. "Thanks again for the ride and for getting me set up here. I really appreciate it."

Maria came back around the serving side of the counter and wiped down the spot where Caroline had been sitting.

"No, thank you," Peter said as he smacked David on the shoulder and got up. "I have another run that takes me through here in about three to four weeks. I'll be sure to stop by and check in."

"I'll hold you to it."

Peter headed out the front door of the store and the two men that had been drinking coffee headed out the side door nearest them.

Charlotte sighed just a bit as she cleaned up after them.

"Maria, I am going to sit in the back for a little bit. You make sure you come get me if it gets busy and you need help."

"I will, Miss Charlotte," Maria answered.

"Does it get busy enough for you here that you need to get her?" David asked as he took another look at the breakfast menu.

"No, but she likes to say that anyway," Maria replied as she pinned her nametag on her dress. "Sometimes she will rest and fall asleep in her chair in the back there. She needs more rest, anyway. I honestly do not know how she does it. I am one third her age and I have a hard time keeping up with her."

"So she's about eighty," David replied without looking up.

"About," Maria answered.

"That's it? No answer?" David asked wryly.

"Well," Maria responded playfully, "you just got here and it would seem as if you might actually be here long enough to uncover other surprises, but I would think you would not want to learn them all in one day."

"Well," David said trying to quickly change the tone of the conversation, "I am sort of hungry, but I could use a better rest than I got in the cab of that truck so I think I'll just head upstairs."

Peter came back in the door and brought in David's duffle bag from the truck.

David turned around in the stool at the sound of the door and stood to meet him part way. He took the bag and extended his hand to shake Peter's when Peter pulled him forward and gave him a bear hug.

Maria watched the exchange, raised an eyebrow, and leaned on the counter. She reached back to the hair catch that was pinning up her long, black hair and adjusted it slightly to tighten it up.

"You take care now," Peter said as his eyes welled up just a bit. "I know you might move on in a bit, but make it at least through my next trip. Three or four weeks. You were figuring to be here at least eight, right? This way if you need another ride, I am around."

"I'm figuring as much. I am sure I'll see you. Safe travels."

Peter waived to Maria, turned, and left the store.

David carried the full-size bag that was nearly bursting at the seams to the counter.

Maria looked at David inquisitively.

"Something wrong?" David asked as he leaned the bag on the stool , sat on the adjacent one, and slid his coffee back over.

"What happened with Peter?"

"I'm not sure I follow."

"He has been coming in here for years," Maria replied as her accent came through a little more strongly again. "I have never seen him express himself like that. What happened to him?"

David studied the look on Maria's face for a moment before responding.

"He had some things going on, some personal things. I did what I could to help him."

Maria responded a little quieter and a little less demanding. "He often spoke of people he met in his travels on the road. He has never mentioned the likes of you and I have never known him to give anyone a ride in his truck. How long have you know him?"

"About eight weeks," David said, smiling just a bit. "It might be a little more, I forget exactly. Not long, that's for sure."

Maria simply stared at David.

"Am I not meeting some approval?" he asked sipping a little more coffee and reaching for the spoon on the counter.

"I am not sure I understand the question," Maria replied, leaning backward into the counter behind her.

David glanced around to the mirror behind her, which basically took in the whole view of most of the now empty store. "You seem to me to be somewhat motherly about people. You have a lot of empathy for others, but caution as well. You were concerned for Peter because he engaged in an uncharacteristic response, one you never saw before, and a stranger that he gave a ride to, which was also uncharacteristic."

"You presume much of people you have just met. But in saying so you are not wrong either," Maria responded as her Mexican accent again became more predominant and her comments became more pointed. "Peter is a very kind man, a man with a good heart. He is the kind of man that is easily taken advantage of by the wrong kind of person."

David sat up a little. He wasn't expecting to be locked into a contentious conversation, but decided to engage. "With respect to your point of presuming much of people, you have just met me as well. It would seem I could make the same counter claim of you," David responded quietly and calmly. "I am a pretty good read of most people, so I feel comfortable with most of my assumptions. When I am wrong, I own up to it. What makes you believe I might be the type of person that is the wrong kind of person?"

Maria realized she might have judged a little and been a little harsh so she backed off her position a little and softened her tone. "You are right. I am sorry. It is like I said, Peter almost never gives anyone a ride in his truck and then you say you have barely known him two months.... Still, he seemed to express sincerity about something you appeared to have helped him with so I will take it at face value."

"Thank you," David responded as he smiled. He noticed that Maria's face softened with her change of tone.

"Besides Carolena seems to like you and she is a pretty good judge of character on first glance," Maria said as she began to tidy up behind the counter.

"So is it Carolena or Caroline? You've called her both," David asked.

"Well, that is a long story I will not bore you with. The short story is her father was set on the name. It was his grandmother's name and had some significance to him. Not enough to stick around for us, but ... anyway, being a Mexican American, the name would be Carolena so I will call her that when I am being endearing to her."

"Or when she's in trouble," David said with a slight smirk.

"Yes," Maria responded softly. "And she can often be that," she said as she smiled a bit.

"So I am going to head up and get some more rest. I will come down a little later and check with Miss Charlotte on what she wants done and when she wants me to get started."

"Rest well then," Maria responded clearing the coffee cup. "Are you sure you do not want anything to eat? Peter did ask that you eat something."

David paused for a moment. "I think I'm okay for now."

Maria stared for a moment with a hard focus. "I will come up to get you in a couple hours. You need something to eat. If you prefer some rest now that is fine, but you also need to eat."

David smiled a little as that motherly characteristic came through in her statement. "I don't suppose if I tried to argue that point that I would win."

"You would not." Maria smirked.

David took a few steps toward the door with his bag in his hand and he stopped and turned back to Maria who was still looking at him.

"So the long story that you didn't want to bore me with. If I wanted to hear it, would you tell me?"

Maria paused before responding and simply stated, "Why would you want to hear it?"

"One of the best ways to get to know someone is to ask them to tell a little about themselves and then listen to them tell their story."

"And is that what you want? To get to know me?" she asked in a more guarded tone.

"Well, I will be here a little while. I think it makes sense."

"A while. And then?" Maria said as her tone shifted.

David sensed he hit a nerve. "You never know what tomorrow brings. You plan your life like you might live forever, but you need to live it like it might end sooner than later. That is the best way I know to try to get the most out of it. It doesn't make sense for everyone, but it does for me."

David backed up more toward the door, but he kept is gaze on Maria's face. "And yes to answer your question. I would like to get to know you, but I am not going to pry and I leave that up to you."

David stepped out the door and headed for the stairs for the apartment to rest.

Maria continued to stare at the door as David walked away.

"Interesting man," Charlotte's voice called out of the back room as she slowly got up.

"He seems nice enough," Maria responded as she moved more into a work mode behind the counter and then made her way to the other side. "He seems out of place."

"Everyone that is not from here is out of place," Charlotte replied as she turned down the small grill. "He sounds like he's from up north. Probably New York."

"That is not what I meant. I meant more like lost I guess," Maria stated as she just looked out the door puzzled.

"Ah," Charlotte replied, putting dishes into the sink to clean. "That would be the soft Maria, trying to save the tortured soul of another but not saving her own."

Maria turned around from the doorway and looked at the old woman. "That is what I do, is it not?" she said as she sighed. "I often feel like I can help. And I never can."

"You never let them in," Charlotte responded as she leaned over the counter. "Not everyone is William."

Maria rolled her eyes slightly as she moved toward the counter. "That is not what I am talking about. How I am is not about Billy and what happened."

"No, it actually is," Charlotte said as she sat. "That's the root of it with you. People disappoint. You put too much faith in them, and then, when they let you down, it ruins you. I remember when you were pregnant with Caroline. You were so happy. Even though it disappointed your father that you were not married first and you really didn't want to disappoint him. You wanted to be pregnant and have a family and you were so happy for it, despite how it happened."

"I have a daughter. I lost the family. Here and in Mexico basically as well," Maria said as her tone saddened.

"William had to take his own path. It is unfortunate. But you've only gained, not lost. We all wish you'd see that."

"We?" Maria asked.

"Your family. All us folks around here. I know we are different from the people you knew from your village in Mexico, but you can erase some of that borderline that separates our two countries. Inside, we're all the same. We love you just as much."

Maria slowly guided herself onto the counter stool. "I am not that young, eighteen-year-old girl anymore."

"Bah! I'm old. You're going to be, what, twenty-eight?"

"Next year," Maria said and cracked a little smile.

"That stool you're sitting on is older than you."

Both women laughed out loud at the statement. Charlotte made her way around the counter and walked over to the front door of the store. "I remember when Henry and I opened this store decades ago. 'It will be a nice little way to earn some extra money to supplement what I make at the mine' he told me. Who knew it would be all we'd have left when the mine closed up. Who knew it would keep me into my eighties."

Maria turned on the stool and noticed the time. She got up to make coffee as more of the regulars would be on their way in shortly.

Charlotte turned from the door and noticed Maria getting the coffee ready. "Good thinking. We are working after all. Folks will be here shortly and the customers are not going to pay good money for only my wit."

Maria smiled as two customers crossed the street and approached the store and another pulled their car into the lot.

Chapter Two

David woke to the sound of light knocking. As he opened his eyes slightly he wondered if he imagined the sound when it lightly repeated.

"Mr. David, it is Maria. I have something for you to eat."

David got up quickly off the beat up, brown couch and walked over to the door and opened it.

"Hi," he said standing in the doorway in only his jeans. "I guess you weren't kidding on the food. Thank you. Come in."

Maria stared at his chest for a brief moment, looked away, and then stepped into the room. "It is ten o'clock. I really cannot stay very long as Charlotte will need me back down there when the lunch folks come in," she stated looking back at him. "She tries to do everything on her own, but she really cannot any longer as I mentioned to you before."

David took the bacon and egg sandwich from her and smiled. He took a bite from it and set it on the kitchen table in the room and walked over to pull a clean shirt from his bag. Maria watched him snap the shirt open and then put it on. Her eyes quickly drifted over his body.

He is not particularly fit nor out of shape, she thought as she drifted her gaze up into his brown eyes. Still, she found herself wanting to stare.

David caught her looking and responded. "So I can eat that quickly and go downstairs and give Charlotte a hand."

"Oh," Maria said as she paused, snapping herself back into the conversation, slightly embarrassed. "I think she needed help from you for things like the shelves in the backroom and the scrub brush out back and other things on the property. Less inside the store."

"I see," David said grabbing his socks and sneakers. "Well, there seems to be enough to do inside as well. Things outside can wait for after hours. You have good daylight here in the later summer to sometime after eight I would presume?"

"Yes," Maria answered as she folded her hands in front of herself.

"So, Miss Maria Romero, you live on the second floor? And Miss Charlotte lives on the first?" he asked as he finished lacing up his sneakers.

"I see you can read the mailbox labels," Maria said.

"Yes, well I am loaded with many little, hidden talents," David said with a smile as he took another bite of his sandwich and walked toward the door with it in his hand. "Shall we?"

David opened the door and gestured for Maria to pass first, which she did with just the slightest smile on her face.

David took another bite of the sandwich when they both headed down the stairs. As he turned the first landing to the second floor he paused his pace as a touch of vertigo hit him and immediately dissipated. Maria turned around and David looked up and stepped forward.

"Did you forget something?" she asked in a soft voice.

"No, why did you ask?" he asked as they both continued down to the first landing and then outside.

"You stopped walking. I thought you needed to go back for something."

"Basically everything left that I own in the world is in that bag upstairs and there's really little else other than clothes. Nope, I'm all set," he said as he smiled a bit and they rounded the building corner to the front door of the store.

The two walked into the store. David looked up and noticed three people sitting at the counter and one walking the small aisles with a basket picking up household items.

Maria continued to the counter while David paused to read the items on the small bulletin board on the wall near the newspapers and magazines while he ate more of his sandwich.

He could hear Charlotte's voice drifting in and out of the conversation with the three people at the counter. She was discussing David as the new tenant and worker at the store.

David scanned the notes on the bulletin board. Items posted for babysitting, fixing autos and trucks, hauling services, and so forth. They were all local numbers, as much as he could tell, and while there were pull tags for the numbers for someone to take with them, most were intact and not pulled.

His eyes drifted to a colorful mini poster titled *Our Library*. David pulled the tack out of it and took it down to read. While he was doing that Charlotte had walked over.

"I know I have things to do and for you to get started on, but we really hadn't discussed pay or anything so I suppose we should."

"That's fine," David responded as he turned around and smiled. "I am going to do some work, you figure out what the value of that is to you and what you can afford and I figure I'll be fine with it."

"Really?" Charlotte questioned loudly. "You strike me as someone from up north. And I know a few folks from that way. Always wheelin' and dealin'. How do you know I won't under bid your work if I know you're so willing to allow me to set the rate?"

"You simply don't strike me as the type of person to take advantage. I trust you'd be fair and offer what you could," David responded as he looked at Maria briefly taking the order from the woman at the counter. David looked up at the menu on the wall and then back down to Charlotte. "I'm going to give Maria a hand with that order. If you need me to do something else, let me know."

"How were you planning to help Maria take an order?" she asked as David pinned the flyer back up and walked toward the counter.

"Well, I can cook what the folks have ordered, that's helping," David said with a smile as the customers and Maria were now listening to the conversation.

"That's all well and fine," Charlotte responded as she walked over to the customer side of the counter, "but I traditionally do all the cooking and the sandwich making around here."

"I am sure you do and I bet it's fantastic. But why not let me give it a try for them? If they don't like the way I do it, you can always take it back." David turned to the customers. "Care to give my skills a spin? You're guaranteed to like it or I'll pay for it."

The three folks looked at Charlotte who shrugged her shoulders as if to respond 'why not'. Charlotte sat next to Mel Porter, a retired doctor and one of the regulars at Charlotte's Place, on the customer side of the counter.

Mel looked like an average, every-day older gentleman in his early seventies even though he had yet to hit sixty-eight years old.

Diana Canton was a single mother in her fifties. Her hair was long, graying and thinning and she looked a few years older than her age.

Carol Campbell was a recent widow in her sixties with dark black hair.

"Well, I would like to try it," the woman walking the aisles and picking up items said. "I don't believe we've met," she continued as she sat on an empty stool a little away from the others and placed her basket of items on the counter. She looked up at David intently with her deep blue eyes.

"My name is David. It's nice to meet you," David said as he extended his hand.

"Sue Ann," the middle aged woman responded as she extended her hand lightly to be taken more than shook. David responded appropriately for the gesture and then let her hand go.

He turned to look at Maria who was staring with a certain level of disdain. "Ah… where are the menus, Maria?"

"Yes, Maria, please be a dear and get me one please, won't you?" Sue Ann interjected with a slight tone of disrespect as she removed her wide brimmed, white hat.

Maria handed a menu over to David. Sue Ann pulled a brush out of her purse and combed her medium length strawberry blonde hair as David set the menu down in front of her.

David noticed that she was rather well dressed as compared to the few other people he had seen so far. It wasn't so much that she was over dressed, but her clothes were newer and a grade above the others. He paid little further attention to it other than recognizing the difference. He also noted that from appearances that she might be around fifty, a few years older than him.

"So, David, what brings you to Westville? It certainly can't be to cook eggs for all us Texas folk, native and non-native alike." Sue Ann flirted as she pushed the menu back slightly.

"Well, for this very moment it is," David said as he smiled back. "So how would you like those two eggs?"

"Surprise me," she said as she leaned forward a little allowing her top to gape open a little further. David saw the gesture and made it a point to not acknowledge it as he walked away and toward the grill. Maria came down to the others and took their orders. She glanced over at Sue Ann once she was done.

"Anything the matter, Miss Romero?" Sue Ann asked.

"Good morning, Mrs. Kurtvow. I was going to ask you if you would like me to ring up your purchases separately or with the breakfast," Maria responded quietly as she lowered her eyes.

David looked up from the food work area as he put the apron on and seasoned the grill. He took notice of how disarmed Maria acted. It was uncharacteristic of how he had seen her earlier.

"You can ring these up now on my husband's account. I will pay for breakfast separately," Sue Ann responded as she turned toward David.

Maria removed the basket from the counter and totaled up the items. She then went over to a ledger near the register and entered information into it. After that, she put the items into a cardboard carrier box and walked over to the counter.

Sue Ann put her keys on the counter. "Be a dear and place those into my car, please, Miss Romero."

David turned down the burner and moved the pan over to the warmer and came around the counter. "Which car is it, Mrs. Kurtvow?" David asked and then turned toward Maria. "I'll take that for you, Maria."

"I can handle it on my own, thank you just the same," she responded to David as she took the keys off the counter.

David turned to Charlotte taking in the exchange and deflected with a neutral question. "Do you have any cinnamon?"

"In the back room on the shelf on the far wall. We use those larger ones for food prep," Charlotte responded.

David walked away and into the back room. He saw the cinnamon right away on the shelf. He took it into his hand and stood for a moment, digesting the exchanges that just took place beyond the doorway.

"Let me offer you some free advice, Maria," Sue Ann interrupted as Maria began to walk out. "While some men like confident women, virtually no men like a woman that does everything themselves. If you're not going to let them do things for you, they will find another woman that will let them."

"Mrs. Kurtvow, with respect, I am not looking for a man to do anything for me."

"Well, that explains many things," Sue Ann responded quietly as David emerged from the back room and headed back over to the grill.

Maria looked at Charlotte who had a slight look of concern on her face.

"Mrs. Kurtvow, would you like these in the trunk or the backseat?" Maria asked with a little more vigor in her voice.

"The backseat, dear. I am sure you're familiar with that area of the car," Sue Ann answered curtly.

David looked up suddenly as the comment ended and came around the grill area quickly. Almost on cue, Charlotte stood briskly. Suddenly, David sensed a need to not follow his initial instinct to say something and continued beyond the counter. "Here, at least let me get the front door for you, Maria."

"The car is off the side door, David," Sue Ann responded.

David cut across the store to the side door as Maria walked over toward it. He didn't offer to take the box, but he got out in front of her and held the door open.

He watched Maria make her way over to the car with the box in both hands. He knew she'd either struggle with the keys or set the box down to complete the task. He let the door go behind her and stepped up and took the box.

She looked at him sternly. "I am more than capable of putting a simple box into the woman's car," she said abruptly and almost as if she was insulted. A little more of her Mexican accent slipped out in her response.

"I realize that you are quite able and capable. I wanted to help make it easier for you to do."

Maria opened the back door of the car and jerked the box from David's hands. "I do not need a man to come running to my rescue."

"It's not that," David said almost defensively.

Maria interrupted and continued. "It is never with the correct intentions and it comes with the want and need of other expectations."

Maria slammed the door and walked away back toward the store.

"Hey!" David yelled out, which stopped Maria in her tracks. She didn't turn around, but she closed her eyes, realizing her rudeness. "A really strong and independent woman is one that knows full well she can do it all but is confident enough in herself to allow someone to help."

Maria took a step forward and then stopped.

"You're better than that exchange we just had," David said in a softer tone as he walked up and past her and held the door open.

Maria walked in past him and paused for a second. "I am sorry," she said quietly.

David softly touched her arm to keep her from walking further past him "We can talk about why that happened some other time," he said reassuringly and with a slight smile.

As they both walked back into the store everyone was looking in their direction. Maria kept her head down and went around the counter to get the coffee and David headed back over to the grill area to tend to Sue Ann's eggs. He then looked at the orders up for the other customers and started all the core items for each.

"Well, I really must know, because you're like a breath of fresh air around here already. How long will you be here in Westville?" Sue Ann asked loudly to be heard from the counter to the grill area.

"To be honest I am not really sure," David answered without looking up. "I tend to travel around. Sometimes I am in one place for a while and sometimes I am here and gone."

"Sounds interesting," Sue Ann added as she adjusted herself in the seat and with some effort to get David's attention. "So what's the change up factor? What makes you decide it's time to go?" she asked with just a hint of southern accent coming out.

"When I figure my work is done," David said with a slight smile and as he prepared all the plates for the orders.

"And what work is that?" Sue Ann asked almost on the spot.

David looked up and he realized the others were not talking among themselves but listening in on the public conversation. "What needs to get done," he responded quite assuredly.

Almost on cue Sue Ann followed up with, "And that would be?"

"Now, Mrs. Kurtvow," David answered slyly as he came around with the orders. "If I told you everything today, you would become far too quickly bored. The best stories take time to unfold."

Maria folded her arms when David delivered over the orders to all the customers instead of handing them over to her. He then went back around to get the final plate that went to her. Maria was confused about the plate. She looked at him as if she needed to serve it, but everyone had a plate.

"That one is yours," David said with a smile.

"How do you know what I like to eat?" she asked smartly.

"I'll tell you what," he said with a smile as he walked back toward the grill area. "Try it. If you don't like it, you can tell me, and I can work from there. I think you'll like it."

"You seem pretty sure of yourself," Maria said defensively.

David looked around at the others enjoying their first bites. "There's a fine line between confidence and arrogance. I usually know what side I am on at any given time."

"I don't care which side it is," Mel said out loud. "Anyone that can cook like this can dance all over the place. Holy Mary!" Mel turned to Charlotte. "I'm sorry, Miss Charlotte, and you know I say no one cooks as well as my departed wife other than you, but if you're eating what I'm eating...."

"Well..." Charlotte said slightly defensive and a little in jest. "It is pretty good considering a man cooked it."

Carol and Diana both smiled at the comments. They were enjoying the food so much they could only smile and take another bite.

Sue Ann looked up from her dish and directly at David. "What is in this? It is excellent. How did you learn to cook this?"

David flinched slightly as he recalled the exact time he perfected the egg breakfast meal he served the patrons. He looked around quickly as he responded. Charlotte noticed the pause and his reaction. "It's actually an old family recipe," he said with a strained smile that he forced harder to maintain for show.

"Impossible, they don't cook like this up north," Charlotte interjected, trying to break David's uneasiness.

David responded in defense of the comment, as Charlotte presumed.

"I think I might surprise you on some of those stereotypes and dispel a few of them," David said as he moved from the grill area back toward the counter. His entire attitude shifted from the moment prior.

"Will you be here long enough to do that?" Maria asked as her Mexican accent thickened up slightly. "As you indicated, you may be here and then you may be gone."

"Well, as I said," David replied moving past her and around the counter to the customer side. "I stay until everything I need to do is done."

"Yes, I recall," she replied as she looked at Sue Ann who enjoyed the cross stare. "And what exactly is that? And who are you anyway with a comment like that?" she added defensively. "We have had enough false saviors here…" Maria said as she trailed off. Sue Ann took notice of the comment and sat up.

David noticed the reaction and tried to store it to digest later. He quickly followed up to remove the sudden additional tension he could feel in the room. "All these complex questions and assumptions when the real burning question for me at least is, Miss Maria, how do you like your meal?"

Maria looked at him sharply and squinted her eyes just slightly. She then softened her look a little and responded, "It is very good, I must admit. Perhaps not as good as I might make…"

"Very well then," David replied quickly and turning to measure the attention of the others at the counter. "Please let me know when you're willing to show me how it is done. I am more than happy to learn a new thing or two."

Maria wasn't planning on that type of response. Charlotte smirked slightly, grinned, and looked away. Mel Porter moved up on his seat slightly for any follow up response.

Carol smiled slightly as she leaned forward to pay better attention.

"I was not implying I could show you or that I was free to invite you over for something to eat," Maria said.

"And that is because you live so far away from me, down on that second floor and all. And I suppose your calendar is full, too," David responded playfully with a warm smile.

"I have a lot to do with Caroline. She is a handful. I am busy here and with her. And to be quite blunt, Mr. David, it is sort of presumptuous of you." She responded in a standoffish manner. "Basically, you invited yourself over."

"Of course it was presumptuous. How very north of me. Despite all my travels in recent years I am still not totally adept at understanding the nuances of southern hospitality and kindness. My apologies, Miss Maria," David said kindly with a smile. He bowed slightly and made his way back around the counter.

Diana turned and mumbled to Carol, "He'd only need to make one pass at me."

Carol practically giggled like a schoolgirl at the comment as Charlotte smiled. Mel grinned at over hearing it as well.

Sue Ann finished up the last bits of her meal. David went beyond the back grill area, through the back room and out the back door.

Maria moved around the counter and began to walk through the store and pull stock forward on the shelves. Her mind raced. *How rude of him to be so presumptuous*, she thought as she tried to maintain her focus on that emotion. Her heart also raced. The more time she spent thinking about him the more attractive he became. He was nice to look at, but there was nothing exceptional. He was a middle of the road looking man, she thought.

She walked from the end of one row to the next one.

He is not someone I would otherwise or normally find attractive, she thought to herself as she worked the stock in the next row. She

33

looked up at the back door he exited from. *He is not from here and he has already indicated he is not going to be here for any real length of stay. There is no point in investing the time.*

She looked up at the wall beyond the shelves she was working and whispered out loud to herself. "Por qué estoy gastando todo este tiempo pensando en él?" She moved her eyes back to the rear of the shop and to the back room, wondering where he went.

Maria came slowly around the row and walked toward the counter entrance from the customer side to the work side. Sue Ann stood from the last bits of her meal. She took cash out of her wallet far in excess of the meal and addressed Maria as she slowly stepped around with her eyes still peering into the back room area. "Please cover my meal and give my regards and the change to the cook. I can't wait to find out all there this to know about our new visitor."

Maria collected the money. Sue Ann took five more dollars out of her wallet and left it on the counter. "Thank you for putting the groceries in the car for me."

Maria looked at the tip and measured the tone of the comment. It seemed nearly genuine.

"Thank you, Mrs. Kurtvow," Maria responded in a hopeful tone that it might have been just that.

Sue Ann looked at the back door of the store and then leaned forward and over the counter. "If you're not going to take advantage of that, I can certainly tell you others will. Consider that an add-on to your tip."

Sue Ann smiled to the remainder of the folks in the room. "Good day, people. I am sure I will be seeing y'all around," she said and headed out the side door to her car.

Maria slowly walked into the back room and noticed that David wasn't there and that the rear door was open. She walked into the doorway and stood on the threshold and saw David looking around the immediate property and at the rear entrance of the residential side of the structure.

"Are there more people?" David asked as he walked toward Maria.

Maria waived him off. "No, Mrs. Kurtvow just paid and left and the folks from before are still there."

David stopped his approach and looked up the back stairs and the small deck off the back of his apartment from the ground. He then turned his view to the west and then looked back up.

"Are you expecting to find something?" Maria asked pointing in the general direction of the deck and then further west.

"I realize the sun came up a few hours ago. I was wondering what the view looks like at sunset and dusk," David replied looking into the sun and in Maria's direction.

Maria stood quietly for a moment before responding. While she paused David continued to look at her. With the sun behind her and shining around her David couldn't move his gaze.

"Is there something significant about the sunset you are hoping to find or see from your deck?" Maria asked as she shifted her small frame slightly and recognized that David had extended his look at her.

"I always try to take the time at the end of the day to watch the sun go down if for nothing else than to view another sunset. People's lives are blessed in all kinds of little ways. For me, I take a little comfort in seeing another day is done and watching another sunset."

Maria wanted to say something, but the words were stuck on her. She tried to translate the Spanish thought in her head to say it to him in English, but she could not. Part of her was enamored by the comment. Such depth for a man, but at the same time, she became defensive, thinking he was a smooth talker. Still, she couldn't help but notice the softness of the tone he used to say it and the innocent deflection of his attitude when he turned his gaze away and then stared south over the immediate dusty land and scrub brush.

"How far is it to Mexico?" David asked pointing south.

"Maybe twenty-five miles or so," Maria replied softly as she looked into the direction of her home country.

"I take it you miss it," David said as he slowly turned and began to walk forward.

"America has been my home for a long time. Mexico is where I come from and where my family went home to. Despite the troubles here, America offers opportunities one cannot find for the most part in the rest of the world. Choices needed to be made for myself and for Caroline. They were in the best interest of us so I make no apologies there."

"And you shouldn't," David said strongly as he approached the steps at the base of the door where Maria was standing.

A shallow burst of wind ruffled Maria's dress and carried some sand along with it. Maria lifted her hand with the bill from Sue Ann's breakfast. She cleared her throat loudly. "Ahem, well, Mrs. Kurtvow paid for her six dollar breakfast with a fifty dollar bill and wanted me to pass along to you her regards and the change."

"I'll tell you what. I'll take the regards, thank you very much for passing them along. Why don't you keep the change?" David responded as he slipped into the remaining space in the doorway and stood very closely to Maria for a moment and then passed the threshold of the doorway and turned back toward her.

"It is not mine to take," Maria replied holding up the fifty in front of her.

"It's mine to give away, so go ahead and take it," David said wondering in his head if that was the button that was going to set her off.

Maria reached over, grabbed David's hand, and stuffed the money into it. "I will ring you out later. You will keep that tip," Maria replied, agitated.

David laughed as she slipped out of the doorway to storm off past him, which caused her to stop short and turn around.

"What is so funny?" she asked impatiently.

"You are far too easily spun up. What did I do wrong there?"

"That is forty-four dollars," Maria replied as her voice got louder and her accent got heavier. "The average tip most folks can afford to leave is a dollar and the change. It takes me a week to get that much, if I get that much at all, and you want me to just take her money? In all her time she has never left me more than five dollars after taking a dig or two at me so I look at it like combat pay."

She folded her arms in front of her, which caused her to lift her breasts slightly. David forced himself to not look at them. It was difficult for him to keep his glance up.

"And what is the issue right now?" David asked softly and calmly with a slight smirk.

"No one gives almost forty-five dollars away!"

"Mrs. Kurtvow did. I am simply passing the same money along to someone else. I have what I need. I earn what else I have to in order to pay for a place to stay. Beyond that, the money isn't going to buy me anything I don't already have."

Maria was surprised by the explanation and took a moment to gather a response.

"Okay" she said, softening her tone. "If that is your explanation then why pass it along to me?"

The immediate thought that went through David's head was that she was a single mother and could probably use the help, but he figured that would upset her and he already poked his little bit of fun at her. "I simply figured you might be able to put it toward something that you and Caroline need. Perhaps if the bills are all caught up, you might put it toward a simple want instead."

Maria was absorbing the response.

"That and I figured that you have this disdain for Mrs. Kurtvow that it would be fitting that you spend her money," David added as he smiled at her.

Maria smiled a genuine smile, not the customer polite ones she presented before.

"Ah," David said as he turned away to walk out of the back room. "That's what an honest smile looks like on you. It looks good. You should share it more often."

Maria stayed in the back room for a moment to let everything soak in. It was the first time in a while she felt genuinely happy.

Chapter Three

Mel Porter came back into Charlotte's Place in the late afternoon.

David had finished up what there was to do inside the store and was out back clearing some of the scrub brush growth on the back part of the property.

Maria was doing some light restocking and cleaning near the front door and was looking up the road for Caroline's bus to return.

Mel walked up to the serving counter and sat across Charlotte who was resting in the high server chair on the work side.

"So I see the young lad is out back now," Mel said as he moved and got comfortable in the chair.

"Yes, a lot a piss an' vinegar in that one," Charlotte quipped. "No moss on that stone. We keep calling them young, but they really aren't, are they." Charlotte gestured over toward Maria.

"No, I guess they are not, not so much anymore. Where does the time go? Well, at least for them they still have much of their lives to go." Mel adjusted himself in the chair a bit more. "Us, we have more days behind us than in front of us."

"Speak for yourself, old man. I am not planning on going any time soon," Charlotte snapped with a small smile knowing she was fifteen years his senior.

"Are you almost finished with David? I was going to walk him over to Davenport's to introduce him and so he could pick a few things up," Mel said with a slight smile.

"So a couple things," Charlotte said as she stood to collect a few things behind the counter. "I was done with David half an hour ago.

He just keeps doing work. Secondly, you and I both know that half your interest is to walk around with him and chew his ear off."

Mel smiled widely at being called out. "Guilty as charged, Miss Charlotte."

"Go around back and grab him anytime you'd like. I know he'll need some stuff for the apartment. I am not sure of his cash situation so if needed have Davenport extend him credit and I'll back it up if needed."

"Jim's had to tighten down like we've all had to. It'll make him comfortable that you're willing to back up David's credit."

"And you wouldn't?" Charlotte responded as she turned around from what she was doing.

"You and I are old-school. We would regardless. Still, there's something about the boy's honesty and openness that makes it easier to do," Mel said as he hopped off the stool and headed behind the counter to cut through the store to exit out the back.

"Yes," Charlotte responded and trailed off. "There is just something about him...his situation for lack of a better term. I just can't put my finger on it."

"Well, Charlotte," Mel replied as he reached the back room entrance, "you've been a pretty good read of people over the years. I am sure within just a little bit of time you're going to know our young friend better than he knows himself."

Charlotte smiled at the compliment as Mel exited toward the rear door.

Maria set her dust broom down and stepped out the front door of the store as the school bus pulled up to the intersection. The older bus breaks squealed loudly as the vehicle came to a full stop.

David looked up from the far end of the property upon hearing the sound. He glanced over at Mel coming out of the back of the store and then looked back at the bus.

Caroline bounded out of the bus and ran toward the front of the store and just out of David's view. He smiled and turned toward the western horizon and peered at the skyline, mentally judging the remainder of the day.

"Mama," Caroline called out as she cleared the street. "Today was such a fun day. I am so happy to be able to go." As Caroline hopped in place her four-foot height cleared her mother's five-foot frame.

"It is okay, honey. I am happy you are having fun. Come inside and tell me all about it."

The two stepped through the entrance of the store as another brisk wind kicked up more dust and sand from the street and the dry land area.

As Caroline ran up to the counter Maria turned to watch the bus drive away. Her thoughts turned to the remainder of the costs for the summer program. "Dios mío, where am I going to come up with the one hundred dollars for the final two weeks of the program?" Maria whispered to herself as the bus pulled out of view.

Maria slipped her hands into her pockets when she realized she still had Sue Ann's guest check to ring out along with the remaining forty-four dollar tip. Maria walked over to the register to clear out the guest check David had returned to her and made the change. "Miss Charlotte, can Caroline sit here for a moment while I go out back?"

"Of course, dear. I haven't heard everything that happened at school today," Charlotte responded with a smile.

Caroline reached over the counter and kissed her mother and threw her arms around her neck. "I love you, Mama. I have the best Mama."

Maria pulled back tears and hugged her back and looked at Charlotte who herself fussed a little to keep from getting stupid sentimental, as she would put it.

Maria let go and headed back behind the counter and toward the back exit of the store.

Mel approached David as he turned away from the western view he was taking in.

"Quite a sight, isn't it?" Mel asked as he finished his approach.

"It is a very nice view. I have this funny thing about sunsets. I try to take them in at the end of the day, when the day allows," David responded as he fully turned to face Mel.

"Of all the habits there are out there, and plenty of them are bad, that is a good one to have. Charlotte is going to let me steal you to go over to Jim's for your things before he closes up for the evening. Why not head up, clean up a bit, and change out of those clothes now that you've managed to get them good and dirty," Mel said as he expanded his already wide smile.

Rebecca Wilson walked alongside Main Street from the west and toward McNally's Grill and Pub where she worked part time as a food server and bartender. As she made her way she peered over to the Cassidy property.

She slowed her pace slightly before crossing the street when she immediately noticed someone unfamiliar with Doc Porter. At the point where Maria came out of the back of Charlotte's Place, Rebecca walked out of view of them in the yard and crossed the street.

She adjusted her denim skirt at her trim waist and tightened down on her button up shirt, intentionally popping the next button open.

She smiled slightly as she shook her short blonde hair that barely touched her shoulders and said aloud to herself, "Yes, this twenty-five-year-old server is going to crack the fifty dollar tip threshold tonight. Positive thinking."

On the rear property of Charlotte's Place, Maria approached David and Mel.

"Gentlemen," Maria said softly as she approached.

"Maria," Mel said slightly surprised. "I was just telling David to head on upstairs to clean up so I can take him over to Davenport's before they close up."

"Yes, that would be good. I am sure David needs a few things for the apartment," Maria replied. She slid her hand back into the pocket of the skirt where the forty-four dollars and change remained. *He will need this for the things he needs*, she thought to herself.

"I'll head up now to get cleaned up, Doctor Porter. Can I meet you inside Charlotte's?" David asked as he wiped a little sweat off his brow.

"It's Mel or Doc, please," he said as he turned to walk back into the store. He smiled at Maria. "Take your time, but he closes in about an hour."

"Hi, Maria," David said as he began a slow stride back toward the rear entrance to the living side of the building. Maria walked along with him.

"I am not very good at this so I will just say it. Are you certain you want me to have that tip from Mrs. Kurtvow? I know you have items to buy for the apartment."

David turned and let out a small smile. "I am pretty good at always saying what I mean and meaning what I say. Yes, I think you will find more good use for it than I. I have some cash and I will earn more."

Maria softly touched David's right arm and pulled him to a stop. "Thank you," she said softly as the emotion of being able to better afford Caroline's classes nearly overtook her.

David could sense her emotional level so he wanted to deflect her out of the emotional state she was entering. "Ah," he responded lightly, "so you already have a good use for it. Tell me," he inquired as they walked up the stairs to the third floor.

Maria's voice perked up slightly. "Well, as you saw this morning, Caroline has those summer classes she loves. There are a couple of weeks left before regular school begins two week afterwards and they are fifty dollars a week. It was getting a little tough to come up with the additional money. If your offer is genuine, it will make it far easier to just come up with the difference over the weekend to pay the full bill."

David walked into the apartment and into the kitchen area and removed his shirt. He sat in the chair and took his boots off. "How will you make up the difference? I was talking to Charlotte earlier before I headed outside. She said on Saturday she is only open until about 2 p.m. or whenever she feels like shutting the grill off. And she's closed on Sunday."

"Yes, I was thinking of asking over at McNally's if they needed any additional help for one of the shifts on Saturday," she replied softly as she watched David walk over to the kitchen sink and run the hot water. "They also, like most everyone else here, are closed on Sunday."

"Well, that's refreshing. I come from a land of twenty-four hour stores. People need to force themselves to stop. I think part of the problem is they can do anything at any time and as such they never take a break. When everything is closed, it sort of forces them," David responded as he ran his hand under the water. It was room temperature where he was expecting it to be hot.

"Yes," Maria said with a smile. "Folks are calling you Mr. New York since no one really knows where you came from." She was as much making the statement as she was asking in a probative manner.

"Really?" David responded playfully. "You can tell them Mr. Boston is a little more accurate in a particular context."

Surprised, Maria responded, "So you are from Boston?"

"As wicked as that sounds," David said playfully with a Boston accent, "no, but I am a big Red Sox fan."

Maria smiled. While she was not much of a sports enthusiast she understood the baseball reference. "So from that area of the country I thought the New York Yankees were the favored team."

David paused for a moment and looked at Maria. He knew if he said too much he could give away more of the area from where he came from. "Miss Maria," he said softly and playfully, "you will find I am always pulling for the underdog."

David turned off the water which never got warm and walked over to his duffle bag that was on the adjacent sofa bed. He fused around and pulled out sixty dollars and handed it to Maria.

"What is this?" she asked.

"The forty-four dollar tip covers part of the class and that sixty handles the rest."

Maria immediately handed it back to David like it was on fire. "I cannot. I do not like taking the forty-four you have given me."

"Okay, look. I would prefer you not lose part of a Saturday with Caroline to give her two weeks of classes away from you. The forty-four dollars from Mrs. Kurtvow's tip is yours to keep. If the sixty dollars is too much then just pay me back down the road. It's not like I don't know where you live seeing as how you're one floor down and all."

Maria looked blankly at David as she was suddenly overwhelmed by the kindness of the stranger she met less than twelve hours before.

"Since it was such a discussion piece before, I promise to not leave town before you have the opportunity to pay it back," David replied lightly and with a smile in an effort to come off funny.

Maria tried to restrain her emotions, but one tear got away from her left eye. David quickly turned away and stepped toward the sink to afford her the chance to clear it without getting caught.

"So I guess I am going to have to change without cleaning up," David said looking at the sink. "Seems to be no hot water."

Maria wiped the runaway tear the moment David looked away and upon the registration of his words she turned and walked over to the power breaker box in the apartment. "Miss Charlotte turns off the hot water tank when the room is not rented to save on the electricity," Maria said as she cleared the lump in her throat and threw the switch on.

"Smart woman. Well, at least it'll be ready for the morning," David said as he walked over to the duffle bag and pulled out some clean clothes.

"Please bring your clothes downstairs. You are welcome to use my shower," Maria said quietly as she turned and stepped toward the door.

"Are you sure?" David asked looking back from the bag. "I don't want to impose."

"I insist," Maria responded assuredly as her accent came out hard in the comment. "I will let you in, but then I need to run down to get Caroline."

"Thank you, Maria," David said as he grabbed his things and moved toward the door.

"No, thank you, Mr. David," she said as she walked out and down the stairs ahead of him. "You are beginning to restore my faith in people, strangers no less."

David smiled as he shut his apartment door. Following behind her down the stairs to the second floor he whispered quietly to himself, "And I'm just getting started."

Chapter Four

David walked across the street with Mel Porter toward Jim Davenport's General Store.

"Jim's place is the last of the General Stores," Mel said as he pointed east up Route 385, the town's main artery. "Time was, when the mines were open and the cattle ranches were at full tilt, fifteen years back and over the prior fifty, this whole street was packed each night with local people coming and going. I suppose not as much as you've seen back where we all assume you're from…"

"New York," David said with a smile.

"Well, it's been said back East, but I have heard a couple people call you Mr. New York," Mel said as he smiled, the wrinkles in his face becoming a bit deeper with the expression.

"As I said to Maria earlier, Mr. Boston is a little more accurate in a particular context."

Mel's expression got a little more enthusiastic. "Ah…well, back twenty years ago this town was nearly six thousand in population. We actually were one of the few areas out here that was able to maintain a town government and not have to fall under county rule. Seems like a lifetime ago now…" Mel's voice trailed off.

The two men entered Davenport's General Store. Mel looked up and saw Jim right away and smiled. "Hi Jim," he said and stuck his hand out to shake it.

Jim was in his early sixties. He was taller than David at a little over six foot tall. His mostly white hair was combed backwards and was thinning slightly on the top.

David took a quick scan about the store from where he was standing. With the exception of food items that can be found over at Charlotte's Place, Davenport's General Store had many of those every-day items that you might need right next door rather than traveling to a bigger town to pick them up. Linens, towels, kitchen items, small hand tools, yard items, and so forth.

Mel turned to David and introduced him.

"Jim Davenport, I'd like you to meet…"

"Mr. New York," Jim said with a smile.

"Boy, that nickname sure does travel fast," David said with a smile as he firmly shook Jim's hand. Jim's grip was tighter than David expected, and it actually took him a little by surprise.

"Small town. Friendly town," Jim said with a smile.

"Yes. And I've seen a few of them along my way while traveling. Were I judging a contest, I am thinking that Westville would have already captured that credit and I'm not even here one full day."

"Thank you. We take a lot pride in our town. That is kind to hear from a stranger," Jim said as he smiled even more.

"I mean it. I don't normally toss around a lot of praise," David responded as he quickly pulled out his cell phone to check the time. He moved it around a little and then put it back in his pocket.

"If you're not getting a signal for a call …" Mel pointed over toward the pay phone near the courtesy desk.

"No, no. I just wanted to see what time it was so I knew how long I had. You close up in about thirty minutes at 7 p.m."

"If you need a little more time, it's fine. I am only closing up and heading over to McNally's for something to eat anyway."

"I'll try not to hold you up. I did notice the cell service is spotty here, forget the data network. Are there better locations for reception?" David asked as he grabbed a small cart to hold his purchases.

"The closer you get to the Kurtvow property the better the signals get. Brian Kurtvow paid out of his own pocket to restore that part of the infrastructure."

"I'm not sure I follow," David said as he sharpened his attention regarding the topic as he had some familiarity with it.

Mel edged his way into the conversation. "Five years ago, just as they were wrapping up a major infrastructure project to expand the cable television, cellular, and Internet fiber networks in this rural area off a federal grant, a storm rolled through with a large series of tornados. We were spared as were many towns, simply because we are so spread out. Problem was, the damage that was caused from the storms took out many of the overhead lines, where they were, and some of the substation platforms that housed the systems and their main junction points. Other than the area around the Kurtvow property and the satellite connections he personally maintains, unless you have the money for the personal satellite dishes there's really not much more out here but land phone lines and dial up service to this day."

"Ok, I guess I can understand the set back of a storm but, five years later, nothing?" David said as he scratched his head.

"We are too small a town," Jim added as he turned and looked about the store a bit. "The next town is San Pecos twenty miles up 385 and they are even smaller than us. Fort Alpine is the town east of here. They are smaller than us, too. The closest larger town is East Sanderson with fourteen thousand residents and they are nearly fifty miles away. The lack of population density doesn't allow for the service companies to recover their installation or operational costs for decades even if everyone took the service, which more than half the folks can't even afford. The only reason they were going to sign us up, those that wanted it and could afford it, was because the federal government was paying the installation costs. Once the storm took out that infrastructure...." Jim's voice trailed off. David understood the rest.

"Well, that is too bad. It must be hard on the school kids not having the connectivity to help out with their studies." David began to walk away with his carriage and then stopped and turned back to the two men at the front of the store.

"Say, Doc. What about the library? I saw a little poster on Charlotte's bulletin board that said *Our Library*. I recall something on that flyer about bringing a steady Internet connection to the library. That's the building easterly on 385 on the same side as Charlotte's Place, right?"

Both Jim and Mel smiled. "Yep. Right near the old Town Hall and the other municipal buildings in that small plaza." Jim responded first. "That is our little spitfire Caroline and her dream for the library. She has the Internet access at county school in East Sanderson with the rest of the students from there and the surrounding area. Of course, like most of the other kids, when she comes home, it's either dial up or nothing as most folks, as I mentioned, do not have the dish data connections or even dial up generally due to the expense of it."

Mel continued. "Caroline has this dream to find a way to get the connection back to the library. I believe the building is all set up for it from the wiring side. We had a grant for computer systems, too, but once the storm took out the external infrastructure and the remainder of the project was cancelled, the grants for the computers were pulled."

David looked at both men for a moment. "Do you think her project has any merit?"

Neither man responded right away. They both looked at David as if to quantify the question. Jim finally chimed in "Well, it's not without its merits, but most of us don't have the money to donate to a project like that. A few folks have the wiring know how, but you still need to purchase the computer hardware. And even if that could be done, you have to have the money to service and maintain it monthly."

"Money helps," David responded as he smiled. "But it isn't everything. You can have all the money for something, but without the will to do it, it will fail. When people feel like they have skin in the game and some ownership, it is more powerful than any other currency. There was money for the project before the storm. The storm was a setback. More money could have been lobbied for and I bet there was some level of insurance coverage. Whoever sponsored the bill for the original money lost their will. Either that or something else happened."

Mel leaned back against the checkout counter as he offered his reply. "Senator Foreman. He wasn't reelected. He actually didn't run again. He retired. Said his bit for the people was done. He sponsored the original bill and got the original funding. After he left, no one picked up the ball."

"You said this was all about five years ago?" David asked.

"Well, the bill passed about ten years ago. Then there was setup and so forth. I guess the major work began seven or eight years ago. They were just about done five years ago like I mentioned when the storm took everything out."

"So this is Caroline's idea?" David asked.

Mel smiled softly and replied with a little skip in his voice. "Who else but a child could dream that big?"

David smiled back. "Children are not held back by the obstacles of adults. They are too young to see them."

David grinned a bit and then departed down the aisle to pick up his items as the two men stood in silence over David's comments.

Chapter Five

Maria walked upstairs with Charlotte and Caroline to her second floor apartment. Caroline skipped past her mother and took her things to her bedroom while Maria looked down the hall to the dark bathroom and then pulled out a chair in the kitchen to sit down with Charlotte who had already taken a seat at the table.

"Anything the matter, dear?" Charlotte asked as she got comfortable.

"Oh no, Miss Charlotte. I was wondering if David was finished and it looks like he has and left as the washroom door is open and the lights are off."

Charlotte looked slightly puzzled at the statement so Maria continued. "When he got to the apartment, there was no hot water because he never turned the hot water tank on. Since he wanted to go with Doc to pick some things up, he really did not have a lot of time to spare waiting for the water to heat up so I offered to let him use my shower."

"Ah," Charlotte replied as she leaned forward onto the table with her arms. A little bit of her gray and white hair that was all tightly bound slipped out of the tie and draped loosely down.

"Would you like some tea?" Maria asked as she got up from the table.

"If you're going to put the water on, I don't mind if I do."

Maria got up and filled the kettle with water, put it on the stove, and turned the gas burner up to high.

"If you would excuse me for a moment, I would like to change," Maria said as she began to slowly make her way out of the kitchen to her adjacent bedroom.

"Take your time, dear. I know you want to get comfortable at the end of the day."

Maria smiled and disappeared into her bedroom.

Caroline came out of the other bedroom with a book and walked over to Charlotte. "I was able to borrow this from the school the other day. I think I need to return it soon. I am not sure. Just in case, I think I will finish reading it today."

"That sounds wonderful, dear," Charlotte replied looking the book cover over.

Maria peered out of the room in just her jeans and bra to check on her daughter. She smiled and then grabbed a pink top that was slightly faded and pulled it over her head.

"Won't it be so nice to get our library online, Miss Charlotte? Then not only can we borrow the books, but if we can get the portable e-readers, we will be able to download them from libraries everywhere and read them. Instead of checking out an actual book, we would be checking out a digital copy. We would check it back in the same way when we are done so someone else can borrow it to their e-reader."

Maria walked out of the room at the tail end of her daughter's comments as Charlotte asked a question.

"I thought the school library already allowed for that."

"It does Miss Charlotte." Caroline excitedly continued. "But there are too many kids that want to borrow the e-readers and not enough of them to go around. That and the school is over an hour away on the bus. If we had our own e-readers here at our own library, I could walk there in just minutes to borrow a digital book since we don't have the Internet here at home."

Charlotte was excited for Caroline and her desires to move beyond the few books that were available at their little library branch that she was at a reading level to read. She also was fully aware that hopes of bringing their library online were dashed several years ago with little hope for another round of funding.

"Well, you sound very excited Caroline. I do hope that something comes from the work that was planned for the library."

Maria prepared the teacup for Charlotte as Caroline continued. "Oh, but Miss Charlotte, it will. I have some ideas. You remember. I put up the flyers in your store and over at Mr. Davenport's and Mr. McNally's. I also sent the letter to Mr. Kurtvow. Also, I sent the letter to Governor Green. And Mr.—Mr.—Mama, who was the man I wrote? The one who was originally going to supply all the computers. You told me his name when I asked before and I wrote the letter."

Maria scrunched up her face for a second because she couldn't remember the name off the top of her head. "From Zee Technologies?"

"Yes, Mama. You said he was the owner."

"Ah yes. That was Zachary Taylor."

"Mr. Taylor, Miss Charlotte. Between all those people and all of us I am sure we can do it." Caroline smiled and kissed Charlotte and took her book into the living room and began to read it on the couch.

Maria sighed and looked at her daughter for a few moments and then redirected her attention to the stove as the kettle of water came to a boil.

Charlotte just stared over at Caroline and then looked at Maria who had taken her hair down from the workday. Her long black hair cascaded over her shoulders midway down the length of her back.

"You know," Charlotte said with a sigh, "I remember when you were that age and your mother brought you into the store. I can't believe almost twenty years has come and gone like that."

Maria heard what Charlotte said and nodded slightly, but basically didn't respond as she placed the teacup on the table.

"You were a lot like her, always on fire, always with some mission. She is your daughter." Charlotte turned her attention away from Caroline and looked at Maria. "Something on your mind, child?" Charlotte asked as she slid the drink forward. "Your thoughts seem to be elsewhere."

"Oh, I am so sorry, Miss Charlotte," Maria replied as she snapped out of her thoughts. "I was just thinking of something Mr. David said earlier."

"Which was?" Charlotte asked with additional interest.

"He made some suggestion as to where he was from. He was still being vague. I am not sure what to make of it. It seems odd that Peter would give a stranger a ride in his truck. He never does that. It is out of character."

"It would have to be an extraordinary stranger knowing Peter," Charlotte responded with a slight smile.

"Yes. It is strange. He seems like an honorable man on the surface. Somewhat trustworthy. But he hides things of himself. As if to be closed," Maria responded as she pulled out the chair and sat back down.

"Like many men."

"I do not know many honorable men," Maria responded coldly.

"I didn't specifically mean any one part," Charlotte replied, "but most men play things close to the vest. And when they do, there is often a good reason, even if only they know that reason."

Maria didn't respond to the comment but simply dwelled on it until Caroline called out from the living room.

"Mama, can I go on to the deck to read while the sun is still up?"

"Sure, Caroline, but stay on this floor. We cannot go up to the upper deck as that is Mr. David's deck while he is renting the room."

"Yes, Mama," Caroline replied with a smile as she went over to the sliders, onto the small deck outside the door, and sat on the wicker furniture.

Maria turned her attention back to Charlotte and looked at her but said nothing as thoughts moved in and out of her head.

"You don't usually get this lost in thought, child. As a matter of fact, at the end of the day you're usually a tad chatty until about an hour or so later."

"I am sorry, Miss Charlotte. This David is so puzzling. And then his stay? He may or may not stay some length of time, but he was willing to pay in advance the five full months to the end of the year. It might be one thing for Mr. Kurtvow to do something like that but not David … I do not know his last name."

"Stephenson," Charlotte responded. "He signed my little makeshift lease with Stephenson."

"Okay. So it might be one thing for Mr. Kurtvow to pay a few months ahead like that with everything he has and owns, but not David Stephenson with his whole life in a duffle bag."

"If it meant getting away from Mrs. Kurtvow," Charlotte said in a low tone, "I'd give Brian the room for free to the end of the year."

Maria smiled and then covered her mouth as it became a slight laugh at the comment.

Foot falls made their way up the first set of stairs, past the apartment, and then up the next flight.

"Well I guess all the shopping is done," Charlotte said before taking a sip of tea.

Maria listened for the closing door to the apartment, which she barely heard and then looked up at the ceiling.

"He is very light footed," Maria said as she continued to look at the ceiling. "The prior tenants that have taken that room over the years, you could always hear them walking around. Their footsteps or at the very least the creaking in the floor boards."

Charlotte was about to respond but then stopped herself.

Maria suddenly popped out of her chair. "Excuse me," she said to Charlotte as she went into her bedroom and went into the pockets of her uniform. A moment later, she returned with money from her outfit and set it on the table.

"This was another thing that puzzles me," Maria said pointing to the money. "He clearly has some money because he paid you in advance, but he needed some work to keep up I suppose. But then he rejected Mrs. Kurtvow's tip."

Charlotte glanced over the money quickly. "She left that much? I know she was flirting with our new tenant, but I've never seen her throw one hundred dollars before."

Maria looked down at the money and then looked back up.

"Oh no," Maria responded. "There is more to the story there. So, Mrs. Kurtvow being how she is, left fifty dollars for her five dollar and change breakfast, leaving David the remaining forty four and change. He then proceeded to give it to me when I tried to give it to him."

"And what reason did he give?" Charlotte asked as she leaned in, listening more intently.

"Mr. David said the money wouldn't buy him anything he didn't already have. And then he added something about that he can earn more if he needs more."

Charlotte said nothing and took a moment to let the words settle it.

Maria continued. "Then he also said I might be able to put it toward something that we need or maybe a simple want."

"Did you have something in mind?" Charlotte asked as she eased back in the chair.

Maria moved forward in her seat and leaned on the kitchen table with her arms out in front of her. "That is where there is more to the story. As you know, I have the last two weeks of Caroline's class, one hundred more dollars. So I decided to ask David if he was genuinely offering the tip to me, because if that were the case I was going to put it on the side for that as it would put me about half way there. He said it was a genuine offer. He wanted me to simply take it." Maria leaned back in her seat and then scooted it closer to the table. There was some wash of emotion that came over her face. Charlotte noticed it right away.

"I thanked him and said that I would use it for Caroline's class. I said I would be checking with Mr. McNally to see if he needed any extra help so that I could get the rest of the money right away rather than ask you if I could be a little late with the rent as the payment for the class was due and there was no flexibility on the date. I really did not get into that part with David."

Charlotte reached across the table and with both hands touched Maria's left hand as she was becoming overwhelmed and tears began to stream down her face.

"What happened?"

"He gave me another sixty dollars. I really believe he intended to give it to me, but I insisted on paying him back when I was able," Maria responded through the tears.

"What did he say?"

Maria snickered out a small laugh and responded with a slightly humorous tone. "He agreed and promised not to leave before I had the chance to pay him back. After all, I know where you live, is what he said."

Charlotte smiled at the comment and let Maria's hand go so she could wipe her eyes up.

"This man walks into our lives here…Who is he that he is gracious like this? It is wonderful, but I am so cynical. What kind of man does things like that?" Maria asked as she reached for a napkin on the table to dry her tears.

Charlotte slowly got up and walked over to the slider door to the deck. "An old, troubled soul, perhaps looking for redemption, or maybe resolution. Or maybe, just maybe, a kind soul adrift in the world looking for a place to anchor him," she said softly.

She peered out and noticed Caroline wasn't there. She glanced up at the stairs that lead up to the third floor.

Maria finished composing herself and walked over. "Did you want to sit outside?" she asked Charlotte as she also peered out the window looking for Caroline.

"Oh no," Maria exclaimed as she attempted to head out the door past Charlotte. "Caroline must have gone up."

Charlotte stopped her and put a hushed finger over her lips and pointed up above her as the two stepped out on the deck.

As they moved out and listened, Caroline's voice became clearer as she addressed David.

"…. and so you see, Mr. David, this is why we would like to raise the money for the library. What do you think of my ideas?"

"Well, Caroline, I really must say, your mother was absolutely correct in telling you that you are precocious. I am going to give you a gift Caroline, would you like that?"

Caroline paused and a look of confusion and concern came over her face. "I am not sure. Mother says I cannot take gifts from people."

"That's a good policy, but this is a little different than an actual thing. What I am going to give you is an honest answer that has no bias. That means I am going to answer you without any real opinion of my own on the matter, something I believe most people do not do for anyone let alone little children."

Maria and Charlotte looked at one another. Maria slowly stepped over to the stairs.

David continued. "I think that you are undertaking something very important and something very selfless for the most part. While you do personally have something to gain in getting that library online because you will use it, it will also be available for anyone else that wants to use it. Instead of doing something small and simple to solve your own problem for yourself, you're willing to take this on in order to try to help everyone."

David moved around on the deck slightly and Maria moved away from the stairs back toward Charlotte so as to not be seen. "Should we be listening?" she whispered to Charlotte.

Charlotte only smiled a little.

"What you're trying to do is going to be very difficult, Caroline. Times are trying for most people and around here it might be a little harder on most folks than perhaps elsewhere. Getting local people to help out may only get you so far."

A look of disappointment came over Caroline's face. In all the times she mentioned her ideas to people no one ever responded to her like this. David could see his words saddened her so he continued with some encouragement. "Hey, Caroline," he said softly, "all I wanted to do was to let you know that it will be a difficult task so that you could be properly prepared to take it on if that is something you want to do. Have you ever heard of the Wright Brothers?"

Caroline looked at him with a little puzzlement. "The men who made the airplane?"

"Yes, the men who made the airplane. They crashed a lot of airplanes and were told by a lot of people they would never get one into the air."

He looked at Caroline as she took in the meaning of the words and then continued after a moment. "After being told by a lot of people it couldn't be done and that they should give up, after a lot more hard work and continued effort, after crashing even more planes, one finally got off the ground. The lesson in that story is to never let people discourage you from chasing a dream. Some dreams become realities. Did you understand all of that?"

"I think so," Caroline responded.

"Excellent. So how can I help you take this on?"

Maria and Charlotte looked at one another and Maria turned and headed up the stairs and called out, "Caroline, are you up there?"

Caroline gasped. "Oh! My mama said to stay downstairs." She jumped up and basically hid behind David.

When Maria rounded the corner, David was standing facing her. He smiled slightly with a look of child-like guilt on his face.

"Carolena, hiding behind Mr. David is not going to work. I am so sorry she came up here. I did ask her not to bother you. She had gotten used to coming up here when the apartment was empty."

"It was no problem at all. I came out to watch the sunset and she just made her way up the stairs on her own and we got to talking."

Caroline did not move from behind David but maintained her still position behind him, holding both of her hands on his belt.

David smiled at Maria and Maria smiled back. "I have this funny feeling she is not going to come out," David said as he took a step to the left and like a shadow, Caroline matched it. Charlotte had quietly come up behind Maria and stepped over to the side.

David slowly stepped backwards so he was positioned a little closer to the wicker two-seat bench that was on the deck. "Well," David announced loudly. "I bet I can see the last of that beautiful Texas sunset if I sit right here," he said and he slowly began to sit down "on" Caroline.

Caroline giggled and very quickly let go of David's belt and scampered out of the way toward her mother. David completely sat once she was clear. Caroline went over to her mother and hugged her.

David looked at the two of them and smirked. "I thought that might work."

Maria was still smiling very widely. Caroline looked up at her mother and smiled widely, too. It has been a long time since she saw her mother this happy.

Charlotte also noticed the smile on Maria as she walked over to the single wicker chair and took a seat.

David got up from the bench seat. "Here, girls, sit here. I'll go get a chair from the kitchen."

Maria's expression quickly changed as she responded, "Oh we do not want to bother you."

"Yeah, you're not bothering me. Come sit."

Caroline didn't need to be asked twice. She made her way over to the spot on the bench seat closest to Charlotte.

David smiled at Maria when he walked past her to the kitchen to get a chair.

Charlotte touched Caroline's hand and she looked over to her. David walked out with the chair and was just about to set it down when Charlotte slowly gestured to Caroline and pointed to the chair.

Maria sat on the couch and when David set the chair down, Caroline jumped out of her seat and grabbed the kitchen chair away from him. She slid it to the opposite side of Charlotte and sat in it, leaving the only place to sit next to her mother on the couch.

David looked at the open seat and did not break stride; he walked right over and sat as if it were nothing.

Maria was turning red despite her deeply tanned complexion and she looked right at both Charlotte and Caroline. Charlotte had a "no apologies" look on her face where Caroline could only giggle as little girls do.

Ignoring everything because it didn't faze him, David turned to Charlotte and then Maria. "Well, I would offer you something, but seeing as how I have not here a full day, the fridge is empty. I can get you some water if you like."

"We are fine," Maria said with a smile. The extra color started to drain out of her face. "Caroline may not be later but ...." Maria said jokingly staring at her daughter, which only made her giggle more.

David glanced over at the sun as it was dropping behind the range of hills to the west. Daylight would last a little while longer, but the sun would set shortly.

"Well, David, did you get everything you needed?" Charlotte asked.

"Yes I think so, at least to get started. I hate to buy more than I need. If I need more or something else, I can always go back."

"So Doc introduced you to Jim Davenport I take it," Charlotte continued.

"Yes, and then we walked over to McNally's as Kevin McNally was outside and Doc wanted to introduce me. Then we walked all along Main Street here. He talked about how there used to be more stores along the road and that how there used to be more occupied houses along the feeder roads."

Charlotte smiled and thought back in her head and looked down off the deck to the street below. She spent several minutes thinking about how Main Street looked when her departed husband first bought the store and added the living dwelling space to the building.

"Doc mentioned how the town used to be a strong municipality form of government and as time and the downturn wore it away, Westville and the other remaining communities more or less were forced out of necessity to follow the county-based system. He made it sound like a personal loss or a loss of pride. I could hear it in his voice."

Charlotte silently agreed.

Maria looked over inquisitively at David and asked, "Up North it is all local town and city governments, is it not?"

"It is," David replied. "I am not sure how or where the shift is in the country, but it seems like the Boston to DC corridor and all those states seem to allow for town or city based governments and then as the population spreads out it turns to more and more to county-based systems. I believe the western states follow the northern and northeastern ones with some exceptions."

Maria adjusted herself on the couch and David moved away a little to give her some room.

David grabbed his phone off his belt to check the time.

"Are you expecting a call?" Maria asked.

"Out here? Not with the lousy signal. This is truly a glorified watch out here," David said with a smile. "I wanted to be mindful of the time. Doc and Jim are over at McNally's and they wanted me to stop by for a drink with Kevin McNally. Apparently, there are more stories to tell the newcomer."

"When are they expecting you?" Charlotte asked smiling.

"I told Doc after I finished up at Mr. Davenports, chatted with Mr. McNally for a bit, and took a stroll with him that I wanted to drop the things I bought off and then I would head over. I told him around eight so I'll get going in a few minutes or so since it's after that already."

David stood and looked at Caroline and then turned and pointed west. "There it goes."

Caroline looked at the setting sun as it disappeared over the hill. "Another sunset?" she asked.

"Another day done," David said as he smiled and walked past everyone and toward the stairs. "Well, I am going to head over. Caroline, as long as it is okay with your mother first, you are more than welcome to come up here and sit."

Caroline jumped up and hugged David at the waist. "Oh thank you Mr. David. It's okay, right Mama?"

"As long as Mr. David has no issues with it I am fine," she responded looking as David who lightly shook his head no.

Caroline squeezed David even harder. David instinctively ran his fingers through part of her hair. The color drained away from his face when Caroline let go and looked up at him. A heavy weight came over him when he looked into her dark brown eyes. Suddenly concerned that the way he felt was visible he knelt down in front of Caroline. "Now remember what I said, if you want to do this library thing, you count me in. You tell me how you think I can help you take this on. You sleep on it and maybe think about it over the weekend and let me know. And then..."

"And then our plane will fly," Caroline added.

"That's right. Crash as many as we need to make one fly. I am all yours, little lady." David smiled and stood. "Good night, ladies."

Caroline smiled as David made his was down the stairs.

"Excuse me," Maria said softly to Charlotte and pointed to Caroline. Charlotte nodded and Maria followed David down the stairs.

It took her to the ground level to catch up with David's long strides.

"David," Maria called out as he landed on the dirt at the bottom.

David turned around and smiled at her.

"It is very kind of you to offer to help Caroline, but it is not really necessary."

"I am not sure what you mean. I would only help and work with her when you were around. Unless you disapprove of me being around in general."

"Oh no, it is not that. I just wanted to let you know that you do not have to entertain her."

"Okay, but if I wanted to work with her on this, you don't have an issue, correct?"

"No, I would not have an issue with it, but I am certain you have other things you would rather do."

David reached down and took Maria's right hand and held it in both of his. "Like what, Maria? All I have is some work here and little else. It isn't that I don't have anything else better to do, but rather even if I had other actual things to do, I cannot think of anything better I'd rather do than watch a little girl fight to reach her goals."

David let Maria's hand slip away and he took a couple steps back.

"Do you think it is really possible? What Caroline wants to do?"

David smiled a little a first and then much wider. "Anything is possible. You need to believe and you need to keep getting up and pushing forward."

"Are you not concerned with failing?"

"I don't fear failing, Maria," David replied as he turned to walk off the property and across the street. "The only thing I fear is the one time I fail so badly that I do not want to try again."

Maria stood and watched David walk across the street as the setting sun glinted off the windows of McNally's.

Chapter Six

David stepped into McNally's and immediately saw Mel Porter and Jim Davenport sitting at the bar along with a few other regulars. Kevin McNally came around the bar and introduced all of the regulars to David and he made acquaintances with them.

As Kevin walked around to the few folks that were eating dinner at tables around the bar area to ask them how their meals were he introduced them to David.

Over the first hour in the place and over three drinks bought by some of those regulars, David met close to thirty people before he finally settled into a seat at the bar with Mel and Jim.

"Wow, I feel like I am running for public office or something off a whistle stop," David said as he laughed and pulled his beer toward the end of the rail. "So Rebecca, you're effectively the only one I haven't really talked to, so introduce yourself."

Rebecca, who had been working tables earlier until another waitress came in, was now pouring drinks behind the bar. She smiled wide at being asked. She tossed her short blonde hair with her hand. "Well, the short, short version is I grew up here and twenty-six years later I am tending bar for my next door neighbor," she said in a sassy tone as she smiled at Mr. McNally.

"Okay, is there an extended version of that story that you can tell in sixty seconds between drink orders?" David said as he finished off his fourth drink and then pointed to another. "Good thing I am only walking across the street."

"Sure," Rebecca replied as she went over to the tap to refill David's beer. "I was from the last high school class locally here in town before we shut down and went to the regional system. I wanted to go to Western Texas College, but things happened at home, money got tight, and I did what I needed to."

Rebecca's voice trailed off just a little as she finished. David knew it was a disappointment to her to have not been able to go. Generally, he would read a little more into it, but he was untrusting of his own perception of the conversations as the drinks were settling in on him. He decided to try to change the subject until Rebecca continued on her own. "Now there's a little bit more of a possibility to go as far as the demands on my time, but not so much on my ability to pay. I would say I am resigned to my fate, slash, future, but I don't look at it as such a bad thing." Her voice picked up as she brought David's beer over to him. "There are worse fates in the world and I've made my peace with the path I'm on and the direction I'm heading."

David listened to the tone of her words and her body language. As much as she as speaking them, she was trying to convince herself that she was alright with the outcome of her life to this point. David was less convinced but let it be for now.

From his seat he could see out the front windows of the bar and across to Charlotte's Place. All the lights were still on at Maria's. He looked at his phone. "Almost nine thirty," he said aloud as he hopped off the barstool and over to the pile of newspapers at the far end of the bar.

"That's our little monthly newspaper," Rebecca said as she walked down that end of the bar on the server side. "We don't have all that much going on for even a weekly so I write that once a month and I publish an extra issue around Memorial Day and then Labor Day. You know, the unofficial beginning and end of summer."

"So this is your work?" David asked as he took the small periodical and folded it up lengthwise to put into his back pocket to read later. "How much? I'll read it at home."

"Oh, I don't charge for it. I print a few dozen copies each month and leave them here and at Mr. Davenport's store, Charlotte's, and a few of the other merchant places up and down 385 here in town. Customers take them to read as they want. I sell the ad space. I make a few dollars but mostly it's just covering costs. The merchants are actually being kind by taking ad space. It's not like we have any other place to really go locally and none of the businesses compete."

David took in Rebecca's comment as he sat. It hadn't occurred to him up until that point that there was only one of each type of business. While there was a little overlap of some items from a convenience factor, there was only one hardware store, one barber, one pub and restaurant, one convenience store, and so on.

"So the newspaper and the writing, I take it that is a hobby or passion of yours, or was it something you were hoping to do?"

Rebecca turned her blue eyes in the direction of the door. "Yes, it is a passion of mine. I was hoping to get a degree in journalism."

David turned to the door as Rebecca's gaze was still locked there.

Sue Ann Kurtvow stepped in and moved her way over to the bar area. She set her purse down on the bar and slid it along toward where Mel, Jim, and David were sitting.

Kevin immediately got up. "Mrs. Kurtvow, would you like your usual?" he asked as he pulled out the chair for her. She passed by it and pulled the chair out next to David and sat.

"Of course, darling," she replied, leaning her left side into the bar and looked to her right at David. "What a wonderful surprise to see you here, David. I trust your first day in our little town has been okay for you."

"It's been just fine, Mrs. Kurtvow," David said with a smile as he looked around at folks. Most were cautiously polite to her, but he could sense the tension. Part of it was dislike for the woman and part of it was something else he didn't understand.

"I do believe I had said it's Sue Ann," she replied in a sickly sweet southern tone. "I don't need you to be so formal with me. I am actually hoping you can get quite familiar with me," she replied. She put her right hand on his left knee and slowly moved it up his thigh.

David looked at Rebecca who didn't know how to react. Sue Ann was known for this, but she was generally not so brazen or public about making an advance.

"Mrs. Kurtvow, were you out with Mr. Kurtvow this evening?" Rebecca asked softly.

"That stick in the mud?" Sue Ann replied harshly. "He doesn't like to even go out to the mailbox to get the newspaper. Oh, not your little publication Rebecca; the real one that comes each day out of Dallas."

David flinched at the comment. It was the same type of cutting remark she made earlier to Maria. David had to breathe in and count. He was losing his social filter having the few drinks he had in such a short amount of time. He wasn't as worried about the getting home part as he was about speaking his true mind at the time.

"So, do tell me David, did the gentlemen show you around properly? It would have been better to have a proper escort for the earlier evening, but I was tied up with other matters. I am now free however."

David just smiled as Sue Ann's hand was now all the way up his thigh and she slid it to the inside.

Kevin came out of the kitchen with a bottle of champagne in an ice bucket and filled a glass for Sue Ann.

"You can mark me up, Kevin, and get David his drinks on me," Sue Ann replied as she removed her hand from David and took her drink.

Rebecca moved to the register, went over to a ledger much like the one Maria marked up at Charlotte's in the morning, and entered information into it.

"David has about four more drinks coming from other people this evening. I am not sure he's going to get through all of them tonight," Mel interjected politely.

"Well, that is just fine, Doc. Those can be put on credit for him on a bar tab. The rest of the night he is mine," she said with a wicked tone.

Mel turned to Jim and said quietly, "This is not going to end well. He's drinking and she's somewhere between persuasive and demanding."

The house phone rang and Rebecca answered it behind the bar. "Jim, it's for you. The Mrs."

Jim pulled out his cell and looked at the zero bars and put it away. "Thanks," he said as he took the phone from her.

Mel got up and went over to the kitchen and walked in behind Kevin.

"Uh, we need to get him out of here," Mel said when Kevin moved around the corner.

"Him who? David? He's fine. Sue Ann is only going to push so far in public and David seems like he has the type of personality to deal well with her as long as he slows down on the drinking. What are you suggesting?"

"I'm not sure, but she is not the best this town has to offer. Besides that, I like David and whether he stays just a little while or longer than he planned, it's better she doesn't get hooks into him. Never ends well," Mel replied.

"Has to offer what? You heard him. He's here for a while, but he is not staying. Brian Kurtvow is resigned to the way his wife is and there's no stopping her anyway. You deliberately yank him out of here and piss Sue Ann off and it'll be way worse than anything she's going to dish out on her own."

Jim poked his head into the kitchen. "The little lady wants me to come home so I'm leaving. Good luck with this mess." He smirked as he pointed over his shoulder with his thumb. "Think you two knuckleheads can get him back across the street okay so he's not a statistic?"

"We won't let him get hit by a car," Mel said with a grin.

"I mean a Sue Ann statistic. He'd be better off if he got hit with the car," Jim said with a laugh. "Good night, gentlemen."

"Jim," Kevin called out.

"Yeah," Jim responded coming back into the kitchen.

Kevin thought for a moment and then followed. "Can you stick your head outside? Let me know if she drove herself or if she had the driver take her."

"Sure," Jim replied as he backed out of the kitchen and walked toward the front door.

The two men stood silently for a moment waiting for Jim to come back. Kevin looked at David who was now alone with Sue Ann with only Rebecca at the bar.

Jim came back to the kitchen. "She has the driver. She's up for maximum mischief. Sorry, gents, I need to leave."

"Why does she do this?" Kevin asked out loud.

"Because she can. On top of having nice features she has money and power. So with all that, she's always starved for whatever she doesn't have and right now her current interest, for whatever reason, is David," Mel replied.

"Well, maybe it doesn't really matter," Kevin responded. "Brian knows what is going on. Sue Ann could care less. David clearly is here by himself. He's probably the best-dressed drifter we've had in a while. Let Sue Ann sniff him up. It distracts her from the locals who are trying not to piss off wives and girlfriends. If he knows how to screw really well, perhaps he can change her entire disposition."

"No one has that much skill and talent," Mel huffed as he walked toward the kitchen phone. He picked it up and dialed a number.

"Who are you calling?" Kevin asked, peering out the window of the kitchen again.

"Charlotte. I thought maybe I could have her call the bar with something for David to do and maybe he'd leave on his own. She's not answering," Mel responded. "She might be upstairs at Maria's. She often goes up there after work to visit."

"So call Maria's," Kevin responded.

"Maria doesn't have a phone. I'll see if I can get him to go over there," Mel said as he walked out of the kitchen and over to David. He partially wedged himself between Sue Ann and him.

"David, Charlotte needs help with something over at the store. Can you head over and give her a hand?"

David sharpened up at the comment and sat up more in the chair. Sue Ann put her hand back on his thigh.

"Charlotte isn't here," Sue Ann responded sharply. "Whatever it is can wait for the morning, I am sure. What was the issue?"

"She didn't say," Mel responded.

"Well, then it can't be a very large emergency and it can wait. I didn't hear the phone ring a second time. There was only the one for Jim to scamper home, which he quickly did."

David slipped back into a casual posture in the seat. Kevin walked over and pulled on Mel's arm and brought him over to the front of the bar by the front door.

"Look, Doc, I don't want her pissed off at me again. Remember last year? The sales guy from Kansas City? His car broke down and he was stuck here for a couple days?"

"Yes. The blonde fella," Mel said with a laugh.

"We all tried to save him and Sue Ann caused all kinds of problems with the ledgers, including mine and others that tried to help. She can deal with being outsmarted. She views it like gamesmanship or something perverted. But if it is a brute outflank like just yanking the guy out of here she gets mad and gets even. So either outsmart her or let her be."

Mel looked out the window and across the street. Maria's lights were still on. He turned to look at David and then to Kevin.

"Don't let him leave with her. I'll outsmart her, but I need a minute."

Kevin said nothing and just stared at him.

"Give me your word. You'll keep him here."

"I'll do my best, Doc. I can only do so much. She's not likely to leave the champagne bottle. It's still half full and I don't allow her to take it with her."

Mel crossed the street under the only floodlight on Route 385 in town and made his way over to Charlotte's Place. He headed up the stairs to the second floor and knocked on the door.

Maria opened the door quietly. "Doc? Why are you here so late?" Maria asked in a soft whisper.

"Pardon me, Miss Maria, I was looking for Miss Charlotte and she wasn't answering her phone."

Maria pointed over to her couch. "She fell asleep. Caroline was reading aloud. It happens often, actually, and she just stays overnight on the couch. It is a nice role reversal, instead of the adult reading the little one to sleep. I actually just put Caroline to bed."

Mel frowned.

"Is something the matter?"

"I feel stupid even mentioning it to you. Charlotte would understand."

"Can you try?" Maria asked softly.

"Bottom line?"

"Of course."

"You remember the incident with the sales guy from Kansas City and Mrs. Kurtvow?"

Maria stood for a second to try to recall the events and then responded. "I believe so, not every detail and every time someone told the story it changed a little. But I do remember generally what happened."

"David is stuck at the bar with her right now. Same situation," Mel said as he looked at her plainly.

Maria was motionless at first and then asked, "Can you stay here in case Caroline wakes up?"

"Yes, but what are you going to do?"

"I am not certain, but I will try to get David out of there," Maria said as she headed down the stairs.

Maria went across the street in a hurry. Mel looked out the window.

Rebecca watched Maria enter the bar past Sue Ann's driver who was sitting right outside the front door.

Sue Ann looked over and pulled her hand off of David's leg despite the fact that Maria clearly saw her.

"Excuse me, David," Maria said over the din of the conversations of the remaining patrons.

David set down his sixth drink and slowly turned around. "Maria?"

"I am sorry to bother you this late…"

"Yes, Miss Moreno, what is so important that you are interrupting us?"

Maria took a deep breath. Sue Ann normally disarms her and she backs down, but she wanted to stand on this.

"I am sorry, Mrs. Kurtvow. David, Caroline fell asleep and then woke up upset and she asked to see you. I generally would not impose on someone…"

David popped right out of the chair "Rebecca, Mr. McNally, if I owe you money I'll square up in the morning."

Maria quickly followed as David bolted nearly full speed out of the bar.

Kevin stopped Maria short. "He's had a lot to drink in a short period of time. Make sure he's okay."

Maria nodded as she entered the street. David was already headed up the stairs. Mel barely got the door open.

Maria felt incredibly guilty. She hadn't expected such a dramatic reaction from the white lie to get David out of the bar.

When she got into the apartment, Mel asked, "What did you say? He couldn't get in here any faster if he flew."

Charlotte woke up from the commotion and sat up on the couch. Mel walked over and helped her up.

Maria stood in Caroline's door way. David was kneeling on the floor and looking her over and he turned to see Charlotte and Mel approach.

"She's all set. She fell back asleep," David said addressing the others.

David slowly got up as the adrenaline rush and the alcohol messed with his ability to stand correctly.

Maria stepped forward to help steady him and took him by his arm.

David softly touched her hand and they walked out of the room.

Mel closed the door behind them.

David approached the kitchen table and put both hands on it and leaned forward. His vision went totally out of focus and a warmth filled his nose.

"Doc," Maria called out.

Mel looked over as the blood ran out of David's nose. It was a heavy volume and it spotted on the kitchen table.

Maria grabbed a dish towel and covered his nose. "I used to get these. It will be okay, tip your head back."

"No!" Mel called out. "There's too much volume. It'll back up into his lungs." Mel kept the rag under his nose but kept his head forward. Maria got a clean towel and wet it with hot water.

After a moment, the bleeding stopped. David was still disoriented and didn't move.

Maria washed the blood off his face.

As the foggy feeling lifted, David was less aware of the bloody nose he had than why he had come over in the first place.

"Caroline," he said as he lurched to move.

"David, she is fine. You just checked on her. Thank you very much for coming right over," Maria said softly. She was still wracked with guilt for using Caroline as the motivator for getting him over.

"Damn nosebleeds. They are happening more and more often. I'm sorry. I'll replace your towels."

"I am not worried about towels. Are you okay?" Maria asked as she continued to clean him up.

"I'll be fine. I always am." David was suddenly more and more aware of his surroundings and who was present. Despite not feeling well mixed with what he had to drink he started to move toward the door.

"Are you sure you will be okay? You had a bit to drink and that was a sudden and nasty nose bleed," Maria said when he made his way to the door.

"I'm sure. I'm good."

"Just as well, I am going to come up in the morning," Maria said sternly.

David smiled a little and headed out the door and up the stairs.

Charlotte looked at Mel. "You didn't like that nosebleed?"

"No," Mel replied. "That was not a small blood vessel rupture like you might see in a normal nosebleed."

"What should we do?" Maria asked.

"I'll try to talk to him in the morning," Mel said as he headed to the door. "I am not his doctor so I don't have his history, but I can try to see if he'll let the retired doc look at him."

"Thanks, Doc," Charlotte responded.

When Mel left, Charlotte slowly made her way toward the door. She turned and smiled at Maria. "I was napping for a bit and missed some of this. I trust you'll tell me the rest of the story in the morning?"

Maria smiled back and said, "Of course."

Maria watched Charlotte walk down the stairs and let herself into her apartment and then she closed the door.

Chapter Seven

It was early morning with the sunlight just barely coming in through the apartment windows. Charlotte moved about her first floor apartment.

She looked at the clock on the wall in the kitchen over the sink that read 5:45 a.m.

As she headed over to the slider door to her deck, she could hear Maria's footfalls overhead.

Charlotte opened the slider and stepped outside with the keys to the rear door of the store when she noticed David already working on more of the overgrown area she wanted cleared on the south side of the property. She slowly made her way off her deck and over to him.

"Good morning, Miss Charlotte," David said as he looked up from what he was doing with the hand tools.

"You don't need to be out here so early doing this work," she said as she looked over what he already cleared.

"Well, I couldn't sleep anymore. I only sleep a few hours each night and I was restless so I figured I'd get started on this. The hand tools are quiet. I am sure I didn't wake anyone up."

"It's not that," Charlotte said, her voice trailing off slightly.

David stopped what he was doing and turned around to look directly at her and pay full attention. "I think I have a pretty good idea what's at issue," David said with a smile.

Charlotte looked at him and squinted. "Okay, go ahead. I'm listening," she responded a little coarsely.

David took a moment and sized up the response and how he wanted to say it. "I am going to make the presumption that you had the apartment for rent and you were only able to afford the work for the hired hand based off the rental take. It makes it a wash, but it's why you wanted or needed to help Maria since you're able to do less and less to help her in the store."

Charlotte didn't say anything, but the response was all on her face.

"I'll presume that is your 'you're a smart ass' look," David said jokingly as his smile grew wide.

"As funny as this all is" Charlotte responded lightening her own disposition, "you're right. I don't have enough money to afford all the work you're doing. At least not at the rate you're doing it."

"Look, Miss Charlotte, it's fine. I'm here, the work needs to be done, and honestly, what else do I have to do? The work keeps me out of trouble. As you saw from last night, I can pretty quickly get into it."

"Oh, I wouldn't sweat Sue Ann all that much. That's her being her. We can do little about it other than deal with it," Charlotte said as she turned to look up at the second floor apartment. Maria was standing out on the deck looking down at the two of them.

David turned in the direction of the house and waved. Maria smiled and waved back.

Charlotte turned slightly to David as she was about to step away and head to the store. "You make sure you don't overdo it out here. It can get surprisingly hot before you realize it. Come in when you need to and have a drink and to cool off."

"I'll make sure," David responded as he was about to start working again. Charlotte hadn't moved so he looked back up at her. "Was there anything else?"

Charlotte was trying to put the words together, which was unusual for her. If she had something to say, she just often said it. She drew in a deep breath and just opened her mouth. "You gave us a bit of a scare last night."

A look of concern came on David's face. Charlotte studied it quickly as it was uncommon for him from what she saw up to this point.

"Thank you for the concern, really. It's nice to have people that care and are concerned. But it was really nothing more than a bloody nose." David continued in an effort to be more convincing. "It's dry here, drier than I am used to. I am sure folks around here have their share of bloody noses."

Almost on queue and without missing a beat Charlotte responded. "It was enough to cause Doc to be concerned."

David sighed audibly. "I'll take it easy. I promise, no one will have to come out here today and pick me up off the ground."

Charlotte paused and studied David's response carefully as felt she was starting to understand how he talked.

"It's not today, necessarily, that I am worried about," she replied as she slowly turned and walked toward the store.

Maria had been watching the conversation from her deck and made her way down the stairs as Charlotte walked away and into the store.

While she was happy to have been able to pull David away from the drama that was Mrs. Kurtvow, she felt badly about using Caroline as the lure, especially since it provoked such a dramatic response from him, much more than she had expected.

When she landed on the ground level and made her way over to him, she was also concerned about his well-being after the incident with his bloody nose and Doc's response to it.

As she approached, David stopped and looked up at her. "Good morning," he said, smiling slightly.

"How are you feeling?" she asked quietly. A slight breeze moved her uniform skirt about.

"I'm fine. I don't hangover. Or I should say, if the beer is going to impact me in the morning, there needs to be more of it than what I had."

Maria paused for a moment. "That is good to hear, but I was more concerned about your overall well-being. That bloody nose gave me quite a scare last night."

"Yes, well I am sorry about that. I didn't mean to do that," David responded softly.

"I am sure it is not something you can control. As long as you are feeling better…."

"I am. Are you headed to work?" David asked. To be funny, he pointed to her waitress uniform.

"Oh no. Today is my day off. These are the only clothes I have," she replied plainly.

David stood for a moment unsure of how to react until Maria cracked a bashful smile and tucked her head down a little to try to hide it.

"That was pretty funny," David replied. "Given some folks around here, yourself included, that could be an actual case."

"Well, yes, I do suppose so. I thought you would like a little humor from me," Maria said turning slightly to walk in.

"It was unexpected. Say, how did Caroline sleep? No more problems?"

The guilt washed in on Maria again. "Yes, she is still asleep."

"I take it she is used to you being in the store and her alone in the apartment."

"Yes. I used to wake her up and take her as needed or go in later, but she has adapted to getting herself up and settled. She comes down on her own after she dresses herself," Maria said smiling.

"She is quite responsible and independent. You must be a proud mother."

Maria smiled at David's comments. "I am. Sometimes I wish I could do more."

"Each to their own ability," David said softly. "If you do everything you can, and I believe you are, then you are doing as much as possible."

Maria let David's words sink in rather than respond to them. What he said and how he said it comforted her and removed a little bit of the self-doubt that she had this morning on the job she was doing raising her daughter alone.

"How do you do that?" Maria asked.

"Do what?"

"Know exactly what to say to put someone at ease? You did it yesterday with Caroline when you talked with her about the reality of what she wanted to undertake with this fundraising. You were honest with her on the reality of it, which naturally upset her, but you immediately explained it and put her fears to rest and encouraged her to continue anyway."

"So you were eavesdropping?" David said as he snickered.

Maria suddenly realized she tipped her hand. She had forgotten she heard the conversation from the deck below. She became embarrassed and blushed slightly.

"It's okay. To answer your question, I'm not really sure how or what it is that I am doing. I like to think that for the most part I am either telling people the truth, being honest, or simply speaking from the heart. If you start there, you really can't go wrong. Don't worry, at some point I'll have to do that, speak a truth that will be ugly. It'll upset someone for sure."

Maria again just took in the words and then asked, "So you do not lie?"

"Everyone lies. I try to avoid it. It usually serves no one well and generally in the long run the truth is better."

Maria firmed up her stance on those words and then spoke freely what was directly on her mind at that moment. "Why are you here?"

David paused for a moment. "I really don't understand your question."

"You blew into this town like a tumbleweed. And you are affecting people's lives."

David's voice moved to concern. "I'm sorry. I hadn't realized my arrival was a bad thing or causing some concern."

"You misunderstand. You are not affecting it in a bad way. People that have met you speak kindly of you. People in the store. I am sure the sentiment will be the same of the people you met in McNally's last night."

"Sue Ann really seems to like me," David said to be funny and off set the mood. Maria didn't bite into the misdirection.

"Even Caroline, I do not often see her warm up to someone so fast."

"You're not used to it either," David said in a deadpan tone.

"That is a little presumptuous," Maria responded a little defensively.

"Perhaps. But the assessment is correct," David replied assuredly.

"To take a page out of your book, as they say, it would serve me little to not be honest. But you did not answer my question."

David paused for a moment to consider how he wanted to answer a question like that. "Well, everyone needs to be somewhere. At this point in my life I am just drifting along. I ended up here." David turned and looked at the rising sun over the eastern hills. "I have simply decided that as I drift along I would try to give more than I take and take some opportunity to stop and reassess what is really important to others and help them find ways to realize those things."

Maria didn't know what to say at first. She smiled and watched him look into the sun.

It was a few moments before she spoke again.

"Caroline's effort," she said, thinking about what he just said. "Do you really believe she can accomplish that?"

David turned away from the morning sun and looked up at Maria's second floor apartment. "People don't understand the power they have. They can do anything."

"Things like what she wishes to do, it costs a lot of money. Other than the Kurtvow's, no one here has it."

"People need to step up and do. The money will follow if money is the solution. Parts of all efforts require more than just money."

"But without money it will not happen," Maria replied.

"Without any one part it won't happen. Look at the original infrastructure effort around here," David said as he turned his gaze from the apartment to Maria. The money was there. After the storm, the priority shifted. If someone kept their eye on the prize and the pressure up, that effort could have been continued and completed."

"Caroline is in this all by herself. People speak to her kindly about it, but the reality is no one is in a real position to help her. She is only eight."

David turned and smiled. "She'll be nine in two months. She said so herself."

Maria smiled that he remembered her saying that. "Yes, on October tenth."

"And the part about being all by herself, that's not true. You'll help her. Miss Charlotte will, too. I am sure Jim Davenport will. And Rebecca. And Doc. There's plenty of help."

"And you, too," Maria smiled.

"Yes, me, too."

"And you really believe she can do it?"

David was cautious on his follow up. "I believe she can bring the effort together. This town gets behind its people from the stories I heard last night at McNally's. They care enough to help each other out like with Rebecca's little newspaper. They cared enough to help the stranger out of the local cougar den."

Maria smiled and then covered her mouth as it became a laugh. The smile dissipated and she looked back at David with a level of seriousness.

"So, I have asked twice and you have not answered. Do you think it is possible for Caroline to make some progress on this?"

David decided to take on a position of strength on his final comment.

"Well, back to my Wright Brothers analogy that I used last night," he said as he turned and began walking away back toward the apartment. "I think enough planes have crashed here. I think you are all due to get one into the air."

Chapter Eight

It was a little after two in the afternoon when Charlotte decided to close up the store for the day. Not many folks were coming in for much of anything. The ones who were going to already had in the morning.

Maria headed out the side door and around to the dumpster to throw the last of the trash away when she spotted David and Caroline at one of the picnic tables near the front of the store where patrons would sometimes eat their lunch.

She realized they hadn't seen her come out the door so she quietly made her way back over to the side door and into earshot of the conversation.

"...so we'll start with that after we get all the information we need." David pointed to his laptop screen. "We will talk to Mr. McNally and Mr. Davenport and see if they can help us, and if so with how much, and then we'll speak with the Sherriff about what we can and cannot do on Route 385. Whatever we can't, we'll do on all the cross streets."

"That seems like a lot of work, Mr. David," Caroline said with some concern.

"Well, Caroline, the reality of it is that it is a huge undertaking. However, if you set your mind to most things, no matter how difficult, with enough help, time, effort, and persistence, a difference can be made."

Caroline looked at him carefully and then back at the laptop. "I'm afraid. What if I can't do everything?"

"Well, you're not going to be doing everything alone. People will help and do their part."

"Will you help me, Mr. David?" Caroline asked as a warm, stiff breeze blew her hair back behind her.

"I did say to sign me up first," he responded with a wide smile. "Of course I will help you."

Caroline stood a little on the picnic table bench and hugged David around the neck tightly. "Oh thank you. I can't wait to tell Mama. I want to do this. I want it to be a success. I want her to be proud of me."

Caroline squeezed a little tighter and then let him go and sat back on the bench.

David had to compose himself slightly. Caroline's hug brought up an emotional response of happiness he long thought he had buried in the past.

Maria was still listening behind them in the doorway. Charlotte had come out and was listening now as well.

"Listen, Caroline, Maria, your mother, she is already proud of you. You want to learn so you study hard. You read more than what's assigned to you because you like it and all that does is make you smarter. You try your best. You're polite and helpful. You are kind. You think of others before you think of yourself. These are many of the things your mother is trying to teach you and give to you of herself. You are taking what she teaches and gives and making even more out of it. Whether you succeed or fail in this effort is not going to make her any less proud."

Caroline smiled.

Tears ran down Maria's face. She turned to Charlotte and stepped back into the store before she was seen. Charlotte followed.

"Are you okay?" Charlotte asked, poking open the facial tissues that were at the aisle and handing the box to Maria.

"Who is this man? He cannot be real. He is not as old as an elder, but he speaks like one."

"Clearly, he is real and I don't understand the question," Charlotte replied looking at her.

"How does a man with that kind of depth and capacity not belong to someone? Not have a family of his own? He is out here, in the middle of our nowhere, all by himself. I just feel like there is something missing. It is almost to the point of him being dishonest," Maria responded still crying and wavering on being upset.

"Maria, everyone keeps some secrets. Generally, no one knows everything about anyone. I am sure my Henry kept a secret or two from me with good reason. Whatever David's are, he is keeping them. We need to accept that and perhaps, maybe, when he feels comfortable enough, he will share some of them."

"I do not feel I have kept things from people," Maria said as she was still upset. "This man has such a level of caring and love, look at him," she said gesturing to the window where they were in full view. "Have you ever seen a man like that before? That took to their own child, let alone the child of a stranger, with that level of compassion and caring?"

"No I haven't. I believe in God and I've never seen Him either," Charlotte replied quickly. "What I do know is that he is here and he is a good influence. On more than just Caroline."

"What do you mean? I do not understand," Maria asked as she dried her tears.

"I've seen you joyful around Caroline, but it's always subdued on some level. You always have this undertone of worry and concern when it comes to you and your lives. I have seen you happy and a tear or two come down your face. But you tell me child, when was the last time you were really this happy? When was the last time you worried less as it seems you have over these past two days?" Charlotte moved toward the front of the store to lock the door.

"Seems to me he's as good an influence on you as he is on Caroline. And again, what's so wrong about that? Sometimes a sunny day is just a sunny day. There is no ulterior motive to warmth and bright sunshine."

Maria let the words sink in as she saw Caroline bound around the side door to the store. Meanwhile, Mel Porter crossed the street and approached David. Maria quickly dried up her eyes and took the now open box of tissues over to the counter.

Caroline walked in and headed over to her mother.

"Is everything alright Mama? Have you been crying?" Caroline's happy look changed to one of concern.

"Oh honey, I am fine," Maria replied softly.

"Mr. David was wonderful. He is such a smart man. He has so many ideas of ways to try to raise the money for the Library."

"Do tell, child," Charlotte said as she walked over to the side door to lock it up and then headed over to the counter to take a seat.

Caroline hopped up on the counter and sat facing the customer side as Maria sat on the next stool.

"He has a whole bunch of notes on his laptop, but he has everything there. He talked a lot. There were a lot of things to look into, he said, but he also said he would help and talk to some of the others here in town to see if they could help. He even said he would approach Mr. Kurtvow for help."

Charlotte and Maria looked at one another at that point.

"What?" Caroline asked as she noticed the reaction.

Charlotte slowly spoke up once she figured out how she wanted to say what was on her mind. "Mr. Kurtvow used to be very helpful to people, but that was a long time ago."

"What happened to him?" Caroline asked.

"Mrs. Kurtvow," Maria quipped as a look of disdain overtook her face.

"I'm not really sure what that means, but Mr. David seems to think Mr. Kurtvow is a good place to start after..." Caroline responded, leaving the rest of the thought unfinished.

"After what, honey?" Maria asked.

"Well, I can't remember it all. Mr. David talked very fast. He mentioned needing to understand how far the work had gotten at the library itself. He thought that maybe if enough of the wiring was done and if it was the right type of wiring that maybe those dishes could be used for the Internet. You know, from the satellite."

Maria nodded. Charlotte, not really sure of the technology, simply sat and listened to more.

"There was more, but I can't remember it all. Miss Charlotte, are you coming over to eat tonight?"

"I do most nights, dear. Your mother is always good enough to have me over," Charlotte replied as she tweaked Caroline's nose. "That, and I like the company."

"Why do you ask, Caroline?" Maria asked as she took her waitress apron off.

"Well Mama, I thought maybe we could invite Mr. David over for dinner. He could tell you more about what he was thinking for the library."

"That is probably a little forward of us, Caroline," Maria responded cautiously as she headed farther behind the counter to put the apron away. "Perhaps he is already busy with something else."

"Oh he's not Mama. I asked him already," Caroline responded without missing a beat.

Charlotte put her hand over her mouth as her smile from the exchange became laughter.

"You asked him over to eat? You know you're not to invite people over to eat without asking me, Caroline. Especially adults." Maria replied, somewhat upset as she took her hair catch out and let her hair down.

"Yes Mama, I know," Caroline said, somewhat subdued. "I didn't ask him over, I asked him what he was going to eat tonight for dinner and he said he wasn't sure. He never got the chance to look the menu over at Mr. McNally's."

Maria walked around the customer side of the counter and toward the front of the store. She looked out the front windows to the right where David and Mel were standing and talking.

"So tell me, David," Mel said as he settled down onto the bench seat of the picnic table. "I saw you out here with Caroline for a little bit while I was over talking to Jim Davenport. You were serious when you said you were going to help her with her little idea."

"I was. I am." David smiled and the afternoon sun beat down on them.

"Any particular reason? I mean, you're basically just passing through. It's an extended stay, sure, but it's still short. Why invest the time?"

"Why not? I have little else to do with my extra time. Caroline's cause is as good as any. She's worth the investment."

Mel looked David over a moment before responding. "You seem like a pretty stand-up man and, as one, I expect you're a straight shooter, too."

"That's a fair assessment, Doc," David said in a more serious tone as he sat opposite Mel at the table.

"Maria and Caroline, they are like family to a lot of us. I think of them like a daughter and granddaughter. Maria is very guarded so I am less worried about her. Caroline is very empathic and attaches very quickly. She cried for a week about a wild coyote that was hit by a car. It didn't die on impact and we tried to nurse it back to health, then it died a couple days later."

"I understand what you're saying, Mr. Porter. I am not trying to inject myself too much. You are correct. At some point I will be going."

"From the sounds of what little Peter told Charlotte, you do a lot of that. Coming for a bit and then going," Mel said cautiously.

"That sounds like some concern there. What can I do to settle your mind? If you have questions, please ask them. I have little to hide and I will never respond with anything less than an honest answer."

"It's interesting that you say that as you really haven't offered up much to folks," Mel said as he leaned in a little.

"I'm not much on talking about myself, to be honest. But again, if you have questions..." David responded, leaning back slightly.

"Okay—what *are* you doing just wandering around? You seem to have a number of core skills and you don't seemingly need more money than to cover a place to live and food. You're not traveling around looking for work."

David thought for a brief second on how he wanted to respond. "I've spent a life making plans for the future. That future never materialized. I swore I would continue the rest of my days living in the present. I've simply decided that I am going to live my life as it comes at me. I am going to try to do the right things, take the necessary risks when I need to, and the rest will happen on its own—with or without a plan."

Mel thought about the answer for a moment. It wasn't exactly what he might have thought would be a typical answer to a question as he asked it, but since it revealed more about David, he decided to accept it.

"So is it just that you can't stay in one place or you just don't?" Mel asked as he leaned forward a little bit more.

David smirked a little. "I'll answer that if you can tell me why the pointed questions."

"Fair enough. In two days Caroline has quickly become attached to you. And Maria can be as tough as she wants. If you are touching Caroline's heart, you are touching hers."

David softened his position quickly. He hadn't realized that particular dynamic. "I generally don't stay long because my tasks at hand, wherever I am, are finished. Sometimes it is just a few days. It's never been more than three months. And then I move along."

"What tasks?" Mel asked, somewhat confused.

"Whatever comes. Someone needs help with something wherever I am. I help them and then I move along. I never know what it is. I travel until I find a place to stop and the task finds me. Like Caroline's library project, which to be honest, will be the biggest task to date since all of this travel started."

"So how long have you been travelling?"

"2014... It's been four years. Wow. I hadn't realized that until just now."

"So why not stay somewhere? You help people. You could continue to stay and help them," Mel added as he softened his tone.

"I don't want to keep helping people. My concern is they become dependent on it. I help them complete a task, show them they can do it on their own, and then I let them. At that point they don't need my help anymore so I move along to the next person that needs it."

"Somewhere totally different?"

"Generally," David responded.

"Is there anything that could 'make' you stay somewhere?"

David paused and looked Mel right in the eye before answering. "Not anymore," he answered simply.

"You know you're answering questions as ambiguously as possible."

"Yes, I know, but they have been honest answers," David said. "I did say I had nothing to hide and that I would answer honestly."

"Do you have family?" Mel asked.

"Blood relatives?"

"Yes," Mel responded.

"No I don't. I was adopted. I never met my birth parents. My adoptive parents were an older couple. They passed over a decade ago when I was thirty-five," David responded, withdrawing further.

"I am sorry," Mel responded as he looked up and saw Maria and now Charlotte looking out the window at the two of them talking.

Maria looked back at Caroline, who was coloring.

Charlotte was studying David's face when Maria spoke. "You are trying to assess something."

"Yes. Doc must have decided to do a little digging and David is playing along. That's the most serious look I've seen on his face since he got here."

Doc pivoted on the bench slightly and continued. "So I am going to ask you a favor and I am going to be about as forward as is likely permissible right now, so I hope you'll excuse me if it's a little out of bounds for you."

"Fair enough, provided I can ask you something first," David interrupted.

"Sure," Mel responded, smiling just slightly.

"I need a favor next week, during the work week. Any day is fine. I need a ride to the County tax and County planning offices. I want to look up what I can on the original infrastructure project that was cancelled after the storm. I know it's a couple hour haul. I don't expect you to wait for me. I can figure out another way back, but it's more cost effective for me if I can arrange only one ride. I can pay you for your fuel and a little extra."

Mel was still unconvinced that this stranger was willing to go through all the expense and time to help out. "What are you hoping to figure out from all the records up there?"

"There is a better chance to steer the future if you can better understand the past. I need to know what was in order to help Caroline try to drive this effort."

"She's eight. How much driving do you think she's going to do?"

"She'll be nine in two months," David said, snickering, realizing he has said this more than once now.

"I'm serious David," Mel said as his look became slightly concerned. "She's had her own disappointments and as you say, she's not yet nine."

"There's a lesson here regardless of the outcome. It's not just Caroline's lesson either. When your chances are one in a million, strive to be *one*, even if the chances of success are very low. You will still be better for the effort."

There was a short pause as the two men looked each other over with differing levels of respect.

Mel stood. "I can give you a ride next week. Let me know what works around Charlotte's schedule for you."

Mel waved to the women in the store as he turned. David looked over and, for the first time, realized they were watching.

"I thought you had a favor to ask of me," David called out to Mel as he began to walk across the street.

Mel stopped and turned around before his foot hit the curb. He looked at David kindly, who stood and walked around to the street side of the picnic table, leaning against it.

"I was going to ask you to do the right thing by Maria and Caroline. I don't need to ask anymore. I don't need to ask you to do something that is already a part of your character."

David nodded slightly and said nothing.

Charlotte opened up the front door of the store and Maria walked outside and over to David.

"Well, that looked like an interesting conversation from where I was standing," Maria said as she smiled slightly.

"You folks need to get some more televisions around here," David quipped, trying to be funny.

Maria looked at the ground and then stepped a little closer toward David.

"Caroline mentioned to me that the two of you discussed some plans regarding the library effort."

"Yes, we were going over some of the leg work that has to get done in order to get started. I just asked Doc Porter if he can give me a ride next week so that I might get some of the data I need from the County seat."

Charlotte stepped back into the store and walked over toward Caroline as a semi roared down Route 385 and kicked up sand that the hot summer wind carried over to the parking lot. Maria looked up at David and straight into his eyes. "So Caroline was doing her best to explain things, but she only remembers so much of the conversation."

"She is only eight," David replied calmly.

"Well, she will..." Maria began and then they both finished "...be nine in a couple of months."

They both smiled at one another as an uncomfortable silence set in.

Maria could feel her heartbeat quicken a little. *Just ask him to come over for dinner*, she thought. *It is innocent and Caroline and Charlotte will be there*

David went to back up a little and realized he was against the picnic table. While he was calm, he could sense Maria's uneasiness.

"Charlotte generally has dinner with us. I would like to know if you would mind joining us if you do not already have plans. Perhaps you can tell me a little more about the research that needs to be done at County?" Maria asked as the wind stopped as suddenly as it had started and her black hair stopped flowing in the breeze.

"Oh, I could stop by anytime and tell you about it. I don't want to impose."

"You are not imposing. I am asking. I think at this point Caroline is looking forward to it as I believe it was in her mind when she asked you what you were planning to eat tonight. I think unless you already have plans and you were to decline, she would be disappointed."

"And you?" David asked in a deep serious tone. "If I simply declined without reason, would it disappoint you, too?"

Maria's pulse quickened. She opened her mouth slightly to respond and then said nothing.

"That's fine," David said as he smiled slightly and looked deeply into her eyes. "The lack of an answer is answer enough."

Maria was upset. She actually didn't like David's perceptiveness of her. She was also upset at not being able to respond honestly.

"What time should I come by?" David asked as he slipped out between the picnic table and where Maria was standing.

"I usually try to sit down for six o'clock on Saturdays. You can come by anytime you like after four as we will be home if you would like to visit earlier."

"Can I bring anything?" David asked as he slowly backed up in the direction of the apartment entrance.

"I might only have a couple of beers in the fridge. If you could stop by Mr. Garcia's place and pick up some Cerveza Pacífico Clara that would be fine."

David turned around to look west down Route 385 to make sure he knew where Garcia's Wine and Spirits was. He pointed in the general direction and Maria nodded.

"Will do," David said as he smiled and turned to walk to the stairs to the apartment. He just about rounded the corner when Maria called out.

"Yes."

David stopped at the stoop and looked at her.

"Yes?" David asked, genuinely confused.

"Yes, if you simply declined without reason, I would be disappointed, too."

David smiled. "I would have been disappointed if you weren't disappointed," he finished as he waved at Caroline, who was now looking out the front window of the store.

Caroline happily and rapidly waved back.

David smiled at her and turned to Maria, where his smile grew a little wider.

"I will see you later then, David."

"I'm looking forward to it."

Chapter Nine

David pushed back his dinner plate and looked over to Maria. "I'm stuffed. I couldn't take another bite."

"Did you enjoy the meal?" She stood and walked over to take his empty beer bottle away.

"It was great. I don't think I've ever had chicken that tasted like that. It was different. It was very appetizing."

Maria shook the empty beer and motioned toward the refrigerator. David nodded his head.

Caroline was licking her fingers as Charlotte reached over with a napkin for her hands.

David got up from the table and took his plate over to the sink, and then stepped back to get Charlotte's as well.

Caroline got up from her seat and cleared all of the items from her setting. Maria smiled and handed David another beer while she opened her new one.

"Thanks," David replied as he helped Caroline finish clearing the table. David looked around under the counter and noticed that where a dishwasher would go there was nothing but a place for the small kitchen garbage pail.

As Caroline walked out of the kitchen and into the dining room, David moved toward the slider to the deck, past the humming air conditioner in the wall.

Maria ran the water in the sink and let it fill up so that the dishes could soak.

"Mr. David, it looks like the sun is going to set soon. Can we go outside and watch together?"

"Are you going to join us?" David asked back into the kitchen.

"Go ahead, we will be right out," Maria responded.

David and Caroline stepped out onto the deck. David closed the slider behind him and walked over to the west side of the deck.

"What do you think, Mr. David?" Caroline asked, pointing over at the western horizon.

"Oh I don't know," he responded taking another sip of his beer. "Maybe another half an hour or so."

"And then we'll have another sunset?"

"Yes Miss Caroline, we will," David said with a smile as she sat in one of the two single wicker chairs.

The slider door opened and Charlotte and Maria stepped out. Charlotte walked over and sat in the other single chair closest to the western deck wall.

"We have to stop meeting like this," David joked as he motioned Maria to the two-seat wicker sofa. "People are going to talk."

Maria smiled and sat comfortably. She was less embarrassed than yesterday.

"I guess it's a good thing I picked up two six packs seeing as how you and I have managed to finish off one already. These Mexican beers go down pretty nicely," David said as he took the seat next to Maria.

Charlotte looked over the deck wall and toward the direction of McNally's. She could see the fancy car out front that belonged to the Kurtvow's. "So David, you never did get the chance to tell us what you were thinking might work as far as raising some funds for Caroline's effort. She tried to explain it as best she could, but she said you were the idea man."

David smiled at the comment. In an earlier time in his life, he had often been referenced as such. It was nice to hear it again.

"Well, there are a lot of things I have to take a look at. As I explained to Caroline, it might not even be possible to undertake. If the storm caused a lot of damage and they were stopped really short of the completion point and then stopped with the effort, you know, in the hundreds of thousands of dollar range, then it would take a long time, like a decade, to do it if it could be done at all," David responded as he took another sip from his beer. "If it was a lot closer to completion, we might be in better luck. Or, if the case is that the library is fully wired, then all we might need to do is install the service dishes to catch the data stream off the satellites that host the services, and then route that to the network in the library and to the wireless access points. Then the services would be available. That way, we are looking at a much lower cost of equipment."

"Are you able to guess the cost?" Maria asked as she leaned forward.

"I need to gather some information. That's why I asked Doc if he could give me a ride next week to the County seat, so I can look some things up. But I have some experience with technology. I am no Zachary Taylor…" David smiled at Caroline.

"Do you know Zachary Taylor of Zee Technologies? His company was one of the sponsors of the original project," Maria added.

"Caroline mentioned," David responded without directly answering her question. David looked at the western horizon where the sun sank further. He motioned to Caroline with both of his hands open, so as to signal ten minutes.

David then continued talking. "My best guess, without looking at everything and making the assumption that the library was basically all set to go, is that we would need to raise about fifty thousand dollars to get the satellite system purchased, installed, wired into the existing network, as well as adding the wireless access points throughout the building."

A look of disappointment washed over Maria's face. Charlotte's as well.

"Well, that was a mood killer," David said with a small laugh.

"It is just that fifty thousand dollars is a lot of money," Maria responded as she took another drink.

"Yes and no. There are about six hundred or so occupied homes here according to Doc and Jim Davenport. That is part of what I am going to review up at County. If we do a public fundraiser, along the lines of what I discussed with Caroline—a weekend bazaar with arts, crafts booths, and food—we could, possibly, pull in an average of ten dollars per household."

"Yes, but that's just six thousand dollars toward what you said was needed," Charlotte said, "and not every family has that kind of spare money lying around."

David looked over as Caroline's expression became plain. She didn't understand all of the conversation, but she did understand that it didn't seem likely that the money could be raised, given the caution her mother and Miss Charlotte were taking in their conversation.

"Yes, Miss Charlotte, that's true. But 'casual' money is spent at Mr. McNally's and at some of the other places in town. I'm hoping on a weekend like that, and with some advanced warning, the families that can spend a little 'fun' money would choose to do it for the cause. At the same time, I am hoping from there we can engage some of the local business owners. I'm thinking that they might be willing to work together to help raise an additional six thousand, five hundred on top of what I am estimating from the citizens."

Maria looked at Charlotte who was doing the math in her head. "That would mean, on average, each business owner would have to kick in about three hundred to make that grand total. I can tell you right now, many of them couldn't."

David was still pushing and maintaining his optimistic stance. "Yes, I do get some of the general idea around here of how difficult things are, but this bazaar weekend would earn them extra money possibly through higher than normal business traffic and extended hours. They could take a portion of their sales from those two days and donate it."

"Even that," Maria said, "if it were as you suggest, would still leave the effort short by over thirty seven thousand dollars. How could you hope to make that up?"

"I'm planning to have a conversation with Mr. Kurtvow to see if he could grant the effort twelve thousand five hundred dollars."

Charlotte leaned forward in her chair. "As hopeful as that is, and it might not have been out of the question ten years ago, Brian was a lot more helpful to the town before the days of Sue Ann. It's a lot less likely now. Most of us haven't seen much of him off that ranch of his in the past five years."

"Have any of you gone over to see him?" David asked. "I mean, you're all friendly and neighborly to each other, and even to me, a total stranger. But it seems like everyone shuts him out. You all clearly deal with Sue Ann because she comes into town, but you seem to have no problem engaging her despite the social status difference. Still, for whatever reason, Brian withdrew... Did any of you go and ask him why, or see how he was doing?"

Maria and Charlotte just looked at each other because they realized that none of them had.

There was a long silence as David finished his beer and walked away to get another one. He motioned to Maria, who was nursing hers, and she politely waved off a refill.

"Mama, is it really possible that Mr. Kurtvow could help that much? I don't understand all the money amounts, but if it is as much as what everyone else could maybe do, isn't that a lot for one person?"

"Child," Charlotte interrupted as David stepped back out onto the deck, "do you remember when some coins felt out of your pocket last week into the living room couch when you got up?"

Caroline nodded rapidly.

"Well, when Brian Kurtvow gets up off his couch he loses that kind of money when he goes to stand."

Caroline looked up at the deck roof above her, puzzled. She'd taken the comment literally. Maria looked at her. "What is wrong, *hija de mi alma?*"

Without missing a beat, but still looking up, Caroline responded, "I'm trying to figure out how much change that has to be and how Mr. Kurtvow can walk around with all of it in his pockets."

Everyone snickered and then laughed. Caroline was unsure of what she'd said that made everyone laugh, but she was glad to see all the smiles.

David turned to look into the setting sun as it just dropped below the horizon ridge.

"Another sunset?" Maria asked.

"Another day done," David said, glancing back at Maria and then turning back toward the sun and the western sky.

"Well, with that passing thought I'll ask just one more question then," Charlotte said as she adjusted herself a bit back into the chair. "Even if you could get Brian to go along with it, because we all know he can certainly afford it, the cause would still be about twenty five thousand dollars short."

"Yes, it would be," David responded without turning around. "Another obstacle to overcome. There will be other hurdles, too. We'll just have to jump at each one and try to clear it if we are to keep running with this." David turned around to see Caroline staring at him intently. "Right little one?"

"Yes!" Caroline responded excitedly.

Charlotte slowly got to her feet. "Well as much as I am coming to like watching the sun set these days, I have to get back inside. The heat may be a bit less than earlier, but I'm still uncomfortable."

David stood in case Charlotte needed some help, but he didn't move forward at all. He was only going to do so if she needed it. Charlotte looked at him and smiled so as to thank him for offering the "little old lady" a hand if she needed it, but also letting her do it on her own.

"*Pequeña hija*, it is time for you to get ready for bed."

"Oh Mama, could Mr. David read me a story tonight?"

Charlotte stopped walking to the sliding door and looked back at Caroline. David looked at Maria, who nodded at him, but then she addressed Caroline. "That is fine with me if it is okay with Mr. David."

"I would like it if he read to me tonight if that's okay, Mama," Caroline responded.

Maria looked at Charlotte and then back to Caroline. "Instead of reading yourself, like you often do for Miss Charlotte, you would like to listen to Mr. David as he reads you the story?"

David wasn't exactly sure of the cause for the confusion, but he decided to not let it bother him. Since he already got the "okay" from Maria, he scooped Caroline up, popped open the sliding door, and plopped her inside. Then he motioned for Charlotte to walk in ahead of him.

Charlotte stepped inside after her, also somewhat confused by Caroline's change. David looked at Maria and asked her, "Are you coming in?"

Maria responded by suddenly moving toward the door and into the apartment.

David walked in and closed the slider behind him, then made his way toward Caroline's room as she entered in ahead of him. "Is there a book you wanted me to read?" David asked as he looked at the few she had on the shelf in her room.

Caroline looked them over, picked one, and handed it to him. "This one, please."

David looked at it as he took it from her. It was a really long children's book and the type was small. It was certainly not something he could finish in one night. He smiled and looked at her as Maria and Charlotte approached the doorway. "Okay, I'll tell you what, let's get you ready for bed and once you're all settled, I will read until nine fifteen. Wherever we are, we're going to stop and, if you like, I can pick up from there some other time. Does that work for you?"

"Yes. Thank you, Mr. David," she said as she hugged him.

"Okay, so why don't you grab your pajamas then and head into the bathroom to change. You can get your last drink of water in there, go to the bathroom, wash your hands, and brush your teeth, and then when you're all set you can come get me out in the living room. Deal?"

"Deal!" She grabbed her things and headed out of the room past her mother and Charlotte in the doorway.

Maria smiled at the exchange and then looked up at David and smiled more. As he stepped out and into the living room area she turned and leaned on the doorway to Caroline's room and watched her daughter get ready from that spot.

David walked over into the kitchen and finished his beer, then set the empty bottle on the counter.

"You are welcome to another if you would like it," Maria said to him as she gestured that hers was empty.

David walked over to the refrigerator and pulled one beer out for Maria, opened it, and then walked over to give it to her and to take her empty bottle away.

"Are you all set?" she asked him. "I am sure I have something else if you would like it."

"Oh, I'm fine," David replied as he headed into the kitchen with the empty bottle. "Maybe when I'm done with the story I'll have another one, if I am not too tired."

Charlotte smiled slightly as she took a seat in the living room.

After a few minutes in the bathroom, Caroline emerged in a yellow nightgown with pink flowers. Maria watched her daughter come out and head over to David. Charlotte was paying attention to David's reaction, which she seemed to feel was fully guarded.

Maria suddenly realized that her face was hurting from smiling so much.

"Are you all set?" David asked Caroline.

"Yep," she responded.

"So you won't need to get out of bed for water or to go to the bathroom?"

Caroline shook her head.

"Hands are all washed and teeth are all brushed?"

Caroline nodded.

"Okay then," David said as he took her daytime clothes from her. "Give Miss Charlotte and your mother a kiss and then head to your bed."

Caroline bounded over to Charlotte and gave her a hug and a kiss and then quickly went over to her mother and squeezed her tightly, kissed her on the cheek, and then stood on her toes to whisper in her mother's ear, "Thank you for inviting Mr. David over. I had so much fun. I hope you can invite him again and he can come again."

Maria looked down into her daughter's eyes and she felt like she could actually see joy. It made her happy and slightly over-emotional. The addition of the beer was making it slightly harder for her to contain herself and she was consciously aware of it.

Caroline went into her room and got into bed as David walked up to Maria with Caroline's day clothes. "I'm sorry, I don't know where these go."

Maria smiled and took them from him without saying a word. In the exchange of the clothes her hands touched his and she felt a rush of emotion come over her as she let go.

David walked into the room and grabbed the book. Caroline scooted over to one side of the twin bed and patted her hand on the space she had made.

Maria laughed and put her hand over her mouth as David looked up playfully at her. He then sat on the bed to take his shoes off and then moved alongside Caroline and opened the book.

"Good night, princess," Maria said as she began partly shutting the door. "No fuss at nine fifteen."

"Yes, Mama," Caroline responded as she smiled.

David began to read aloud to Caroline from the book as Maria went to the easy chair in the living room. As she sat, she and Charlotte listened for quite some time without saying anything to each other. As the minutes passed and David read the story, different characters were introduced and he would change the way he talked so that each character had their own voice. Caroline giggled a couple of times as David mixed the voices up.

After some more time passed, Charlotte spoke up in a hushed tone to Maria so as not to draw attention from David. "So it would seem that Mr. David would be at least an uncle if not a father. Doc had mentioned that he was adopted and an only child so that leaves only father."

"How could you know that?" Maria asked as she put her beer down on the coffee table.

"The suave bedtime negotiation on the time regarding the story. The laundry list of things for the child to have done before going to bed so they don't have an excuse to get up after they are down. The water. Going to the bathroom. Brushing the teeth. Kissing everyone good night. Most men can't remember to put the bathroom seat down but a father, a good father … does what he just did earlier."

Maria hadn't considered any of those things. She was so happy that Caroline was happy that she didn't give any of that a thought. It was at that point she started to as she looked back to the door way to Caroline's room. David's voice was getting quieter and calmer as he continued the story. Once she completed her thoughts she looked at Charlotte with a softness in her eyes.

"It would explain some things about him. It might explain his reaction yesterday leaving McNally's so quickly when he thought something was wrong with Caroline," Maria said quietly to Charlotte. "Now I feel worse having said that to him and provoking that reaction. It was the only thing I could think of on the spot."

"I think he unintentionally gave that away," Charlotte added quietly. "I spoke with Doc a little bit this afternoon. He said he played a little twenty questions with him. David indicated he'd answer honestly which Doc said he seemed to be, but he was giving ambiguous answers. Without asking David something directly, I think he's said a lot."

Maria went to respond when Caroline's door creaked open and David slowly backed out of the room. David turned around and smiled to the two of them. "She fell asleep." He looked at the clock on the microwave across the living room and in the kitchen. "With a minute to spare" he said as he pointed to it as it changed to nine fifteen. Charlotte smiled at David as she stood. "Well, I think it is about time to get ready for bed myself," she said quietly as she looked at Caroline's room. "You did a wonderful job getting her to bed and settling her in."

David became suddenly self-conscious about how far he had let his guard down. "At one point, I spent my time helping out at the foster home that I came from. I guess some habits die hard."

"It's a good habit to keep," Charlotte responded as she turned away to head out, not fully convinced of his answer as being directly genuine toward his demeanor with Caroline.

Maria walked past David and let Charlotte out and watched her get down the stairs to her apartment, stepping out the door to have her in full view.

David quietly made his way out the slider door and up the stairs to his apartment at the same time.

Maria walked back in to find David was gone from the living room. She peaked into Caroline's room where she was fast asleep.

She decided to head out and up the stairs to David's deck. She stood outside his sliding door just off the top of the stairs as she watched him pull the sleeper sofa out. She stepped back and out of full view of the doorway as he took his shirt off. As she peered into the room from her vantage point she could see his large duffle bag neatly folded in the corner of the room on an old wooden chair with everything removed from it, his two pairs of shoes and his work boots lined up at the base of the cabinet.

David sat on the bed in just his slacks and used his hand to wipe one stray tear away. He breathed in deeply and held the breath for a moment before letting it out. He said something out loud to himself, but with the door closed, she could not make it out.

David walked over into the kitchen. Maria was trying to decide whether she should knock on the slider or not. She turned to walk away and then changed her mind and knocked.

David came over from the kitchen and opened the slider. "Hi," he said as he stepped outside and closed the slider behind him. "I'm sorry I just left. I figured with Charlotte leaving company time was over so I would just get going."

"That is fine. I wanted to make sure everything was okay. When you leave without saying good night, it might mean your evening was not a good one and I wanted to make sure it was. Caroline enjoyed having you over and I am sure she would want you to come over again."

Maria paused as she looked up at David. He was looking at her, but she sensed an emptiness in his eyes, almost as if he was distracted and elsewhere in his thoughts.

Maria cleared her throat slightly and continued. "I enjoyed having you over. I would like to have you over again some time."

David appeared more lucid at her comments, but his thoughts were clearly elsewhere. "It was a very nice time. It was probably one of the nicest times I have had in the past year. Thank you very much for inviting me."

The two stood together on the deck for a moment without saying anything.

"I do not like to pry. Doc and Charlotte, they are going to do that simply because it is their nature," Maria said as she let the loss of inhibition from the beer take over her better judgment. "If you should need something of me, please know you can trust me. I do not judge and I do not speak to others about private matters."

David felt a rush of feelings come over him. He worked hard to push it back. He said nothing and stared into Maria's eyes.

Maria reached down and touched his left hand, picking it up and holding it in both of hers. "If you would trust me ..."

"I do," he responded with just a hint of break in his voice. "You will have to trust me when I tell you that I haven't let anyone this close to me in a long time. And at the end of it all, I really can't. I am not staying after all."

Maria let his hand go.

"It has only been a couple of days," Maria said very softly, now wondering if it was a mistake to throw caution to the wind so suddenly, regardless of the excuse. "You did say you would be here for at least a couple of months. Westville might grow on you and you might decide to stay. Perhaps even just for a little longer than originally planned."

David said nothing and continued to fight what was going through his head as another awkward silence set in.

"I might grow on you," Maria said plainly.

David opened his mouth and then closed it. It took him a full minute to respond. "I'm sure your life is already a happy one."

"It is a good life. It has been happier over these past two days," Maria responded quickly and without thought.

"Your life will remain better, happier, if this is as close as you get to me."

Maria was embarrassed and confused. "I do not understand ..."

"I know. You don't know everything and that makes it difficult for me to define it for you. It has nothing to do with what I feel. It has everything to do with knowing what I am capable of giving to someone."

"And what can you give?" Maria asked basically fighting back tears.

David slid the slider open and stepped backward through it. "Nothing. I have nothing left to give. Anything I had is long since gone."

Maria stood in silence on the deck. She didn't know what to say and she couldn't walk away. "Good night Maria," David replied as he looked away from her, closed the sliding door, and drew across the curtain.

Maria stood on the deck and quietly let the tears flow.

Chapter Ten

The Tuesday morning sun had already started to make its way into the sky by the time Maria and Caroline made their way into the store.

Charlotte was already there heating up the grill and making the morning coffee.

Caroline took her bag over to the counter, sat, and waited for the bus. While she had a happy look on her face, looking forward to the County school summer program again this morning, Maria's look was more sullen.

As Maria went behind the counter to get her apron, she looked past Charlotte into the back room briefly.

"He's not here again," Charlotte offered. "He actually asked for another day off which I didn't mind, considering all the work he's already done. It was more than I was figuring. He wanted to start on the efforts for the library and needed the free time to do it."

Maria stopped looking into the back room and looked into the old woman's eyes.

"I do not know what I saw when I talked to him late on Saturday night, but I know it was a part of his soul. He seems terribly broken. I believe he has done some of it to himself. I cannot figure out what he feels he has done to deserve the isolation he is putting himself in ..." Maria had more to say, but her voice trailed off.

"I didn't see him at all on Sunday or yesterday except in the morning when he asked if he could defer some of his work to later in the week," Charlotte said quietly. "I walked up to the third floor deck and peaked through the slider late yesterday, just before I came down to eat with you. He wasn't home at the time. With no car, I figured he couldn't get all that far, but no one from church services saw him all day Sunday."

Maria continued to settle herself down. "I saw Doc. I asked him if he managed to speak to David about the bloody nose. He indicated he meant to while they were conversing outside on Saturday, but they moved away from the subject and then it slipped his mind."

Henry Baylor Jr., the owner of Baylor Appliances, was coming across Route 385 with his hand truck, a large brown box, and his tool belt draped across the top. He smiled and whistled as his thirty-nine-year-old feet scuffed across the dirt-blown highway to Charlotte's Place. He walked past the entrance to the store and over to the stoop at the apartments, where he dropped the hand truck.

Charlotte and Maria walked over to see where he went when he made his way to the front door of the store.

"Good morning ladies," he said in a very chipper voice, one that was a little loud for just after six in the morning. "I have a special delivery for first thing this morning for Miss Maria, and this is about as 'first' as it gets." He waved "hi" over to Caroline at the counter, who was now getting up to come over and see what the commotion was.

"I am sorry, Mr. Henry, but I do not understand. I did not order anything from your store," Maria said as she looked out the front window and over at the box on the hand truck.

"Oh, yes, Miss Maria, that is a discontinued floor model. It's never been used and it's in perfect shape. Mr. David wanted it brought over in exchange," he said proudly as he scratched the three-day-old brown stubble on his face.

"I do not understand," Maria responded. "In exchange for what?"

"Well, you might not know. We ordered four of these inventory and point-of-sale machines to make cataloging, pricing, and discounting everything in the store easier, but let me tell you—there's nothing easy about getting a system like that up and running. It's been sitting in the stock room for weeks."

Caroline took her mother's left hand and listened in.

"So anyway, Mr. David came in to talk to me about Caroline's effort for the library," he said as he tweaked her nose. "I knew about it because y'all came in a few weeks ago asking us to post the flyer and all." He looked at Caroline and smiled. "Well, he asked if there was any interest in Baylor Appliances sponsoring a booth or helping out and so forth." Henry slid and scuffed his feet on the floor as he looked down. "I said to him I wish I could, but with things being as they are and all— He said, 'That's okay, I understand.' He really is a nice guy for a Yankee."

Charlotte looked at the hand truck again and then tapped Henry on the shoulder and flicked her thumb at the window. "Henry—the box?"

"Oh yes!" Henry exclaimed, stepping over to the coolers to get a can of soda. "So I got to talking about the bills and expenses and how we just spent this money on a new system that I couldn't figure out how to install and how I might need to come up with money to have someone professionally do it. Well, David spent all day Monday setting up the sales units, the scanner guns, inventorying all the stock. The guy is a whiz. I wanted to pay him. I would have needed to spend eight hundred dollars to have the company come back out and do it. I know because I have the quote and all."

Henry popped the soda can open, took a sip, and continued. "I was really appreciative and I wanted to offer something for his time, but David said he didn't want the money. I really insisted. I had to. I would have been cramped even harder on this month's bills if I had to part with that money. So he was leaving while I was still insisting when he stopped in front of the dishwashers. I had the sign on that one because it was a discontinued floor model I wanted to get rid of anyway and he asked me how much would it be for it and to have it installed. I told him that it was all his and that I would set it up personally. Then he said he didn't need it for himself and that it was for you, Miss Maria."

Henry fumbled around for the loose change in his pocket to pay for the soda when Charlotte waived him off.

"So, Miss Charlotte, can I borrow Miss Maria for a few minutes to let me into her place to get this all set up?"

"I do not know if I can accept this," Maria said cautiously as she looked at Henry then over to Charlotte.

"I can't say I fully reckon what's going on, Miss Maria, but I can tell you that Mr. David has taken a shine to you. He seems like a good man, too, if you don't mind me saying so. He did all that work for me first before even knowing I would barter square with him. That is a man that just wants to help someone. A man like that simply figures the world will square up with him all on its own."

Charlotte touched Maria on the shoulder and took Caroline by the hand. "Go on up and let Henry in. I will make sure Caroline gets on the bus if it shows before you get back."

Maria was still uncomfortable accepting the gift of a band new dishwasher, but she relented and walked ahead of Henry, taking his can of soda so he could pull the delivery up the stairs.

"Miss Charlotte, that was a thoughtful thing Mr. David did, wasn't it?" Caroline asked as she headed back to the counter area.

"Yes, it was, child," Charlotte said as she poured herself some coffee.

"I like Mr. David. He was very funny on Saturday with the bedtime story. I really hope Mama sees fit to ask him over for dinner again sometime," Caroline responded as she took her backpack from the counter and unzipped one of the pockets.

Charlotte didn't respond as she looked out the front window from the counter and glanced up Packer Road. She wondered where David had gone to today, since no one really knew where he was.

The two sat in the store in silence until Millie Perkins came in with Sherriff Donna Neely for coffee on their way to work.

Maria opened the unlocked door to her apartment and cleared out the space under the cabinet where the dishwasher needed to go.

Henry finished pulling the hand truck backward up the stairs and backed into the kitchen with it, and then took a look underneath the counter where it needed to go.

"Yep," he said as he took his baseball cap off to scratch his short brown hair, then popped it back onto his head. "Looks like all the water and drain connections are there already," he said, crouching down to look under the counter.

"Yes," Maria replied as she sat for a moment in the kitchen chair. "One used to be installed there, but the motor burned out some time ago and I had it removed. I never had enough money to replace it, and with just Caroline and me there was really little reason to do so."

Henry looked up at her and then stood upright. "I am sorry, Miss Maria. Had I known, I am sure I could have taken care of this for you in the past. I am sure you could have paid me a little bit over time or something."

"That is very kind, Henry, but I don't even really have the little bit extra. You know how it is."

"Yes, ma'am, I do." He looked at her somewhat shyly. "Well, I have my tools there and I would think that unless I need something from my shop I should be all set. You don't need to stay if you want to get back downstairs," he said softly.

"Yes, of course," Maria said quietly as she put her hands on the table to push and stand up. She then removed them and put them at her side. "Henry, could you please sit for a moment?"

"Certainly, Miss Maria," he responded gladly as he took the seat across from her.

"Henry, you and I have been friends for some time."

"Yes, we have Maria. You've always been very kind to me," he said with a slight smile.

"Can you please tell me what you meant when you said 'David has taken a shine to you'? I want to know what you meant by that."

"Well, Miss Maria, when I asked him about how he was settling in, and how he liked his place, and working here, and so on, you came up a lot. Now, I'm not much of a study on people, but I know that when a man keeps mentioning a woman by name and does a lot of referencing to her it means she's on his mind a lot."

Maria let Henry's words sink in a bit and was about to ask another question when Henry spoke up again. "It might not be my place, Maria, but I think it's okay to take the dishwasher. I know what you're thinking, that when a man spends that kind of money on a woman, it comes with strings attached and all. It wasn't his money. It was his time and actually, it was time spent helping me really. He just wanted to help and he had the time and skill to do that. When I offered money in exchange for his time, he didn't want it. But when the idea was there to help you, that is what he did."

"So it was not 'special,' as they say?" Maria asked.

"Oh, it was," Henry said as he smiled. "He thought of you first before he thought of himself. Most people don't do that anymore." Henry's tone dropped a little. "It is even starting to be the case around here now, too. I know times are tough. But there is a fine line between a reason for something and an excuse for something."

Maria smiled a bit. "That is a very wise saying, Henry."

Henry smirked a little. "Mr. David said that yesterday. I think he was trying to tell me something in a kind way."

"Oh?" Maria asked.

"Yeah, he knows that he could have asked for more to be fully square for everything, but that getting this for you was enough. He wants me to consider taking a little of whatever I think the difference might be to put it toward the bazaar he is helping Caroline set up for the library."

"You said he asked initially, but I assume he did not bring it up again after you explained how tight money had become."

"Yeah, that's true," Henry said as he stood from the chair and looked out the kitchen window. "That David is a smart man. He knows he didn't have to ask me twice."

"So you are considering helping?" Maria asked softly as she stood and touched Henry on the arm.

Henry turned to Maria with a humbled look, took off his hat, and crumpled it a bit in his hands in front of him. "The man comes into our town and seems to be more willing to put more blood and sweat into it than we all are currently, all because of a little girl with an idea. I simply have to if for no other reason than it's the right thing to do."

Maria smiled at him.

"I didn't tell him. As I said, he never spoke of it again. But I am going to pay all the bills that are due this month and get my ledger payment down a little and whatever is left I am likely to put to the cause."

"Thank you, Henry," Maria said as she got up and walked to the door. "Would you please let me know if there are any problems hooking up? I will be just downstairs."

"Of course, Miss Maria," Henry replied as he put his hat back on and turned to start work on the installation.

Chapter Eleven

Caroline was playing out behind Charlotte's Place as her mother stepped out the back door. Maria watched her daughter hop from spot to spot on the baked ground as a slight breeze of hot summer air blew across the edge of the building.

Maria stepped off the stairs and walked slowly past her daughter, touching her hair as she walked by and allowing Caroline to hop along and play.

Maria turned toward the west and the sinking sun in the late Wednesday sky and said aloud to herself in a quiet voice, "I never used to really pay attention to the setting sun at the end of the day. Now because of you, I really cannot avoid doing so."

"What did you say Mama?" Caroline asked as she hopped again.

"Oh, nothing, *miel*. I was just saying something aloud to myself."

"Mr. Jim from the general store said to Doc that it's what crazy people do," Caroline said innocently.

Maria just smiled.

"Mr. David said back to them, 'Sometimes I have to talk to myself, it is the only way to have an intel…. intel….'"

"Intelligent?" Maria asked.

"Yes, that was it," Caroline said as she tried to deepen her voice to sound like David. " 'I have to talk to myself, it is the only way to have an intelligent conversation.'"

Maria was puzzled by the comment. It didn't sound like something she felt David would say, as it almost sounded insulting. "David said this?" Maria asked.

"Yes. When he was done they all laughed," Caroline said as she continued to play without looking at her mother.

"When did you see Mr. David? I have not seen him even come home the past three days," Maria commented as Charlotte came out the back door and pulled it closed.

"I saw him when I got off the bus today. I walked over to Mr. Davenport's store because he was there. I wanted to talk to him and find out how I can help him with the library effort."

Charlotte walked over and stood next to Maria as they both watched Caroline continue to hop around.

"David stopped at all the remaining businesses today that he missed on Tuesday because he spent part of the day up at County. More than half of them are willing to pitch in the three hundred dollars at this point. I suppose at this rate he is going to be able to get at least the business buy-in on the effort. Even if people are a little stretched, they don't want to be the one or two to be left out," Charlotte said as she smiled a little. "He makes it seem easy, but I know that it's not. Getting folks to come up with money like that. He's offering to do a little work for folks to help them save some costs on things to make them meet that three hundred threshold."

"Oh? There were others that needed help with technology?" Maria asked.

Charlotte looked a little confused so Maria continued. "It would seem that was his strong point with Henry Baylor. David helped him in that manner. I presumed he did that with others."

"Oh," Charlotte said as she smiled. "It seems our Mr. David is skilled at a number of things. He went over to Garcia's Wine and Spirits and spoke with Jose about his books and bookkeeping. Somehow the subject came up. Well, I guess David showed him how to manage some of his payments in another manner than he was doing and saved him fifty dollars in fees and interest. I think the interest was about thirty dollars or so. Then David asked him if he'd participate in the bazaar and he couldn't say yes fast enough."

Maria smiled slightly as she looked at Charlotte. "He does seem to have a way with everything he does. He is very influential."

"What's on your mind, child?" Charlotte asked as she took her gray and white hair down and let the evening summer wind gently blow it back.

Maria sighed. "Well, for one, I would like to not feel so soft. I was fine with the way I was before he got here. Somehow, without even his trying, I opened up to thoughts and feelings I have not had in some while."

Caroline looked at her mother and then went back to playing.

"If it were not for all the good he is doing, I would almost wish he had never come," Maria said as she lowered her voice and turned slightly toward Charlotte so that Caroline could not hear as much of the conversation.

"I think you and I both believe that you really don't feel like that," Charlotte said as she huffed a little at the comment.

"What is there to wish for? The man does all of these presumptuous things and then makes it impossible to thank him where we find those efforts kind," Maria said as she turned away and looked at the early evening sunset. "I was just thinking a moment ago how I never gave much thought to the setting sun and now an evening cannot come without me looking forward to it."

Charlotte stepped around to stand in front of Maria. She could see the tears welling up in her eyes as her face was bathed in the setting sunlight.

"*Dios mío*, I do not want him in my head and yet I cannot get him out of there."

"I think those are your first and second problems," Charlotte said slyly as a smirk grew across her face. "You think he's in your head. He's not. He's seeped into your heart."

"And my second problem?" Maria asked defensively.

"You think you control the ability to get him out."

Maria looked between the scrub brush down the south side of Route 385 heading west and the apartment side of the store. She saw Rebecca walking along the road edge with David. As they neared the property threshold Rebecca stopped for a moment, put a pad of paper and a pen back into her bag, and said a few more words to David before heading across the street.

As David began to cut into the property toward them a car pulled across Route 385 and settled, parked in the wrong direction on the opposite side of the road. It was out of view in front of the building, so Maria stepped forward to see it as David stopped his approach and walked toward it.

Charlotte followed Maria forward and recognized the car immediately. It was the Kurtvow's car. The back window was down and David was talking to the backseat passenger.

Caroline looked over and saw David at the car and yelled out at the top of her lungs, "Mr. David! Hi, Mr. David!" She waved wildly to him.

Maria and Charlotte were both so startled by Caroline calling out that they turned to her. As they both turned back they noticed David finishing his wave to her and then entering the car door that was now opened for him.

Maria suddenly felt her stomach turn as the car pulled back onto Route 385 and turned in the road to head back east and over to Packer Road and the Kurtvow property.

"Now he might just be heading there to talk to Brian," Charlotte said to try to reassure Maria, as she seemed distressed. "He did mention that, you know."

"I saw the Kurtvow helicopter leave today and head west to El Paso, I presume. I am sure it was Mr. Kurtvow and business. I have not seen nor heard it return. That leaves very little to the imagination as who was likely in the car and who he left with," Maria scoffed as she turned and headed into the house. "Caroline, please come along for dinner."

"But, Mama, I was hoping to play outside for just a little longer. Until the sun set," Caroline responded as she continued to hop along the dirt patches.

"No backtalk, young lady," Maria responded harshly. "I said to come along."

Caroline looked at Charlotte. Both were surprised at her tone. Caroline generally never heard her mother get upset and scold anyone so she immediately stopped and followed behind her.

Charlotte sighed, closed her eyes, and slowly followed them to the back steps of the apartments. She looked in the general direction of Packer Road and thought, "You tend to do the right thing automatically, David, without the small prayer. I am giving you one now, in case you need it for some other reason."

Kurtvow's driver turned the car as Rebecca entered McNally's and headed back around and up Packer Road.

David moved about in his seat a little bit to get comfortable. It had been a while since he rode in a stretch limo and faced the opposite direction of the travel of the car.

Brian Kurtvow was dressed in a full suit and jacket. His salt and pepper hair was slightly thinning and slicked back, but he looked a full ten years younger than his sixty-six years of age. He looked at

David with his deep blue eyes and then leaned to the left to the small bar area in the car.

"Would you care for some scotch?" he asked David as his deep voice seemed to boom in the small space.

"To be honest, sir, I am not much of a spirits drinker, but please don't let that stop you from enjoying one."

Brian smiled slightly at the comment. "Well, according to my wife, you do drink."

"Well, yes, sir," David said without missing a beat. "I do enjoy a good beer or three, that is for sure."

Brian stopped reaching for the scotch at the comment and opened the cooler compartment. He took out two Founders Imperial Stouts and handed one to David.

"Thank you," David responded as he opened it up and raised the bottle toward Kurtvow.

"So I was in town by chance today," Brian said as he opened his drink and took a sip, "as I am generally not often in town anymore these days, and Mel Porter mentioned to me something about this effort that the little Romero girl has been championing."

"Yes, do you know much about it?" David asked as he glanced out the window. All of the remaining houses disappeared to the south of their travel as they continued north. All that David could see on both sides of the road was open ranch land and a dot way off on the eastern side of the road to the north of them.

"All I know about it is what I read in the prior issue of Rebecca Wilson's little monthly paper. What Doc Porter spoke to me about was something new about the effort and it involved you."

"Yes, and as a matter of fact, Rebecca was asking me about what we were up to. I presume to publish it in her next monthly edition."

"From the conversation that I had with Doc Porter it would seem at some point you were going to come to have a conversation with me," Brian said as he took another drink from his beer.

"Yes, that was the case. So I make the assumption this wasn't really by chance that you were driving by as I was walking back," David responded.

"Actually, it was. My driver spotted you because he recognized you from Friday evening," Brian said plainly.

David looked out the window to the easterly direction trying to make out the building that was coming up on the right as more and more daylight faded away. He turned to the west and realized that the sun was setting.

"Something amiss outside the car?" Brian asked as he took another drink.

"Oh no," David replied as he turned to face Brian again. "I was just noticing that it was getting darker out."

"It does get dark pretty quick out here shortly after sunset. Not a lot of pollution in the atmosphere to scatter the light."

"So I understand your curiosity in finding out what it was I wanted, but why are we driving back to your ranch?" David asked as he took another drink.

"Are you sure that's where we are going?" Brian asked with his voice still loud and over powering.

"Well, there's nothing out this way except your estate as far as I am aware, and I have to make the assumption if you wanted me shot for the exchange with your wife, you would have sent the driver or a cleaner to do it," David said in a simple, quiet monotone, looking directly at Brian.

Brian guffawed loudly and slapped David on the knee. "You've lived up to your reputation. You're damn funny!"

"I didn't realize that I had a reputation already, being out here less than a week," David said as he smiled slightly.

"Yes, we are headed up to the ranch," Brian said still laughing and wiping a tear out of his eye. "I hate to call it an estate. I know that's what it is, but I like to think it's a ranch."

"So why head out here? You could pretty much talk to me anywhere if you had questions. This car is bigger than some rooms."

"Yes," Brian said still snickering a little, "I do suppose you're right. Having said that, there are a lot of ears out there and regardless of where I go, short of the car I suppose, people talk."

"I have said they need some more televisions around here," David said as he finished his beer and set it down.

"Would you like another?" Brian asked.

"If you're going to have more, I'll have more."

"I do believe I will be having more," Brian responded as he fished another one out of the car cooler. "So to my point of a lot of talk for lack of other entertaining things, I know you were fishing around the County records to research what was going on prior with the infrastructure project and the library. I also know you were looking into the municipal tax shift of the properties and their tax burden to the County system from a few years back."

David was listening, but he was also looking out of the window as the car turned off Packer Road, which this far out was now called Rural Route 2, and onto the Kurtvow ranch.

Four miles outside of the town center and nearly one mile off Rural Route 2 was the huge estate Brian Kurtvow lived in with his wife, Sue Ann.

"So this is what eight hundred million dollars affords you to live in?" David said quietly.

"It's nine hundred million now," Brian said with a measure of true pride in his voice. "The stock market has been running hot. I am really looking forward to the potential to crack that tenth digit perhaps in the next couple of years."

"So are there forty-four rooms or forty-five?" David asked slyly without knowing the room total at all.

"Fifty-five rooms scattered across about thirty-thousand square feet," Brian replied proudly again as the car pulled up to the circular covered entrance.

"One helicopter or two?" David asked as he saw the split road leaving the driveway area to the landing area and the accompanying garage and maintenance hangar.

"I actually have two. Sue Ann has the other one. She took it to El Paso," Brian responded plainly.

"For business?" David asked in a serious tone as the driver opened the door of the car.

Brian guffawed again loudly. "Boy, I like you. You're funny as hell. Mitchell," Brian said as he climbed out of the car and looked at the driver, "our good man here thinks Sue Ann headed to El Paso for something work related."

David stepped out of the car with a slight smirk as he was content with the way he was steering the conversation. He looked at Mitchell who barely cracked a smile at Brian's comment.

"My good man," Brian said as he slapped David on the shoulder, "if spending money uselessly is a business then my wife runs the most effective business there is."

Brian started stepping in the general direction of the house as David looked southwesterly across the property and in the general direction of Westville. He then glanced up at the sun as it disappeared over the hills and he whispered to himself, "another day done."

"So tell me, Mr. Kurtvow—" David started as Brian interrupted.

"David, please. Everyone 'Mr. Kurtvows' me, even the older folks in town when I should be the one paying that respect to them. Yes, I have more money. I've tried to not make the distinction too well known as I am proud of my accomplishments, but I basically put my pants on the same way they do."

"Well, Brian, you have to admit that being as self-made as you are, to the tune of nine hundred million dollars in the span of twenty-five years is a pretty big accomplishment," David commented as they turned and entered the house and went into the first floor study.

The room was large and full of books and some computer and networking equipment. There was a small bar and two semi-circle couches that faced each other and a large round table in the center.

A server walked in the room and exchanged David's beer that he just started with a cold one and handed a fresh one to Brian. Another server set down some sandwiches and a few hot items as Brian motioned for David to take a seat.

"So, David, yes, I do have some questions, but I bet you do, too. As I mentioned, you looked up a lot more than you needed to at County."

"Well, it is all public information," David responded plainly.

"Yes it is, but you're on a mission and I don't believe there is much that someone of your caliber does without a reason in mind," Brian said in his commanding voice as he sat across from David.

"Well, I won't try to defend with any pretense. It seems to me as if it would be a complete waste."

"That would be wonderful and refreshing," Brian said as he reached forward for something from the serving dishes and nudged it toward David. "I sit in rooms during my work day with people who do everything from butter me up to bullshit me. It seems like a guy like you," he said as he smiled, "could give two shits whether or not I was impressed by him."

"I doubt there's anything I've done in my life that was so grand that I could impress you, so why bother you with it?"

"You'd be surprised what impresses me. The simple fact that you're not trying to impress me, that impresses me."

David smiled a little. While he was happy to be able to steer the conversation, Kurtvow's character and demeanor was not what he had expected. It certainly wasn't what he briefly read online at County when he had access to the Internet to review his biography and background, which led him to consider the fact that Brian either intentionally shielded the information, or no one took the time to dig in and find out.

"So I'll tell you what, David, you and I, we can do a little back and forth on our questions. This way we both can find out what we want and I can have Mitchell bring you back to town when you're done. How does that sound?"

"That sounds fair enough," David replied after grabbing something off the hot plate and grabbed his beer and leaned all the way in.

"So, I have to know," Brian asked as he too leaned in. "What made you leave McNally's so fast the other night?"

David didn't immediately answer. He wasn't expecting the question, so he hesitated.

"I mean, most people that travel through, Sue Ann makes some sort of move on them. She stopped with the locals a long time ago. The very occasional traveler is all she has when she's in town and most are or become willing participants. El Paso is a different story of course ... men by the dozen there ... So anyway?"

David sized up Brian and then spoke "Okay, it wasn't the question I was figuring on, but I'll answer it honestly if you'll allow me a rebuttal question on the topic."

Brian looked right at David and shook his finger lightly, smiled, and then took a sip from his beer. "Ah ... I like your style. Nothing to lose by going for it all and then if nothing else, backing down and regrouping. Sure—answer and then follow up."

"Maria came in and said Caroline woke up and was upset and asking for me. I got up and bolted across the street. When I got there, she was settled and back to sleep. I've come to believe now, because I thought about it later as Doc was at McNally's then suddenly over the apartment for no real reason, that is was all a ruse to get me out of the bar and away from Sue Ann."

"And the fact that you got manipulated via subterfuge, that doesn't bother you?" Brian asked.

"It was done with good intentions in mind. People cared enough to trick me to leave before I did something I might regret, which by the way I wouldn't have regardless, or end up in a situation that caused everyone else an issue with respect to all the ledgers."

"Ah. So is that your rebuttal question? What are the ledgers?"

"I actually think I know what they are and I was going to ask about them later if I could get to the topic, but the question I have concerning the central topic of your wife would be, why do you let her do this to you?"

Brian paused for a moment to give David a chance to either back off or dig more. He wanted to see which way he'd go when silence was initially offered.

"You made the comment before that everyone 'Mr. Kurtvows' you, even the older folks in town when you feel you should be the one paying that respect to them. Don't you think there is a certain level of respect Mrs. Kurtvow should be paying to you? I mean, unless the two of you have an arrangement that allows for this, at the very minimum she should not flaunt it."

Brian smiled and spoke. "Only a man like you would ask me a question like that. You have nothing to really gain or lose by going to the wall. Oh I suppose you could have pissed me off with a question like that and then perhaps I wouldn't get involved in the fundraising effort. Of course, at the same time, I never committed to it, so you might not get a dime from me anyhow. But how many chances in your life do you get to take a man of success and stature to the wall?"

"Believe it or not, I've danced to this tune before with other partners," David said with a slight grin.

"I believe you have," Brian said loudly and confidently.

The two men sat in a brief moment of silence as they picked at the food and finished the beers. Brian pointed to David's empty beer and motioned. David pointed back to Brian's and with that the server came over with two new beers for them.

"I noticed you allowed me to ask the question, but you never really answered it," David responded as he started the next beer.

"That is true," Brian quickly answered. "I really don't know why I permit it. I guess I don't have a solution for the issue, so I have sort of capitulated to the situation."

"Fair enough for now, I suppose. If I think of something, I can always follow up. So I guess it's your turn again, Brian."

Brian smiled and leaned back in the seat a bit with his beer in his hand. "So tell me, if you're traveling through with no intention of staying, why get involved at all? Why not let the little girl make her way on her own and let the townspeople figure out what they can or cannot help with on their own library?"

David sat for a minute to decide what he wanted Kurtvow to know and then sat back to answer. "I've seen a lot of things in my travels over the years. One of the things that seems to be universal everywhere I go is that people feel powerless and directionless. They feel like they have no ability to guide themselves, that they are rudderless. I know that is not the case, but in the absence of a leader, someone to follow or show them the way, that is exactly how they are."

"And you're the man to do it?" Brian asked inquisitively.

"Not always, no. Sometimes I have found someone in the place that I am at the time that can do it much better than me. I have to convince them that they have the skill and ability to take that on. Absent that, if not me, then who?"

Brian smiled. He appreciated the candor of the answer. "Okay, your turn."

"The ledgers. It's a multi-part question if you'll indulge it."

Brian nodded and then David continued.

"I figured them out when I reviewed all the tax records at County. It was as you said, I was looking into the municipal tax shift of the properties and their tax burden to the County system from a few years back. Almost no one could afford the special assessments that were being levied in over the three years to get the properties under that management and operational structure. People were being hit with liens on their properties and at eighteen percent annual interest, compounding monthly at one point five percent, it was wiping out the town faster than the loss of the cattle ranchers and the closing of the mineral mines. You stopped it by buying up all the liens so the County, and in some cases the banks, wouldn't foreclose on any more properties and force even more people out."

"Yes," Brian said solemnly.

"So what happened? You did this to help them. At first you really were not tallying the interest any longer—that has since stopped and the interest is being applied again. You held the notes and you let the people pay their bills, mortgages, and current County taxes as due, and you took payments from them leisurely and as they had them. What changed?"

Brian sat forward. He then waved his staff out of the room. "Because you are the man you are, I am going to give you an honest answer," he said as the last of the staff exited and the door closed. "I lost my way. I married a greedy woman who uses those bills due to us from the townspeople like a personal piggy bank, and I haven't stopped it because I really have lost the will, all my will, in my personal life. That is the truth. I used to think I could make a difference in the lives of others. I can't even make a difference in mine."

David stood, drank all the remaining beer in his bottle, and then set it down on the table. "You are a five percent shareholder in three publicly traded small cap companies from what I could review online. One of them pays a dividend. You earned six million dollars last year in dividend payments."

Brian wasn't totally clear on where David was going with his comments.

"All of the liens you hold, they now amount to slightly less than six million dollars."

"And so I should just forgive all that debt? Not everyone spends so wisely. Some could afford to do better managing their checkbooks and their spending. Forgiving debt like that doesn't magically make people smart," Brian said with a certain amount of irritability.

"That's true; I have seen that, too. But total futility doesn't make them want to dig in and try harder either. They all decide, 'I'll never get out from under this all, so I might as well just try to maintain and make my way and when the house of cards falls, it falls. I am expecting it anyways.' There is nothing worse for a person than feeling as if there's no hope."

"Okay, I'll tell you what, convince me with one sentence why I should consider making such a bold and grand move like that and I'll consider it," Brian said in a challenging voice as he stood. "I am not going to commit to doing it, but I want you to make such an impeccable point that I am compelled to sit and contemplate it."

"Fair enough, I'll take my best shot at it if you'll commit a match of twelve thousand five hundred to Caroline's library effort. I figure I can get twelve thousand five hundred dollars out of the businesses and residents, I'd like to have you match it."

"Done. You have my word. Now, hit me. Why I should consider making such a bold and grand move like forgiving six million dollars of debt like that?"

Without hesitation David replied, "Because someday when you die, there will be no armored car following your hearse."

Brian took in David's entire comment and after a comfortable period of silence he said, "Well, it looks like I have something new to think about."

David reached over and extended his hand. Brian shook it firmly and then pointed over to the door to the study. "If you're ready, I'll arrange a ride back for you."

"I'd appreciate that," David said as he smiled.

The two men walked out to the foyer and Brian signaled Mitchell over. "Bring the car around and take David back or wherever he wants to go."

"Thanks. Back to the apartment is just fine."

"So I have to ask you, David, with all the skill, ability, gusto, and tenacity that I have seen in this short exchange tonight, why are you wandering? You could settle here, anywhere, and have it all. Hell, you could work for me. Why are you living the life you live?"

David slowly stepped in front of Brian toward the door, then turned to face him and answer before heading out to the car waiting for him.

"Because my life right now is more of a life worth living than the one I left behind not so long ago. What I have left right now is having it all."

Chapter Twelve

Maria partially loaded her new dishwasher with the plates from the evening. It had been a long while since she was finished up in the kitchen early enough to sit down in the living room and listen to Caroline start reading to Charlotte. Generally, she would come in part of the way through.

After Caroline came out of her room with a book, she sat on the couch next to Charlotte and opened it up.

Maria sat in the single chair that faced diagonally toward the kitchen. She curled her legs up under her and rested her left arm on the armrest of the chair.

As she listened to her daughter read aloud to Charlotte, she would look out the window of the apartment to the street below where Packer Road intersected with Route 385. Occasionally, she would look about, at Davenport's, all shuttered and dark for the evening, as well as McNally's and the few people that were coming and going. For the most part however, she kept her line of sight down the darkness of Packer Road for what little she could see.

Caroline read for about half an hour as Charlotte listened and asked the occasional question about the story as well as helping out with a word or two. Charlotte also watched Maria stare out the window.

"Mama? I'm all finished. Can I color a little bit before I go to bed?"

"Certainly, Caroline," Maria responded without really turning her gaze away from the street below. "Did you want to color at the kitchen table or on the storyboard in your room?"

"On the storyboard," Caroline answered as she got up.

"Okay. Just for a little bit then."

Caroline kissed Charlotte and then walked over, and gave her mother a kiss. From there she headed to her room.

Charlotte sat up a little in her seat, just enough to turn her head and peer out the window herself and then she turned to face Maria.

"You can keep looking out the window, but it won't make him come back down that road any earlier or faster."

Maria turned slightly to look at Charlotte but still tried to keep part of her line of sight out the window. "I just cannot believe after the trouble we went through to get him away from her that he would just get in the car and head off."

"You don't even know if he got in with her, child. You're getting all upset over nothing at this point."

"I am not upset. I am disappointed at a poor decision. I assumed he was above making them in that manner. Clearly, I gave him too much credit," Maria responded looking over a McNally's abruptly and then slowly turning her head.

"You need to have a little more faith in people," Charlotte replied as she got up and walked into the kitchen. "If David did get into the car with Sue Ann, he may have had a legitimate reason to do so. As you might recall, part of his plans for this library fundraiser that he's helping Caroline with called for him to get in touch with Brian Kurtvow. Maybe she was a means to an end for that."

Maria turned and looked at Charlotte feeling slightly guilty now.

"It's okay, child," Charlotte continued. "It is never easy when someone special enters your life and turns it upside down."

"My life is not all that different this week than last from before David came into town," Maria defended.

"No, of course not," Charlotte responded insincerely.

"It really is not," Maria continued. "I still get up for work the way that I do. I take care of Caroline. She goes to summer school on time and she will go to regular classes as they start up again shortly. I help her with her homework and I go outside and play with her a little bit. Then we come in, have dinner, the three of us, and then she reads and goes to bed. That is pretty much the same as it has always been."

Charlotte just smiled as she headed back into the living room, taking a quick look out the window herself as she rounded the table to the couch.

"I'm glad you are able to dismiss David as not affecting your life all that much and that it's just 'business as usual' for you. When he decides to depart, then it will be that much easier on you," Charlotte said before pausing slightly on her follow up. "And for Caroline, too."

Maria sighed as she looked at the second floor of McNally's. The lights went off in the living area where Kevin McNally and his wife lived. "I just do not understand why he cannot be a little more—"

"Simple?" Charlotte interrupted.

"Yes. Perhaps. I understand he is a very dynamic and complex person, but he could slow down a little and perhaps be more regular. I do not know," Maria said as she squinted a little as she looked back out the window into the darkness down Packer Road.

"You mean to say that perhaps he should slow down a little, take in a little more of what a simple life might offer. Like taking the time to stop and smell the roses, as they say," Charlotte added with a smirk.

"Yes, that is a very good example," Maria agreed, looking down at McNally's as Mel Porter headed out the front door and down the street to his apartment above his closed doctor's office.

"I am glad you agree," Charlotte said with a slight smirk, "seeing as how this is a man who takes a little time out of the day to do nothing at the end of it but stop and watch the sun set."

Maria turned back to Charlotte and then looked down a little bit. She realized she was overlooking some of the little things he does do to simply take life in.

"There is nothing wrong with a busy man, especially one that does more for others than himself," Charlotte continued. "He takes a little time each day, as we have already seen, for the simple things and the important things." Charlotte looked in the direction of Caroline's room.

Maria breathed in a little as her emotions began to rise to the surface. "I cannot afford to feel like this. The man is going to leave. He has already done this in other places he has been. He has already told us he will do the same at some point here."

"Perhaps he's never been given a reason to stay and he's gotten used to that."

Maria jerked her head toward the window as a car approached. It was an eastbound traveler on Route 385 and she slowly turned her attention back to Charlotte.

"I just do not know, Miss Charlotte. It has been such a long time since I felt anything for any one."

"I know, but you can't let your history totally guide your future," Charlotte said as she moved to a seat closer to Maria and then placed her hand on Maria's knee. "Yes, there is a better chance to steer the future if you understand the past, but you cannot let the past control the future. If you have any feelings for him, you may need to say something before the opportunity passes."

Maria took a deep breath and then looked at Charlotte. "I did try somewhat. From a few days back when he had dinner and put Caroline to bed. It really has touched me how much attention he has paid to Caroline. And me. He spent his time over at Baylor's and when he had a chance to help himself, he helped Caroline's cause and me as well."

Maria paused to catch her breath. She looked over her shoulder to make sure Caroline was still playing in her room and was not likely to come out, as she did not want to have her daughter see her crying.

"I told David that I did not want to pry, but that if he should need something of me that he could trust me. I told him I do not judge and I do not speak to others about private matters."

Charlotte sat in silence for a moment and then spoke. "Did he say anything back?"

Maria sniffed. "He said that he did trust me and that he had not let anyone close to him in a long time."

"Well, that is a good thing. At least it was an honest response."

"But he implied that, despite what he might feel, that he could not allow it, that in the end my life would remain better, happier, if we did not become any closer."

Charlotte let Maria's words settle in and then decided on a measured response. "I can't say I understand all people, but I am a pretty good read. I must admit I am a bit surprised at the level of honesty that seems to come out of his conversation. Many men, when they are being truly honest, feel like they take more than they give. They often realize that they are somewhat selfish in a lot of areas. He may feel like he is 'intruding' on your life and Caroline's and he might take more than he can give."

"But he has already given so much without seeming to try," Maria interrupted. "When we were younger, William and I, and we were together, he promised the whole world, or at least as much as he thought we could have together at the time. It certainly seemed like the whole world. And then I got pregnant. You remember. As much as it seemed embarrassing at the time with how religious both our families were, I was genuinely happy. I didn't care how things fell in the matter of time. I just wanted them to unfold. I was secretly happy. I wanted to raise a family. I wanted to be a mother. I wanted to be a wife. I wanted to be a partner. It suddenly didn't matter to me that things occurred out of someone else's expected order."

Maria's light tears became heavier.

"How could he see his own daughter, hold her in the hospital and kiss her lightly, and then tell me that he was going to leave and go back with his parents?"

Charlotte reached over and pulled Maria forward and comforted her as best she could.

"It is so difficult every time Caroline asks about her father. 'Why is Papi not here? Will he come some day? Is there a way for me to meet him?'"

Maria suddenly seized up as she saw the car coming down Packer Road. As Charlotte pulled away to also look out the window Maria wiped the tears off her face and stood.

The stretch limousine pulled up to the "T" where Packer intersected Route 385 as Maria walked over and crouched a bit to see out the window. She stepped to the left slightly so as to remain unseen from the street.

Charlotte got up and headed into Caroline's room to sit with her.

David stepped out of the car next to McNally's and closed the door as the limo turned right onto 385, then circled around and pulled back down Packer.

David stepped forward toward 385, then looked westward down the dark state route. After a moment, he turned and looked back at McNally's and then checked his phone for the time. Maria watched him as he then crossed the street.

Maria walked over to the kitchen door and stood quietly near the door listening for his footfalls coming up the stairs.

Maria stood for several minutes at the door without hearing David come up. She moved over more into the kitchen area, wondering if he came up so quietly that she didn't hear him. She looked up at the ceiling and listened a little more intently.

Charlotte stepped out of Caroline's room and pulled the door mostly closed behind her. "Go ahead," she said in a loud whisper. "I'll get Caroline ready for bed. Go talk to him."

Maria smiled and then slowly opened the door. She went into the hallway to turn and head up the stairs when she glanced behind her and looked down the stairs and out the screen of the storm door. She noticed David sitting on the front stoop, leaning back against the side and looking to the west, so she slowly made her way down the stairs, quickly thinking about what it was she wanted to say in her head. As she reached the bottom of the stairs she placed her hands on the door.

"Good evening, David. I saw you come back from the Kurtvow's. I am hoping it was a successful conversation regarding the bazaar."

David didn't respond and continued to look diagonally away down 385.

"David?" Maria called out a little more loudly as she turned to flip the outside light on.

Maria looked through the screen and saw David had closed his eyes. *He must be exhausted and fell asleep,* she thought as she stepped out onto the stoop.

"David?" Maria called out quietly as she knelt down beside him and touched his arm. He still didn't move.

"David," she said a little more loudly and shook him a little.

Charlotte came to the door of Maria's apartment and stepped into the landing. "What is it, Maria?" she asked as she paused to step Caroline back into the room.

"He's not moving. He's breathing, but I can't wake him."

Rebecca stepped outside of McNally's across the street as they were closing up for the evening and heard Maria call out. She stepped part of the way into the street and called over. "Maria?"

Maria looked up and saw Rebecca and then looked at Doc Porter's place and saw the lights in the apartment were still on. "Becky! Go get Doc!"

Rebecca turned quickly and ran over to Doc's place as Maria shook David a little, trying to rouse him. A slight trickle of blood came from his nose, nowhere near what occurred the last time. She wiped it away with her thumb as she began to get upset. "David," she whispered harshly. "Wake up. *Maldita sea.*"

Maria looked up the stairs and she saw Charlotte on the landing. "Please don't let Caroline see him like this."

Charlotte moved Caroline further back from the doorway. "Come, child, it's time to get ready for bed," she said as she moved her in and closed the door.

Rebecca made her way across 385 with Doc who was carrying a small bag. "... and she called out and I came right over to get you," Rebecca finished as the two of them reached the stoop.

"He won't wake up, Doc," Maria said as she held David's left hand in both of hers.

Doc took a quick read on David's pulse of his wrist. "His resting pulse rate should be about seventy-five," Doc said as he stopped and shined a small flashlight into his bag.

"Well, what is it?" Rebecca asked as she knelt down on the ground below the stoop.

"It's over ninety," he said looking up at Maria. "Was his nose bleeding again?"

"Just a small amount, nothing like before. I wiped it away with my finger and nothing more came," Maria responded as she closed her eyes and squeezed her hands tighter around his left hand.

Doc pulled out a small stick and waved it slowly under David's nose. His body flinched and then moved more. Doc pulled it away and then held open one eye and then the other, shining the small flashlight in them as he went along. David felt someone holding his hand and he squeezed it lightly. Maria smiled slightly at his response.

David began to stir and then attempted to sit up and move into a standing position. Maria and Doc held him in place. Doc noticed how strong David's reaction was to stand and was relieved that it was a forceful attempt.

"Hold still, son, give yourself a minute. Did you fall? How do you feel?" Doc asked as he began to rummage in his bag for other items and pulled out a blood pressure cuff.

"I'm … yeah, um …" David responded as he began to get his wits about himself. He looked over to Maria and smiled slightly and then looked at Doc and Rebecca. He moved a little less vigorously and tried to stand again. Doc pushed him back softly and then maneuvered David's right arm to take his blood pressure.

Maria rubbed David's hand and forearm. Rebecca looked at Maria and smiled a little and mouthed, "It'll be okay. He's okay."

Doc took the blood pressure a couple additional times for comparison reads after short rests and then took David's pulse again which was slowing into the normal range.

"Okay, David, now that you're a little more lucid, can you tell me what happened?" Doc asked as he started to put his things back into his bag.

"Well," David said as he sat up a little bit and swung both of his feet slowly off the stoop and onto the dirt. "I finished up my conversation with Brian Kurtvow and his driver dropped me off at the corner," David said as he pointed across the route.

"I was walking across the way, my heart was pounding, I could feel it. I presumed a little bit of adrenaline rush," he turned from Doc and looked at Maria excitedly. "Kurtvow pledged the twelve thousand five hundred for Caroline's effort for the library."

David attempted to stand again and while Doc and Maria tried lightly to hold him still he pushed back with more strength and got up despite that so they quickly changed independently and helped steady him. Rebecca stood as he continued.

"When I got over to the stoop to head upstairs, I felt funny so I sat and put my head back on the porch. Next thing I know you were all here. I am sorry for the scare but trust me, I'm fine."

"People who are fine don't normally have to be woken up with smelling salts," Doc replied, a little annoyed. "It doesn't have to be tomorrow, but please let the old, retired, town doctor take a proper look at you, will ya?"

"Sure, Doc. How were my stats?" David asked.

"Well, your pulse was initially high and your pressure was low, but they both seem to have stabilized."

"So it could have just been the excitement?" Maria asked.

Doc didn't want to brush off what happened too easily in consideration of the heavy nose bleed the other day, but he didn't want to worry them unnecessarily either. "It could have been, but I would be more comfortable with a stress test and a little blood work. Also, I think it makes sense for someone to stay with you or at least check on you once or twice."

David nodded. "Thanks, Doc, I am sure I'll be fine," he said as he shook his hand. He turned and nodded to Rebecca, then went to head upstairs when he realized Maria was still holding his left hand.

When she realized it, too, she released it quickly as if it were hot to the touch.

David entered the breezeway and the others said their good-byes.

He slowly made his way up the stairs and Maria quickly caught up with him. She walked with him up to the third floor landing and into his apartment.

David walked over to the recliner that was in the room and sat. He put the leg rest up as Maria went into the kitchen and got him a glass of water. She went over to the freezer and took a couple of cubes of ice out for the drink.

"Thanks," David said as he took the water from her and took a sip. He was holding it out in front of him slightly for a moment while he slowly blinked his eyes.

Maria took the water from him and set it on the side table next to the chair. David followed her movements with his eyes and then closed them.

"Will you be okay for a few minutes by yourself?" Maria asked as she pointed over her shoulder with her thumb. "I want to go downstairs and check on Caroline. Miss Charlotte was getting her ready for bed."

"Sure. Go ahead. I'm tired, I am not going anywhere," David responded with a slight smile and then closed his eyes.

Maria backed up a little still watching him for a moment. David's eyes drifted open somewhat and then closed. He waved her off lightly with his right hand. "Go. I'll be right here when you get back."

"Before I go and while you are still awake, I wanted to thank you for the dishwasher. It was really unnecessary, but I do appreciate it."

David seemed to perk up a little at the comment and opened his eyes. "It was totally necessary. You didn't have one."

"I simply meant that it was a little much," Maria said as she tried to defend her independent nature and be accepting of the practical gift.

"It wasn't a lot of trouble," David said as he slowly closed his eyes. "And even if it were, I would have wanted to do it for you anyway."

Maria smiled and slowly made her way out the door, leaving it ajar for her return.

As she came down the stairs to the second floor landing Charlotte opened the door.

"Is he settled? What did Doc say?"

Maria stepped in and headed toward Caroline's bedroom. "Doc really did not say much. David's vitals were off but returned to normal as we sat there and as he woke up. He would like him to go in for more of a formal checkup."

Maria entered her daughter's bedroom quietly, but Caroline was sitting up in the bed. "Did Mr. David come in? Could I go say good night?"

"Another night, little one. Mr. David is exceptionally tired and is resting right now. I am sure you can see him tomorrow," Maria responded as she sat on her daughter bed and shifted her down slightly. "Keep the light cover on you. I'll turn the air conditioner in the living room down, but I want you to stay covered."

"Yes, Mama."

Maria smiled at her, kissed her on the forehead and stood. She turned to walk away when Caroline called out to her again. "Mama?"

"Yes, honey?" Maria asked as she stopped in the doorway.

"If you're going to go back upstairs, can you invite Mr. David to dinner again?"

"Would you like that, Caroline?" Maria asked as she smiled.

"I would, Mama. Please?"

"Then I will ask him. Go to sleep now."

Caroline smiled and closed her eyes. "Can you kiss him good night for me? Tell him it is from me?" Caroline asked with her eyes closed.

Maria stood in silence looking at her daughter for a moment. Caroline opened her eyes and smiled. "Can you? Tell him it's from Caroline?"

"I will," she responded, smiling at the request.

Maria closed Caroline's door most of the way and stepped over to Charlotte. "Can you stay a few more minutes? I would like to go and check on David, and I would be more comfortable if you could wait."

"Of course, child. Go on up," Charlotte said with a smile.

Maria went out the door and headed up the flight of stairs. As she entered David's apartment she did so as quietly as she could in the event he fell asleep which it appeared he did as he didn't stir at all as she entered.

Maria closed the door most of the way and turned the two room lights that were on off as she turned the night setting on the light over the microwave.

She went over to where David was sitting and touched his forehead, then placed her hand lightly under his nose. She then placed it lightly on his chest over his buttoned shirt. She decided to try to wake him partly and get a response from him.

"David," she whispered, "are you okay?" Maria gently shook him.

"Hm?" David responded groggily. "What?"

Maria stopped and stood quietly and just watched him for a few moments and then spoke again. "Are you awake?"

David didn't answer, but Maria was satisfied that he was simply sleeping again and not blacked out like before.

She slowly moved around to the opposite side of the chair and unbuttoned his shirt and spread it open so that he could be a little bit cooler. She stepped away and checked the temperature setting on the through the wall air conditioner.

She moved back to him in the chair and removed his shoes and placed them with the other pairs near his neatly folded duffle bag. She then went back and removed his socks carefully so as to not wake him.

Once she had him as comfortable as she could make him in the recliner, she stepped back and looked at him and smiled lightly. She turned to step away and then stopped and went back over.

She leaned down, touched his arm, and kissed him on the forehead and whispered quietly, "That was from Caroline. She said to say 'good night.' "

Maria stood and looked at David quietly for a moment, then she reached down and placed her hand on his bare chest. Leaning in, she kissed him on the lips lightly and backed up. "That one was from me. Good night, David. Rest peacefully."

Maria then stood and walked quietly out the door.

Chapter Thirteen

Caroline finished coloring the poster she was working on as David peaked over his laptop screen to see how she made out.

"That looks perfect," David said as he stood from the kitchen table and walked over to stand behind her for a better look.

"Do you really like it?" Caroline asked.

"It looks wonderful. No one else could make a poster exactly the way you do. Maria, come take a look," David said as he looked up.

Maria was in the living room folding laundry and she set it aside to come over to see.

Charlotte sipped her tea, kept her seat, and looked into the kitchen. Maria had walked over and stood behind Caroline next to David to look over the finished poster. Charlotte closed her eyes for a moment and then opened them again. She knew it was unlikely to last for them given David's plans to leave, but she wanted to try as best she could to remember the three of them as they were at that moment. If she could freeze time, this would be when she would do it.

"That looks very well done, Caroline. I do believe with that poster it makes the twenty we wanted to get done," Maria said with as much pride as she could have for her daughter.

"And more or less on schedule, with four weeks to go to the bazaar," David replied.

Caroline smiled widely as she began to put the markers and crayons into their boxes. She glanced over at the clock, which read 9:10.

Maria saw her daughter look at the clock and smirked herself because she knew what was next.

"Mama, if I hurry up now and get ready for bed, can I have one story from Mr. David?" Caroline pleaded sheepishly.

David looked at Maria and pointed his thumb over his shoulder.

"We discussed this before, Carolena," Maria said as she took a slightly authoritative tone with her. "I let you stay up past your regular bedtime to help finish the posters. Mr. Peter is back in town tonight. He has been gone nearly four weeks and Mr. David is going over to McNally's to get something to eat with him. Because of the time of the evening and the other obligations there will not be a story tonight."

"Listen, kiddo," David said as he shut down his laptop, "as long as tomorrow is a good day, I promise I'll read you a story. But right now you follow up on your mother's wishes." David smiled as he turned to kiss Caroline on the top of the head.

Charlotte slowly got out of her seat as Caroline dashed by, gave her a kiss goodnight and then headed into the bathroom to change and brush her teeth.

"David," Charlotte called out as she began to make her way into the kitchen, "why don't you take Maria over with you to have something to eat with Peter?"

David smiled slightly and looked at Maria. "Well, you're more than welcome to come over. It's not like we are talking State Secrets or anything."

"I know I am just across the street, but I could not leave Caroline here alone," Maria said as she leaned on the back of the kitchen chair.

"I can watch her," Charlotte said as she waived her hand in the air. "Half the time I am in this apartment well past my bedtime anyway."

Maria and David just looked at each other quietly for a moment until Maria spoke. "It would be nice to go out. Are you certain you do not mind? I do not want to impose."

"I offered. You didn't ask," Charlotte responded as she headed back to her seat in the living room.

Caroline bounded out of the bathroom. "Are you really going with Mr. David?" she asked excitedly.

"I guess I am now. I will just need to get ready." Maria turned to David. "You can head over if you want. I can just meet you there."

"Well, how much getting ready do you need to do? You look fine like that," David said as he grabbed his things and head toward the door.

"I would like to clean up some. It was a long day and I feel a little grubby."

"I can come back down for you if you like," David said as he stood in the doorway.

"I do not want Peter waiting much longer by himself. I know he headed over after 8:30. Go over, I will meet you there."

"Okay," David answered. He turned to leave the apartment and Caroline dashed over and pulled on his shirt to get him to lower himself. David bent down and Caroline kissed him goodnight. With that, David stepped out into the hallway and headed upstairs.

Caroline ran over to her mother and hugged her. "Mama has a date. Mama has a date," she sang.

"It is not a date. Get into bed, you stinker," Maria teased as she tapped Caroline's bottom.

Caroline giggled and headed off to bed. Maria took her purse and walked into the living room. She began to brush out her long black hair. "I am wondering if I should not just take a shower."

"But it's not a date," Charlotte laughed.

"I smell like today's special and a day's worth of sweat. It would be pretty awful if Peter smelled better than me having driven in the truck all day," Maria defended.

Charlotte just grinned.

"I have the time to take a quick one. And I will not be shaving my legs," Maria responded to be funny.

"Perhaps you should consider it," Charlotte said plainly.

Maria opened her mouth, but she was so surprised by the comment she couldn't form a thought. Charlotte laughed as Maria turned and headed into the bathroom.

David put his things down in his apartment, took a few minutes to change into clean clothes, and then headed back down the stairs. On the way back down, he peaked into Maria's apartment.

"Shower," Charlotte said pointing from the couch down over to the bathroom.

David waved and smiled and then pointed in the direction of McNally's. Charlotte nodded her head. "I'll send her right over."

David made his way down the stairs and out the door. He could see Peter's truck parked in Charlotte's lot as he headed across the street.

Maria quickly went from the bathroom to her bedroom in just her towel. Charlotte looked out the window and saw David crossing the street below.

A few minutes later, Maria came out carrying a pair of shoes. She was dressed in a yellow camisole top and wearing a denim skirt, her hair still wet from the shower. She sat in the living room and combed out her long black hair. "I don't have a lot of time to do something with my hair," Maria said to Charlotte as she continued to use the brush and long strokes to comb it out. "Maybe I should just put it up."

"David likes it down," Charlotte said confidently.

"Did he mention this to you?" Maria asked as she put the brush down.

"No, but I see the amount of time he likes to look at you while you're working and your hair is up and when we are here and elsewhere when your hair is down. If I had to place a bet, I would go with 'likes hair down'."

Maria just shook her head slightly and then continued to comb out her hair, leaving it down.

She put the brush back into her purse and she rummaged through it to pull out her wallet and an envelope. She counted up the money in the envelope and then took a few more dollars out of her wallet and added it to the money in the envelope. She then closed it up and took out a pen and wrote "David $60.00" on it and walked it over to the kitchen, where she placed it on the top shelf to the left of the sink.

She walked back to the living room and grabbed the things she took out of her purse and began to put them back. "Are you sure about this? I feel badly having you babysit."

"Stop, before I put you over my knee," Charlotte said as she motioned back to the kitchen. "What is that for?"

"That is the sixty dollars I need to return to David from when he first got here. You remember, he gave me Mrs. Kurtvow's tip and then another sixty, and I used it for Caroline's summer class. I told him the tip was fine if he wanted to pass it along to me, but I insisted on paying him back the additional sixty dollars," Maria explained as she headed into the kitchen to leave.

"Are you going to take the money to him?" Charlotte asked.

"No," Maria replied softly and unsure.

There was a long pause until Charlotte spoke. "I don't understand."

Maria breathed in deeply. "David told me to take my time and to just get the sixty dollars back to him when I could. He promised to not leave town before I had the opportunity to pay it back."

Charlotte just looked at the woman in front of her and imagined in her mind to the little girl she remembered. "So you're thinking to just leave it up on the shelf. You'd rather not give it back to him."

"No," she said softly. "If I do that, he would be free to leave. Selfishly, I would like him to stay."

Maria turned and headed out the door.

Charlotte looked at the shelf when Maria placed the envelope and then walked into Caroline's room to check on her.

David walked into McNally's and found Peter at one of the small tables in the bar area. He walked over as Peter got up out of his chair.

"How are you doing?" Peter asked loudly as he bear-hugged David off the ground.

"Wow," David exclaimed. "Hey, yeah, I'm doing good." He laughed.

Peter dropped him and David slid into the free chair. "Maria is going to come over in a little bit. I figured you wouldn't mind."

"Absolutely not. That's great," Peter said as he went back to his beer and pushed the menu forward to David.

David picked it up and looked it over. He also took a quick look around the pub. It looked like a slow night, but it was a pretty normal night with around twenty people in the place. He glanced over at the door that entered the kitchen area and he could see Kevin McNally moving about in the back.

"So I see things are really taking to you here. You're all involved in this library effort. I told you this town would grow on you."

"Yes," David said as he looked out the windows to McNally's. "It has."

There was a short pause while David looked over the menu, but Peter was waiting on anything additional.

"It doesn't change anything," David responded sounding despondent and without looking up from the menu.

Some of the happiness washed away from Peter. "I was hoping this place might be the exception to your rule. The place that would make you stay."

David set the menu down and looked at Peter. "I can't tell you everything, but you know more than most. I cannot stay. Four weeks, do or die, I am leaving. But this is my last task. There is no more work for me to do after Westville. I am comforted that Caroline's effort will be my last. There's always a 'final' to everything people do. I find her efforts here to be a fitting end to the work I have been helping people do for the past four years."

Peter was unsure what everything meant. "You're right. I reckon I don't understand it all and I'm good with what you have told me. I won't tell anyone else, but where will you go? I mean if you're all done and this is the last you do, why not stay here? You're going to go to some other location to just disappear there. Why not make here, there, and stay?"

"The unintended consequences of getting deeply involved with a large effort is that you become emotionally committed and passionate to what you are doing, who you are helping, and the people you are with."

"I know," Peter said, "but you're committed to getting this done and I bet you'll figure it out. So let Caroline get the brass ring and then stay to enjoy things? It's not written anywhere that you help people realize some of their potential and then you *must* leave."

"I can't explain everything to you my friend. You'll just have to trust me when I tell you it has to be like this."

Peter could only sigh. He knew David was not going to be convinced by him to stay. "You're willing to walk away and leave Westville behind?"

"I have little other choice things being what they are," David responded as he took another glance at the menu.

"There's nothing to change your mind?"

"Oh, I could easily justify it. I just can't stay despite the justification," David said as he turned again toward the door.

"I see," Peter replied quietly.

"You do?" David responded as he turned back around.

"Yes," Peter said as he finished his beer and held up his bottle so Rebecca could see him. "Your justification to stay would be Caroline and Maria. Somehow, despite that justification, you're going to leave them anyway."

Rebecca was listening in as best she could, but she had other customers to attend to.

"They are not mine, Peter. Caroline is Maria's daughter. Maria is her own person."

Peter sat up in his chair a little. "I don't know Maria very well, admittedly. Kind of hard, even with five years of coming and going. I talked at the counter at Charlotte's Place with Doc and Charlotte after the place closed tonight and after Maria took Caroline upstairs. They tell me that without really trying, you've restored Maria to the woman she used to be. And Caroline... she's never known a father or someone that could be one. Not really. Until now. Until you. This burden, this cross you bear, I can't presume to know what it is. I really think you've done your penance. If any man has, you have."

"Thank you, Peter. But you're right. The time is here to let all of that go. So I finish here, I move along, and the rest becomes lost to time and history."

Rebecca walked over with Peter's drink and brought one over for David.

"You will never be lost on the people you've touched to time or history. That moves forward without you there."

"Good. That was the end result I was looking for."

Peter looked up at the door as Maria walked in. David turned his head.

Maria walked in with her long hair still somewhat damp about her shoulders and her camisole top. She smiled at Rebecca who gave her a hidden thumbs-up. Maria smiled even wider.

David got up and gave her his chair at the two-seater high rise pub table and took another one from the bar rail and squeezed it in.

"Thank you," Maria replied, taking the seat.

"Rebecca," David called out, "Cerveza Pacífico Clara for Maria, please."

Rebecca smiled as she went into the long cooler for Maria's beer.

Kevin McNally left the kitchen area and headed into a partitioned private room off the main dining area. While watching Kevin walk away and because of the tight quarters where they were sitting, David accidently bumped Maria's knee with his.

Somewhat startled, David responded, "Sorry about that."

Maria just smiled.

The rest of the evening over dinner was uneventful as Maria and David caught up with what Peter had been doing over the past month since they last saw him.

Rebecca came by to clear their dinner plates away and Maria took the dessert menu from her.

Peter stood and stretched. "Well, it's time for me to get going. I need a little shut-eye and it's getting late."

Maria smiled and put the dessert menu down.

Peter picked it back up and handed it to her. "You want dessert, you stay and have it. I know you don't get out a whole lot and he's not going anywhere tonight." He pointed at David, who just smiled at the comment.

David stood and shook Peter's hand. "Good night, old man."

Peter rapped David on the head with his baseball cap. He gave Maria a peck on the cheek and left.

David moved around to take the third chair away from the table and sit where Peter was when Maria placed her hand on it to keep him from easily moving it.

"Was there something wrong with the seat?" she asked a little playfully with a hint of her accent coming out.

"No," David responded with a slight smirk.

"Then sit where you were."

David just looked at her for a moment.

"Please," she said with almost a seductive smile.

David suddenly became aware of her emotional state as he sat. She had been slowly letting her guard down over the past few weeks and tonight with the rounds of beers the remainder of that guard was gone.

They sat for a short time more as they had another round of drinks and Maria had a piece of chocolate cake.

As Maria was finishing up David turned to Rebecca. "Check, please."

"Oh, Peter said to bill him tomorrow for it."

David just smiled. "Thanks, Rebecca. We're going to get going as we're just about your last customers."

"Oh, don't worry. The Kurtvows have been back there all night. I'm still waiting on them," Rebecca said as she pointed back to the private room where David saw Kevin McNally head earlier.

Maria and David looked at each other with a surprised look and then both looked at Rebecca.

"Good luck with that," David said smiling.

"Gee, thanks," Rebecca said, being funny about it.

"Good night, sweetie," Maria said as she stood on the rail and leaned over for a hug as David turned and started stepping toward the door.

While holding each other, Rebecca whispered in her ear, "I believe tonight would probably be a good night to get a really nice kiss out of him."

"I believe you might be right," Maria responded out of character, much to Rebecca's surprise.

The two let go and giggled at each other. David shook his head.

Maria and David walked across the street and back to the apartment. Maria walked up the stairs ahead of David to the second floor landing.

"Well, this is me," she said playfully as she stood with her back to the hallway wall just beyond her door.

"Yes, well, good night, Maria," David said uncomfortably as he was fighting what he instinctively wanted to do. She stepped forward slightly, her heart racing in her chest since she was in his personal space.

David took one step back to gain a little more comfort zone.

Maria reached forward and wrapped one finger through a belt loop on David's jeans at his hip and tugged slightly.

"Don't," David said, barely protesting. "This ends at some point."

"So you have said, but you are still here," Maria said as the heat in the hall from the summer evening started to make them both sweat.

David tried to straighten out all his thoughts. He was trying to be rational and practical about things after having a few drinks and with his emotional state becoming more exposed.

"This ends at some point," David repeated.

"Yes, you said that. That day is not today. I am not living 'some point' today. I am living *today*, today."

Maria stepped forwards and lightly kissed David on the lips. David kissed her back. He left her hand in his belt loop and he wrapped his arms around her as he pulled her all the way in.

Maria felt the electricity as both of their bodies pressed together. The more pressure David applied kissing her, the more she responded.

It was already hot in the hallway. Both of their bodies together just made it even hotter.

David reached his right hand up to Maria's face and touched it, running his hand over it and into and through her hair. He lowered his left hand around her waist and pulled her up and tight. He was aroused. She could feel him against her and through his jeans.

Overcome in the excitement and the heat of the moment, Maria's knees started to give out. It was David's grip around her waist that kept her standing. Her mind went totally blank and all she could do was respond to his kissing.

David slowed down and reduced the pressure and speed and slowly and softly pulled away.

Maria's eyes were still closed. Her finger slipped out of the belt loop and David slowly let go.

Maria slowly opened her eyes. They darted around David's face as he slowly backed away and she leaned back against the wall behind her.

"I'm going to go upstairs. You're going in to your apartment."

Maria went to say something and David kissed her lightly again.

David slowly backed away.

"David, I—"

"Don't," David interrupted. "Not tonight. Not like this."

Maria was unable to think clearly for a variety of reasons and said nothing more at that point.

"Good night, Maria," David said as he backed away to his stairwell.

"*Buenas noches*, David," Maria said softly.

David smiled as he disappeared around the corner and went up the stairs.

Maria softly touched her lips as a bead of sweat rolled off her forehead and down her cheek. "*Te amo*, David," she whispered aloud as she closed her eyes. "*Por favor, elegir permanecer.* If not for me, if that is not enough, then for both of us. Please choose to stay."

Chapter Fourteen

David stood out on his deck as the morning sun hit his back. His cup of coffee was sitting on the rail edge as he leaned on it with both hands.

A small burst of warm wind blew about the sand on the ground below, carrying some of it out to Route 385 as his thoughts drifted to last night with Maria.

I know better than that, he thought to himself. *I can't let what I feel get out in front of me. I can't let it overtake me. I can't stay. The time is ticking down. I will need to go. I should go. I can't let things catch up with me here. I can't do this to them.*

David took another sip of his coffee and walked over to the opposite side of his deck to where the sun was rising. As his floor of the residence rose above the store, he had an unobstructed view of the eastern sky as well. The warm morning sun hit his face, and he looked down to the large lot below and Peter's truck.

It was Saturday, so he was likely only staying the one additional day and leaving sometime in the morning on Sunday.

David pulled out his phone to check the time. He was actually surprised to see a phone signal, since there was generally more "no network" than signal, but this morning it was there.

"Almost 6 a.m.," he said aloud as he walked back to his slider door to go inside. He closed the slider behind him and changed the setting on the air conditioner to seventy-six and moved the control to the economy setting.

Downstairs in the second floor apartment, Maria went in to check on Caroline who was still fast asleep. Maria walked over and kissed her gently to try to rouse her just a little.

"Hi, Mama," Caroline said as she peeked a little then closed her eyes.

"Good morning, *pequeño*. Did you sleep well?"

"I did, Mama. Are you going downstairs to work?"

"In a minute or two," Maria said as she slipped into the bed beside her daughter.

Caroline smiled, snuggled against her, and turned onto her right side a little so she could drape her left arm over her mother. Maria raised both of her hands up from her sides to touch Caroline's arm.

"Mama, I have a question," Caroline said, wiggling a little.

"Go ahead," Maria said as she closed her eyes and listened.

"I have asked you before about *mi padre*. I know you gave me reasons why he is not here, but I wanted to ask you, if he is not able to be with us, does that mean we could ask Mr. David?"

Maria opened her eyes and sat up, knocking Caroline's arm away. She turned and faced her.

"Did I say something wrong?" Caroline asked as she opened her eyes and sat up startled. "I'm sorry, Mama, I didn't mean to upset you."

"It is not that I am upset," Maria said as she tried to collect herself a little and prepare for follow up questions. "That is a sensitive subject with many people. I trust you never asked Mr. David this."

"Oh no, Mama, not without checking with you first," Caroline said as she smiled. "It's just that Mr. David likes to do things with us, like Melissa's dad does with her. You know, my friend from Freemont Road who takes my bus. I just thought since Mr. David seemed so interested in doing things with us and since *mi padre* wasn't, that is was okay to ask you."

Maria smirked a little as she thought the person that could come up with the best answer for this was the only person she really couldn't ask—David.

"So I guess we cannot ask him if he wants the job." Caroline said quietly.

Maria smiled at the label Caroline gave the topic. "It's more involved than that, Caroline. Let's start with your side. Why would you want David to apply for the job?"

"Well," Caroline said as she leaned forward and moved some of the hair out of her eyes, "he seems to enjoy spending the time here. He reads stories very well with the voices and all. He helps me when I get stuck on my math. He likes to watch the cartoons and movies on the DVDs that we have with me on the couch."

Maria smiled at all the reasons Caroline listed. "He does seem to do a lot of the right things, doesn't he?"

Caroline took her mother's right hand in both of hers. "But mostly, Mama, it's because he makes you smile. You smile a lot when he is near you. That makes him smile a lot. And then I smile. Even Miss Charlotte smiles more, too. I like that the best. All the smiling."

A small wave of emotion rushed over Maria. She needed to pull that back a little because she knew she still had to face David this morning, after last night in the hallway, and she wanted to remain as even-keeled as she could be.

"Well, little one, for now let us keep this conversation a secret of ours. What do you say?"

"Okay, Mama," Caroline said as she leaned in and hugged her mother.

"I have to head downstairs now. You know the rules; you can lay here for a little while, but when you're all set to get up, get cleaned up and dressed, and then come down with a book."

"Yes, Mama," Caroline said as she let go and laid back down.

Maria stood, leaned in, kissed her daughter, and then walked out of the room.

She looked at the clock in the kitchen. She had just about five minutes or so to be on time downstairs. As Maria headed to the door, she could hear David's light footfalls come down the stairs, so she stopped short of the door. She listened for a moment. It didn't sound like he walked past and all the way down, so she remained still near the door. She also remembered that he walked pretty lightly and that he might have walked by already.

Maria turned her head back toward the clock and realized that she basically didn't have any real time left to stand behind her own door. She turned to open it and was surprised to see David standing directly in front of it in a knocking stance.

"Hi," David said, slightly surprised. "I was going to knock and walk down with you, but I wasn't sure if I heard you or Caroline. The footsteps were light and suddenly stopped."

Maria smiled and put her hand over her mouth as it turned into a small laugh.

"Caroline is still in bed, but she was talking about you before I left," Maria said naturally and then suddenly became worried about mentioning it.

"Oh, what did she say?" David asked as he stepped out of the doorway and waved Maria past.

Maria tightened up a little and replied, "She just wanted to make sure I said good morning to you for her."

"That was very nice of her," David said as he followed Maria down the stairs. "That alone makes it a good morning."

Maria hit the bottom landing and continued right out the door without looking back. She smiled at the comment David made but said nothing of it.

Charlotte was already inside and getting the morning coffee ready. "David, I wasn't really expecting you this morning. You did plenty of work already this week."

"Well, you know, Miss Charlotte ... nothing else really to do and all," David said, happy to not have to address his comment to Maria.

Maria stepped behind the counter first and grabbed her waitress apron, then turned around to face the customer side of the counter, which meant that David would have to squeeze by across her front.

David stepped up, thinking Maria was going to keep moving to the back where there was more room in order to get by, but she stopped. He got up to where she was and waited a moment.

Maria stepped backwards just a hair, as that's all the room there was, and pulled the ties to the apron behind her. David slowly turned to face her and squeeze past her. She intentionally stepped forward.

David's face took a momentary turn to discomfort as their bodies brushed up against one another, then he brushed it off as best he could.

As he turned and walked away Maria smiled, proud of herself, because her deliberate step forward threw him off a little.

Charlotte continued making the coffee and getting the serving area all together. She grinned widely as she watched the entire exchange unfold in the mirror at the counter.

A short while later, a few of the locals came in for Saturday morning breakfast.

Rebecca was up early. She was seated at the far right end of the counter. Beyond the open stool at the counter to her left was Doc, and then Peter.

Sherriff Neely came in, but she took her breakfast to go since she wanted to head up Route 385 to patrol.

Charlotte sat between Peter and Doc since Maria and David were working everything fine without her.

Caroline was down the far left end of the L-shaped counter coloring.

David came around from the grill area once all the orders were done and no one new was there to order. He stepped over to talk with Peter, Charlotte, and Doc, occasionally looking over at Maria. Jim Davenport walked in, got a coffee, and took a seat as well.

The store was full of active chatter and Charlotte closed her eyes for a moment and just soaked in it.

Maria walked over to check on Caroline.

"Well, this ought to be interesting," David said loudly above the conversations as he looked out the main windows and straight up Packer road over the concrete barriers at the "T" in the road.

Rebecca swung around with the others to see the Kurtvow limo coming down the road, followed by one of Brian Kutvow's private cars.

"Oh my God, I forgot to mention it," Rebecca exclaimed excitedly, basically looking at Maria but turning to also address David and the others.

"Peter, you left a little earlier and then Maria, you and David left, but the Kurtvows were in the private room until after midnight. I couldn't hear the whole conversation, but it was colorful. Mr. McNally looked agitated over it."

Mitchell pulled the Kurtvow car into the side lot and Brian roared in behind it.

Sue Ann stormed in through the side door.

"You son-of-a-bitch," Sue Ann yelled looking right at David.

Maria went over to Caroline and took her around to the serving side of the counter. "Take your things," she whispered, "and head out the back door, up to the apartment. I will come up in a little bit and have you come back down."

Caroline quickly kissed her mother and scampered out the back way.

Everyone turned to Sue Ann as Brian walked in the side door.

David took his apron off and walked around to the customer side of the counter. He immediately started to count backwards in his head to keep himself at least calmer than her.

"Sue Ann, look," Brian said as he attempted to lightly touch his wife's arm. She jerked it away.

"Quiet and hold this," she exclaimed as she shoved her oversize purse into his hands.

"New York, you've got some brass ones. I'm not sure what the entire conversation was last month, but it was clearly way more than getting Brian to contribute to this stupid bazaar."

David stood quietly. He decided to let Sue Ann vent more.

"And I thought you were a smart man, but I gave you too much credit. Suggesting to him to write down six million dollars' worth of investments as losses."

David still didn't say a word but was still watching her intently. Everyone else was watching like it was a tennis volley. Brian was fixed on David.

"You had a lot to say last month. Nothing now?" Sue Ann shouted.

"I was just going to let you keep going with all the 'rope.' I'm wondering how much you're going to take up and how much is really needed to hang yourself."

Charlotte looked at Jim and both of them held their breath. Charlotte looked past him at the brown ledger book at her register.

"Hang myself? Your stupid thought process hung you, not me."

"Okay," David said very calmly, "how did I hang myself?"

"If you think Brian is going to write down six million dollars on your suggestion, you're crazy."

"Brian is free to do what he wants," David said in a quiet monotone. "I don't see how that validates your comment that I am hanging myself by, I presume, overstepping my station."

"He will not be granting the fund raising effort the money either," Sue Ann continued.

"Well, that would be a shame, since we already announced the matching pledge," David said calmly. "But that is Brian's right if he chooses it."

"I'm telling you," Sue Ann yelled, "he won't be."

"With all due respect, Sue Ann," David said as he began to raise his voice, "you are not in a position to tell me shit."

David's words almost reverberated in the room. It was so quiet.

"You come in here like you own the place, much like you do when you go into all the places in town where Brian holds the tax liens. You demean people and treat them poorly as if that commands to you some level of respect from them, when all they are doing is responding out of fear."

Sue Ann went to respond, but David moved right up to her, into her personal space, and spoke even louder.

"You haven't got a single thing to hold over me and I don't fear you. If you talked Brian out of the donation and he wants to tell me so, then I will continue to work on another way to get this done, but I'll hear it from him. I will give him the courtesy and respect he deserves to say it for himself and either way, I'll thank him for the original consideration."

David stepped away from Sue Ann and walked over to Brian. "Brian, as you know I have a lot of different things I am working on with respect to Caroline's effort. It is counting in large part on your help. If you need to change your decision, I understand. I would need to know now so that I can try to have another solution before the four weeks go by. As you know, we are still about twenty-five thousand short with your help."

Brian looked at Sue Ann, whose eyes were practically popping out of her head. He then turned to David. He knew what he wanted to do—he wanted to help. His wife was exerting the pressure.

"Oh, come on," Sue Ann yelled. "I handed you my purse. Reach in there, grab your balls, and tell him."

"You know something, Sue Ann?" David said as he turned and approached. "You came storming in here saying you thought I was a smart man, but suddenly my actions showed you something different. That rope from before? Here's where I hang you with it. Without your husband, you are nothing here in the town. In this county. Hell, the whole state. He holds the liens in his company holdings, which you really don't have access to. He's allowed you to muscle control from him, but he owns it. That means at any time he can shut the whole thing down on you."

David paused and looked at Sue Ann, over to Brian, and then back to Sue Ann. He gave her a chance to speak, but she realized he was outflanking her.

"My comment before," David continued, "about how you haven't got a single thing to hold over me and I don't fear you. He should feel the same way," David said as he threw his thumb over his shoulder. "What are you going to do to him? What other shoe could you possibly drop? Are you going to spend shitloads of his money? You already do that. Are you going to screw around on him? Check, always and whenever you can. Are you going to insult him and humiliate him in public? Well, we were all witness to that already. So really, what could you possibly threaten him with? Making his life hell in a divorce where you try to take half of everything? You already make his life hell."

David took his tone down a notch. "Funny thing, when I was doing some of the research regarding the tax liens. I went back to when the last cattle ranch closed and you two got married. The press outlined an overview of the prenuptial agreement that was filed. Seems you only get fifty percent of what he earned while you two were married. Not a chance for half of everything but just half of what he's earned while you were married over the first ten years. That paperwork was filed seven years ago. In the past seven years he's earned two hundred million dollars according to the financial article I read online. Half of that is one hundred million."

David walked back into Sue Ann's personal space again.

"Where I come from there's a saying that goes, 'divorce is expensive, but that's because it's worth every penny.' That fully applies to you."

David backed up, turned, and went back behind the counter.

Brian dropped Sue Ann's purse on the floor and took his wedding ring off.

"I told you the boy makes an impressive argument," Brian said as he took Sue Ann's right hand and placed the ring in her palm, closing her fingers around it.

Brian turned to the others and smiled just slightly then looked at David. "I won't be making a donation to Caroline's fundraiser for the library for the twelve thousand five hundred as we previously discussed, David. It is too much of a short fall for the town to make up. I will match two for one rather than one for one. Raise the twelve five and I'll match twenty-five."

Maria put her hands up to her mouth and looked at David who was trying as hard as he could to contain his enthusiasm over what just happened, as it was unexpected.

"Yes," Peter yelled.

Rebecca took out her reporter pad and started scribbling notes.

Brian smiled as he walked out the side door, giving a thumbs-up to David.

Charlotte turned in her chair and looked Sue Ann dead in the eye and said nothing as she simply stood there, stunned at the series of events that just happened to her.

David came back around the counter. "Charlotte is too polite and refined to say it so I will," David said as he picked up Sue Ann's bag and handed it to her. "Get the hell out of here and don't come back until you've learned some manners and you show the respect to others that they deserve."

Sue Ann became emotionally upset and her hands shook. She went to slap David, but he stepped backwards and her swing missed.

"I can see that will be some time from now," David said as he walked away with his back turned all the way behind the counter and into the back room.

Sue Ann looked at everyone in the room and was visibly shaken.

"Stupid podunk people. Stupid podunk town," she yelled as she stormed out of the building.

Once the door closed completely everyone in the store celebrated excitedly regarding the turn of events for the bazaar.

Maria ran into the backroom. David was standing outside the backdoor.

"Are you okay?" she asked him as she circled around in front of him.

"Yes," David said with a certain amount of relief in his voice. "I had no idea where that was going to go, but she just pissed me off."

Maria smiled. "I do not know how you do it. You fly on the wings of angels."

"Fate protects fools, little children, and ships named Enterprise," David said with a grin.

Maria looked at him puzzled.

"Sorry, quote from a television show I used to watch. It basically means the hand of fate favors certain things and somehow my mouth never happens to write a check my ass can't cash." David said as he put his hands on Maria's shoulders.

Maria still looked at him uncertain of the additional meaning.

"I just always seem to get lucky," David said as he smiled widely.

Jim Davenport got up from his seat and slapped Doc on the back. "Come on, we have to head over to McNally's and fill him in on what just happened here."

Doc shook his head and stood. "I know. I've never seen anyone put that woman in her place. That was amazing."

Doc and Jim headed out the door and waved to Kevin who was over on his property across the street.

Rebecca was still writing notes in her pad as David and Maria came back into the store.

"David," Charlotte said, "please take the rest of the day off. I don't care where you go or what you do. That was a wonderful display of forced karma if I ever saw it."

"I'm sorry about the grandstanding, but I couldn't control it once she set me off," David said as he started to take his cook apron off.

"She does that to everyone. No one has even stood up to her. We've all been afraid to. It took a drifter to set us straight," she said with a smile.

"Well, I do suppose that if you can spare me, there's more I can do with the fundraising effort."

"Please," Charlotte replied. "You've just doubled the Kurtvow pledge and gapped the effort that much more. This might actually happen after all."

David looked at Maria and smiled. "Tell me how excited Caroline is later when you tell her."

"You can see for yourself when you tell her tonight at dinner," Maria responded with a smile.

"Six?" David asked as he walked out the door, and Maria nodded.

Charlotte moved away from the customer side of the counter and walked toward the side door. She gave Peter a short little tug. "Walk with me."

Peter grabbed his coffee and headed outside with Charlotte.

Maria leaned on the counter near Rebecca looking out in the direction that David walked off.

Rebecca finished up her notes and put her things away.

"Okay, so off the record, as the reporter has put her notebook away, what happened after you left last night?"

Maria looked at her and tried not to smile, but it took over her face. "Oh my goodness. In one move I was giddy like I was sixteen and in high school again," Maria said as she practically giggled.

"Really?" Rebecca asked.

"Yes. The anticipation, it was intense. It was exciting. I do not even know how to fully describe it, but when his lips touched mine … if his arm was not already wrapped around my waist, I am certain I would have collapsed."

"I've never been kissed like that," Rebecca said as she leaned into the counter.

"I had not either. That was a first for me," Maria said as she pulled the stool of the serving side forward and down.

"Was there more? Or are you not telling?"

"Nothing further than the hallway. But that only made everything more memorable."

"Would you have? If he asked or pressed?" Rebecca asked intently.

Maria just sat for a moment looking up and recalled the entire event in the hallway. She smiled and a shudder went through her entire body. Rebecca sat, watching the expression on her face.

"He could have done anything," Maria said with a deep seriousness turning back to look her in the eye, "and I would have let him. I wanted him to. He knew it, too. He could have done anything he wanted. Somehow he knew the best way to make the biggest impression with me was to leave it where he did."

Rebecca giggled. "I want him now."

Maria just looked at her dead serious for one second and then they both burst out in laughter.

Charlotte walked outside with Peter around his parked truck and into the back property.

"Well, I tell you, Miss Charlotte, I've seen David in a couple of situations, but I ain't never seen him like that before. I don't know all about that Mrs. Kurtvow exceptin' what you tell me, but it sounds like he went and totally put her into place," Peter said grinning from ear to ear. "And then getting that extra money like that! I am going to tell every trucker I see all about this little bazaar."

"It really was something to see, someone properly handle Sue Ann. It's been a long time coming that is for sure."

"Thank you again Miss Charlotte for letting me leave the big rig on the property while I am here. I certainly do appreciate it."

"It's not a problem, Peter. We enjoy when you come to visit and I'm happy for you to have a place to park it."

Charlotte walked over to a small rock outcropping at the eastern edge of her property where it abutted the old municipal properties and sat on one of the flat rocks. There was room for Peter to sit as well, but he was so charged up and excited over the events he wanted to stand.

"So, Peter," Charlotte said as she firmed up her speaking tone while lowering her voice, "I want to ask you some questions about our young friend."

Charlotte looked up at Peter and noticed some of the excitement wash out of his face.

"Miss Charlotte," Peter replied, "you know I always try to be honest and upfront with you, but there may be things I can't talk about."

"Things David specifically asked you not to mention."

"Yes, ma'am."

"I won't ask you to break your word."

Peter sat quickly. "Thank you."

"I remember you telling me you were having issues with your truck with the back taxes. Property and income and so forth."

"Yes, ma'am."

"You never mention it anymore. At one point it was so critical you were concerned you might lose the truck. Did David help you get that taken care of? Is that how you came to meet him?"

Peter thought about things for a minute. The things he was asked to not repeat and then he answered her. "Yes, ma'am. He helped me reach the right people at the federal government to get on a payment plan. He put me in touch with an accountant he knew that knew all the rules I didn't know. The lady taught me what I needed to know so I don't get into that kind of jam again. They worked with the IRS fella to stop the additional interest and penalties. As long as I make the agreed payment on the amounts I owe prior, I will be fine and, as a matter of fact, I'll be completely paid and done in March."

Charlotte nodded. "And do you know anything about how he is? He's had a couple of nasty spells while he's been here."

Again, Peter paused to think and then asked "the nose bleed thing?"

"Yes," Charlotte said as she moved over a little on the rock outcropping.

"It would happen once in a while. I never asked him. I figured a nose bleed is a nose bleed."

"Have you ever seen him black out?"

Peter laughed out loud. "Have I? He likes his beer. That is for sure. He never drops on the floor, but he gets comfortable and he'll go to sleep really fast."

Charlotte wasn't exactly sure that was the same thing she had seen, but she looked at the store and was worried someone would come over and she wouldn't be able to finish questioning him so she moved along.

"Clearly he leaves. He goes somewhere, helps someone with something, and then he leaves. Has he ever indicated how or if he might stay?"

Peter thought harder this time. "Well, he helped me two towns ago and while he left those places he's stayed with me giving him a ride. He got around just fine before. He could again. So I guess you say he does allow for an attachment if it meets a need."

"So he could change his mind?"

"Miss Charlotte, I will tell you this, I have never seen him take to most of a town like he has here. He helps someone, a group, a family, a congregation. He stays at arm's length, does his thing, and almost sneaks away like a thief. I don't mean that he takes anything. He just disappears on them. He never says good-bye. He's disappointed some people by doing that. They still talk about him in Clearwater, Arkansas. Every time I go through, the folks he helped there, they ask me if I've seen him. David asked me to always answer no, so that is what I tell them."

"How did he help them?" Charlotte asked.

"A family was going to lose their home to a developer because they were going to build a mall or something. The developer was lying to the people, telling them they had the sell or the federal government was going to take the land away and give them nothing. David knew what the laws really were. He got a state senator involved. The developer got pinched. The family was offered the full amount for their home and relocated to a nice home farther away from where all the building was going to take place. And the place they bought was a little newer and a little cheaper. There was some money left over. Not a whole lot but some. They were so happy they weren't tricked. And it was only because David was there. No one else knew the laws or even knew enough to ask."

Charlotte got quiet thinking the things through. Peter thought for a moment too, then stood in front of her, removed his hat, and spoke some more.

"I don't profess to know everything, Miss Charlotte, but I do know this. The man is searching. I don't know what he's looking for, but I have never seen him attach himself. He's gone to great lengths to avoid it. Maybe he's found it here. Maybe he'll help with this bazaar and stay when it's all over and not leave like he otherwise might."

Peter turned to slowly walk away but then stopped and turned back.

"Caroline and Maria. I've seen him with Maria mostly, but I know he's done little things with Caroline too from what Doc said. He's never done that before either. To sit and engage with a woman. I think he was badly burned or something. Maybe in some way like Mr. Kurtvow. Really rolled over and taken advantage of. Maybe that is why he got so beside himself and really let Mrs. Kurtvow have it. Maybe it was something he never could do before for himself. He's really good at helping others. Perhaps helping himself and taking care of himself, maybe he's bad at that."

Charlotte smiled a little. "Maybe," she answered as she watched Peter start to back away a little. She went to get up and Peter came right over to help her and she brushed him off.

Peter smiled at being swatted for trying to help.

"Maybe you're right, Peter. Maybe he has been searching. I really hope he's found what he's looking for here. If it's the need to help others, he'll always be in demand here that is for sure," she said as she looked across to Davenport's and McNally's. "And if it's being taken care of, I believe Maria is signed up for that. All he has to do is tell her."

Chapter Fifteen

The afternoon sun heated up the late September sky as a warm breeze blew. Cars moving along on Route 385 past Charlotte's Place stirred up dirt that had blown off the surface properties along the side of the route.

David made his way along the north side of the route and crossed over at McNally's.

Maria was kneeling and arranging items in the window at the time and stopped to watch him walk along and start to make his way across. Caroline hopped into the window area and waved vigorously to him. As David looked up, he traded his dour expression for a friendlier one and waved back. Maria smiled and waved as well. David turned his attention to her and his smile got a bit wider.

Caroline looked at her mother smiling and then looked back out as David was smiling and crossing the main road.

"See, Mama? All the smiling. Can we ask now?" Caroline asked as she smiled.

Maria shook her head and mouthed the words "no" as she became slightly embarrassed. David stepped into the store and turned to the window display where they both were.

Caroline jumped off the raised partition and right onto David's chest.

"OooF!" David gasped as he caught her. "I think by the time October tenth rolls around in three weeks or so and you turn nine, I won't be able to pick you up any longer."

"Oh, Mr. David, you're big. You'll always be able to pick me up no matter how big I get."

Maria smiled at how excited Caroline was to see David. Her mind drifted to her daughter's words from the prior moment. She continued to hear in her head, *Can we ask now?*

David set Caroline down on the ground at the edge of the laundry detergent and soap aisle and turned toward Maria. "I thought I would do a little work."

"Okay. Did you want a sandwich or something before you get started?"

David smiled, hesitated for a moment, and then answered, "A sandwich would be great. Turkey with some lettuce and tomato and—"

"I have made you a sandwich before. I do know the way you like it," Maria said playfully as she stepped a little closer to him.

Caroline stepped in between them and hugged her mother.

David smiled and started to back away to the counter.

"You seemed like you wanted to say something else," Maria said as she stroked Caroline's hair.

"You said 'did you want a sandwich or something' and I was going to be funny and say 'something.' I wasn't sure how it would sound, so I didn't."

Maria slowly let her daughter go and went around the counter to make the sandwich for him. Caroline sat one seat over from David.

"You should simply speak your mind instead of thinking about it first. I would think by now you would realize I know you well enough. I do not believe something you might say would offend me," she said as she smiled and looked at him.

David returned the smile and replied, "Okay, I will."

"Just be David. I find it hard to believe you could go wrong just being you."

David pulled his laptop out of his side bag and put it up on the counter.

"Where were you just now?" Maria asked as she worked on the sandwich for him.

"I was over at Garcia's Wine and Spirits. I needed to pull my e-mail to my local e-mail client and Mr. Garcia's credit card system is not a direct dial connection to the company. It's a connection to the Internet that tunnels there and that allows me to use it to sync my e-mail."

"Ah. Were you waiting on something in particular?" Maria asked as she finished up and came around with the sandwich and a glass of water for him.

"Thank you," David replied as she put the sandwich down. "All the final numbers were sent in from County. I will now know exactly what we'll need to raise to get the library online," he replied as he looked at Caroline and smiled.

David turned and looked at Caroline. "Are you ready? This is now the final goal," David said pointing to one of the unread e-mails.

"Yes!" she replied excitedly.

"Do you know?" Maria asked in a voice just above a whisper.

"No," David silently mouthed back.

David turned and opened the e-mail as Maria came around to their side of the counter. He scrolled through the list of items outlined to the total at the bottom.

"Sixty-four thousand and change," David said quietly and withdrawn.

"I do not understand," Maria said disappointedly. "You had indicated earlier that the estimate was closer to fifty."

Caroline looked at them both but didn't say anything. She was unsure what the new numbers meant.

"I didn't have all of the information. Also, some of the records I had showed the wiring part of the project inside the library as farther along than it actually was. Also, the systems that need to go into the library, the cost for the equipment, as well as all the e-readers, were higher than I estimated." David responded.

"So what does that mean, Mr. David?" Caroline asked. "I don't understand."

David turned to Caroline. "Well, we have about seven thousand from the businesses between advertising and booth space. I am estimating that we can earn about six thousand from the people as they come to the event. We have to hope for good weather now, but that is a fair estimate over the sixteen hundred people here in town. So with that thirteen thousand and Mr. Kurtvow's pledge of twenty five thousand we should have thirty eight thousand."

Maria quickly did the math in her head.

"So how much more would we need?" Caroline asked.

"About twenty seven thousand, honey," Maria said softly.

"Is that a lot?" Caroline asked.

"It is enough to make it very likely this won't be completed. At least this time through," Maria answered.

David sat looking forward at the wall while they talked. His mind was racing.

"Well, could we just continue to try? Over time? I'm sure if we keep trying we would eventually get there," Caroline insisted.

David looked at Caroline and responded softly, "That is absolutely correct."

David took his wallet out of his pocket and, from one of the inside sleeves, took out a few hand written notes, one on a yellowing piece of paper. Moving it to the side, he returned the others to their place.

David got up, walked to the phone, and dialed the number on the paper. After a few rings, a female voice on the opposite end of the call answered.

"Yes, good afternoon. Is Mr. Taylor available?" David asked.

"I'm sorry, sir," the woman responded, "but he is not available at this time."

"Can you please forward him a message now? I know you can reach him."

"I'm sorry, who is this, please?"

David looked at Maria and Caroline, who were both listening. David paused for a moment and sighed. "David Stephenson."

The woman began to look over the exception list she had for direct access to Zachary Taylor and she could not find David Stephenson listed.

"I am sorry, sir, but I do not have your name on the list. I can take the message to give to his executive assistant."

David paused for a moment and again looked at Maria and Caroline. "Please, I am under a tightening deadline and it is really important that you give him a message for me. Please give it to him exactly as follows. I am confident he will take the call or directly follow up on his own. Here is the message: 'You're only taller than me when your mother makes you wear your combat boots.'"

The woman on the other end of the phone was silent for a moment and then spoke up. "Is this a joke? This is a direct line bypassing the switchboard. How did you get this number?"

"I have this number because I am supposed to have it."

"Then why are you not on my list?"

"I actually am," he said again looking at Caroline. "And if you pass that message, you'll see for yourself."

"'You're only taller than me when your mother makes you wear your combat boots.' That is the message you expect me to forward?" The woman sounded agitated.

"Or don't. Eventually I'll get through to him and I'll mention to him the issues I had getting through on this line," David said calmly.

The woman was again silent for a moment and then responded. "Hold one moment, please."

David smiled and looked at Maria. "I'm on hold," he said in a loud whisper.

"Who is Mr. Taylor? What are you doing?" she asked.

"I'm calling in an old favor to see where it might get us."

The woman looked at Zachary's schedule, which was set for "planning" and then viewed the call extension to his office, which was dark. She got up from her desk and knocked on his office door and entered slowly.

"Yes, Beverly," Zachary said as he looked up from his desk and the presentation he was working on.

"I am very sorry to bother you, Mr. Taylor. I have a caller on the direct dial line that is not on the list, but he is fairly insistent to pass a message to you," Beverly responded as she stopped a few feet from his desk and then folded her hands in front of her burgundy skirt.

Zachary looked up, a little puzzled, as his assistant knew what the protocol was. "Well that had to be an interesting message then. Who is on the line?" he asked as he ran his hand through his short brown hair.

"I have David Stephenson holding, sir," she replied, somewhat nervous.

Zachary stood to stretch as he had been sitting working for some time. "No…" he said aloud, thinking to himself and tugging down on his button down white dress shirt. "The name is not ringing a bell. Maybe the message?"

Beverly cleared her throat. "Yes, sir. It is an … unorthodox message."

A small smirk came over Zachary's face. "Go ahead. I'll forgive you if it's something otherwise embarrassing. It's probably Christopher from the club playing a joke."

"Yes, sir," Beverly said more relieved. "The message was, 'You're only taller than me when your mother makes you wear your combat boots.' "

Zachary thought about the comment for less than a second. "Did you say Michael?"

"No," Beverly said with a little doubt in her voice. "I am nearly certain he said David."

"Put the call through," Zachary said as he prepared to take the call on his wireless headset.

Beverly went back out, closing the office doors behind her and took the phone again.

"Mr. Stephenson?"

"Yes," David responded as he turned to Maria and put his finger over his lips to her.

"I can connect your call now."

"Thank you."

"Connecting now. Mr. Taylor, David Stephenson is now on the line," Beverly announced as she connected the two and then disconnected her end of the line.

"Good afternoon, Mr. Stephenson, is it?"

"Yes," David responded. "I take it you understood the message, otherwise you would probably not have taken the call."

"Michael," Zachary said quietly and plainly. "It's been a really long time."

"It has," David responded as he looked at Maria and Caroline.

"So it's David, is it?" Zachary asked.

"It is," David replied as he began to become a little self-conscious that Zachary's voice over the handset might be loud enough to hear in the now quiet store.

"I take it you're in a place where you cannot fully respond to everything openly."

"That would be correct, Mr. Taylor."

"I presume it's time for you to call in that favor," Zachary said with a wide grin.

"Well, truth be told, the call-in is small against why I have it in the first place, but I am running out of other options and time, so I have to play this card since I have it to use."

"I understand," Zachary said as he looked at the caller ID on the phone console. "You're in Texas, whereabouts?"

"I'm a couple of hours outside of El Paso in Westville."

"If you can get to El Paso, I can send the plane and have you here in Houston before nine. We can meet in the morning, catch up, and you can let me know how I can help."

David thought about it for a moment. "Okay, I'll have to get to El Paso, but I'll figure it out."

"Perfect," Zachary replied. "I'll get Beverly to set the arrangements and send them to your phone."

"It'll have to go to my e-mail account. I don't have that phone anymore," David responded.

"Good enough. I'm sure I still have the e-mail. It'll be good to see you again, Michael."

"See you then, Zachary."

David turned and hung up the phone.

"Taylor," Maria said. "Zachary Taylor? From Zee Technologies?"

Caroline looked surprised. "Did he get my letter?"

"I am sure he did, Caroline. I will ask him," David said as he smiled.

"You are leaving? To go to El Paso?" Maria asked with a sinking feeling. The words "you are leaving" did not set well with her when talking to David.

"And then to Houston. I have to get to El Paso first," David said as he fumbled his wallet to return the paper to its place and then pull out a business card. David turned to use the phone again.

"Hello," Brian Kurtvow responded on his cell phone.

"Mr. Kurtvow, it's David."

"Hi David, and please, it's Brian. How are you?"

"Well, to be honest, I am in need of a favor. You're already doing so much for us but—"

"How can I help?" Brian asked as he set his work aside for the moment.

"I need to get to El Paso as quickly as I can. I need to catch a plane to Houston."

"I am in El Paso now. I can send Mitchell to get you and he can drive you there in a couple of hours. Do you already have a flight?"

"That would be more than fine. I do have a flight. A private jet I presume. Zachary Taylor is sending it for me."

Brian let out a hearty laugh. "And here I thought I was the richest person you knew. You are one surprise after another, boy. I like your style."

"Believe me, I would have preferred to have gone another way with this," David said as he looked at Caroline, "but the lesson here is not just money to get things done. It's leveraging people and their skills and abilities."

"I think I follow a little. That's fine. If the car ride will help, I am happy to offer it. I'll have him fuel up and be there in thirty minutes. Will that work?"

"It'll be perfect, Brian. Thank you." David hung up the phone as Charlotte came in from outside by way of the back door of the store.

"Ah, Miss Charlotte, perfect timing. I will need to ask for a couple of days of not being at work. I need to leave."

Charlotte stopped short in her step at the comment and looked at Maria. Since Maria didn't seem overly concerned, Charlotte quickly buried her initial reaction. "Oh? Going on a short trip?"

"Yes, but I am in a rush so I'm afraid Maria will need to fill you in," David said as he smiled and began to slowly come around the corner of the counter area.

He turned and looked at Maria and then down to Caroline. While still looking at her he extended both of his arms. Caroline got up and ran to him and hugged him. "Safe trip," she said as she squeezed him tight.

"I will have one now that I have a proper sendoff," David said as he kissed the top of her head and let her go.

Caroline went back to the stool she was sitting on and then looked at her mother and back to David.

David wanted to walk over and say good-bye properly, but he was having trouble committing to the action as he stood there and could only back away a step.

"Would you be able to give the store a call when you arrive in Houston? So that I do not worry and I know that you arrived off the flight okay?" Maria asked.

"Of course. I'll call first thing." David said trying to give her some reassurance. "It's not a long flight. I'll be perfectly fine."

"I will feel better… once you are home."

The words fell on David like bricks. He hadn't used the term "home" or referred to any place as home in a long time. As hard as the words sounded, they rang in his ears at a certain level of comfort as well.

"I'm coming back," David said as he turned to leave.

"You have to," Maria said with a smile.

David turned at the door to look at her.

"I still owe you sixty dollars."

David smiled as he went out the door and up to his apartment to pack.

Chapter Sixteen

David was sitting in the lobby of Michael's, the restaurant where he was waiting on Zachary Taylor to arrive for their lunch meeting. While he was waiting, he was reading some legal papers he had long ago scanned into digital format. As he looked up, he saw Zachary's car pull up front. He resaved the current file "Berucci_Samson_ATTYs_2009" to "Berucci_Samson_ATTYs_2014," attached it to an open e-mail, and sent it off as Zachary walked in.

David closed the laptop and stood.

"So, should I call you David your entire time here or is Michael fine?" Zachary asked as he shook his friend's hand.

"Honestly, it doesn't really matter. I guess it doesn't make sense for you to call me David right now but, to be honest, I stopped being Michael a long time ago."

Zachary motioned toward the private area of the restaurant as the server walked with them. "Yes, I know. Everything that happened … Let's get seated and we can catch up. It's been four years since you basically disappeared."

"It's behind me as best as it can be. I've gotten through what I needed to and continued on by leaving it as part of the past," David replied stoically as he took a seat in the enclosed room. "But I guess you're right, I probably should catch you up."

The server entered the room and stepped over to Zachary. "Can I take a drink order to get you started?"

"Yes, we'll have a couple of Sam Adams, Boston Lager please, and my usual business lunch menu, adjusted for just two attendees." Zachary said as he sat. "Once you bring it please notify the remainder of the staff that, until called for, we should not be disturbed."

"Of course, sir."

"I take it you do a lot of lunch business here?" David asked.

"I own the place," Zachary said plainly. "The restaurant is named after the man who saved my company from a hostile investment takeover."

David smiled just slightly. "I was just doing what I knew how to do."

"You were an investment analyst. I bumped into you at a technology trade show and once we got to chatting over beers I asked you some advice on my personal investments. You said you'd take a look, but from the conversation alone you thought I was too leveraged from a personal aspect in my own company as far as my long-term investments were concerned. Afterward, you went digging around you uncovered the underpinnings of that takeover attempt that most of the financial sector had no real knowledge about. No one else, but you saw that because the groundwork on it was being done in such a clandestine manner. As a matter of fact, other people I asked said you were way off, being beyond highly speculative, and that you were seeing things that were just not there."

David just smiled. "Guess we know who was right in the end."

The server came back in with the drinks and a small cart with six more on ice. "The food will be in shortly and the staff has been informed that until the serving light comes on at the floor manager station that no one should come in."

"Thank you, Diane," Zachary replied.

David took his beer and had a large sip of it and set it down on the table. He looked around the private dining room quickly. It was just the two of them in the decent sized room, sitting at one end of a long table that could host up to eighteen people in total if people were seated on the short ends. David quickly counted the chairs and noticed sixteen.

"Do you ever actually have sixteen people in here?"

"I have on a couple occasions," Zachary said as he took a drink from his beer, "but we are not here to discuss my restaurant or my business. First, what do you need?"

"There is an eight-year-old girl trying to get her town's library brought into the twenty-first century. Your company was involved with the larger project several years ago."

"The West Texas Infrastructure project?"

David nodded his head.

"I thought all the funding from that was pulled after the natural disaster."

"It was. The little girl got the idea in a very generic way on her own and was trying to restore the project via a grassroots effort in her hometown."

"That sounds like an impressive little girl."

"Caroline," David said quietly as he tightly clenched the beer bottle. Zachary watched his hand shake and almost thought if he squeezed any tighter that it might shatter. He touched David's arm and he began to settle.

For a short while both men sat in silence and then the servers made their way in and put the various serving platters on the table between the two of them. Once everything was set and the two emptied beer bottles were taken away and replaced they left the room.

"Look, Michael," Zachary said as he picked a little at the food on his plate, "as far as the project goes, e-mail me the specifications of what you need and it's done."

"It won't be a lot. I estimate we may effectively be a little less than \$30,000 short. For that little town, it's a lot. For you, it's likely the tip you leave here on a good night."

"Like I said, e-mail me what you need. As far as I am concerned, it's done."

"Thank you."

"No, thank you. As I said, if you hadn't caught what you did, I would have lost my company. Yes, I'd be well compensated by the overall buyout effort as the stock ran up, but for me it's always been about the technology, the company and the good people that helped me build it. The money has always been a nice fringe benefit. It was never the most important thing of the things I wanted to make my life a success."

"That was a lesson I needed to learn earlier in my life. I learned it once it was too late," David replied as he fought back more emotions.

"Normally, I would say it's never too late to learn that lesson, but like with all the things you do, I would have to say that you are the exception. I am so very sorry about that."

There was another long silence and they both took advantage of the pause to eat some more and finish another round of beers. "So I know what happened, obviously. What happened after?"

"I don't know, really. A lot of the first year was a fog. I spent almost that whole year anywhere but the house," David said as he slowly recalled the details he had worked so hard to try to forget. "I stayed at the cottage. Down the marina. On the boat. Up north in the cabin. All the places we bought and had never really been. All the places we said we wanted to go and never did for all the justified reasons I gave at the time. Then one day I just went home. I put everything up for sale. I put everything I felt I really needed to take with me in my huge green army duffle bag and left. I haven't been back to Connecticut since. I made my way down the Atlantic Coast states and then along the Gulf Coast states basically and into Texas. I've spent about four years just wandering."

Zachary sat a while and thought about all the things he remembered about Michael's situation and the life events that occurred, the man himself, and what he'd just told him.

"I'm sure doing good things the whole way through," Zachary said as he finally spoke. "I know you always locked tone on 'business', but you were a Boy Scout with impeccable radar for finding problems and coming up with solutions."

David finally lost his grip and tears began to stream down his face.

"I spread myself too thin. I never burned the candle at both ends. My whole world was always on fire. And I liked it like that. Always in demand. Always needed. Always the one that was called when something needed to be resolved or solved. Then when it was time for me to do those things for myself ..."

It was painful for Zachary to see his friend this emotional. It was a side of him he never saw before. He didn't know what to say or how to respond and he felt powerless to help him.

"I met a woman. Maria. Caroline's mother." David couldn't say anymore. He didn't have to. Zachary understood.

"Michael, I'm good. You don't need to say anymore. I get the general idea. You don't need to live it again. Once was more than enough for anyone. If you'd found someone and a place to rebuild—"

"I won't be staying. I do what needs to be done. The problems, they find me. The people often don't ask for help, they don't know how. They struggle and try to overcome. I help them get there."

"And then you leave?"

"Yes."

"Why?" Zachary asked. "I understand you are a problem solver for target issues. It sounds as if you found not one person but two people whose lives you are affecting for the positive. Why not keep doing that? Why not be there for them the way they seem to be there for you? You can allow this for yourself. You can afford to be selfish and to be happy again."

David fought and struggled with himself to get the words out. He had to say them out loud if only just the one time.

"Because this is not about me. It's about them. I will not bring onto them and into their lives the same losses that happened in mine."

Zachary watched his friend completely break down and sob uncontrollably at the table. He thought about what Michael said and recalled the events in his life that he was aware of.

Zachary slipped against the back of his chair, totally emotionally deflated.

Chapter Seventeen

Caroline sat in the living room looking out the windows to Route 385 below while Charlotte sat in the single chair. Maria put the last of the dried dishes and pots away and walked into the living room.

"Mama, when will Mr. David be home?"

"He called us at the store when he landed around closing time," Maria answered as she turned to the clock in the kitchen. "I would think he would be here fairly soon."

"I can't wait until he gets back. I want to hear the news."

Charlotte looked at Maria as she sat. "Seems like David is one surprise after another. I thought it was interesting that he was able to handle and manage a rich man like Kurtvow with some level of ease. Now it makes a little more sense. He knew an even richer one."

"I must admit," Maria said as she set her beer down on the table, "I was also surprised. I seem to be getting used to it. David being full of secrets and surprises. I would not have believed I would ever be comfortable with someone who was not entirely upfront, but for some reason I seem to continually allow him this courtesy."

Charlotte smiled and said quietly, "Love does that to people."

Maria turned slightly defensive at the comment. "I never said that," she whispered loudly so that Caroline would not respond to it.

"Some things don't need to be said out loud, child. You know what you feel. You don't need to tell me. However, you should admit it to yourself and make sure David knows."

"There is nothing to tell," Maria said complacently.

Charlotte only smiled.

"He's coming! He's coming," Caroline yelled as she jumped up and ran for the door as the long car slowed and pulled along the south side of Route 385 East.

Maria followed Caroline down the stairs as Charlotte turned to the window and cracked it open to listen.

David got out of the car and grabbed his bag. "Thanks, Mitchell," he said to the driver.

"Anytime, sir."

"Pass along to Mr. Kurtvow my thanks once again."

"Will do."

David closed the door of the car and turned to Caroline who was hopping in place on the dirt next to the road.

"Tell us. Tell us. Did Mr. Taylor get my letter? Can he help us?"

David looked at the two of them as he stepped forward. Maria looked at him and was concerned as his look was very sullen and withdrawn.

"Yes, Caroline," David said very plainly as he bent down just a little. "He did say he could help us. All we have to focus on now is the event itself. I believe everything else will fall into place."

Caroline was so excited that she screamed and ran up the stairs to tell Charlotte. "Miss Charlotte. Miss Charlotte. It's good news."

Maria smiled a little at David while he just looked at her plainly.

"Are you okay? You left late the other day; you had the meeting today and then travelled back. I am certain you are tired. Can you come up so that I can make you something to eat?" Maria asked as she reached over to take David's left hand.

"I'm really kind of tired," David replied as he drew his hand away from her advance. "I was thinking to just deliver the news and then go up to my apartment."

Maria paused for a moment, unsure of what to say. As David stepped toward the building she slowly followed. "Of course, I understand. It has been a long two days. You have let Caroline know the news and I am sure she is telling Miss Charlotte all about it. I will head up and get her ready for bed and allow you to get settled."

"Thank you," David said as they reached the second floor landing.

As David rounded the corner and began to head away to the third floor Maria continued, "I would like to stop up for a few minutes after Caroline is settled. I would like to talk to you."

David stopped at the start of the third floor stairs and sighed just slightly. "Yes, that would be fine. Just for a short bit."

Maria smiled slightly to him as she entered her apartment slowly. David continued upstairs without much additional expression.

Maria closed her kitchen door behind her and leaned against it. She could hear Caroline excitedly telling Charlotte how David's trip was a success.

Charlotte focused her attention on Caroline, but she glanced over at Maria and saw the look of concern as it began to wash over her face.

Maria shook it off and then walked into the living room to spend the short remainder of the evening with her daughter and Charlotte.

Afterward, Maria got Caroline ready and off to bed and then spoke with Charlotte for a moment.

"I am going to head upstairs to talk with David. If you need to go down that is fine, just please close the apartment door before you head down," Maria said as she moved into the kitchen and got ready to leave.

"I'm sure I can wait a little bit. It won't be a problem. Is anything the matter? All the news sounded good," Charlotte commented as she took a seat in the kitchen.

"I am not sure. He seemed withdrawn, which I find unsettling given the good news that Mr. Taylor is going to help the effort. That and the fact that David is generally full of enthusiasm and very animated when he is working on things of this nature."

"You know," Charlotte said as she sat forward lightly and leaned her arms on the table, "it may be time for total truth between the two of you. You are both somewhat stubborn. He is protective of himself and his past, which is why he keeps it hidden. You are much the same although you seem to be opening up around him. You may need to let the rest go. If you want him to open up, to allow you to perhaps help him however you might be able to, you may need to reassure him that you have no secrets."

"I am not sure I totally understand," Maria said as she went to turn the knob on the door.

"If you want him to open up and fully trust you, you have to show him that you are fully open and trusting," Charlotte said as she eased back into the chair.

Maria didn't respond as she slowly made her way out the door and up the stairs to David's apartment.

At David's door Maria paused for a moment before knocking to gather her thoughts together.

"David, are you still awake?" she asked through the door as she knocked lightly.

"Yes," David responded. "It's open. Come on in."

Maria turned the doorknob and slowly walked in. She closed the door behind her, but it clicked back open a little. Maria remained standing for a moment at the entrance and saw David lying on the sofa. He hadn't pulled the sleeper bed out yet. As he looked up and saw her come in he began to sit up to make room for her to sit down.

As she made her way over she glanced down at the papers on the kitchen table. She saw envelopes and letterheads from Zee Technologies as well as a letter from a law office with an address from Hartford, Connecticut. Her heart skipped a beat at seeing that letter. *Could that be where he is from* she thought as she sat.

"So Maria," David said warming up a little bit more than how he was before. "What's on your mind?"

"Well," she said as she sat and adjusted her skirt on her knees, "a couple of things, but I would understand if you are too tired to discuss both. I could wait on one of them for the morning or another time."

"Let's see how the first one goes," David said as he worked himself backwards just a little bit more into the armrest.

"I would like to know how everything went at Mr. Taylor's offices. It would appear you somehow knew him to call in the favor, get an appointment to see him, and then be able to arrange his company to help out."

David sat quietly for a moment. He wasn't exactly sure how he wanted to answer her. *If I am too direct in answering, she is going to have too much information,* David thought as he turned away from her for a moment and glanced over at the paperwork on the kitchen table. He suddenly remembered the legal papers that he had received and continued to himself, *I guess in short order what she does or does not know isn't really going to matter.*

"David," Maria said as she moved just slightly closer to him, "I know you are a very private man. I presume you have your reasons. I believe I have seen enough of your nature and character to know that whatever you are keeping and why are for a good and fair reason and not a deceitful one."

"It's okay, Maria. There are reasons why I don't tell you everything, but I do want to share things with you, so I am just taking a moment to figure out what I want to say."

David sat quietly for a moment to collect his thoughts and Maria reached over and put her hand on his right knee.

"Okay," David said as he sat up a little and touched Maria's hand.

"Before I decided I was going to take the time in my life to travel around I dealt with finance and investments. I met Zachary Taylor at a technology event because technology was a hobby of mine and I was a pretty big enthusiast. Also because I was connected with some investment firms that wanted to invest in disruptive technologies and those owning companies I often got sent along to review both aspects. The financial side of the company, their products, their research and development groups and their product pipelines."

David paused for a moment and just looked into Maria's eyes as she listened intently on his conversation.

"So long story short really, I got the opportunity to meet Zachary, became friendly with him, took a look at his personal finances at his request and then helped him with some uphill financial issues that his company was facing. After all the dust from the events settled, he was very grateful and said that if I ever needed anything of him to just get a hold of him and ask, so that is what I decided to do here."

"Well," Maria responded after a short pause, "I am happy that you found Caroline's cause so worthwhile to the point that you would want to use that favor."

David smiled just slightly as he responded, "I am very fond of Caroline. I am having a difficult time separating my feelings when it comes to her."

Maria leaned forward just slightly and said, "Then perhaps you should not fight so hard to do that."

"There are tasks at hand to focus on and I cannot afford to get lost in the way I feel if I am to get them completed successfully," David said as he sat forward slightly.

"It would seem to me, David, that this effort is effectively completed. If I may be so bold, you have buy-in from two very wealthy men in Texas. Your influence has sold them both on this comparatively inexpensive project. I would go as far as to say if not a penny more came in from the residents that this effort would be a success regardless as you could get either or both of those men to commit the remaining funds. What I think you want is to show Caroline and some of the people that anything is possible when enough people pull together. That it is not just having the money that gets it done as you have steadily said."

David didn't respond to her comment but continued to look at her.

Maria cleared her throat. "As far as going back to your comment of separating your feelings and mine of perhaps you should not. I want to tell you why I am the way I am."

"You don't have to do that, Maria," David interrupted. "I've gathered some of the story here and there from people in town that have shared what I would call the public sides of stories when telling me a little of the history of people, places and things around Westville. I know some of it may be difficult for you to relive just to share it with me. You don't have to."

"You see, though, David," Maria said as she moved a little closer to him, "I do know that. The truth of the matter is, I would like to."

David smiled at her a little more and leaned back to listen.

"My family came to America when I was about Caroline's age. My older brother, Juan was fifteen at the time and came with us. My two older brothers were unable to come. While my father was able to get us visas and eventually green cards to be in America, my two oldest brothers were adults already and would not be considered under my father's visas."

Maria collected herself slightly as she started to get upset.

"Work here in Westville was fair to moderate. None of us were going to get rich, but if you worked hard, you were paid fairly and there was always work to do. Then as we got older and times got harder decisions to perhaps go home to Mexico were becoming easier and easier to justify. While there was still some work it was not as plentiful. When we would go back to my village to visit, my mother would become homesick. My brothers got married and had children and my mother wanted to stay and help. My father did not like splitting so much time and staying away from the family. My brother here got into a little trouble with illegal drugs and my family thought if they were back home he would have less availability to them, but that is always questionable."

Maria wanted to continue, but she started to get a little shaky and her eyes began to fill with tears. David leaned forward and kissed Maria very softly on the cheek and then gently pulled her to him so she lay partly on him and on the couch.

"If it's too much, you can stop and just lie here," David said softly.

Maria cried a little from being sad about the part of her life she was reliving telling David. At the same time, the comfort she felt lying in his arms also calmed her.

"Then I met William. His family was from Mexico as well. A different part from where my family is from. His mother was very enamored with the United States. So much so, she named her children more Americanized names. His sisters were Margaret and Natalie. William and I were in school together. My father basically forbid us to see one another as both of our families were discussing about going home. My father felt that there was no way both our families were going to stay in America so if one did and the other did not or if we both went back to our respective villages, we were never going to be able to be together. That and he did not like the idea that I was dating a boy at sixteen."

Maria moved a little bit to get a little more comfortable. David moved so that he was now totally lying on the couch and Maria also lifted her feet off the floor and swung them onto the couch.

"We were young. We were in love. You know how that story goes," Maria said softly as she continued. "I became pregnant with Caroline. I fought with my family to stay here with William. I told them I wanted my child to be born here so that she would be a citizen. She could come and go as she pleased when she was older. My father wouldn't hear of it. He wanted me to go with them home. Then William decided that he was too young to be a father. He basically said he wanted nothing to do with the unborn child."

Maria became more upset and David held her a little tighter.

"I talked with Miss Charlotte about my problem with William and my family. She offered me a place to stay here because I was about to turn eighteen and was determined to live my life for the best of myself and my child. If there are hard times here and in Mexico, it tends to be worse there and for a longer period of time. America always tends to prosper and recover faster and better. There is always opportunity for people that want to work to take it. I wanted that opportunity for my daughter and me. So my family left me behind and I am here."

Maria lay for a little bit and started to relax. David just sat and listened to her breathe until she continued softly.

"I do not hear from them regularly. I believe it has been a year since I have seen them. I really cannot afford to travel there, I have no car and I really only make enough for food, clothing and shelter, but it is enough."

Maria's voice became weaker and softer. David could tell she was getting tired and falling asleep. Rather than move, he just held her and listened.

"Because of that, because of all those things, I have become very guarded and untrusting, especially of my feelings and of any hopes and dreams. And then David Stephenson walks into Westville and upsets that entire balance."

David listened to her breathe some more as he began to get a little sleepy himself. He perked up just a little as Maria began to speak again.

"I was all set. I had my life set plainly. My daughter was happy and it was the two of us. And then you arrived. She has never been happier. I have not been this happy in a very long time. Caroline's birth was not the perfect happy moment that it could have been with all the disappointment and family turmoil, but it was still joyous for me. At the time, it was the happiest I had ever been. Until now."

David didn't say anything. He wasn't sure what he could say or even what he should say. He was fighting his own feelings while listening to hers.

"I loved William as a schoolgirl does. I love Caroline as a mother does."

Maria lifted her had just slightly and looked into David's eyes.

She wanted to say what she felt, but she was so afraid to admit her feelings aloud. She hadn't done so to herself and now she was on the edge of telling him.

David leaned forward and kissed her softly. He then leaned back and held her more firmly.

Nothing more was said and they both fell asleep on the couch.

A short while later, Charlotte quietly entered the apartment looking for Maria. As quiet as she was, David opened his eyes and attempted to move, but Charlotte quickly raised her hand.

"Stay there," she said as she slowly turned around. "I can mind Caroline. Maria's couch is more comfortable than my bed anyway," Charlotte whispered as she slowly walked out of the room.

David looked at Maria sound asleep on his chest as Charlotte clicked the door closed. He thought about their conversation, and he smiled slightly as he closed his eyes.

"I love you, too, Maria," he whispered.

Chapter Eighteen

David looked out the front windows of Charlotte's Place as the resident and business owner volunteers put the finishing touches on the booths and other setups on Packer Road.

Sheriff Donna Neely had already set up the detour further north on the road to pipe local traffic around to get down to Route 385 as needed. Deputy Mendoza set up the portable "slow" signs and speed humps for the main route to further cut their speeds down.

Sam Crenshaw offered up his large empty lot nearest to the event for all and any needed parking.

Brian Kurtvow walked to the old municipal building center just east of Charlotte's Place to set up the stands where his big cardboard check would go, as well as one for Zachary Taylor's pledge.

Charlotte and Maria were out in the parking lot setting up what would be the tables and booth area for Charlotte's Place, which were going to double tonight for refreshments and the celebration for Caroline's birthday.

Maria walked into the store from the parking lot and stepped over to the side, where David was standing and looking out.

"You did it," she said and smiled. "This is now going to be a reality, all because of you." She wedged herself in front of him and put her arms around his waist.

"The people did this. I led and influenced where I could," David said as he looked up at the graying sky. "I just hope the rain holds off."

"Rain or no rain, this is going to be a weekend that Westville will talk about for a long time," Maria said as she put her head against David's chest.

David just nudged her away a little bit to look at her. "As long as Caroline enjoys her birthday tonight, that is all that matters to me. The rest is going to just take care—" David stopped mid-sentence.

Maria looked up at him. "The rest is going to just take care of what?"

David refocused and finished. "—of itself. Excuse me, Maria. I want to head upstairs for a little bit before we start with the birthday."

David removed Maria's hands abruptly and hurried off to the apartment, exiting through the back door.

Maria was taken aback and was prepared to follow him when Caroline came in through the front door and distracted her.

"Look, Mama, Mr. Peter made it back," Caroline exclaimed as Peter's big rig slowly pulled into the parking lot of Charlotte's Place around the bazaar set up.

David got into the second floor stairwell as his stomach turned. He leaned hard against the wall and used the banister railing to pull himself along as his vision blurred.

"This is not good," he said aloud as he turned the corner.

He approached the third floor stairwell as he heard someone enter on the first floor.

David made his way up and into his room. He closed the door behind him and fumbled for the lock. He turned it, not knowing whether or not it engaged, as he never used it the whole time he had rented the apartment.

He turned and steadied himself by leaning on the kitchen table as warm blood ran out of his nose. He focused his vision on his large duffle bag that was still neatly folded in the corner of the room on the old wooden chair where it had sat since the day he unpacked it.

Suddenly Maria knocked on the door. "David? Are you in the room?"

David heard her, but he couldn't focus enough to answer.

Maria tried the doorknob, but the door was locked. She said something to Charlotte who was in the hall with her and then her voice dissipated.

"David, can you open the door?" Charlotte called out.

David felt like he was going to throw up. He wanted to get over to the sink, but he couldn't let the table go. His heart was pounding in his chest. "Move," he said to his own feet, but they wouldn't budge.

Maria raced in through the sliding doors, which were still unlocked.

"*Dios mío!*"

David looked up to see Maria's horrified look, and he lost all his vision and balance. As he started to black out Maria moved forward and guided as much of his weight as she could bear to keep him from impacting the table or the floor at full, dead drop.

As soon as he was down, she reached over and fumbled for the lock. Charlotte came into the room and then immediately headed back out. Rebecca was half way up the stairs at the time. "Rebecca. Run! Go get Doc right away. Keep Caroline downstairs."

Rebecca turned immediately and went back down.

Maria propped David's head into her lap as she sat on the floor trying to clean the blood off his face with her hand as it continued to come out of his nose.

Maria sobbed and began to pray quietly, something she had not done in a long time. "Please help him. He means so much to so many. He means so much to Caroline and I. We have not been the same since he came here. We will not be the same if he cannot get better."

Maria's final words resonated loudly in David's ears and he forced open his eyes. He tried to look up to her, but he really could not focus. The words echoed, "We will not be the same if he cannot get better" as his line of sight spun.

"Don't ... don't let ..."

"Shhhh, *amado*, Doc is on his way. Just rest. Do not try to talk."

"Don't let Caroline see me ... like this ... on her birthday. Give me a minute and I will be fine."

Maria cried more. It had been some time since she had seen David like this. So much so, that she had forgotten that he never did follow up to see Doc or go in for the blood work.

"I don't care if it is my place to say so or not, but on Monday you will go to County for the blood work. Do you understand me?"

"Yes." David said and he struggled weakly to sit up. Maria pulled him back down easily.

Doc came in through the door with Rebecca as Charlotte moved over to make room. "I'm going back down to keep an eye on Caroline. She's with Peter," Rebecca said as she headed back down the stairs.

"Stubborn man. He never did come to see me," Doc said as he huffed. "Did he hit his head at all?"

Maria shook her head. "No. As he began to fall I guided him away from the table and down to the floor."

"Was he drinking at all today like the episodes over the summer?" Doc asked as he looked to Maria and then Charlotte.

"No," Charlotte said. "As a matter of fact, when he was helping earlier today with the tents on Packer, the volunteers kept passing him a beer and he would open it and set it down. Now that I am thinking about it, he never drank it. He eventually would toss it into the barrel with the cans without having any."

David struggled more and more to focus as Doc shined the light into his eyes to watch his dilation.

"One side?" Doc whispered out loud.

David aggressively attempted to get up. "Maria, please let me go."

Startled by David's uncharacteristic response, Doc backed up at the same time Maria released him.

David rolled off and forced himself onto his hands and knees.

Everyone in the room was paralyzed. They all wanted to help him, but no one wanted to touch him.

The warm blood coming out of David's nose slowed and finally stopped dripping after a moment. He very slowly raised his right hand onto the seat of one of the kitchen chairs to steady himself and tried to press up off the furniture to stand. Maria reached over finally to help him. When he didn't respond aggressively, Doc also helped.

David stood all the way up and leaned on the back of the kitchen chair. Maria got up under his right arm and supported him.

Doc looked at him sternly. "County. Monday. No bullshit."

"Yes, sir. I am out of excuses," David said weakly.

Doc leaned in and very quietly whispered, "You may be out of options. And time."

Charlotte looked at Doc, who tipped his head to motion her out of the room. Maria helped David over to sit down. She then walked over to get a clean towel and soaked it with hot water.

"David, please, please go with Doc Monday. Something is seriously wrong."

David heard her but didn't answer. *I am too close to them and I needed to leave. I wanted to see this through. This was my last chance to make a difference*, he thought and he looked at his now blood stained T-shirt.

Maria cleaned off his face with the towel. She still had tears in her eyes.

"I am sorry that I upset you," David said as he touched her hand softly.

"You upset me because you do not take care of yourself and you do not let me do it either," she said loudly as her accent crept into her response. David attempted to speak, but she cut him off. "You should eat a little better. I try to have you come to eat with us, but you sometimes excuse yourself. I do not push because it is not my place. But then I want to come up and make sure you are okay and you have fallen asleep on the couch. I do not wake you, but I should and make you sit until the bed is pulled out and properly set."

Maria began to get more worked up and upset. David caught a pause and was going to say something but was unsure if she was mad or upset so he said nothing at first.

"I know you come up and try to take care of me. I appreciate it. I don't thank you enough, so thank you for it."

"I do not want to be thanked with the words," she responded as she finished cleaning him up and put the towel down on the table with some force. "I want to be thanked with respect. For yourself. You are not alone anymore. As much as you may still wish to be. When you are hurt, Caroline is hurt. I am hurt. We love you. If you want to do the right thing, it is not a thank you that we need. We need you to do for yourself that which you do for others."

"And that is?"

"Everything and anything. You do, selflessly, for everyone. Do something for yourself. Go to the doctor."

"I have had a long life of being selfish ..." he began until Maria cut him off.

"Which I know very little about. I have accepted that you have put that life behind you. I know only the man you are today. If you say you were once selfish then I ask you to be that way just a little bit for perhaps a week so that you might tend to your own needs," Maria scolded as she turned around and sobbed loudly.

David stood, took his bloody shirt off and tossed it on the floor. He then stood behind Maria and put his arms around her.

"Please tell me that we are important enough to you that you will take care of yourself."

David paused for a minute and responded with, "I will do what needs to be done."

Maria spun around in place and looked into David's face.

"Do you love me?"

David said nothing but continued to look right at her.

"I see it in everything you do, but you never say it. There are women who would be glad to never hear the words but instead receive all that you have given to my daughter and me. I need to hear it, I am sorry. I do not want to mistake the kindness you have for everyone as more than it is for us unless it is in fact more. As I said before, I only know the man you are now." Maria paused for a moment and just stared into his eyes.

The words sat at the edge of David's mouth. He knew what he felt. He knew he had shown her. He knew that if he said it, it could never be unsaid.

His mind fought with his heart. His past fought with his present. He could taste the future in the back of his throat. One stray tear got away from him.

"I do," he said as his voice trembled just slightly. "I do love you."

"But?" Maria asked immediately.

"There are no buts. Not today."

Maria closed her eyes and laid her head on his bare chest for just a moment as David digested what he just admitted to her.

"I need to get a clean shirt and we need to get downstairs. I am not going to let this episode ruin Caroline's birthday."

Maria nodded and let David go.

Doc and Charlotte had reached the bottom of the stairs and stepped off to the side to discuss what happened.

"Okay, Doc, what was the one side comment that made David jump?" Charlotte asked.

"Well, I can't be sure, but his left eye dilated differently than his right eye. That can mean any number of things. In some rare cases it means nothing, as it is a personal, physical idiosyncrasy, but his reaction to it makes me believe he knows there's more to it."

They both stood in silence for a moment in each other's company. Doc looked up occasionally at the third floor apartment from the ground.

"It's funny," Charlotte said as she also took a look up, "I remember a conversation Maria and I had not too long ago where she commented on David something along the lines of, 'He is not as old as an elder, but he speaks like one,' or something to that effect. She was reflecting on how wise David was despite his age. Older than her but younger than you and I." Charlotte smiled a bit as she continued. "I think that's what makes them such a good fit. She has a lot of wisdom and empathy for just twenty-seven years old."

Doc said nothing but did turn his gaze away from the apartment to the final touches on the bazaar across the street on Packer Road.

"Someone needs help with something wherever I am. I help them and then I move along. I never know what it is. I travel until I find a place to stop and the task finds me," Doc said as he stared off at the bazaar.

"What did you mean, Mel?" Charlotte asked as she touched his arm.

"It was something David told me a little after he got here and I got to talking to him. 'I generally don't stay long because my tasks at hand, wherever I am, are finished. And then I move along.' He said he's never helped out with anything this large before."

"And on Sunday evening, it'll be done," Charlotte replied.

The two stood there quietly as Maria and David came downstairs and began to head over to the parking lot tent. Maria was holding David's hand and she turned back to them. "Are you coming? Caroline is going to be so surprised. I made a large sheet cake to let everyone setting up have a piece."

"We'll be right along, child. We won't miss it." Charlotte responded.

As they rounded the corner of the building the street floodlight turned itself on as the photocell engaged.

Doc sighed. "We can't force him to stay."

"Will he leave? With everything he's gained? With all the potential of what he can still have? The life that is yet to unfold in front of him. The love of a woman with that kind of strength and devotion. What kind of person walks away from that?"

Doc thought about it for a moment. "Someone that had it all before and lost everything and doesn't want to go through that again," Doc said. He then paused before continuing. "I don't know enough about the man. I can only guess. Some scars run too deep and time does not heal all wounds."

The two of them stood in silence for a minute and then Doc continued. "I do know that in the here and now, there is a little nine-year-old girl counting on everything to be the way she wishes it to be on her birthday. We best do our part to see that through."

Charlotte nodded as they both made their way to the parking lot.

Chapter Nineteen

Caroline walked to her mother as her birthday party wound down. "Mama, it was such a wonderful party. And there were so many people here. I don't think the party has ever been this large."

Maria smiled just slightly as she stood next to Charlotte. "Well, Caroline, we do always have the party here. We just never had a situation before where we were setting up a bazaar at the same time. But that is why I made such a large cake in Miss Charlotte's big oven in the store."

"I was going to ask you, Mama, if you made smaller cakes in our oven and then just lined them up together and put frosting all over them so they looked like one."

Charlotte covered her mouth. "So precious," she said as she laughed a little.

Maria kissed Caroline on the top of the head. "Wait here a moment and I will go get David. And we can walk to McNally's and bring some of the cake there to Rebecca and her parents."

Maria walked away and over to Peter's truck. Peter had been over where the main body of people were at the party for most of the gathering, but David remained near the truck.

"Is everything alright?" she asked as she approached.

"Oh," David said looking back toward her and away from the night sky. "Yes, things are fine. I was talking to Peter earlier and I just sort of stayed over here as he walked over to the party-goers. I did come over when it was time to sing."

"Yes, I did see you," Maria said as she smiled slightly. "Are you feeling better?"

"I am. I'm sorry to put a scare into you like that."

"You do not do it on purpose," Maria said as she took his hand. "You do have the control of seeing the doctor."

"Well, I don't suppose I do anymore. Between you and Doc, I have marching orders for Monday."

Maria smiled slightly. "I suppose that is true."

"I am sorry. I don't like to cause people worry or pain. There really is enough of that."

Maria pulled on David's hand just a little. "Come with us. Caroline and I have a little bit of birthday cake to take over to Rebecca."

Maria walked with David over to the table. "Miss Charlotte, we are going to head across the street. Please leave these few things. I will come down early in the morning and finish clearing them and setting the rest up."

Charlotte just nodded a little. Maria shook her head slightly knowing that Charlotte wouldn't leave until everything was cleaned up.

"Go," Charlotte said abruptly with the smallest hint of a smile and pointed across the street.

David, Maria, and Caroline walked across Route 385 to McNally's. Caroline was holding a small disposable tray with a little of her birthday cake left over on it. Kevin McNally was just helping clear the last two tables, and Rebecca was wiping down the bar where her parents were sitting and talking to her.

"David," Rebecca said as she waved them over. "I don't think you've ever met my parents before."

The three of them walked into the bar area as Rebecca made the introductions. "This is my mother Mary Wilson and my father Thomas."

"Pleased to meet you," David said as he shook the older gentleman's hand. Thomas was still seated at the bar on the raised stool. He appeared to David to be a shell of a man he imagined he once was. Thinning, graying hair and pulling a portable oxygen tank, Thomas Wilson looked on the frail side. But David could see a gleam in his eye and a former robustness in his handshake that told more of a story about the man than who was sitting in front of him now.

"David, we are so glad to get the chance to finally meet you in person," Mary Wilson said as she leaned forward and grasped his right hand with both of hers. She was noticeably younger than her husband and little on the heavier side compared to her daughter and husband. "We really don't come into the town center all that much with Tom's health being a little shaky, and when we have we always seem to have missed you. We have lived here our whole lives. Time and tide have worn the town down. We were so hopeful when we moved to the county system that it might recharge the town some. We thought the same when Mr. Kurtvow eased some of the tax pressure when he stopped all the liens and so forth. But I will tell you, your presence and efforts have done more."

David was slightly embarrassed at the praise. "I just wandered into town a couple months ago and helped a little girl with an opportunity to see something of her doing through. That's all. The people got behind her," David said as he put his free hand on Caroline's shoulder.

"You got them engaged," Thomas replied. "Leaders do that. We haven't had that. You came here with that."

"Thank you, sir," David said as he smiled.

"Miss Rebecca, could you cut this up into six pieces?" Caroline asked as she lifted her tray. "I would like to share with your parents, you, Mr. McNally, Mr. Kurtvow, and Mr. Taylor, if they are still here."

229

"That was thoughtful of you. They are still in the private dining room," Rebecca said pointing into the back. "Let me cut off those two pieces and you can take them into there."

With the cake cut and on two small plates, Caroline walked with her mother and David.

David knocked on the closed door.

"Come on in," Brian said.

David opened the door and the three of them walked in.

"Hello. You were unable to come over earlier so I wanted to bring you both a piece of my birthday cake," Caroline said as she walked the cake over to each of them.

"Well, thank you very much," Zachary Taylor said as he stood to formally meet Caroline and Maria.

"Mr. Taylor, Mr. Kurtvow, I cannot express to you enough how much your involvement is appreciated by Caroline, myself, the whole town," Maria said as she folded up her hands in front of herself. She was not comfortable talking to either of the men because of their wealth and social status.

"I was happy to help once I was fully made aware of what was going on by David here," Zachary said as he looked at the man he knew as Michael.

"Yes," Brian chimed in, "and I am glad to get back onto a track I once set off on my own some time ago. I let too much of my own things get out in front of me, but no more. I have my chance at another shot. I am going to get it right this time and I will start with Caroline's fundraiser," Brian said as he took a bite of the cake. "Wow! This cake is perfect. Just the right amount of white cake and chocolate frosting. It's sweet but not over the top."

"Thank you," Maria said quietly.

"You made this?" Brian exclaimed loudly. "It's wonderful."

"It is very good," Zachary said with a bite in his mouth.

Maria just smiled.

"Well, gentlemen, we are going to let you be. It's a little later than Caroline normally is awake and she has a big couple of days coming up. We'll get going so Maria can get her ready for bed," David said as he smiled.

"Big three days coming up," Brian said with a slight smile.

David looked at Maria and then back at Brian. In his head he counted two, for Saturday and Sunday. Brian just smirked a little and nodded and said, "Three."

David wasn't sure what to make of the comment, but he just nodded and responded, "Very well, then. Good night, gentlemen."

Zachary and Brian stood as the group turned to depart. Upon leaving the room, David pulled the door closed.

As Brian finished up his cake, he leaned over to Zachary a little. "That boy, dynamic as hell. He could sell water to Neptune and sand to Egyptians."

Zachary turned to the closed door and then back to Brian. "It goes beyond simple selling. I've seen salespeople do what he does. He reads people magnificently. He doesn't even realize he's doing it. It's like genuine observation to him. Then when he speaks, it's disarming. It's like nothing I've ever seen before. He had a way of getting me to look at things against the better judgment of my own experts without being combative or derogatory. When I did and discovered he was right, in spades, I might add, he was fairly humble about it."

"You know, you never did tell me exactly how it was that you came to know him," Brian said plainly.

"No, I didn't," Zachary responded. "I am bound by a promise."

"I understand," Brian said as he held up his hand.

"Still …" Zachary said, thinking for a moment, "there is a story to be told." Zachary stood and looked at Brian. "Would you excuse me for a moment?"

"Certainly," Brian said with a small chuckle. "If you run across more of that cake out there, buy me another piece."

Zachary walked out to the bar area where the Wilsons were and sat.

"I am sorry, Mr. Taylor," Rebecca said looking surprised. "I didn't know you needed anything else back there. I should have checked in."

"Oh no, we're fine back there. Mr. and Mrs. Wilson, Rebecca, I would like a few minutes of your time, if I may."

"Oh certainly," Mrs. Wilson responded.

"Rebecca, when we were chatting earlier this evening about the bazaar and you took some information regarding the story you wanted to write for the Westville Press, you mentioned that you never went to college for journalism."

"Yes, sir. Things here at home needed my time and attention. We needed to use some of the money up that we had put aside. Even if I could get the student loans, my folks needed my help. Someday I may still get my chance."

"So with some respect to that, I may have a small, temporary project in Houston that I could use your skills on. It will help me complete a task that really only someone of your talent can do the right way, and it might give you some exposure to what you're looking to do."

Rebecca looked to her parents. Her thoughts immediately went to the help that they needed from her. Brian Kurtvow walked out of the private dining area and stood behind the dividing wall between the bar area and the public dining area.

"Well, you see, Mr. Taylor, part of the issue is my parents need my help. Mostly my mother can handle my father for a short period of time alone, but she needs my help over an extended period with him and the house. The money I earn here helps out with paying down the tax bills, and of course, the day to day items as well."

"Well, I believe in short order we might have an overall solution for some of that," Zachary said as he looked at Brian who nodded once. "Regardless, I would be willing to pay you for the work, obviously. I would expect you to be able to complete this project in four to six weeks. I would cover your travel and work expenses and be able to pay you five thousand dollars for the expected six weeks of work. I can front you two thousand and then, upon the completion of the project, I can give to the additional three thousand."

Rebecca looked at her parents, stunned. "Mr. Taylor, I don't know what to say. That's more than twice what I would make over six weeks here."

"I don't need to know right now. Think about it. Talk it over with your parents and then you can let me know tomorrow morning, or at least by the end of the day on Saturday. There are a few conditions. If you decide to take on this project, you need to see it through to completion. I'll need you to start immediately—Monday, basically. Finally, you will not be able to discuss the nature of the project with anyone, including your parents. Once you agree to the work, I'll need you to sign a non-disclosure agreement and you'll basically be committed to the project for the period with no contact for the project period. If you'd need to contact family for an emergency or the reverse, it would be done through my offices."

Rebecca just took all of Zachary's comments in.

"Well, good night, folks. Rebecca, thank you for the consideration. I'll look forward to your thoughts tomorrow."

"Yes, Mr. Taylor. Good night."

Zachary walked over to the front window of McNally's and looked out across Route 385 to the second floor of Charlotte's Place, where the lights were still on.

"Sounds like something interesting there, Mr. Taylor," Brian Kurtvow said playfully as he walked up alongside Zachary.

"It's something that's needed. A story that needs to be uncovered fully and told."

Maria and Caroline stopped at their apartment door as David walked past.

"Mr. David? Can you please come in for a few minutes? I know I need to go to bed because tomorrow is an early and long day, but maybe just for a few minutes?"

David looked at Maria who only smiled and tipped her head slightly toward her daughter.

"Sure, Caroline. Why don't you go in and get all squared away, and I'll be back down in a few minutes."

Caroline smiled and ran into the apartment.

Maria stood in the hallway for a moment and just looked at David as he backed away slowly to head up. "Anything the matter?" he asked as he stopped.

"I was wondering how you felt. You gave us quite the scare earlier."

"I know, Maria. I am sorry."

"Will you please promise me that you will go to County on Monday?"

David weighed his response and then said, "I will make sure to get things taken care of on Monday."

Maria went to turn to go into the apartment when she stopped short. "Promise me."

"I promise to address everything on Monday," David responded.

Maria smiled and entered her apartment. "Come down in a few minutes. I don't want her up very late."

"Of course."

Maria stepped in as Charlotte began to walk into the kitchen. "I just gave Caroline a kiss goodnight. It's going to be a long weekend. I am going to head downstairs and get some proper rest. I loaded the flatware of yours that we used outside into your dishwasher, but I didn't turn it on, as it wasn't full."

"Of course, Miss Charlotte. Thank you for everything."

Maria walked away and into her bedroom to get ready for bed.

Charlotte paused in the kitchen before turning to leave. Mel Porter's words echoed in her head. *I generally don't stay long because my tasks at hand, wherever I am, are finished. And then I move along.*

Charlotte looked on the top shelf to the left of the sink and saw that the envelope for David was still there. She lifted it and felt the money still in it. She sighed just a little and set it down to head back downstairs.

A short while later, David came downstairs in a T-shirt and a pair of loose fitting shorts. As he entered the apartment, Maria called out from Caroline's bedroom. "We are in here."

David headed over with a gift for Caroline in his hand and entered the room.

Caroline sat up and Maria looked over. "David, you have done plenty. A gift was not necessary on top of everything else."

"I wanted to. It's a fitting gift," David said as he smiled and handed it to Maria.

Maria looked at the tag. *To: The Birthday Girl. From: Mama & Mr. David.* Maria smiled and handed it to Caroline to open.

Caroline quickly took the wrapping paper off and opened the plain cardboard box and shouted excitedly, "It's an e-reader. My own e-reader!"

"David, that's fairly expensive."

David shook his head. "It's fine. I wanted to," he replied as Caroline started it up. "It's all set up for auto sync when there's a network to connect to and cached mode for when there isn't. I checked with the school logs and downloaded all the books she put on her wish list."

"Oh, thank you so much, Mama and Mr. David."

"There are two head phone sets in the box to use. A spare one if the first one breaks," David said as he leaned in and poked at the screen. "And here—"

"*Iron Giant*. My favorite movie," Caroline squealed.

"I bought it and put it on the device. It'll be there for you to watch as much as you want. What does Hogarth say?"

"'You are what you choose to be. You choose.'"

"Always remember that, little one. For your whole life, there is no message that is more important to remember," David said as he messed her hair a little. "Now, I know you're excited, but put that aside for tomorrow."

"Yes, Mr. David," Caroline said as she turned it over, shut it off, and reached up for a kiss.

David kissed her and said good night, then turned quickly to steal a quick kiss from Maria.

Caroline giggled a little as David exited the room.

"Good night, Caroline," Maria whispered and she kissed her, then also left, closing the door behind her.

"David," Maria called out as he reached the door.

David turned back before turning the knob. He looked back at Maria, who was standing just outside Caroline's room in her long pink T-shirt.

"It was a very long day and a little traumatic. Would you mind terribly staying here tonight?"

David shrugged as he went back into the living room and sat on the couch where he had fallen asleep on prior nights. As he got comfortable he just looked up at her, waiting to see how she planned to sit down.

Maria watched him settle on the couch and then walked over. She took his hand and pulled him gently.

David moved a little bit on the couch, which prompted her to pull a little harder.

David stood and Maria took him by the hand into her bedroom.

Chapter Twenty

People gathered around the reviewing stand as the second and final day of the bazaar came to an end.

Brian Kurtvow stood near the stairs of the stand with County Commissioner Sanchez and Zachary Taylor as Rebecca discussed with them what they were about to speak about. She wanted to have everything all recorded and typeset for the next issue of the paper, as she would be leaving it with Kevin McNally to get printed while she was away for Zachary's project in the upcoming weeks.

"So Mr. Kurtvow," Rebecca said as she put away her notepad and glanced around a little. "I didn't see your car or Mrs. Kurtvow. Is she coming?"

"Well," Brian said rather plainly with just a little pitch in his voice, "right now the Mrs. is staying at our El Paso residence. At least for the time being."

"I'm sorry, Mr. Kurtvow. I didn't mean to pry. I meant the question innocently," Rebecca replied apologetically.

"Oh, I know. I suppose it's better to kind of just say that to someone before the talk just starts on its own," he said with a faint smile.

Maria and Caroline were seated on the raised reviewing stand. Caroline kept popping out of her seat to wave to friends she rode to school with as they walked nearby.

Maria scanned the crowd looking for David.

The dignitaries came up on the stand and Brian made his way over to Maria and Caroline. "Okay, ladies, so Commissioner Sanchez is going to say a few words and then at some point he may call you up, little lady," Brian said as he addressed Caroline directly, "and then you may have the chance to say a few words if you like depending on the flow of things. Do you want your mom to come up with you?"

"I do," Caroline replied. "And Mr. David."

Brian looked at Maria and then looked around for David. "I don't see him. Do you?"

"No," Maria responded, "to this point I have not."

Brian walked over to Zachary and Maria stood and walked over to the far end of the stand, looking around for David. Kevin McNally approached her at the lower side and she knelt down. "Have you seen David?"

"He was with Peter before. Maybe about half an hour ago," Kevin responded as Jim Davenport approached.

"Peter was talking about his upcoming delivery schedule and his next time into town with him about twenty minutes ago over in front of Garcia's," Jim said as he looked back and pointed. "I saw them both as I walked by."

Maria became very anxious over that conversation and being unable to find him.

Sherriff Neely walked over on the conversation. "I think Deputy Mendoza was over that way. Did you want me to call him and have him send David over?" she asked.

"Would you please? I am sorry to ask, but we are about to get started." Maria said.

"We can wait a moment or two if we need to," Brian responded as he came over with Caroline.

"He's on his way over," Sherriff Neely replied.

"Thank you," Maria said as her nervousness dissipated.

David approached the near perimeter of the gathering crowd and circled around to come over to where the stairs were.

"I didn't know I was supposed to be up here. This is Caroline's thing," he said to Zachary as he came up top.

Zachary extended his hand to shake David's. "Maybe so, but without you here it never would have moved up the radar like it did and had the response that it got."

"You give me too much credit," David said as he shook his friend's hand.

"And you do not take enough nor a compliment when given one," he said with a smirk.

"Fair enough. Thank you, Zachary," David said with a smile as he walked over and sat with Maria and Caroline.

Commissioner Sanchez began with the first speech of the evening.

"Friends and neighbors," he started over the public address system, "tonight we close out the Westville Library Bazaar and announce its complete success."

All the people that had gathered clapped and cheered and Commissioner Sanchez paused to let them settle back down.

"We of course know about the major pledges and sponsors, and we will let them speak in just a moment. The important thing to not miss here is that this all started with an idea from one of our own children who stepped up, with some help and guidance, where adults seemed to fear to tread. Perhaps it is because children do not see the same obstacles and difficulties that we see as adults. Simplistic wonder of their presence of thought. It is a shame that through the natural course of the events of growing up that we lose that."

The Commissioner paused for a moment to collect his thoughts and then continued.

"The many booths set up here from the local businesses like, McNally's Pub, Davenport's General Store, Garcia's Wine and Spirits, Barker's Hardware and all the others contributed to the effort. There were also the smaller personal booths, where Mrs. Bradfield sold her afghans, where Mr. Brumstone sold his birdhouses and so forth. All of the booth costs, sponsorships and percentages of sales generated a total of $14,692."

The crowd again erupted into applause and cheering as many of the folks realized that the goal of twelve thousand five hundred had been soundly eclipsed.

Commissioner Sanchez fished around his wallet as the applause subsided.

"Seems to me that's a hair under $310 off of a nice round number like $15,000," he said as he took the sum from his wallet, turned, and walked it over to Caroline. He walked back to the PA system as people in the front began to cheer.

"$15,002. That's more like it."

As the crowd erupted in more applause, Commissioner Sanchez wrapped up by shaking everyone's hand and giving Maria and Caroline a kiss. At that point, he turned the microphone to Brian Kurtvow, who waited for everyone to settle down.

"I was supposed to go now and Mr. Taylor last, but I am going to let him go now because... well, I guess because the 'visiting' team should go before the 'home' team," he said with a smile, waving Zachary up.

Zachary took the change up in stride and changed places with Brian and started his speech.

"Thank you very much, Brian," he said as he looked out over the large crowd that was still getting larger, people trickling in from the closing booths.

"As some of you may be aware, years ago Zee Technologies was part of the original infrastructure effort in this part of the state to initialize or otherwise stabilize broadband and data services. At the time we had our share of critics, like any big corporations does, that we were just jumping in on a big lucrative state contract to fill our own coffers. In business, as in life, there is a certain amount of truth in every rumor. Of course we wanted to win that contract and be part of the effort. There was money to earn for the company and the employees that work for us as well. There was also money to be earned for the subcontracting companies and our subsidiaries too. But with all those truths said, we also wanted to do it for the people. Zee Technologies has always felt that simple and reliable broadband and data services is paramount for our citizens all across this great state of Texas and the United States."

Zachary paused as moderate applause came from the standing crowd. As it subsided he continued. "As fate would have it, the storms came that set the project back and then cuts came to the state budget and certain projects, like this one, lost their funding. Time marched on and one little girl had an idea." Zachary paused to motion back to Caroline.

"It was a simple idea. Let's just bring Internet access to the Library if there was no way to bring it to the town. It was an idea that needed backing and support," Zachary said as he paused and looked back at David, who mouthed the word "no" to him.

"As luck would have it," Zachary turned and continued, "David Stephenson came to town and decided, 'This is a cause I can help with,' and he did. He engaged Caroline to better understand the ideas she had. He leveraged his own stills and collected the information from County that was required. He got the people and the business of this town excited, that with their hard work and effort, this is not as much of a long shot as it seems. He then reached out to Brian Kurtvow without knowing him at all and presented the idea. He said, 'We need your help,' and Brian stepped up."

Zachary paused as light applause moved through the crowd.

"The effort was still running short. It was strong but needed more help. So David reached out to Zee Technologies and we are lucky that he did. We were lucky not because it was going to make us any money, as it's actually an expenditure. Yes, it's something we can write off our taxes, but it is way more than that for us. It is an opportunity to reaffirm one of our core business values and that is simple and reliable broadband and data services is paramount for our citizens all across this great state of Texas and the United States. We get the opportunity to thumb our nose at the detractors and say, 'See, we put our money where our mouth is.' "

More light applause went through the crowd as Zachary leaned in and continued with his speech.

"Zee Technologies has pledged thirty thousand dollars to this effort," Zachary said as he pointed to the large cardboard check on the reviewing stand just off to his left, "and we have also decided to up the ante. We are going to make sure that every address in the town of Westville receives a tablet device that will work on the Library's satellite network, and that in addition to that, every registered student, child, or adult also gets their own additional, personal device."

The crowd erupted in applause as people whistled and cheered. Zachary allowed the celebration to continue before he spoke again.

"Before I turn this over to Brian Kurtvow I just wanted to say thank you to the hospitality I have received here in your little community. What all you folks have here, I couldn't buy anywhere even with all the money I have at my command."

Zachary turned and motioned to Brian. "And now, ladies and gentlemen, it gives me great pleasure to turn the podium to Westville's Brian Kurtvow."

More applause came from the crowd as the men shook hands and changed places on the reviewing stand. As Zachary sat, Brian came over and took Maria and Caroline by the hand. "You, too," he said directly to David.

243

"I wanted to take a moment before I get started to make sure all of you understand and realize that this entire effort, all that has happened and all that is planned to happen, has been able to get to this point because of these three people."

Applause came up from the crowd and Brian let it complete before he continued.

"Without any one of these three individuals up here, we would not be here today. Little Caroline is the idea maker. She got it into her head that this was something she wanted. Not just for herself but for everyone. She was going to do, in her capacity and ability, whatever she could. Maria's part is no smaller than anyone else's. The ability to raise a thoughtful, independent, sensitive, and empathic child is hard enough these days, and a factor harder as a single parent. Maria's total commitment and sacrifice to raise her daughter considering others above self, fully contributed to where we have been able to get to today."

More applause and cheering came from the crowd. Maria felt embarrassed to be called out and praised for being Caroline's mother. As she looked over to the people she knew the best, Charlotte, Mel, Jim, Rebecca, and the others, she could see how proud they all were of her.

"And then there's David," Brian continued as a fast silence fell across the crowd. "Three months or so ago we never heard of this man. He wandered into our town as a stranger and most of you good people do what you always do. You welcomed him and made him feel like this was his home and that he lived here forever. As we have seen, he is a man of unparalleled stock. A man that cared more for people he didn't know at the time than himself. A man that still does. A man that will rise up against seemingly any challenge with no idea who or what obstacles are going to be in his way because he is willing to at least try to do what must be done."

Brian paused to look at Mel Porter and collect his thoughts.

"Doc Porter has this saying that goes something like, 'When your chances are one in a million strive to be one, even if your chances at success are very low, no matter the outcome, you will still be better for the effort.' David, I am here to tell you, you are that one in a million."

The crowd erupted in applause and cheering. David smiled nervously as he looked at Maria, who was crying just slightly. Caroline was intensely slapping her hands together and smiling ear to ear. Brian finished collecting his thoughts and continued once the applause quieted enough for him to do so.

"When I grow up, I want to be like David," he said with a slight smile knowing how much older he already was than him. "I almost made it once, a few years ago. When this town started to feel the pressures of its own failing circumstances, I was hoping to affect some change and offer some help once the regionalization occurred. I did what I thought I could to stem the back taxing, interest fees and foreclosures that were escalating. Then I lost my way. This man," Brian said as he pointed back to David, "befriended me and helped me find my way back. He has given me the opportunity to do what I originally set out to do. Give everyone a jump start and a chance to recover and prosper."

Brian turned away from them and looked at Commissioner Sanchez. "Commissioner, I hold the remaining Town of Westville tax liens of an estimated five and a half million dollars on many of the homes and properties that have been in arrearage since we moved to the County system. On Monday morning, I will be at County to wire in all of the funds and clear every lien on all the back taxes. Westville will start the upcoming holiday season next month on a clear slate."

The crowd went wild as Brian walked over to Commissioner Sanchez and shook his hand and said a few words. Many of the people were simply stunned at the comments. Even David was surprised at the announcement.

Maria reached over and hugged Caroline, and then turned to hug David as Caroline held her around the waist.

"I cannot believe all the good fortune you have brought with you. Times for years have been so difficult for so many and now we all have the opportunity for something more than just the hope we were all holding onto."

"I don't know what to say, Maria. It's a perfect storm. I wanted to help Caroline with the library, but I had no idea it would mushroom into all of this," David said as he looked down at Caroline. "I am so happy to have come this way and met you both." He looked back to Maria. "You all have saved me far more than I have saved you."

Maria smiled and hugged him, and the three of them stood there, having a private moment in the midst of all the celebration.

Chapter Twenty-One

David waved his hand over the grill as it heated up for the morning breakfast. As he moved things around he looked up Packer Road at the few remaining tents and tables that were still set up.

He stepped out from behind the grill, walked around the front counter toward the front door, and then stepped outside and watched a couple of the business owners start taking down the remaining setup from the bazaar.

As David looked over to his right toward the municipal buildings, the library, and into the morning sun, he still could not believe everything that had happened all from this singular effort.

The sound of an approaching car got David's attention, and he turned around to see Rebecca getting out of her mother's car, which was now pulled off to the side near Charlotte's Place.

"Going in for some breakfast, Mrs. Wilson? Miss Charlotte is inside," David said calling out to the two of them as he began to make his way over.

Mrs. Wilson waved and nodded. "I'll see you inside," she said to Rebecca as she went in.

Rebecca walked over to David and he turned slightly so that the morning sun was not directly in either of their eyes.

"I guess you're leaving today," David said as he noted that Rebecca's suitcase was visible from the backseat of the car.

"Yes," she replied excitedly. "I talked to my family and everyone seems to agree that beyond just the money, which in and of itself is worth it, it will also be a great learning experience."

"It will be. It may offer you opportunities for the future you never even considered. Perhaps it will take you farther down the journalist path. Maybe Zachary has some work upcoming for a corporate communications person and he wants to see how you can adapt to that. Perhaps another company might need or want you for that. I don't know what he has planned for you, and I did try to ask, but he wouldn't tell me. I'm sure it will be exciting and rewarding."

"I don't know what to say to you. Your being here and stoking the fire, that's what allowed all of this to happen. So many of us are looking at things differently already. A few, like myself, are finding ourselves with new opportunities we never thought possible before," Rebecca said as she choked up a little on the words.

"Life happens while you're busy making other plans. You have to grab onto it when you can and ride it for all it's worth."

"I've never been on a plane before and Mr. Taylor is flying me out of El Paso on his private jet," she said as she turned west and looked down Route 385 toward El Paso. "I tried all night to come up with some way to thank you for all of this and I still can't think of anything."

David breathed in deeply looking for something meaningful and encouraging to say. "Some things are right place, right time. If you had gone away to college, you might have been elsewhere when all of this happened and you wouldn't have been here for the opportunity when it came. Life is full of variables and many of them we have little control over. It's really not necessary to thank me, but if you really feel the need to then take in what's happened here and never forget it. Don't let other people forget it. That's what happens in the fullness of time. Memories fade and fires dwindle on their own. We have to work to prevent that from happening."

Rebecca worked very hard to hold back the tears. "I'll remember. I'll never forget."

David smiled at her. "Go have something to eat with your mother. You won't be seeing her for a few weeks."

Rebecca turned to walk away, then reached back and hugged him tightly. "I hope there are more people like you and that I find them. Each making the world a better place, one person at a time."

David had a response for that, but he didn't like the sound of it, so he kept it to himself and simply smiled.

As Rebecca let go to go inside Caroline bounded off the stoop of the apartment and ran over to David. She was already for school and clutching her tablet. Maria came out and stopped and chatted with Rebecca before she went in. David noticed she was not dressed for work.

"Mr. David, everything was so wonderful. I can't wait to tell the kids from the other towns that couldn't come how great the bazaar was. I am so excited."

David kneeled down so that he was basically looking up at Caroline. He looked at Maria, who was still talking with Rebecca. "Can you do something for me?"

"I can," Caroline said proudly.

"I want you to be you. I don't want you to ever worry about what others think or what their expectations are. You are the only one that you need to live up to. Your expectations, no one else's. Can you remember that?"

"I think so," Caroline said. "I'll keep repeating it to myself like I do with what Hogarth says: 'You are what you choose to be. You choose.' "

"That's a good plan. The meaning will change for you as you get older. Always remember the message," David said as he looked at Maria again who looked as if she was about to come over. "Always remember your mother, too. She has sacrificed so much to give you this life you have and it is invaluable."

"What does 'invaluable' mean?" Caroline asked.

"Depending on how it's said, it can mean a couple of things. The way I use it means that there is no way to put a price on what your mother has given you, and even if there was a way to price it, it would cost more money than anyone has."

"Even Mr. Kurtvow?"

"Him and Mr. Taylor put together, and they would both agree."

"Both agree on what?" Maria asked as she came over.

"We were talking about value and what Mr. Kutvow and Mr. Taylor have put together," Caroline said with a smile.

Maria wasn't completely sure what she meant but turned to her daughter. "Hurry up and go give Miss Charlotte a kiss. The bus will be here soon and we don't want to miss it."

Caroline ran inside as David turned and stood. "We?"

"One of Caroline's teachers stopped me last night and asked if I could come to the school today for an event they are having regarding the bazaar. I spoke with Miss Charlotte and she said she would be fine even with you not here."

David looked at her plainly.

"You are going to County with Doc. You said you would today and that you would not argue."

David paused for a moment and then responded, "I promise, I will not come back until I have seen a doctor."

"I will hold you to that promise," Maria said wryly as she stepped a little closer to him. "I would expect that you would be back in time for dinner this evening?" Maria asked as she placed her hands around and on David's lower back.

"Unless something out of the ordinary occurs, I would expect to be," David said dryly.

Maria placed a soft kiss on his lips and then stepped back as Caroline came back out the door. The sound of the bus engine came up from the silence.

Caroline gave David a huge hug and kissed him. "My birthday, the bazaar, this whole summer and into the fall … I will remember them for the rest of my life."

"I will too, Caroline. I will, too," David said as he smiled at her and touched her face.

The bus pulled up to the stop and they crossed the street to get on.

They both sat together on the bus and, as the bus pulled away, they both waved to David, who waved back and then turned to head back into the store.

A short while later, Rebecca and her mother left Charlotte's Place for El Paso, and few of the other regulars came and went.

Charlotte was slightly more lively than usual and David just grinned a little as he took notice.

All morning as customers came and went, the conversations were all the same. The success of the bazaar and the nullification of all the taxes in arrears dominated all the conversations.

All the business owners which were under the tax debt pressure, and that was many of them, were now talking about using the recovered money to expand their businesses or make other changes and modifications that they could not afford before.

Some of the homeowners who were cutting back a little on things as well as trying to retire that tax debt, now talked about enjoying an extra meal at McNally's or a new electronic device for their living room.

Each time the discussion started, David's name was mentioned. "Were it not for him—"

Inside the store, Charlotte came around from the back room. "David, you might want to head up and get changed. Doc said he'd be by around ten and it's about quarter to."

David nodded and turned off the grill, as it was unlikely anyone else would be coming in for anything hot. Most of the lunches were sandwiches and any of the hot sandwiches were handled using the toasters.

As he was about to head out the back way, Charlotte called out to him.

"I have to tell you, son, in light of this weekend and everything else, when you arrived that day with Peter, looking for work and a place to stay, never in a million years would I have assumed that I would live to see days again like I did this past weekend. If God were to take me today, I would go knowing I lived well, lived fairly, and had the opportunity to actually observe hope come alive."

David smiled just a bit and responded, "I don't know what to say, Miss Charlotte. I am just making my way the only way I know how."

"You do it better than most. Just keep doing it," she said as she eased into the chair.

David responded, "Yes, Miss Charlotte," and headed out the back door.

A short while later, Mel Porter walked into the store and called out, "David?"

Charlotte walked out of the back room upon hearing the bell above the door dinging and Doc's voice calling out.

"Hi, Doc," she said as she made her way around the counter. "He went upstairs to get cleaned up. He'll be down."

"I just came from the third floor, Miss Charlotte. He's not there. That's why I came in here looking for him. I looked out on the back property too. He's not out there."

The color drained out of Charlotte's face as she made her way past Mel as fast as her old legs could take her. They both headed out the door together and around to the apartments. "No, no, no," Charlotte said as she pulled herself onto the second landing and rounded the railing to head for the third floor stairwell.

Mel stood close behind her in case her rushing caused her any issue.

Charlotte crashed the door open to David's apartment and stepped into the kitchen. She looked into the living area. There was no large duffle bag neatly folded in the corner of the room on the old wooden chair with everything removed from it. His two pairs of shoes and his work boots that used to be lined up at the base of the cabinet were missing.

Mel said nothing. There was nothing for him to say.

Charlotte slowly made her way down the flight of stairs to the second floor landing. As she reached Maria's apartment she stopped outside the door. After standing there for a minute, she walked in.

On the kitchen table was the yellowing envelope that had been on the top shelf to the left of the sink. Next to it was another envelope. It was brand new and strikingly white.

Charlotte sat in the kitchen on one of the chairs and her eyes welled up with tears.

Mel looked on. It was all he could do. The last time he saw Charlotte cry was at the passing of her husband.

"Please do me a favor, Mel," Charlotte asked without looking up.

"Anything," he answered plainly.

"Please go lock the store up. We are closed the rest of the day. Family emergency."

Shortly after lunchtime, Maria arrived back at Charlotte's Place. Fernando Vargas's son was at the same assembly and offered Maria a ride back, rather than letting her wait for the afternoon school bus.

As she exited the truck, Fernando headed farther down Route 385 and up West End Road toward home.

Once she was completely across the street, she noticed the store was dark and the door was locked. Confused, she looked around. The tents and tables from the weekend were all gone from the parking lot, as well as Packer Road. Peter's truck was also gone, but she recalled him mentioning he was leaving.

She walked off the store stoop and headed slowly into the apartment side of the dwelling. She stopped at Charlotte's door and knocked. "Charlotte, are you in there?"

"I'm up in your kitchen, Maria," Charlotte responded while partly clearing her throat.

Maria walked up the stairs and into her own kitchen to see Mel sitting in the kitchen with Charlotte holding her hand on the table.

Next to their hands were the two envelopes.

Maria dropped her purse to the floor without moving from where she was.

The tears began to stream down her face. She wanted to move, but she couldn't. She told her feet to move. Either look in the envelopes or go to the third floor, but *move*.

After a few minutes, she slowly moved to the table and sat in the chair closest to the envelopes.

She did her best to focus her vision through the tears as she looked at the yellowing envelope. David's voice echoed through her head: *I promise to not leave town before you have the opportunity to pay it back.*

She finally reached over and looked in the yellowing envelope. It was empty.

"At least he kept his word," she said softly.

It was several minutes before she could settle herself to open the white envelope and read the contents. Without realizing it, she began to read it aloud.

Maria,

In all my travels over these past four plus years, I have never left a good-bye note. I have never really said good-bye. I never had to. It was always understood or implied. This has been the only time I had to remind others, and myself, that I would have to go.

I know I leave you with more questions than answers, and that is pretty much my entire life these past few years. I understand that is not solace for you nor is it justification of my actions, but I like to believe you have come to know and understand me enough to know that I do things for specific reasons.

I hate to use the old cliché "It's not you, it's me", but it is exactly that. It is not anything you did or didn't do. My time and work here in Westville was complete and it was time for me to leave. I know it was on the heels of the successful effort with the library. I hope that some of the remaining work gives people some ability to dig into the effort and get over any hurt or pain I caused in leaving. It was the farthest thing I could want for anyone but especially for you and Caroline.

I have held off emotional connections in my travels. It was relatively easy for me to do that. With you and Caroline it was impossible. I had no ability whatsoever to stay closed off. It was like trying to contain sand in my hand. The harder I tried the more slipped by. I was never going to keep the two of you out of my heart so one day I simply stopped trying.

I was a fairly broken and damaged man before I arrived in Westville. I leave ruined. I walked away from what would have been the greatest thing in my life for what would have certainly been the rest of my days.

There is an old saying that goes "Count your blessings; count the important ones twice." As I walk the rest of my days I will remember all that Westville gave to me, without my asking, and all the love you both had for me.

What you have in your heart, what you pass onto others, while you are here and after you are gone, matters more than anything else.

Please find a way to keep me in yours. You will forever be in mine.

David.

Maria crumpled the paper as she finished reading it.

She looked up at Doc and Charlotte, who were both crying, and then over at the clock.

She sat silent for a moment, then finally spoke. "Caroline is going to be home in three hours. What am I supposed to tell her?"

Neither of them responded as they didn't have a suitable response.

The remainder of the time was spent composing themselves as best they could to break the news to Caroline.

Mel left shortly before her arrival to let Kevin and Jim know. "The talking" would start soon, so they would want to get out ahead of any senseless gossip.

As Maria and Charlotte sat in the kitchen in silence, she suddenly heard the squealing brakes of the school bus.

"Mama? Are you home? The store is closed."

"Yes, honey, we are up here," Maria called out as she tried to strengthen her voice and the resolve in it that her daughter would need.

"Why is the store closed, Miss Charlotte?" Caroline asked as she came into the kitchen. "Mama, did you like the assembly? I was so glad you could go. Where is Mr. David? I want to tell Miss Charlotte all about it. If he is around, I can tell them both at the same time."

"Um, Caroline, can you please sit down with us here?"

Caroline put her book bag onto the floor next to the table and held onto her tablet tightly as she slowly took a seat. She looked at Miss Charlotte and then her mother and could sense something was wrong.

"Did I do something wrong?" she asked nervously.

"Oh, no, honey," Maria answered quickly. "It was not anything you did or are in trouble for."

Caroline continued to sit and listen.

"Mama has some news. There really isn't an easy way to tell you …" Maria's voice broke, but she steeled it back up as best as she could. "You might recall the occasional conversations people may have had where they talked about Mr. David and his travels and how he would come to a place, stay a while, and eventually go."

"Well, yes," Caroline said plainly. "I heard Mr. Mel and Mr. Kevin talk often. I remember them saying if there was ever a place to make it so he would stay, Westville would be the place." Caroline looked at her mother. "Where is Mr. David?"

Maria couldn't maintain her composure any longer. "It was his time to go. He traveled away this morning," she responded as the tears got away from her.

Caroline slowly moved her line of vision away from her mother and just straight forward. Charlotte couldn't add anything. She sat in silence.

Caroline slowly placed the tablet down flat on the table and inched it away from her. "He must be upstairs on the deck," she said very plainly and got up, walking toward the slider. "He wouldn't miss the sunset, it'll be here shortly."

Maria and Charlotte both got up and followed Caroline who went out the door and up to the third floor deck. No one was up there. Caroline looked in through the slider. "His shoes—"

"He wished me off to school, but he didn't say good-bye," she whispered as the tears streamed down her face and the color rushed in.

Maria went to hold her, but Caroline slipped her grasp and bounded down the deck stairs.

Maria followed as quickly as she could. Charlotte knew she could never keep up. She headed back into the apartment and down the stairs.

Caroline tore around the house and bounded across Route 385. A pickup truck had to swerve to miss her. Steve Dipetro working at Barker's saw her and tried to get out in front of her as Maria followed, but Caroline was just too fast.

Kevin McNally jumped into his car as Caroline went past Mr. Garcia's place and onto Arturo Rivera's property.

Jim Davenport came out of his store and onto the street because of the commotion along with the residents that were shopping at the stores.

Maria continued to run after Caroline as she went deeper and deeper off the road and onto Mr. Rivera's property.

Caroline finally collapsed on her knees, unable to run any further. Maria dropped and hugged her daughter tightly from behind as Deputy Mendoza crossed the property barrier of Rural Route 7 at the far end of the property.

"What did I do wrong?" Caroline asked. "What did I say? Was I not a good girl? Why would he go?"

"Oh, no, *has hecho nada mal cariño*. This has nothing to do with you. It is not anything you did wrong. It was David's choice, his, alone."

"Why? Why would he leave us? Didn't he love us anymore?"

Maria was breaking down at the words, but she had to offer answers through her own confusion for Caroline. "I do not totally understand, Caroline, but I think Mr. David loves us so much that he felt he had to let us go so we could grow on our own."

"Mama, will you let me go?"

"Never, honey."

"Why could Mr. David, then?"

"I do not know, honey. I really do not know."

Arturo Rivera moved his car closer to where they were sitting in his open scrub brush lot. Steve Dipetro who followed on foot stopped where Arturo pulled the car over.

"You will stay and take care of me, Mama?"

"I will, always. We will always have each other. And when we really need it, there are others here in Westville that we can count on as well. Look around at all the people coming now to see if we are okay."

Caroline poked her head around just slightly.

"But who will take care of Mr. David? He is gone and on his own now."

Maria just squeezed her daughter tighter, as she had no answer for her.

Chapter Twenty-Two

Rebecca had settled in from the flight and was dressed and ready for her dinner meeting with Zachary Taylor.

As she made her way to Michael's, the restaurant where they were to meet, she was overwhelmed.

In the past four days, she had seen Westville come together to do their part on the ground to advance the services of the library. In addition to that, Brian Kurtvow's release of all the tax liens removed a huge burden from her own family as well as many of the other families in town.

Now, with the additional opportunity of work more in line with what she had always dreamed, and getting there by way of a private flight, it was almost more than she could believe.

As the car service stopped at the front of the restaurant, she was greeted by one of the hostesses who took her directly into the private dining room where Zachary Taylor was already waiting.

As she entered, she quickly glanced at her cell phone for the time. She was concerned she might be late, but she entered right on the dot.

"Miss Wilson, I am so very glad you were able to make it and that you did decide this was something you wanted to pursue. I have as good a feeling about it, as I do the good work and the outcome from the bazaar at Westville," Zachary said as he stood and welcomed Rebecca into the room.

"I am really honored to be asked," Rebecca replied strongly. She was doing her best to be dynamic and assertive despite the fact that Zachary was twice her age and had so much more social status. *Remember*, she thought as she took a seat, *he asked you to consider doing this task. Therefore, he must see in you the ability to do it. Positive thoughts.*

"So I take it from the signing and returning of all the documents my courier delivered that you understood the details of what the terms are?"

"Well," she said as she cleared her throat and took a sip of water from the glass at the table, "I understand the technical terms. I need to surrender my personal cellphone. I will be issued a corporate one and a corporate laptop, a car from the car pool and a credit card for business related expenses. When the assignment is given, I am not to discuss the details with anyone. I am not to call directly back to Westville at all. If I need to get a call to someone, I am to call the provided number, and if my family needs to reach me, they call the same number. In both cases, messages are forwarded if they are critical in nature, and I saw what was listed as critical. Everything else was listed under 'informational' or 'secondary communications' and would be auto-logged for my retrieval after my work is done."

Zachary smiled and was about to say something when she continued.

"The assignment is supposed to start tomorrow on Tuesday, October fourteenth, and I am supposed to have the investigation part of the work done by November tenth, then the work completed fully by the end of the day on the fourteenth."

"See," Zachary said as he smiled. "I knew you had the ability to do this work."

The servers came into the room and left different dishes for them to choose dinner from and then they departed.

The two of them sat in moderate silence while they had a little something to eat. Zachary asked how the flight was and Rebecca indicated she had never flown before.

After dessert was served, someone from operations came in with Rebecca's equipment and took her personal phone from her, leaving her with everything as provided in the laptop bag.

"Are you ready to get started?" Zachary asked.

"Yes," Rebecca said as she sat forward and took out her notepad.

"Over these next few weeks I am sending you on the assignment of putting together and telling David's story."

Rebecca looked up from her notepad. She didn't know what to expect in way of an assignment, but she would have never guessed this.

"I am sure you have some questions. Let me give you, generically, what I can. I know about eighty percent of David's story. The rest, some of the more recent parts, totally elude me. In totality, more or less, I am honor bound to not divulge most of it. That is where you come in. I gave my word never to discuss his details with anyone. He wanted them to remain undiscovered. Technically speaking, I have no control over a young reporter digging up the human interest story of the year, which I believe this is."

"May I ask you something?"

"Sure. As a matter of fact, I have a total open door policy."

Rebecca sat back for a moment and collected her thoughts.

"It would seem to me that whatever life David had before, he's shared it with no one and that life is behind him. He's closest to Maria more than anybody, and she and I are good friends. Other than what we know on the surface and what we've seen since he arrived, there is little else to him. It would also seem as if his drifting days may be over, too. He's happy. Maria loves him, as does Caroline. I would think this is the end of his story."

"You see, I would think that was the end of the story as well. I know most of his history and I would otherwise believe that, had he not met me here a month or so ago to discuss the bazaar and the efforts in Westville. The man you see today was forged from something else that happened to him more recently. That is what you'll find out, as I cannot tell you the parts that I do know and the rest, those details elude me as well. There are some things I know and other things I don't. What you'll answer for me and wrap the whole thing together is what has happened over the last four years."

"Why now?"

Zachary sat back for a moment and smiled. "I did ask the right person to investigate and ask questions," he said as he picked up his drink and walked over to the one-way mirror in the private dining room. "Do you see all those people out there enjoying their dinner?"

"Yes," Rebecca replied as she got up to walk over and get a better view.

"Most of them, if they had to deal with certain truths, say of my life or David's, they would buckle under the weight and pressure. The average person, the everyday citizen, is losing hope for a better world. Hope for a better life for themselves or their kids if they have them. They are at their own tables out there eating dinner and going through the motions like Westville was. Each table out there is its own Westville. It has its own set of problems with seemingly little hope of solutions or resolution. It's not as if they have lost their will to live or anything like that, but they strive for the mediocrity. David mentioned you, at one point to this example. He said you had all these hopes and dreams of possibly going to school and maybe becoming a journalist, but that the needs and demands of life got in the way and you made choices. Now perhaps you would have returned to it someday. A few people actually do. Most never have the time. If they have the time, they don't have the money. If they have both, they lose their will. 'I'm too old now to start' or 'I can't make a difference.' "

Zachary paused and stepped away from the mirror.

"You asked me why now. I started to lose my own faith in the world and the kindness of others and I am the ultimate optimist. It may be slightly presumptuous of me to make myself the barometer, but if the rich guy is having faith in humanity issues, how well is the average person doing?"

Rebecca began to understand what Zachary was getting at.

"You're going to discover that David had every reason to tell the whole world to piss off, and he had the means to totally shut it out. He did the exact opposite instead. He decided to impart on people what he really believes at his core. He fought back that urge to throw in the towel and shut the world out. He knows that the people can do anything if they believe in themselves and in others. That is the main story. When people hear it, hopefully, they will look at their lives through a whole different lens. David can't be everywhere. Also there is that 'something else' that I need you to figure out. There is some other dynamic in there that I don't understand that is affecting him right now. It's pulling against him and what he is trying to do. He will never ask for relief from whatever it is. Oh, he will ask for help like he did with the bazaar. He's being crushed under some other load he is bearing right now. I need to know what that is so we can help him. You'll discover that. The work David did in Westville, it changed the people and their outlook there. I believe his story will, too, and if we can get it far and wide enough, maybe we can effect some change elsewhere with others, too. That is why I want it done before the holidays. Before the people lose themselves in the commercialism of the season, I am hoping they get caught in the possibility of something more."

"I'm in," Rebecca said fully convinced. "I need a way to get started. I cannot get much out of Peter and he's ferried him from his last couple of locations. I believe he is bound to his word much in the manner you are."

"Yes, this is true," Zachary said as he walked back toward the table and then went over to a notepad. "I made a list of things I can divulge to you without breaking my word. It's not a lot, but it will put you on the road east of where Peter first encountered him and where the trail is otherwise non-existent as Peter moved him around, probably unaware he was making a cover for his tracks."

Rebecca walked over and reviewed what Zachary had.

"So that is why Peter was indebted to him. David saved him from legal and tax issues. He could have been ruined financially or even gone to jail if he hadn't properly addressed these things."

Zachary just nodded and let her continue.

"So it looks to me like the starting point for me is Clearwater, and then east from there."

"That's as good a place as any. You drive out with the car, have some conversations with the people he helped and see what they know. Piece together the things they say with what the other locals say. Think about how David networks with people. He mentioned to me something about helping a shop owner in Westville and he was able to leverage the time against a sale floor appliance for I think it was Maria. He does those types of things. If he's helping one person and he can help another by proxy or exchange that's what he does. The good will on the right people, it becomes infectious."

"I'll leave in the morning."

"I know four weeks short a day seems like a lot, but it'll go by like a blink of an eye. You'll need to press hard and long. Don't burn yourself out. Take an hour each day or even two to just totally decompress from everything. You will need it, as you get closer to uncovering everything. Trust me." Zachary took a card out of his wallet and handed it to Rebecca. "That is my personal cell number. I cannot give you any more details without breaking my word. Everything that skirts it is on that pad. If you reach some point of frustration and you need to vent, I know you cannot call home. Mom, Dad, Maria, and so on. If it's that bad, you can call me." Zachary smiled a little and continued. "Obviously, I run an international multi-billion dollar corporation, so you might need to leave a message," he finished as he laughed.

Rebecca laughed, too, which broke up the tension that had started to build in the room.

There was little else to discuss so Rebecca thanked Zachary for the dinner once again, the advice, and the opportunity to do the work. She then left the room to head back to the hotel to start getting ready for tomorrow's departure.

Zachary sat at the dining table, put his feet up for a moment, and reflected on some of the things he felt were problems in his business and in his life. He then pulled out his phone and called his assistant.

"Beverly? Sorry to call you so late. First thing in the morning, please cancel all my appointments after noon and reschedule them. I am going to call my son and see if he has time for me to stop by and visit him, the wife, and see his kids."

Chapter Twenty-Three

Rebecca pulled onto the long rural road in Clearwater looking for the address she has scribbled down on her travel pad. She had left Houston in the early morning hours and stopped for something to eat around noon.

Despite the fact that Zachary provided her with the address east of Clearwater as the start point, she wanted the opportunity to meet the Miller's who David helped when the developer tried to force the sale of their home. She could have her talk with them and still make the Louisiana border and East Oaks for early evening, as it was less than one hundred miles away.

As she slowed down, looking for the address markings and the survey lot markings and comparing them to the GPS in the car, a middle aged woman wandered off her property up ahead of where she was slowing and waived her forward.

"Well, maybe that's Mrs. Miller," Rebecca said aloud to herself as she looked forward and sped up.

The woman in the road appeared to be in her mid-forties. Rebecca pulled the car closer and stopped in front of a single family home.

"Dan," The woman yelled as she stepped back into the driveway. "Ms. Wilson the reporter is here. Come outside."

"Hi," Rebecca said as she turned her digital recorder on and slipped it back into its holder. She fiddled with the Bluetooth microphone and made sure it was clipped high enough up to catch all the conversation. "I guess with that call over I do have the correct address," she said as she smiled and switched her notepad to her left hand to extend her right one to the woman. "Kathy Miller?"

"Oh, yes, hello. We are so happy you could come. After your phone call and the interest in your paper to do a story … We wished our regional newspaper wanted to do the story, but I guess they figured 'no autopsy, no story of value.'"

Dan Miller came out the door followed by their daughter. "Hi," Dan said as he gestured back, "this is Melanie, our eighteen-year-old daughter. Alex, our son, is fifteen and in school right now. His younger sister Sally is as well. She is eleven." Rebecca jotted everything down.

"Thank you. And are you 'Dan' or 'Daniel' or something else?" she asked.

"Dan is just fine, and of course you already met Kathy," he said as they walked into the small yard. Dan extended his arm and offered a seat at a small picnic table just off the driveway. "So what was the name of the paper again?" Dan asked as he sat.

"The Westville Press," Rebecca said proudly as if it were a large industrial paper.

"Well, I will tell you, we are generally not the type of folks that go off running for the TV camera if we ever see one, but we really did want our paper to cover this story. Others were getting pressured by this developer and the crooked contractor in other towns," Dan said as he leaned forward on the table. "We're not unintelligent folk, but when you have numerous people saying the same thing you start to believe what you hear."

Rebecca nodded and took notes. She was happy to have the digital recorder running, but as she had additional thoughts or comments alongside the items, she would make note of them.

"So Ms. Wilson—" Kathy started.

"Oh please, Rebecca is just fine," she replied as she looked up.

Kathy smiled back. "So Rebecca, have you met him? David Stephenson? Were you able to get his side of this for your story?"

"Actually, we are just staring to put together this story based on his doings. He stopped in Westville as he travelled along," she said as her voice weakened a little. "He helped us, too. We didn't know at the time that he had done this elsewhere, too."

"Oh," Melanie exclaimed. "Can you tell us how he helped you?"

"Let's let her get the details from us," Melanie's father replied. "I am sure once the story is done we can read all about it, if it is a story about everything he's done."

"You believe there's more?" Rebecca asked.

"Well, he helped us. He helped the trucker fella that eats over at Stella's when he makes his way through. You just said he helped you."

"The man is a kind soul," Kathy said. "He is terribly troubled, but he refuses to let that tarnish him. At least on the surface."

They were all silent for a moment.

"Okay, so what else can you tell me?" Rebecca asked as she shook the weight of the comment off.

The Miller's went through the details of what Rebecca already knew. That they thought they would lose their home to a developer and how they were lying to as many people they could frighten into bad sales deals.

They explained how the kind drifter they came to know as David knew enough that they were not being above board in their conversations with the property owners, engaged State Senator Campbell and moved everything to the present resolution.

Rebecca wrapped up all her note taking and stood. "Well, I think that is everything I needed. Was there anything more that I should add?"

"How is he?" Kathy asked softly.

Rebecca smiled a little. "I understand your comments about the tortured soul in him. We've seen it in him too. He softened up. We are really hoping that he is planning to stay in Westville."

"Oh I hope so," Kathy continued. "My friend Samantha took an interest in him. We gathered he was a traveller. A few of us hoped he would stay, but we could tell as much as he was willing to help his heart wasn't in on the idea of staying here. Maybe there in Westville he's found his peace."

"Here is a number where you can reach me," Rebecca said as she handed out a business card with her information on it, "if you think of anything you might have left out that you'd like to add."

"Thank you," Dan replied. "When is your reporting due to be published? Is your publication a national one? Will we be able to read your story? Online maybe?"

"I am expecting in about two to four weeks once I make all my stops. I'm on my way to the next one. We don't have an online presence as we are a small publication but I can mail you a print copy if you'd like."

"Well, I am glad you have some sort of bread crumb trail to follow. That trucker fella was tight lipped. Wouldn't say a word. Loyal as hell."

Rebecca smiled as she took her leave and made her way to the car.

Melanie ran up to the car as Rebecca started it.

"Could you get a message to him? When you go home?"

"I'm sure I could," Rebecca answered.

"Could you tell him the Millers and some of the other folks from Clearwater said hello and that we miss him? We think of him often and hope he has found what he's looking for."

Rebecca held her breath for a moment to compose herself and then answered, "Absolutely."

"Thank you," Melanie responded as Rebecca slowly pulled the car away.

Rebecca spent the next couple of hours replaying the conversation with the Millers in her head as she traveled to East Oaks to meet with Lisa Bennett.

Upon her arrival into town she drove around looking for a place to stay overnight and booked a room.

As she sat in the room, a mix of emotions flowed through her. She was excited for the assignment and for the opportunity. Her mind drifted to Westville. She wasn't used to not being able to tell her parents how her day was going. She wondered how things were going now that a couple days passed since the bazaar. She was curious how folks were handling the aftermath of the removal of all their tax debt.

She got up and grabbed her things, then thought of Maria and Caroline. She wondered how things were doing with them. She was a little concerned about completing the project and reporting on it. She was worried how David would perceive it.

She sat on the edge of the bed and thought on it for a moment, as it was the first time in all the excitement that it had crossed her mind.

"David told me that life just sometimes comes at you," she whispered aloud to herself. "He never approached me about anything in confidence."

She stood abruptly and said in a normal speaking voice, "He would respect that I worked hard and honorably and I didn't compromise my principles. He'd approve."

It was nearly seven in the evening when Rebecca arrived at Lisa Bennett's apartment. Lisa stood about the same height as Rebecca but was noticeably older than her, likely in her late forties or early fifties. Her hair was dark with a few streaks of gray.

"Hi, come in, please," she said in a very soft voice.

"Thank you for having me over," Rebecca said as she looked around the simple apartment.

"Oh, it's no trouble. When you said you wanted to talk to me about David, I … Well, I don't even know how to describe it," Lisa responded as she sat on the living room sofa.

Rebecca quickly scanned the apartment from the living room where they were sitting and took in as much as she could see. There were a few older pieces of furniture within her line of sight, but for the most part everything was new or gently used, as near as she could tell.

"Why don't you just say what comes to mind?" Rebecca said in a comforting tone. "This is more a human interest story than a news story, so we are looking for the personal elements as much as anything else."

Lisa looked at Rebecca as her bottom lip trembled and the tears just began flowing.

"Oh, I'm sorry," Rebecca said as she fished through her bad for tissues. "I didn't mean to upset you. I can come back."

"No, please … I'll be okay … I just need a moment."

Rebecca sat quietly and let Lisa collect herself. She understood that for some people the topic of David might be upsetting, given his mode of operation of picking up and leaving, as she understood it.

"Okay," Lisa said as she sighed. "I think I am okay now."

"Are you sure? I am not in a hurry tonight if you have the time, I can wait a bit longer if you need it."

"No, I'm good," Lisa responded as she breathed in deeply and exhaled loudly.

"Okay. Start anywhere you like. I can ask you questions as we go," Rebecca said softly as she opened up her notebook.

"David ... He saved my life."

Rebecca looked up from her notepad and just looked at Lisa as the tears streamed down her face.

"I had been out of work for some time. Months. The factory downsized and there were quite a few of us looking for too few open jobs. Anything, even part time ones. I was a contract worker so the unemployment check was really lacking. I was sure that was the next thing to go. I was selling off things from the apartment trying to pay the rent and even with doing that I was still falling behind. I had a roommate. He left for a better opportunity."

"Work?"

"A thirty-year-old with big boobs," Lisa said as she laughed. Rebecca smiled as a little of the tension left the room.

"So I was looking for a roommate, too," Lisa continued. "I was getting desperate. I was two months behind on my rent. I had almost no real food. The electric was the only thing that hadn't been turned off."

Rebecca went back to taking her notes. She knew the recorder was on, but it was therapeutic for her to take the notes. As long as it felt like work and that she was reporting she could stay disengaged and disconnected. But it was about David and even without him here, his presence, or even the ghost of it, would pull the average person in.

"My landlord told me that I had to stay at least within the two month behind window. If I got any further behind, he would have to start the eviction process. I asked him if there was anything I could do. He asked me what 'anything' meant to me. So yes, I did that. I went somewhere I wasn't proud of. I did it more than once. I had to. I had nowhere else to go. I looked at it as if I was lucky. If I was a man, I couldn't even resort to that with him and I would have been out. He carried me into the third month. I was still trying to find work without much luck. He took more and more advantage. I let him. I didn't even care anymore."

Lisa paused and looked out her window from her seat. Rebecca just watched her stare.

"After a marathon session in bed, which was the worst sex I ever had in my life, I got up, took fifty dollars out of his wallet, got dressed, and walked to Brewers. It's the bar up the street. I was going to drink fifty dollars of booze and then go McKenzie Bridge and jump off it."

Rebecca put her pen and pad down and reached over and took Lisa's right hand.

"So I am sitting there drinking with abandon and this soft voice asks me, 'Is anything the matter or are you trying to add volume to the beer by crying into it? If you need another drink, I can always get you another.' He smiled kindly. I think I told him to screw off. I can't be sure. I was so drunk. I'm not the best drunk normally and I felt totally degraded at that point."

Lisa laughed a little and then continued through the steady stream of tears.

"He didn't say anything. He just sat there. All I could think of was ending it. I know he was still talking, and I have no recollection of what he was saying at that point, but I just stood and walked out. He followed me. I bitched at him the whole way. I said the worst things I could to him. I said every negative thing ever said to me or that I felt about myself and I spewed it all over him. All the way to the bridge."

Lisa started to breath heavily. Rebecca got up as she tried to catch her breath and got a glass of water for her from her kitchen and gave it to her. As Lisa took a few sips and calmed down Rebecca touched her softly on the shoulder and sat back down.

"We got to the bridge and I hadn't even really acknowledged him up to that point except to abuse him. I started climbing onto the over ledge. He didn't stop me. He climbed out there with me. As I stood there ready to jump I turned and looked at him really for the first time. Here was this attractive man standing with me on the ledge and I asked him, 'What are you doing?' He says something to me like, 'I could ask you the same thing.' I remembered saying 'I've had it with this life. I am done.' He said nothing to me. He just looked at me. Eventually I asked him what he was doing on the ledge. He answers 'I'm standing out here with you.' And then I said, 'Why?' So he answered, 'Because I am still waiting for you to tell me what you're planning to do.' So then I said, 'I am going to jump.' And I remember him saying, 'Okay. You are aware you won't survive the fall.' Then I swore at him and called him stupid. Of course, I knew that. And then he said 'Okay, as long as we're straight on that part. So let me know when you're ready.' I turned around and I asked him why. He said, 'So I can jump, too.' He said it so plainly. I still think to this day he actually meant it. So anyway, I remember saying to him, 'Why would you want to jump, too? If it's going to kill me, it will kill you, too.'"

Lisa lost all her composure and it took her a few minutes to regain it to finish.

"He said to me …'No one deserves to die alone and tonight isn't going to be an exception.' I remember standing there for such a long time after that comment and not saying a word. He just stood and waited. The he slowly got down and stood in front of me and said, 'Do you want to come down now?' I said to him I had no reason to come down. And he said, 'I'm here, can I be reason enough?' I climbed down and we sat on the ground for an hour or more before Highway Patrol came by. He got up and talked to the trooper. He said he would take responsibility to make sure I got home and I was safe."

Rebecca wiped her own tears away.

"He took the rent I was looking to fill. He told me he wasn't staying long, but that he'd pull his weight while he was here. He paid all the back rent. He addressed the landlord directly about the 'consensual sex that had been occurring that would never happen again' as he put it. He worked for a few weeks with Mr. Donovan doing deliveries and he bought all this furniture. He found out Mr. Donovan was in need of office help and he spent the time learning the system he was using there and he taught it to me. Mr. Donovan gave me the job."

Lisa wiped her tears away. "I came home from work one day and his duffle bag was gone. I haven't seen him since."

There was a long silence before Lisa finished her conversation with Rebecca.

"I owe him everything and he wanted nothing. The man was an angel when I needed one, and I never got the chance to tell him or even say good-bye."

Chapter Twenty-Four

It was early Friday morning and Rebecca was on the road to Florida for her next stop. She spoke with other people who'd met David over the past year in Louisiana, Mississippi and Alabama, and was now trying to trace his travel back to the prior year.

Each story had the same theme. David would wander in after hitching a ride with someone or coming in on the bus, and he would find a place to settle for a little bit, help out with something or make some sort of difference, and then disappear without a trace.

As she glanced over at her notebook in the small box on the front seat of the car, she mentally went through her recent visits. She thought first about Lisa in East Oaks whom David had talked back from the brink of suicide.

She then thought about John Clement and his encounter with David regarding Cadmus Children's Camp in Mississippi, which had its laptops stolen. David found a local recycler who was willing to give up scrapped systems to the camp. David stayed and taught the teens there how to troubleshoot and fix the laptops by cannibalizing other parts from comparable systems. By the time they were done they had fifteen working systems which was three more than they had before the theft.

In Tidewater, Mary Sevier talked to Rebecca about how David, looking for a place to stay, ended up with her after coming in from Florida, and how he helped her with many of the things in her home that became neglected over the years since her husband died. She explained how he worked with a local mechanic to fix her broken down car so she could use it more reliably to get around. He showed her how to better manage her money between her checking account and he savings account to avoid unnecessary fees and to earn a little better interest.

It was the visit with Mary that put her on the road to Florida. It was getting harder to follow the trail backwards now that over a year of travelling had been logged. People at diners tended to forget the name of the helpful stranger and had to be coaxed to remember it. Employees at the ticket counters of the bus stations were only six months on the job and were it not for other people on shift remembering the trail might have gone cold.

Only a week in and having all this difficulty, Rebecca was worried that she would be not only unable to follow David's path all the way back in the three remaining weeks, or maybe not at all given unlimited time.

As she hit the Florida state line, she decided to think positive and forge ahead as she began to really believe in what Zachary told her: *This story, his story, it has to be uncovered fully and told far and wide.*

Back in Westville, Maria made her way out of her bedroom dressed for work and quietly went into Caroline's room.

"Good morning, *pequeño,*" she said very softly as she sat on the open part of the bed. "It is time to get up and ready for school."

Caroline stirred quietly and opened her eyes. She sighed slightly and got up slowly and went into the bathroom.

Maria sat quietly on Caroline's bed and listened to the water run in the bathroom. She hoped that today would be the first day that Caroline would not go out the backslider and up the stairs to look at the now-empty apartment above them.

As the water turned off, Caroline came out and put her slippers on and walked over to the slider. She stopped short of going out as Maria closed her eyes. Caroline turned around and came back into her bedroom and climbed as much as she could into her mother's lap.

As Maria held her daughter, she looked at Caroline's tablet on the top of her dresser. It was in the same place where she set it on

Monday evening. It bothered her that her daughter suddenly seemed disinterested in something she was once so passionate about.

Caroline squeezed her mother tightly and tried to nuzzle her head more under her chin.

"*Pequeño*, we will have to start getting you ready," Maria said softly.

"Can I stay right here? Just like this?" Caroline asked.

"You have to go to school and I have to go to work. These are just some of the things that we have a responsibility to do," Maria said as she pulled her head back a little to look at her. "How about tonight we go over to Mr. McNally's after we eat and we can order a dessert? Would you like that?"

Caroline waited a moment before answering.

"Was there something else you wanted to do?" Maria asked.

"Could we—"

Maria waited for her daughter to finish, but she needed to ask, "What, *pequeño*? Could we what?"

"Could Miss Charlotte come sit with us upstairs on Mr. David's deck and watch the sunset?"

Maria became upset almost immediately with an equal mix of sadness and anger. She pulled her thoughts together and answered quietly, "Are you sure that is what you would like to do, honey? You would not prefer to do something else?"

"No, Mama that is what I would like," she answered softly as she looked into her mother's eyes. "We did that a lot with Mr. David. Whenever we could. And always on Friday night. Maybe he is not here now, but I think of him anyway. Since I think of him anyway, I would like to do something tonight that I believe he is doing somewhere on his own. I would like to think that as I think of him, he is thinking of us."

The equal mix of sadness and anger became just sadness at her daughter's words. Maria closed her eyes as the tears made their way out and she pulled Caroline in a little tighter. "Sure, Caroline, we can go up and do that tonight."

The two of them sat together quietly for a little longer, with Maria occasionally glancing over at the time.

"Mama?"

"Yes, *pequeño?*"

"Do you think about Mr. David? What do you think about? Can you tell me?"

Maria drew in a deep breath. She needed to collect all her thoughts on what she wanted to say and didn't want to say. About some of the things that really upset her about him leaving and about how she really felt. She thought about his letter and the dozens of times she read it and how his leaving just made less and less sense to her.

"I think about him all the time, Caroline, if I must be truly honest with you," Maria said as she worked consciously to keep from crying or getting mad. "I wonder where he went. I think about how he is traveling. I hope that he is eating well and that he is warm and safe."

"I do too Mama. I keep thinking of a day that he walks back into town like the way he did. He'll just suddenly show up like he once did with Mr. Peter," Caroline said as she hopped down and became more animated. "Perhaps that's it. Mr. Peter will be driving his truck and will suddenly come upon him again and bring him back."

"Oh, Caroline. I would like to think that and hope so too, but please do not get all your hopes on so high about that. If he is unable or unwilling to come back, I would not want you to be disappointed," Maria said as she got up and slowly guided her daughter out of her bedroom to get ready for school.

A short while later, Caroline was ready and off to school and Maria was working downstairs.

Some of the adults were still subdued over David leaving. Most others, having limited engagement with him, were disappointed that he left, but they were now more consumed by the fact that they now had no tax arrearages to deal with.

Henry Baylor was on his way out the door as Kevin McNally made his way in and headed over to the counter.

Mel Porter was seated with Charlotte, Diana Canton, and Jim Davenport.

Maria came over with the coffee pot and a cup for Kevin as he took a seat. She smiled slightly and said a quiet, "Good morning," as she poured and then reheated the cups of the others that were seated.

Charlotte watched Maria as she went about her work. She was a little more stoic than she was originally and it was certainly in contrast to the Maria of the past two months. She was also looking somewhat withdrawn.

Mel decided he had enough of all the uncomfortable silence and spoke up. "You know we've been coming in here today and the prior mornings since Tuesday acting like someone died. I don't want to be insensitive, but we've dealt with people's passing better than the fact that this man walked out of here."

"That is because death is usually sudden, often unexpected, and generally a surprise," Maria said as he accent came out as her tone became angry.

"Are we really shocked he left?" Kevin asked. "He said from day one he wasn't going to stay. I don't want say I am happy to see him gone, but he never mislead anyone," Kevin said to everyone and then turned to Maria. "Maria, I know he became special to you and your daughter. I really am genuinely sorry about that. The kind of man he was, attentive and all, I am sure he became very important to the two of you. I am not sorry however about how he came in here and pulled on the reigns and stirred everyone up. He made things happen that no one else could have. You think Brian Kurtvow was going to wake up all on his own, help save the library, and relieve all of us of our tax debt? That took a visionary and I don't care how much money he has or how successful he is, Kurtvow was more right place, right time with investments than visionary."

Kevin's comments echoed off the walls as no one debated his points.

"I don't care," Diana said after a few moments of silence. "I can think of plenty of people I would have preferred to see walk west than him."

"You saw him walking?" Maria asked aggressively.

"Well, no," Diana replied, surprised, as she never had Maria speak to her with that tone. "I'm just making an assumption. Peter spoke about giving him a ride from Arkansas and East Texas. I just figured he's heading west rather than back the way he came."

Maria withdrew slowly and then spoke again. "I am sorry, Diana. I did not mean to yell."

"It's okay, honey," she replied sympathetically. "We understand. How's Caroline been?"

Maria settled onto the chair on the serving side of the counter. "She often goes up on the third floor deck. She generally did that before when the apartment was empty. She does it now because he used to be up there. She has stopped reading to Charlotte at night. That became a family thing. David was part of the family. She has lost her desire to do it anymore. She has put that tablet he got her for her birthday on the side and does not use it, at least for now."

The room stayed quiet for a few moments and then Maria continued.

"After everything that unfolded, I was so excited for her. It looked like a birthday she would remember forever. Now it is one that I hope she can forget."

Mel adjusted himself a little on the stool and spoke up. "I called Peter on his cell phone after he left as it seemed awfully close to the same time as when David left. I agree with Diana. It's unlikely David traveled east since he came that way. Peter's deliveries were east of here and he assures me he had no idea that David was leaving."

Jim Davenport got up to refill his own coffee, as he didn't want to bother Maria, but she waived him off and took the pot over.

"The problem with Peter being unaware," Mel said as he pushed his empty cup forward, "is that we've totally lost the link. The prior few stops David made he traveled with Peter. Even if he'd never divulge, we would have at least known how he was or might possibly get a message to him. There's no way to right now."

Maria set the coffee pot down and looked at Mel. "Get a message," she repeated and then looked at the phone.

Everyone was looking at her to follow up, but Maria just stared at the phone. Then she suddenly marched over to it, pulled it off the receiver, and started going through the dialed number history. She stopped at a number she didn't recognize and hit redial.

As the phone rang she stood tapping her feet lightly. "Yes, hello," she said suddenly. "Can you please put me through to Zachary Taylor?"

"I'm sorry," Beverly said, "who is this calling please?"

"This is Maria Moreno."

"Yes, Ms. Moreno," Beverly said as she reviewed her list. "I am not sure how you have this number, however—"

"I got it from David Stephenson," she responded quickly.

"I see," she said as she recalled her prior exchange with him. "Well, Mr. Taylor is unavailable at the current time. May I leave a message with him?"

"Yes, please. Could you please inform him that I called and that it is fairly urgent that I follow up with him? It concerns David Stephenson. Do you need a return number?"

"I should be all set, I have it here on the caller ID."

"Thank you very much," Maria said as she hung up the phone.

"Yeah, he didn't rub off too much on her," Jim said wryly.

Maria smiled just a little.

Chapter Twenty-Five

It was near the end of the day on Friday as Rebecca settled in her hotel room and mapped out her plan to head up to Georgia and South Carolina over the weekend. She had three stops in total that took her back almost to the twenty-four-month mark of David's travels, as close as she could estimate.

As she looked over her notes, she recognized that until Peter picked up David that he pretty much hugged Interstate 10. Since she arrived in Florida and the path turned north, she estimated the likely path north to where Mr. New York / Mr. Boston came from would fall along Interstate 95.

She took her notes over to the desk in her room and began to pen out an outline of what she wanted to write.

She took a moment to collect her thoughts and she looked at the cell phone. She really wanted to call home. She missed her parents and working at McNally's and all the people that interacted with her there. As tempting as it was, she knew she was not supposed to so she put it out of her head.

She forged on with her outline so that she could jump start the beginning portion of the writing while still collecting the early parts of David's travels.

She was writing her encounters in blocks, since she wanted to start his story from the beginning from where he came, to the ending of the story, with him settling in Westville.

She paused at the thought and allowed herself to daydream a little. How David might end up together with Maria and have children of their own as they both raised Caroline. How he might work with Mr. Kurtvow to further revive the town. She wondered if a future life for herself might lead to a husband and children.

Life happens while you're busy making other plans. You have to grab onto it when you can and ride it for all it's worth.

David's words popped into her head as she smiled and then got back to the effort at hand.

The phone at Charlotte's Place rang as Maria walked back in from the apartment and getting Caroline started on her homework.

"Charlotte? Did you want me to get that?" Maria called out as she walked toward the counter.

"Go ahead," Charlotte responded from the back room. "I was just going to let it ring. It's a little after six, I was figuring to close up shortly."

Maria reached over and picked up the phone "Charlotte's Place, Maria speaking."

"Ms. Moreno," the man said quickly catching Maria's attention.

"Mr. Taylor," Maria said back loudly so that Charlotte would hear her.

"You seem somewhat surprised to hear from me," he said to her as he took a seat at his desk.

"I was not exactly sure what to expect in calling this number," she answered as Charlotte walked up next to her to listen.

"Well, as busy as I might be, when I get calls on this line, I try to follow up fairly quickly. I see David gave you the number."

"To be honest he did not. I called it off the redial," she admitted.

"That's fairly industrious of you. So now that you have me, what can I do for you?"

Maria swallowed a little and just spoke. "It is about David. He left on Monday. No one has heard a word from him at all for the entire week. He has simply disappeared as if he was never here in the first place."

"I see," Zachary said somewhat disappointed in hearing the news. "I know this is probably not what you wanted to hear, but this is not totally unexpected of him. At least not these past few years, anyway."

Zachary paused for a moment and then continued. "I had hoped that perhaps this stop was different. I had hoped that such a climatic success might get him to consider settling back down and staying in Westville."

"Mr. Taylor, I think you can appreciate how important David has become to many of us here. I am not ashamed to admit a degree more for my daughter and myself. I do not think he fully understood the impact he would have leaving us. He stated that he has always moved along. I do not believe he made this deep a connection before, but we did not have the opportunity to really let him know as he left unannounced."

Maria paused for any response. There wasn't one so she continued.

"Do you have any idea where he went? Is there any way for you to get a message to him?"

"I am sure that if I did know where he went, I wouldn't be able to say where, but I can honestly tell you I don't know. Because of that, there is no way for me to get a message to him for you, unfortunately."

"I see," Maria said as hope turned into disappointment.

"I can promise you that the moment that changes, if it changes, I will let you know, right after I tell him to call you."

"Thank you, Mr. Taylor," Maria said slightly comforted.

"Please call me Zachary and you go ahead and keep this number. If you need to reach me for something, this number is the best way to do it."

"Thank you again, Zachary. Have a good night."

"You as well. Tell your daughter I will make sure she's kept up to date with the work on her library. Good evening."

Maria hung up the phone and looked at the caller ID information to write it all down.

"I take it no new news," Charlotte said as she walked around the counter and headed to lock the side door of the store off the parking lot.

"No," Maria said plainly as she came around and sat on one of the stools on the customer side of the counter. "I could probably use one of your talks where you impart all that wisdom on me."

"To be honest, child, this situation baffles me as well," Charlotte said as she walked back along the aisle and sat next to her. "I don't know why he left. There are far too many possible reasons why but without knowing his whole history there is no way to really know."

"Was there anything more we could have or should have done?" Maria asked as her emotional level rose.

"As I said there are too many things to know except this part. I cannot think of a single thing more you could have or should have done. This was really up to him and his decision making process. I have to hope he had a highly justified reason for choosing leaving as the only option."

A couple of tears ran down Maria's face and she quickly wiped them away. "You of all people know how closed and guarded I have been since William left. I remember you telling me 'You never let people in. Not everyone is William.' Are you still sure of that?"

"I will be the first person to admit, yes, this looks strikingly familiar. William was a boy, too young to be the man he needed to be at the time and likely too embarrassed now to admit the mistake even if he was actually considering to. David feared nothing. Something else made him go. Think about it. The man was very calculating and logical."

"He was quickly becoming everything to me," Maria said as she began to cry openly. "And to Caroline. I would have done anything he asked."

"Would you have gone with him if he asked you?"

Maria had to stop to think about the question. "I really cannot say for certain. I am looking at the future now without him and thinking I would. If he were to ask me, I might want to choose to not leave and try to convince him harder to stay. I have lived without someone in my life for a long time. I am quite capable of doing things for Caroline and myself. I feel as if I had reached a point and place where I did not want to do it all alone anymore. I thought I had found the right man to share things with. I wish he could have seen that."

Chapter Twenty-Six

Rebecca held onto the railing of the subway car as she tried to remember all the suggestions and tips for traveling in New York City that she had read online the night before in her hotel room in New Jersey.

She realized, too, that keeping on the trail from here was going to be the most difficult.

New York City, and its eight million inhabitants, was going to prove to be a challenge for her to find out what David did here, if he did anything at all, and then backtrack farther.

David had mentioned more than once that everyone's assessment of him being "Mr. New York" was off and that it was more like "Mr. Boston," so she knew she still had farther back to go. She also knew that it wasn't much farther. She had estimated she had spoken to enough people to draw the timeline back almost four years and that was about the last time Zachary had heard from David so it was all coming back to the beginning.

Timing was critical as well. It was Thursday, November sixth. Rebecca knew she had just this weekend to get the last of the information together and complete the story for the following Friday.

All she had to go on was the address given to her by Tim Washington, the blackjack dealer from Atlantic City that met David. He remembered David from when he won a decent sum of money that night and he took back his own cash that he started with and gave all the winnings to the dealer tip box for no real reason. Tim talked to him just a little bit before he left that evening for Delaware and he remembered the place he said David used to eat at all the time while he spent his time in New York City — a popular tavern on Third Avenue.

The subway train screeched to a stop at Penn Station and she got off to catch the connecting train heading east so she could take it up to Third Avenue and the general area where she needed to be.

She was amazed at all the people and how fast they moved everywhere. She knew she would be struggling and would have to read the signs to make her way around, having never been to the city, but she thought it was busy in Jersey City where she parked the car.

She was dedicated and focused on the task, but she took a few moments while out and about to just marvel and the surroundings. The people, the traffic, the hustle and bustle, the skyscrapers and the sheer size and volume of everything.

She finally arrived on Third Avenue and went into the tavern to take a look around. She talked to some of the staff and showed them the photo of David on her phone from Caroline's birthday party. No one recognized him. She asked if there were other staff members that might work on other nights, but the bartender indicated that there wasn't anyone working in the place from four years prior any longer and that the place was under different ownership back then.

Rebecca went outside and walked north up and along Third Avenue a bit. Her normal everyday pace was somewhat moderate for her age, but most of the people blew right past her. She was also feeling dejected. She had come all this was and the trail had dried up.

Rebecca stopped when she came upon a bench and she sat. She took out the cell phone and called the one number she was avoiding using the entire time on her journey.

The phone rang only twice by the time Zachary answered it. "Hey, no e-mail status update today? You decided to call? Lucky you, I was between meetings."

"Hi, Mr. Taylor," Rebecca replied quietly.

"Sounds like a big city. You'll need to speak up a little with all that background noise."

"Yes, I'm in New York," Rebecca said as she spoke up.

Zachary sat at his desk in his personal office at home. "Something must be up. You've never used the phone. You've always e-mailed your updates. Talk to me."

"I'm sorry. I've done everything I can think of. I talked to the last person that saw him four years ago in Atlantic City which took me to New York City, but the last place he was seen was a restaurant that is under new ownership and there are no staff hold overs."

Zachary sat quietly and thought for a moment. He thought about how far she had gotten and how little was left to go. He pulled a different cell phone out of his desk draw and sent a text to Rebecca's phone and then pulled the battery from it.

"Something will come up," Zachary said. "That's the thing with Michael's, it always does."

"You mean David?" Rebecca asked.

"Yes, sorry. I'm on my way to Michael's to have dinner. I do have to run but circle back to me tomorrow and let me know if you brainstorm anything. There's still a little time."

"I will. Thank you for the opportunity and the confidence. I hope I don't let you down," Rebecca said mildly.

"I have faith in you. Have a good night."

Rebecca hung up the phone and noticed a text message that contained a single word.

"Wallingford."

She sent several texts back and received no reply so she decided to call the number by using the dial feature, but the number was marked *restricted*, so the app feature could not redial. She also had no way to otherwise identify the number that sent the text because of that setting.

She had given a few people the phone number over her travels in the hope that if anyone remembered anything additional that they might send it along. This might be just the break she needed.

Rebecca started to head back to the subway station, but she realized that if she took it that she'd lose the data line for the phone so she looked at the mapping app on the phone and started walking back to Penn Station.

As she made her way, she looked up Wallingford and got a number of hits. She ruled out the small neighborhood in Seattle, Washington as well as Wallingford, Oxfordshire, in the United Kingdom.

She looked at the search results for Wallingford, Iowa and Wallingford, Pennsylvania. *The one in Iowa was too far away to be a high probability choice,* she thought to herself, *but the one in Pennsylvania is possible.*

She reviewed the location of Wallingford, Pennsylvania against Atlantic City. It wasn't out of the question.

"But David always made comments about how Mr. Boston was more relative than Mr. New York. That might discount Wallingford, Pennsylvania some," she said aloud as her pace quickened.

The other remaining search results were Wallingford, Connecticut, and Wallingford, Vermont. She pulled them up on the map. From Jersey City where she parked the car Wallingford, Connecticut was basically a one hundred mile ride north. Wallingford, Vermont was an additional one hundred and eighty miles north from Wallingford, Connecticut.

Rebecca pulled up her calendar and realized that even if she took a full day in each place, she would still be able to drive back from the furthest point north, Wallingford, Vermont, to Houston over three days.

"Two, if I need to push it," she mumbled as she hustled down 38th Street. "If either of these are the right towns, I can still do it."

Rebecca continued to press on to Penn Station and she began to plan her trip to Wallingford, Connecticut.

Chapter Twenty-Seven

Rebecca hit the Wallingford town line driving the Wilbur Cross Parkway and got off Exit 64. The GPS brought her up into the center of town. She had looked earlier at an online map that detailed a lot of businesses along Route 5 on her way over to Route 68 where her hotel was. She scoped all restaurants along the way in the hopes of finding one or more that she felt might be able to quickly recognize someone from the area.

As she needed to break off toward the hotel, she quickly realized that most of the fast food and fine food chains might not be the best place to start. If David had been from the area and not been around for years, it wasn't likely anyone would recognize him.

The town was very large by her standards but much smaller than the cities she had been recently, certainly much smaller than Jersey City and New York City. Despite that, the town of Wallingford was certainly larger than all the towns in her area. It also wasn't built up like larger cities but more built out.

She decided she'd get settled into her room and then ask someone at the check in desk if they thought the downtown area that crossed Route 5 near the train station was a better place for chatting with the locals.

A short time later, she was headed down Interstate 91 to Exit 14 to the downtown area. Kimberly, the girl at the check in desk, lived in town. She didn't recognize David's name or his face in the pictures she has on her phone, but she acknowledged that being only twenty years old was probably a factor and that a person as old as David is someone her parents were more likely to know.

Rebecca turned off the exit ramp and quickly glanced at the names of the places in the downtown area that she suggested. She gave Rebecca a paper map, the one that all the travelers get, and she circled the local establishments that have been owned by locals for years.

Over the three hours she spent walking from the pub and restaurants to the small eateries and pizza places, it was all the same, for the most part no one knew him. What seemed to be a little different and somewhat encouraging to her was that a few thought the face looked a little familiar, but they really couldn't place the name and the face. Rebecca wasn't sure if she should discount that or not. There were many people in the places and it was some of the older patrons that seemed to get that feeling that they had seen him before or knew of him.

Rebecca passed the Route 5 boundary of the downtown area and stopped at three more pubs. The final one highlighted on the map in the downtown area was a neighborhood Irish pub. It was later in the evening, Irish music was playing, and there were people listening and talking amongst themselves.

Rebecca decided to relax a little and have a drink. She had been "working" every bar and restaurant and hadn't eaten.

She sat at the bar next to an older couple, ordered a Smithwick's, and asked to see a menu.

"Hi," a voice called out. "I'm Paul. I don't believe I've seen you in here before."

"Hi," Rebecca said as she turned around to see the older gentleman with the Irish accent standing behind her. "No, first time. I'm traveling from out of town. Texas, actually."

"Really?" Paul asked as he slipped into the space between the chair and the rail.

"Yes, I am a reporter on assignment," Rebecca said as she began to tell him the details and some of the others sitting in the area began to listen in.

As Rebecca gave out all the details to those that were listening she passed around her phone and let them scroll through the few pictures she had of David.

"You know," Paul said scratching the razor stubble on his face, "the bloke does look familiar. But the name ... It's not ringing a bell."

One of the other regulars chimed in. "I've seen him in here Paul, but not for years now. I can't remember his name and David just doesn't sound right."

As people chatted Rebecca jotted a few notes. It was too loud for the digital recorder. This was the most progress she had made since the city where the trail dried up.

The night wore on and as the crowd got younger, less and less people found him familiar looking and any correlation to a name was gone.

As she took a look at the time and paid her bill, she looked at her digital planner on her phone and her schedule. The trail was warm here, but if she wanted to try Wallingford, Vermont she would need to leave by midafternoon tomorrow the latest.

She said good-bye to the remaining people she talked with earlier, thank them for their help, and handed out a few more business cards. She then left started her walk back up the hill to where she parked her car.

As she walked she thought about the interactions. He gut was telling her that this was the right place. She debated not going up to Vermont. This was more than another stop on her journey. This was the last stop.

Back at the Irish pub, one of the older women that was sitting with one of her friends and listening in on the exchange excused herself and stepped outside the bar. As she watched Rebecca walk up the street she looked at her cell phone and noticed it was nearly 11 p.m.

"Barbara," she texted, "I was going to call you, but I thought it might be too late. Someone came into the pub tonight looking for Michael. Call me. I'll be out until midnight or call in the morning."

Morning came and Rebecca sprang out of bed as she realized it was nearly 9 a.m. The drive up the day prior and the late night took more out of her than she realized. As she walked around the room looking to get into the shower all the events from the final stop last night swam in her head.

She jumped in the shower to get cleaned up and ready so she could head back out. She continued to mentally run through last night's events and conversations. When she got out of the shower, she compared what she remembered to her notes to make sure she hadn't missed anything.

As she was going over the notes and making small notations, her cell phone rang.

"Hello," she said after reviewing the number.

"Yes, hello, is this Rebecca Wilson?" the voice on the other end of the line asked.

"Yes, good morning, it is," Rebecca said as she grabbed her notepad and tucked the cell phone onto her shoulder.

"Yes, good morning," the woman caller said as she cleared her throat. "Can you please tell me why you're looking for Michael Anderson?"

Rebecca jotted the name down quickly and then spoke. "I'm sorry, there must be some confusion. I am from the Westville Press and I am here as part of a news project regarding David Stephenson."

"I see," she said somewhat withdrawn. "You met someone I knew last night at the Irish pub and she indicated something different in a text to me. I do apologize."

"Wait," Rebecca quickly replied. "Have you lived in town a long time?"

"My whole life. I've never lived anywhere else."

"It's possible you know the person I am covering in this story."

"I don't think so," the woman caller responded. "The name David Stephenson doesn't ring any bells with me."

"I'm sorry to impose, but would it be possible for me to meet you? Perhaps after a little conversation with you, and you look at the picture, it might jar you memory. Or perhaps you give me some other information that leads me to another person that can help."

Rebecca listened to the woman just breathe into the phone on the other end.

"I'm almost out of time. The deadline for this story is due shortly and the trail back to this man almost went dry in New York City. I am here in Wallingford on basically dumb luck."

"How long have you been working on this story?"

"About three weeks," Rebecca responded.

"Are you able to discuss the details with me? I have certain … issues … if you will, with some reporters and their reporting."

"Yes ma'am, I can understand. This story is all about a man that has been wandering the country for four years. He's been helping people and disappearing without a trace. Hold on," Rebecca said as she texted over one of David's pictures. "I just sent you a picture of him."

The woman pulled the phone away to look at the photo, and then without further hesitation she said, "My name is Barbara Killingly. I would like to speak with you. I will text you my home address and plan to meet you here."

Rebecca got the address on the phone and then got dressed to leave.

A short while later, she pulled up to a modest ranch home on a residential street. As she got out of the car she took a quick look around at all the homes on the street in the quiet little neighborhood.

As she turned to walk up the driveway, the side door at the driveway opened up by a woman who appeared to be in her mid-fifties, with short cropped salt and pepper hair.

"Rebecca Wilson?" she called out.

"Yes, ma'am," Rebecca replied.

"Barbara is just fine," she said as she smiled slightly and let her into the kitchen.

The two entered the home and Barbara extended her arm in a motion for Rebecca to sit down at the kitchen table.

Rebecca sat at the chair on one of the long sides of the table, turned on the digital recorder, and placed her notepad down.

"Can I get you anything to drink?" Barbara asked as she walked briefly into the adjacent room.

"No, thank you, I'm all set," Rebecca said as she quickly looked about the kitchen. "So did that photo jar you memory at all?" Rebecca asked as Barbara walked back into the room.

Barbara handed two framed photos to Rebecca as she took a seat at the head of the kitchen table.

One was a picture of the man she knew as David in a tuxedo with a bride on his arm and the other photo was of the same two people years later and a daughter.

"Your David Stephenson is my Michael Anderson," Barbara said softly. "His wife there is Carol, my baby sister, and the little girl there is their daughter Penny."

Chapter Twenty-Eight

Rebecca sat motionless in Barbara's kitchen doing nothing more than staring at the pictures she was holding. She suddenly realized she never actually thought much about what the end result of her research might bring. She quickly acknowledged to herself that this was not a scenario that she might have thought of.

"So it appears to me that you're in a little bit of shock. I take it the reporting and investigating has at least a little bit of a personal tie," Barbara said calmly for as much her sake as Rebecca's.

"Honestly, yes," Rebecca said as she slowly set the framed pictures down on the kitchen table without removing her stare from them.

"You surprised me a little, to be honest," Barbara said. "You look a little young to be a travelling reporter. You must be good at what you do."

"My employer has a lot of faith in me to uncover the truth," Rebecca said weakly.

"They should," she said very plainly. "You backtracked a man that the private investigator the family hired couldn't find moving forward from the starting point."

Rebecca looked up and smiled just slightly.

"So since it seems as if you have some level of personal interest and investment, as I do, why don't you tell me what brought you here and then from there I can fill you in on the piece of the story you're missing?"

Rebecca shook her head and took a minute to begin collecting her thoughts. Once she was done, Rebecca spent the next two hours telling Barbara all about the man she and others in Westville knew as David. How he came into the town and almost immediately won the hearts and minds of everyone there. How he connected with Caroline and helped her with the project with the library and how the entire town followed his lead.

She hedged quite a bit about his involvement with Maria. She didn't know what the situation was, and she didn't want to throw David under the bus.

She also outlined Brian Kurtvow's involvement with the library project and finished up with Zachary's involvement with it as well, including his part of the effort for financing the effort to report on David's story.

"Interesting," Barbara said. "So Zachary Taylor sent you on this endeavor without Michael's knowledge?"

"Yes," Rebecca responded, still trying to get used to the new moniker for David. "I take it you were aware of their friendship."

"Yes. Not all the details, of course, but I know he helped Zachary stem a hostile takeover for which he really owes Michael everything. Money is not Zachary's largest driver, despite what everyone reads. He cares about that company and the employees."

"Yes. In some ways he's like Dav… Michael. Underneath all the energy that simply seems to drive him, the man cares deeply," Rebecca replied.

"Too much so, the both of them, really," Barbara offered as she got up for a glass of juice. She offered some to Rebecca, who accepted. "So I would like to know, is Michael happy?"

Rebecca didn't know how to answer.

"Ah," Barbara said. "That's good. He deserves that. I suppose it is my turn to tell you our end of the story."

Rebecca slowly reached for her notepad and also switched back on the digital recorder she had paused prior.

"Michael Anderson met my sister in the summer of 1999. He was thirty and she was twenty-five. It was love at first sight for them both. We used to tease how 'ill' it made all of us, as they were both so sickly sweet with each other. They were married the following summer in 2000," Barbara said as she pointed over to the picture of the two of them.

"Carol was a Business Analyst. A really successful one. Michael was a Financial Investment Analyst. He was the best there was. Not only did he understand the ebb and flow of many businesses, especially technology, their cycles, and the overall economic trends, he understood most people even better than they understood themselves. He could read their emotions, desires, wants, and needs. He'd then either feed into them or deprive them, whichever got him the results he needed or wanted for what he was doing. I used to joke with him, 'Don't ever use your powers for evil,' because it was amazing what he could do."

Barbara sat forward a little and folded her hands on the table.

"They wanted a family. My sister wanted three kids, and I think Michael wanted a basketball team. They got pregnant with Penny, but it was a very difficult pregnancy. It almost cost my sister's life and unborn Penny. That was enough for Michael to call off any others. He used to say, 'Count your blessings; count the important ones twice.' With that episode he was good with just Penny. His daughter was the 'other woman' he loved her so much."

Rebecca smiled and stood for a moment to stretch and continued to listen.

"They made plenty of money on either of their salaries alone, but Michael made much more. So they decided to start taking it easy on their master plan since it was more or less on track. A two or three year delay wasn't a big issue and they lived way below their means. They lived like Joe and Jane Wallingford to a certain degree. He had some expenses and tastes, like a vacation home for example, but they had excessive money for it. No one publicly knew how much money they were actually worth. The overall plan was to set up investments that acted like lifetime annuities that generated an income stream that not only sustained themselves but grew the principle. In effect, they would be perpetual."

Rebecca sat back down as Barbara continued.

"Michael worked ridiculous hours and travelled all over. It cut deeply into their time together as a family, but he was planning to hit that self-set cash target and then turn his back on the world of work and spend the rest of the time with Carol and Penny."

"He raked in more and more deals and bonuses. He paid off the homes, the cars, the boat, and other things. He paid off the mortgage on this house. My parents moved to Florida. He paid for their home down there and paid the movers to ship all their things with them. He stockpiled those investments and he was finally there."

Rebecca leaned in and had to consciously make herself continue to take notes because she would get so engrossed in the story she would stop.

"That day came in 2009, a little after Penny's seventh birthday. He gave notice at work. He was done and ready to retire at forty. His employer as well as everyone else he knew in the financial and technical communities were shocked. This guy was such a mover and a shaker. All the money aside, the man would die of boredom. But the family, we knew better. He loved being a father and a husband. All he wanted was to matter and to two people he was the whole world. It was all he really needed and all he wanted."

Barbara paused for a moment to collect herself.

"It was a Friday evening. Michael was at his final day of work in the offices and everyone was going out afterwards to his retirement party. Chris, Michael's boss, invited Carol to come as a surprise and told her to bring Penny. He figured it was a great way to start the next portion of their lives together, at the ending celebration of his previous one."

Rebecca saw the uneasiness in Barbara's demeanor as she attempted to finish.

"It was around the end of the day. There was some sun glare at play and another driver not paying enough attention. They were unable to react. It was a horrible accident ..."

Barbara couldn't finish as her emotions overwhelmed her and she began to cry steadily. After a few moments, she recovered and continued.

"Michael didn't know they were coming, only Chris did, and he figured they were just running late. Around the end of the party Michael got the call on his cell phone and he raced to the hospital. They both died at the scene. They pronounced formally at the hospital once he arrived."

Barbara got up from the table and walked over to the kitchen sink and looked out the window into her backyard.

"They were buried on the following Monday. We were all devastated. Michael obviously took it the hardest. Everything he worked for, everything he planned, was now off the rails. There was no way that his life was going to move forward in any semblance of what he had originally intended."

Rebecca sat quietly and again recalled the words David had said to her before she left, *Life happens while you're busy making other plans. You have to grab onto it when you can and ride it for all it's worth.* This time those words had quite a different meaning in the context of everything she was hearing. She imagined that he always said it to others with his life in mind.

"Michael became a stranger to himself and anyone that knew him," Barbara continued. "He wasn't the same man anymore. He was depressed and broken, two things that were a polar opposite of the man he used to be. He spent the better part of a full year that way. He shut out our family. He was adopted and had no remaining family from his adoptive parents. I guess he felt we couldn't help him or that he needed to be this way to protect what was left of himself. The shell of the man that remained. He used to drink socially but did so much more often after the accident, but I feel he did it more to self-medicate. At least he never went out, it was just a danger to himself."

"He called me one day out of the blue. It was a little more than a year after everything had happened. He said he wasn't feeling well and wanted to go to the doctor but that he didn't feel confident enough to drive. I told him I would come and get him, so I did. When I got there, he didn't look well at all. He dropped a lot of weight and he looked sullen. I told him that if the doctor wanted any blood work drawn, he'd have to let the booze out of his system for a few days to get a good blood reading. He indicated to me he hadn't had a drink in two weeks at that point. He explained to me that he felt strange and thought it might have been the drinking so he stopped to let his system flush out. I can't imagine what he looked like two weeks prior."

Barbara turned away from the window and looked back to Rebecca.

"So the doctor did request further tests and blood work. In the end the diagnosis was like insult to injury. Glioblastoma Multiforme, a tumor of the brain. The main issues with GBM is that the tumor cells are very resistant to conventional therapies and because the brain has a limited capacity to repair itself, it is susceptible to damage due to conventional therapies. Any drugs that are available to treat the condition cannot cross the blood–brain barrier to act on the tumor. The life expectancy is eighteen months maximum in most cases, sometimes twenty-four. Given that, after he disappeared, I figured he died at least a year ago."

Rebecca again was shocked as she had just seen David about a month ago. "Are nose bleeds with this condition common?" she asked.

"Possibly, as the brain tissue gets damaged. If damage had caused bleeding and it evacuated through his nose, he is lucky.

Usually that bleeding is intracranial, adds pressure in the cavity, and causes additional issues. More common symptoms are seizure, nausea and vomiting, headache, temporary memory loss. There is also the possibility of progressive memory loss and, or, personality changes, when there is temporal and frontal lobe impact by the tumor. If he was fully functional for lack of a better term then he's been very lucky."

Rebecca just started to collect all her things slowly.

"I guess there's not a whole lot more to the story for you. That would be everything."

"Do you know specifically why he left and decided to wander?"

"Not exactly. He technically didn't say good-bye or where he was going to go or what he was going to do. He simply sold everything he had, the property, the cars, the vacation home, and packed some clothes and a laptop into a big green duffle bag. He told me he was going to travel. He wasn't sure where he was going to go but that he only had thirty more days at the time after the closing to vacate the house. When I went by a week later, he was nowhere to be found and no one ever saw him again."

"Barbara, I cannot thank you enough for everything. For me, this now goes beyond doing this story for the sake of the story. It is now about the man that was wandering around selflessly helping people who needs help himself."

"If you would, will you please tell him the Killingly family still thinks of him often. We were devastated to lose Carol and Penny. Losing him, too, was just as much a loss for us."

"I will, I promise. It'll be one of the first things I tell him once I get home to Westville."

Chapter Twenty-Nine

Days later, after returning to Houston and writing up the details of her investigation as a story for publication, Rebecca sat in Zachary Taylor's office to let him review her story outline and the hard copy of the actual story as she intended to print it.

He reviewed the details of Michael's journey as David, backwards from Westville. Zachary had been aware of some of the places he visited and the people he helped, but not all of them. He also was fully aware of the loss of his daughter and wife.

The part that was totally unknown to him was the fact that he was terminally ill—that was the missing piece he was looking for.

Rebecca watched Zachary read over the story. She watched the expressions on his face change, and from them she knew the things he was aware of and the things that surprised him.

After he finished, he got up from his desk and walked over to one of his windows and looked out of it. "You did a fantastic job with this. You really have."

"Thank you," Rebecca said as she smiled slightly. "I needed the help in New York, so thank you for that as well."

Zachary turned around looking as surprised as he could. "New York? I'm not sure I follow."

"No one else had the exact information I needed except you. The trail was gone. If you hadn't helped, we wouldn't have known all of it. Or maybe you could have gotten the rest since you knew the family. I would have been stopped cold."

Zachary said nothing more about it but then needed to broach a new subject with her.

"So I know you have been gone and are looking forward to getting home and being able to directly contact friends and family again. Now that the sequester is over, you're basically free to do so, but there are things I need to tell you first—and given your information here from your talk with Barbara—it's a bad situation made worse."

"Oh no. Did he …?"

"Die suddenly? No, I'm sorry, I didn't mean to startle you like that. Technically, it's worse. He left—the day after the bazaar and the day you came out here to leave on the research. I didn't know until several days after when Maria called me. And of course I didn't know of his being terminal until basically now."

"He didn't contact you?" Rebecca asked.

"No. And it's my understanding after talking to some people that he didn't get any help from Brian Kurtvow and he didn't leave with his trucker friend, either. What bothers me is that I think he knew this was it. Westville was his last stop."

Zachary looked at the article again and looked at Rebecca. "I guess that means you'll have to change the way you ended the article."

"Yes, I will need to in light of this new information. I can get it to you by the end of the day tomorrow."

Zachary nodded in agreement and looked down at his desk. "I can get you transportation back to Westville. Maria and Caroline have taken this very hard. The people have, too, but obviously for those two it was worse. They are going to need to be told all of this. That will not be an easy thing to do nor will it be easy for them to hear."

"Zachary, can I ask you something?"

"Sure."

"Will this story make things better or worse? All of the people I talked to that made little connections to David, knowing more to the story might have brought them some closure. Even if he was terminal, if he decided to stay in Westville, I believe that they would look at it like a peaceful ending. If he is going to die, at least he was surrounded by people who loved him. Now he's off and alone. I don't know that is any better than not knowing, and I have to wonder if that wasn't what David was doing. By leaving, he was trying to spare everyone his dying."

Zachary thought about Rebecca's comments for a moment before answering. "I don't know. I hope we get the chance to ask him."

"How can we if we don't know where he is?"

Zachary just smiled a bit and moved her story forward slightly on the desk.

"Let's get you home. Your parents are sure to have missed you and Maria could use her friend back."

They left the office together. Rebecca spent the time thinking about the story and how she wrote it as they walked down to the cars in the transportation pool. She started to think about getting home to work on the article for the Westville Press and then publishing the edition.

Her mind also wandered to David and then to Maria and Caroline. She was still processing the whole situation. His being married, having a daughter, losing his family, being terminally ill, falling in love again, and then making the choice to walk away. The thought that he might have done that to spare them the fact he was ill echoed in her head.

As she climbed into one of the cars that would take her to the airport, she decided that she would just do what she felt was the right thing to do. She would impartially tell the story as she learned it and let the people make up their own minds. It wasn't her responsibility to make the decisions for them.

Several hours later, nightfall came to Westville.

Maria returned to her apartment after work and was now sitting with Charlotte at the kitchen table.

"It will be nice to see Rebecca again," Charlotte said to Maria, who was a combination of happy to see her friend again but also upset at not knowing what the assignment was until after the fact.

"I am anxious," Maria said as she walked over to close Caroline's door more now that she was asleep. "She said she had so many details to share with me, but she did not want to tell me over the phone from the airport."

"She did say it was complicated," Charlotte responded quietly.

"I am almost at a point where I am uncertain if I want to re-engage. I spent a lot of energy trying to let him go over these few weeks since he left. I am uncertain if this will be closure for me or reopening the wound," Maria said as she sat at the kitchen table. "With the holidays coming up, I have to wonder if it will not make things worse."

A short while later, Rebecca parked the family car in the lot and made her way up to Maria's apartment.

As she entered, Maria hugged her and got a little misty eyed. Rebecca gave Charlotte a slight kiss on the cheek and then the three of them made their way over to the kitchen table and sat.

Rebecca opened up her laptop and called up the document that was to be her article. She sighed as she looked at it. "I don't know if it makes sense to read it aloud to you or just tell it to you. Either way, I know you're going to have questions."

"Until I know where he went, how he is feeling, if he is safe, and if he is happy, I will always have questions," Maria said plainly.

Rebecca decided to read the story she wrote for the paper.

As she read the story, she tried to look up at Charlotte and Maria when she could. She was trying to judge their reactions to her written content as a gauge whether it was good or not.

There was a sense of pride that she saw from the two of them as "their" David helped the Miller's defend their home. Maria also appreciated learning how he helped Peter. There were other small stories that were heartfelt that she read to them. Rebecca did the stories out of chronological order as she tried to stack them up from smaller efforts to larger ones.

Her second to last story was regarding Lisa Bennett. By the time Rebecca finished reading that piece of the article, all three of the women were crying.

"*Dios mío,*" Maria said softly. "What if David was there a day later? She might likely be gone."

Charlotte wiped a tear from her eye. Rebecca stared just a little, as it was uncharacteristic for her to shed any tears.

Rebecca read the next segment, which was all about Westville and that look of happiness and pride returned to both women.

As she finished that section, she looked at Maria and said, "I really need you to be prepared for the next section, Maria."

Maria looked plainly at her.

"It will be unsettling, but you will need to allow me to read the whole thing."

"I do not like the sound of that, but I believe I have little other choice."

Rebecca started with the next section of her article:

"As I reached New England and the large town of Wallingford, I would finally uncover the history of the man we in Westville, and many others along the I-10 and I-95 corridor, knew as David Stephenson.

That man didn't exist in Wallingford. He existed there as Michael Anderson. Michael was a Financial Investment Analyst, one of the best in the industry, a complement given to him by other industry experts and his own peers. He was married in 2000 to Carol Anderson, formally Killingly, of Wallingford. In 2002, the couple had a daughter named Penny. While the couple had hoped for a larger family, Carol's pregnancy was a difficult one and they made the decision to not have any other children."

Rebecca needed to pause to take a sip of water as her throat was drying out. She looked at the look of shock on Maria's face and was concerned about what would follow.

"2009 was to be the family's pinnacle year from a financial perspective. The years of work and investment persistence, as well as living well within their means, allowed the Anderson's to reach a level of financial independence where Michael was able to retire at the age of forty. He gave his retirement notice shortly after Penny's seventh birthday. His plans, with no other major life changes, were to simply spend his life as a father and a husband."

Maria sat motionless and more stoic than she was before until Rebecca slid her left hand over and took her right hand. At that point, Maria's heart jumped and she became anxious.

"Please," Maria said as a worried look came over her face, "I need to know the rest."

Charlotte sat quietly as she really did not know how to respond.

Rebecca took another drink of water and slowly continued. "On the evening of Michael's final day of work, he was celebrating at his retirement party, and Carol and Penny were traveling in the family car the short thirty miles to surprise him. Fate cut their trip short. A wayward driver, who lost sight of the road between sun glare and a pitted windshield, crossed the centerline and collided with the car head on. Before the retirement party ended, Michael was called to the hospital to be with his family. His wife and daughter died on the impact and were pronounced dead at his arrival."

Maria slowly lowered her head and sobbed openly. Charlotte was openly crying as well.

Rebecca was also in tears, as she had been each of the times she wrote and then rewrote this section of the article. After a few minutes, she simply filled in the rest of the details without referring back to the article. "They were buried on the following Monday. His sister-in-law, Barbara Killingly, told me that Michael withdrew himself from just about everything at that point for the better part of a year."

Maria continued to cry without looking up.

"I'm not going to read any more of this because, when I wrote this, I didn't know David had left, so there are changes I need to make."

Maria nodded without looking up. Rebecca glanced over at Charlotte with a worried look on her face.

"Maria, there's more," Rebecca said as Maria slowly looked up. Rebecca closed up the laptop and took Maria's right hand in both of hers.

"He's terminally ill. He found out a year after the accident and was given eighteen months to live. He's past that mark by about eighteen months."

Maria trembled as the words sunk in. She wanted to breakdown and scream, but she didn't want to wake Caroline. *How will I tell Caroline* she thought as her emotions swelled between anger and sadness.

The three women sat in silence and in their own thoughts for a long while after Rebecca finished up.

Charlotte finally stood slowly and spoke. "God never gives you more than you can handle. I am sure David could have gone his whole life not knowing he could withstand what he's been through."

"And he is gone," Maria said angrily as she got out of her seat quickly. "He has gone off to die. He stood on the bridge ledge with a stranger and told her 'No one deserves to die alone' and he refused to let her. Yet he has left all of us who care deeply for him to do just that. I cannot believe the depth of his hypocrisy. I cannot believe he was that selfish."

Maria turned and exited the kitchen for her bedroom where she collapsed on her bed.

Chapter Thirty

Zachary sat in his corporate office reviewing the changes to the article that Rebecca made since she had returned home. Since she had been working on the assignment and sequestered from anything that was going on in Westville, she was unaware that David had left. When she worked on the original article draft for him, it had ended with David staying in Westville.

Zachary pulled his desk chair over in front of the windows that overlook his corporate campus. He took the hard copy of Rebecca's new draft and set it down, and then decided to read the prior one an additional time.

As he scanned through the older article, he compared a few small notational changes she made throughout the piece. He then focused on the ending of the original article.

Michael Anderson, as himself and his alter ego David Stephenson, despite a huge personal loss in the deaths of his wife and daughter and a terminal diagnosis, was many different things to many different people. He was a friend, a confidant, a leader, a hero, and an angel. As a citizen of Westville myself, I counted him as all of the above.

We all hope that he might be able to live out the remainder of his days in relative peace and as much happiness as he might be lucky enough to have. I know we will all try to give him that as much as we are able. In our eyes, just from how he helped all of us, we realize no one deserves it more. Now that we know his whole story, we realized just how right we were.

Zachary set down that copy and sighed.

"Why on Earth would you walk, man?" he asked himself.

Zachary got up from his chair and walked over to his desk and called Beverly, his assistant.

"Yes, Mr. Taylor?"

"Beverly, please call the senior staff for a meeting in the corporate conference room," Zachary paused to look at the time, "at the half hour for a one-hour meeting. If they have other meetings, tell them to cancel them. This is mandatory and a priority meeting."

"Yes, sir," she said as she began looking at schedules on the computer.

"Thank you, Beverly. I will also need the head of HR in here and one of our senior accountants. From them, I will need headcount and daily payroll numbers ready for the meeting. It should be quick for them to pull from the system from last quarter. Also, tell them I want the third quarter numbers and fourth quarter projections. We were discussing last week, so it shouldn't be a big deal for them to have this ready and on hand last minute."

"Will do, Mr. Taylor."

"I'll need someone from Corporate Communications. Debbie Connelly if she is in today."

"Yes, sir."

Zachary hung up and walked to the windows and stood at them and stared back out them. He watched his employees walk around on the campus grounds in the late November afternoon either going from building to building or just to take a break.

He then turned, sat, and reviewed Rebecca's rewrite of the article.

Michael Anderson, as himself and his alter ego David Stephenson, despite a huge personal loss in the deaths of his wife and daughter and a terminal diagnosis, was many different things to many different people. He was a friend, a confidant, a leader, a hero, and an angel. As a citizen of Westville myself, I counted him as all of the above.

It may have been too much to hope that he might be able to live out the remainder of his days in relative peace and as much happiness as he might be lucky enough to have. We had hoped he might have found that peace and happiness with us. After I returned from my assignment, I had discovered that David had decided to move on again, and he did so without leaving a trace as to where he was going.

David's message to Lisa Bennett that night on McKenzie Bridge was crystal clear. It was so pivotal to her that it made her pause and reconsider. No one deserves to die alone.

We can only hope the man that meant so much to so many has the opportunity to remember and heed his own words and come home to Westville.

Zachary spent the next few minutes pondering tasks ahead of him. After some additional time of just staring out the window to the campus below, he took his cell phone out and placed a call to Dennis Lewis out of his stored numbers.

"Dennis here," the gruff voice on the other end of the line answered.

"Dennis, it's Zachary Taylor. How are you today?"

"Zachary, I haven't heard from you in quite some time. The weather's been too random lately to play golf so you must need a favor," Dennis replied sarcastically.

"Well, in a way I do suppose it's a partial favor for me, and also to you."

"Really?" Dennis asked. "I'm intrigued. Go on."

"Thanksgiving is next Thursday, and I know all you editors like to try to be the first one to lock on to that one special interest story that captures the season and gets all the notoriety."

"We do, that's true. Stories like that, especially this time of the year, if they become the one that rises to the top, become the talk of the season."

"I not only have the story, it's right out of our great state and it's already written. The reporter is Rebecca Wilson from the Westville Press. I'll send it to you. Look it over. When you are done, I am sure you'll be convinced that nothing more needs to be done than print it in the Thanksgiving holiday edition and get it out on the news wire as *Special to the Texas Daily News.*"

"Well, then, please do. With all the gloom and doom we've been printing, we could use a story like that, time of the year notwithstanding."

"I'll send it over shortly. Let me know if it'll work for that Thanksgiving holiday edition."

"Who is the reporter, anyway? I've never heard of Rebecca Wilson or the Westville Press, for that matter," Dennis said as he jotted the names down on a pad.

"That is an oversight that I think you might want to take the time to correct. Read the story first. I'm convinced you'll take my word for regarding both by the time you're done."

"Looking forward to it Zachary. Thank you much."

As he wrapped up his call, Beverly called into his office. "Mr. Taylor, everyone is gathered and ready for you."

Zachary put on his suit jacket and headed into the corporate conference room where the senior officers sat waiting for him.

"Gentlemen," he said as he entered the room. "Ladies, how are you?" He went to the front of the room and took a seat.

"Okay, I know this was very last minute and I want to thank all of you for coming. I hope I didn't disrupt too many other meetings or tee times," he said, and a small wave of laughter moved through the room. "I'll make sure we're out plenty ahead of happy hour as well."

Zachary got up from his seat and slowly walked around the room as he spoke.

"Jackie, can you please tell me what our numbers were last quarter, what our projections are for the final quarter, and what that would mean for our overall numbers for the year? I don't need all the details—just the high recap. I think I remember them all from the prior meeting and I just want to confirm that."

Jackie quickly went through the papers she was asked to bring with her and reviewed the numbers.

"Well, we had revenue of $13.3 billion in the third quarter, we are projecting $14 billion this quarter, and we are ahead of target to date, actually. Overall, we are looking at $58 billion for the end of the fiscal and calendar year."

"Diana, can you quickly calculate for me, at a high level, what additional costs there would be, if any, for granting the three additional days off on Thanksgiving week? We already pay on Thanksgiving and that Friday. If we paid the additional three days, what costs are involved?"

"Sir?"

"Well, we'd still need to cover technical support calls, our critical care support lines, as well as sales and corporate paid support. If we gave comp days for the people who still had to work, what is the additional overhead for the company to do that?"

Diana reviewed the data that she had with her quickly. "I can't give you an exact number, honestly. I can give you an estimate. It's a little difficult on the fly, but it's technically no worse than daily payroll. Against our average salary of four hundred dollars a day, ninety-three thousand employees, three days ... It rounds out at $100 million, approximately."

There were some gasps around the room and Zachary held up his hand. "Yes, but this is not a true expenditure of $100 million, correct?"

"Well, that is true," Diana added. "It's sort of like a sick day. Since the majority of the people are salaried, the costs are baked-in costs. This is not new money but just lost work, really. If we simply offered the people who have to work those three days, three other comp days, it is just coverage, shortages on staff, and a little lost productivity. It probably amounts to about $10 million in hard costs to the company. That would be a guess off the top of my head."

Zachary continued to circle the room.

"At the end of the year, I am due another stock share grant as part of my compensation. How many shares am I due?"

"Well, as you know, the number of shares is based totally on company performance and the dollar amount of the grant is calculated at the cost per share at the time. So using the current projections your end of year grant should be about one million shares. Based on yesterday's closing price, that is $14 million," Diana said as she looked up at him from her paperwork.

"What paperwork is required to rescind the grant back to the company to cover the costs we expect against the three days off I want to implement?"

"I would have to research it, as we've never done that before."

"Then let's look into it. We are going to give the employees that week off, but I am not about to have it come on the back of the company."

Zachary walked around the far side of the table and continued. "Debbie, this will get play in the press, I'm sure. It's not my intention to get press play out of it, but it will by its nature. When calling for response, I am going to have you direct them to a news story regarding Michael... David, David Stephenson. We are granting our employees the full week of Thanksgiving off in honor of David Stephenson."

After some more discussion and planning, the meeting ended with Zachary's plan in place to grant all the employees of his company the extended holiday.

He sent along that additional information to Dennis at the *Texas Daily News* along with the corporate communication that Debbie drafted with him. Attached to the press release was Rebecca's story regarding David.

Dennis sat and read the story with his assistant editor and publisher, Margie Kenworth.

As they both finished, Dennis looked at Margie, who was drying her eyes, and quietly said, "I believe we have our holiday story."

Chapter Thirty-One

Caroline sat at the table in McNally's, next to Rebecca and her parents, as Kevin McNally put the big screen on America Nation News. Other patrons in the restaurant sat around the room watching the big screen. Mel and Charlotte were sitting with Jim Davenport and his wife at the next table. Kevin McNally came over and took a seat next to his wife.

"Mama, tell me again why we came here tonight to eat?" Caroline asked.

"Well, do you remember Rebecca wrote her new story for the Westville Press?" Maria asked as she set her beer down on the table.

"Yes. I remember it ended up in the big newspaper," Caroline said proudly and smiled at Rebecca.

"That is correct. The story ended up running in the *Texas Daily News*. As part of that story that she wrote, Mr. Taylor gave his workers extra time off around Thanksgiving. He wanted them to spend a little extra time with their families before the holiday rush began. Those two events sparked news interest. Do you remember the news crews that came here a few days ago to interview people?"

"I do. I answered some questions from the news lady," Caroline said proudly.

"Yes. Today is supposed to be the broadcast on the *America Nation News*. They have the segment at the end of their news each night called 'News from Across America.' "

"Here we go," Kevin announced as the segment started.

The announcer came on the screen and started the segment.

"Sean Layman here, and tonight on our December twelfth edition of "News from Across America" segment, reporter Kelly

Rodriguez traveled from New England to Texas following the journey of Michael Anderson, who was known by most along his journey as David Stephenson."

The news segment cut away from the main anchor desk to Kelly at the assignment desk.

"Thank you, Sean. Our story comes out of the pages of the *Texas Daily News*, Texas' largest daily newspaper, who ran an article special from the *Westville Press* and their local reporter Rebecca Wilson."

McNally's lit up with applause as Rebecca's name was mentioned. She looked at her parents, who were smiling.

"Rebecca travelled on assignment to uncover the journey of David Stephenson, a drifter who arrived two months earlier in Westville, Texas. Normally, a drifter might not normally garner much attention from folks except for some extra scrutiny as a stranger. But that is not how Westville saw him."

The shot moved away from the assignment desk to a video of the outside of Charlotte's Place as the assignment reporter's voiceover continued.

"In the little town of Westville, Texas, they are used to people coming and going along State Route 385. Other than the fact that David indicated he was looking to stay for a bit and looking for some work, he was not much different at first than anyone else coming through."

The shot panned first to a photo of David at Caroline's birthday, and then to Charlotte "We get our share of folks coming and going. When David came into town, he arrived with a regular traveler that more or less vouched for him, so when he asked for work and a place to stay we were able to help out."

The scene cut to Peter Dempsey standing alongside his truck in the parking lot of Charlotte's Place. "I had met David a few months back. He was drifting along I-10, and I met him at a diner. I talked with him for a spell, and he was a good listener. I needed someone to listen to me. I was in a bind."

The story cut back to Peter's truck, panned out and was followed up by a narrative by Kelly. "Peter Dempsey had gotten behind on income tax payments to the federal government and state property taxes where his truck was registered. As he worked to try to get caught up, the interest charges were mounting, and because he was making deliveries and trying to work to pay those bills, his communication wasn't the best with the collectors from the agencies, which only made matters worse."

The scene cut back to Peter at his truck. "I only know what I know. I'm really good at driving safely, being cost effective on my routes, and making my schedules on time. The rest I needed some guidance on, 'specially once I had fallen behind. I was in a jam and I didn't know anyone that had the knowledge to help me. Being a new independent driver was harder than I had imagined."

The scene cut back to a long stretch of Route 385 and Kelly's voice over. "But David Stephenson did. He spent the time helping Peter reach the right people at the federal government to get his payments locked so that he could pay them on a schedule. He also put Peter in touch with an accountant he knew so that he could better learn and understand the taxes and fees he needed to pay."

The report faded away from Route 385 and then focused in on a sign that showed the Clearwater town limits as Kelly's voiceover continued. "It wasn't the first time that David had come to someone's rescue, and it wouldn't be the last. The Millers from Clearwater Arkansas were nearly taken advantage of from a slick developer until David stepped in."

"We basically were going to lose our home to the developer" Kathy Miller said as the segment focused on their situation. "This strip mall was going to be built through here and part of the area was designated by the county for the use and the rest was being taken by eminent domain," she said as she was recorded sitting at her kitchen table. "The developer was lying to the people, telling them that they had the sell or the federal government was going to take the land away and give them nothing. We had no idea that we were supposed to get fair market value for the land and the home."

The shot panned to the outside of their new home. "We almost sold for next to nothing. David knew what the laws really were. He got State Senator Campbell involved. The developer got pinched. We were offered the proper fair market value for our home. In one fashion, we really didn't want to be made to move, but we didn't want to fight and live there near all that new build up. Because David shared with us what our rights were, we were relocated to a nice home not too far away from where we were before and the new place was a little more modern and cost us a little less so there was some money left over."

The shot panned back to Kelly, who wiped a tear away from her cheek. "I don't know what would have happened if David never wandered through."

"The man with tenacity and a lot of fortitude was also filled with compassion ..." Kelly's voiceover continued as the report changed to Lisa Bennett standing outside her home.

"He came into my life exactly when I needed someone to help me. He literally saved my life."

The story scene changed to a view of the McKenzie Bridge in East Oaks as Lisa's voiceover continued.

"I was behind on my rent to the point where I should have been evicted, but instead, I allowed myself to be taken advantage of physically in the hopes that maybe the next break I needed was going to come along in short order. Something, anything that would allow me to get back on track and get caught up. It made things worse. I hated myself and decided I was going to end it all."

The report shifted back to Lisa outside her home, breaking down emotionally. "This man was sitting next to me in the bar while I was drinking everything I could so I could end it without much pain, and he tried to talk to me. He tried to befriend me. I was as vile as I could be and it didn't faze him. I just stood and walked out. He followed me. He was not going to write me off like everyone else had and how I expected him to. We got to the bridge, and I started climbing onto the over ledge. He didn't stop me, but he climbed out there with me. Then he said to me, 'Can you tell me what you're planning to do?' So then I said, 'I am going to jump.' And I remember him saying something like, 'Okay. You are aware you won't survive the fall.' Then I swore at him and said, 'Of course I know that.' Then he said, 'Okay, as long as we're straight on that part. So let me know when you're ready.' I remember turning to him and asking him why. He said, 'So I can jump, too.' He said it so plainly, and I think he actually meant it. So I asked him, 'Why would you want to jump, too? If it's going to kill me, it will kill you.' With that he said very plainly, 'No one deserves to die alone, and tonight isn't going to be an exception.' He just stood with me and waited as I let everything sink in. Then he slowly got down and stood in front of me on the bridge pavement and said, 'Do you want to come down now?' Eventually, I climbed down and we sat on the ground for an hour or more before Highway Patrol came by. He got up and talked to the trooper. He said he would take responsibility to make sure I got home and I was safe."

"There were other acts of kindness and compassion by David during his travels, but Westville would be his greatest accomplishment," Kelly's voiceover continued as the images again focused on Westville. "Upon his arrival, he met Maria Moreno and her daughter Caroline. Caroline had an idea to restore a project to the local library that had been cancelled years before."

The video showed Maria and Caroline talking as Kelly's commentary continued. "A few years prior funding was set up as part of a bill that was originally sponsored by Senator Foreman that would have expanded the local library services as part of the West

Texas Infrastructure project. That project was to expand the cable television, cellular, and Internet fiber networks in rural areas."

"Near the end of the project, a storm rolled through with a large series of tornadoes. The damage that was caused from the storms took out many of the overhead lines, where they were, and some of the substation platforms that housed the systems and their main junction points. And that is where Caroline's idea was born."

"I wasn't exactly sure how to do it, but I knew I wanted to save the library," Caroline said as the images showed the old Westville municipal buildings and the library. "So I made the posters and asked the businesses to help hang them."

"And the businesses did." Kelly's commentary continued and the video cut over to Kevin McNally and Jim Davenport.

"When Caroline approached us to hang the posters in the store windows to help advertise the effort, we were happy to. It's a simple thing to do and that is the sort of thing we do around here," Jim Davenport said as the video showed his store and then cut back to him talking. "The businesses were willing to help in some way, but none of us had the skill or expertise for something of this scale. With everything always being as tight as it was, it wasn't as if we had any extra money to throw at it."

"That is where David Stephenson came in," Kelly continued.

Mel Porter continued as the shot panned to him. "He had as much energy for this as Caroline did. I knew something was going to happen when we were talking with him one day and the comment was made that this was a big dream of a little, enthusiastic, nine-year-old child and he defended it by saying, 'Children are not held back by the obstacles of adults. They are too young to see them.' From that moment on, I didn't know what to expect, but I knew something would get started from the effort."

"And it did," Kelly continued. "David and Caroline got the idea to hold a weekend bazaar to raise some of the funds. The businesses also donated cash. Brian Kurtvow, a local land and mineral ore rights magnate, was contacted to help out with some money and resources. David also called in the favor of an old friend: Zee Technologies founder and CEO Zachary Taylor."

"We were part of the original West Texas Infrastructure project," Zachary said as the shot panned to him in his corporate offices. "We were involved with providing some of the end user devices as the areas were connected. Once the storms occurred and the damage was done, the project stopped. Zee Technologies remained committed that if the effort was ever to continue, we'd immediately be involved again. I just never imagined my old friend Michael Anderson from New England was going to be the man to pull us back into it."

"The man everyone knew, from Atlantic City, New Jersey to Westville, Texas, as David Stephenson was really Financial Investment Analyst, Michael Anderson, a husband and father from Wallingford, Connecticut," Kelly continued. "What makes a successful, self-made, family man travel the country and help others? Personal tragedy."

The shot panned to Barbara Killingly. "Michael Anderson met my sister Carol in the summer of 1999. They were married the following summer in 2000 and Penny was born in 2002. They had hoped for a larger family, but Carol's pregnancy was a difficult one and they made the decision to not have any other children."

Kelly's voiceover continued. "2009 was to be the family's pinnacle year from a financial perspective. The years of work and investment persistence allowed the Anderson's to reach a level of financial independence where Michael was able to retire at the age of forty. He gave his retirement notice shortly after Penny's seventh birthday. With few foreseeable life changes, Michael was going to simply spend his life as a father and a husband."

The image turned to Rebecca who discussed her own reporting of that part of the story segment. "On the evening of Michael's final day of work, he was celebrating at his retirement party and Carol and

Penny were traveling in the family car the short thirty miles to surprise him. Fate cut their trip short. A wayward driver, who lost sight of the road between sun glare and a pitted windshield, crossed the centerline and collided with the car head on. Before the retirement party ended, Michael was called to the hospital to be with his family. His wife and daughter died on the impact and were pronounced at his arrival."

Rebecca fought to keep her objective composure. "They were buried on the following Monday. Barbara Killingly told me that Michael withdrew himself from just about everything at that point for the better part of a year."

"A year later, there was more devastating news for Michael," Kelly continued.

The shot returned to Barbara as her commentary was heard. "Michael called me out of the blue a little over a year later saying that he wasn't feeling well and wanted to go to the clinic but was unsure if he could drive. I picked him up and took him there. They ran a series of tests and blood work. In the end the diagnosis was Glioblastoma Multiforme, a tumor of the brain. GBM tumor cells are very resistant to conventional therapies because the brain has a very limited capacity to repair itself and it is susceptible to damage due to conventional therapies. The life expectancy is eighteen months maximum in most cases, sometimes twenty-four."

"With that," Kelly continued, "David sold everything he owned and set off on his journey. A journey that ended in Westville as much as anyone is aware."

The scene returned to Rebecca, "While I was off on the assignment, David packed up and left."

The camera cut to Maria who was somber in the scene. "It was a normal day like any other. He went upstairs to his apartment and when he did not return, that was when we discovered he packed up and, as far as we know, simply walked out of town along Route 385."

"Life returned to normal for most people in Westville that had come to know David. While they didn't understand his desire to leave being terminally ill, they have dealt with it as best they could," Kelly continued, as scenes from around Westville displayed.

"Unsure of his whereabouts and considering the possibility that his friend had passed from his affliction," Kelly said as the scene shifted to Zee Technologies corporate headquarters and the surrounding campus. "Zachary Taylor wanted a way to memorialize his friend."

"Above all other things and deep down, Michael was always about family. Whether his actual family or the families of others. I share the same sentiment and I wanted to make sure my own employees learned that message—nothing is more important than family—and I wanted to make sure they got a little more time with theirs."

"So on the Friday before the shortened Thanksgiving work week, Zachary Taylor held a companywide meeting and announced that he was going to forgo his planned 2014 stock grant, which is part of his compensation, and return it to the company to cover the costs of all the employees having the full week off."

"The people David helped around the country remembered him at Thanksgiving in their own ways," Kelly continued as scenes faded in and out of the people David helped. "Each of them thanking the man who walked into their lives with simple kindness and consideration that amounted to making major differences in their lives."

"Because of his illness and the stage it is presumed he is at," Kelly concluded in the segment as the image of David faded in one final time, "it is unlikely David is still doing much traveling or acts of kindness for others. For the families of Westville and the people who love him, the hopes are that he will have a change of heart and return."

The final scene showed a shot of Maria's kitchen with Charlotte, Caroline, and Maria sitting at the kitchen table getting ready to eat, and an open seat with a full place setting unoccupied.

The scene faded back to the studio and Kelly at the assignment desk and the shot panned out to take in the main news desk at well.

"A wonderful but sad holiday story," Sean said as he addressed Kelly. "So, as of today, no one knows the whereabouts of Michael Anderson or, as he is known on the road, David Stephenson?"

"No," Kelly responded. "We tried to follow his trail westward in the same manner that reporter Rebecca Wilson did eastward, but the trail was cold."

Sean finished the segment. "In the spirit of the season and that time of year that always seems to get so commercial, our family here at *America Nation News* hopes for the best for David. And we ask all our viewers to take the time to set their own thoughts aside to their families and loved ones."

As the segment finished, there was not a dry eye in McNally's or in many homes and businesses across the nation where the broadcast was viewed.

The news segment impacted each individual that watched it in a different way, as it meant different things to different people.

For the two critical care nurses at the community hospital in Wilcox, Arizona, it meant they finally had a name for their John Doe.

Chapter Thirty-Two

Charlotte and Maria entered the store on Tuesday morning to get it ready for the regulars that arrive. Caroline was close behind.

Mel porter was crossing the street as Maria stepped back outside to greet him.

Maria was about to say good morning when the sound of an approaching helicopter made them both turn.

They looked up and saw Brian Kurtvow's private helicopter flying low and coming up along Packer Road to make a turn to land on Charlotte's back property. Charlotte came out of the store as Deputy Mendoza patrolled by and slowed down at the sight.

As the helicopter came to rest, Caroline also came out of the store.

Brian Kurtvow exited the helicopter as it was down at station keeping. He ran off the back lot and over to the front of the building. "They found him," he shouted to Maria over the roar of the helicopter blades. "He's in a hospital in Wilcox, Arizona. I'm going to get you to my plane in El Paso and we can head straight over to Cochise County Airport."

Maria was stopped in her tracks, but she turned to Charlotte for direction.

"Take Caroline. Go," Charlotte yelled. "We'll make do without you."

Maria looked at Caroline, who started to cry. "We have to go, Mama. He's family."

Maria looked at Brian. "Should I change?"

"Let's go. We can deal with getting the two of you clothes there. Grab a purse or whatever you need for yourself and Caroline, and we can figure out the rest on the way."

A few short hours later, the trio found themselves at the community hospital in Wilcox. Local news crews from Tucson were already on the scene as the news quickly spread that the man taken in a few days prior might be David Stephenson.

Local law enforcement initially stopped them from entering the hospital, but hospital security intervened and allowed them through.

Attendants took them to the ICU, where David was hooked up to a number of systems and monitors.

Caroline ran up to the door and pressed her face up to it to try to see him. "Mama! Can we go in?"

"I have to find out, little one," she responded, upset at seeing him unconscious and nonresponsive.

A woman approached Maria and Brian from the waiting area with a small boy about half the age of Caroline in tow.

"Are you Maria? From the news?"

"I am," Maria responded firmly, despite being confused.

The woman shuddered and broke down crying immediately. Brian helped guide her back to a chair. Maria motioned Caroline over.

"Are you okay?" Brian asked.

"Deanna," she said as she nodded her head. She breathed in deeply a couple of times to try to catch her breath.

Brian walked to the fountain to get some water for her and then asked the station nurse when they could speak to the doctor. Deanna was just about settled as Brian returned.

"This is Patrick," she said pointing to the boy. "He's my son. He will be four in February. He wouldn't be, were it not for David. I let go of his hand for a second as we waited to cross the street, to put my wallet back in my purse. He wandered into the crosswalk."

She became unsettled again and cried some more. Maria sat next to her and put her hand on her knee.

"I don't know where he came from. I didn't notice him in the crosswalk a minute prior, but as I heard the brakes squeal from the car, I looked to see David scoop him up and take the impact of the car. He turned and used his whole body to absorb the hit as he went up onto the hood. When the car stopped, they slid off and David landed on his feet still holding my son. He placed Patrick down and said so softly, 'Always look both ways.' He watched Patrick run over to me. I was in shock, I couldn't move. The second Patrick reached me, he collapsed in the road. That was a week ago."

As Deanna finished up the attending doctor came over.

"I presume you are the folks we saw on the news the other night?" he asked as he motioned to them to step away. Brian moved over and Maria stood, motioning to Caroline to stay where she was a few steps away.

"We are," Brian said as they moved closer to the nurse's station.

"I guess with that I don't need to go into a lot of details on his condition since you are fully aware he is terminal. He was actually highly functional from what I now understand between the reports from Deanna the mother there and what I saw on the news report. Often people who are afflicted by this are gone by now, and in the months prior, are heavily impacted by their condition. For someone that was affected by this to have such a low, quality of life impact level, he was extremely fortunate."

Maria was listening to the doctor, but her gaze was through the glass, into David's room.

"On top of taking the body hit on the car, his head hit the windshield. It might not have caused the average person much more trauma than a mild concussion, but here, it's only complicated and aggravated his condition and made things worse. It's effectively accelerated his deterioration. He really hasn't been awake much since being brought in here. A little bit here and there and then he goes back out. All we can really do is keep him comfortable. To be quite blunt, his time is numbered in days only."

"Keep him as comfortable as possible. Send me the bills," Brian said as he turned to Maria. "Why don't you go in?"

"Can I?" Maria asked as she turned to the doctor.

"Go on. It kind of skirts a couple of our rules in the ICU, but they are only going to fire me once" the doctor said with a slight smile.

Maria waved over Caroline as Brian walked away with the doctor.

Caroline and Maria walked into the room. The sounds of beeping and hissing equipment were the only things that broke the silence of the room. Caroline walked over and put her small backpack on the ground and then took David's left hand in both of hers.

"His hands are cold," she said quietly as the tears ran down her mother's face.

"He is not well, Caroline. He has not been for some time. He never told anyone. There was nothing that anyone could have done for him and he did not want to burden anyone with his illness."

"Why wouldn't he tell anyone?"

"I do not know, really. I cannot ask him. I have to imagine that he was such a strong and proud man that he did not want anyone to see him once he reached this state."

"But the lady said he was hit by the car," Caroline said softly.

"Yes, that is true, but because he was sick he would eventually end up like this. Because he knew that he just wanted to be away from anyone that he cared about."

"But when he did that, we couldn't take care of him," Caroline said as the tears started.

"Mr. David is a smart and kind man. His pride got in the way of him thinking clearly. As fate would have it, we now have our chance. We can take care of him now as best we can."

Days passed through the Christmas holiday as the news crews came and went. *America Nation News* sent their reporter that covered the original story to do the follow up.

Zachary showed up to say good-bye. He made arrangements for Lisa Bennett and Barbara Killingly to be there as well. Barbara's parents were not comfortable traveling, so Zachary sent them regular updates.

In the early morning pre-dawn hours of January second of the new year, David opened his eyes somewhat for the first time since Maria arrived. As he stirred, she woke up and immediately took his hand.

"Is my work done?" he asked weakly without really opening his eyes completely.

"You have done as much as anyone can do. You are entitled to your rest."

He opened his eyes more and stared straight into the small light that illuminated one of the monitors. His field of vision flooded with white light.

"A bright sunrise," he said as the monitors flat lined.

Epilogue

Maria pulled the blinds down on the front entrance door at Charlotte's Place and let down her hair as she turned the lock.

Jim Davenport and his wife were sitting at the counter with Kevin McNally and his wife.

Caroline walked out of the backroom and sat on the serving side of the counter.

"Happy seventeenth birthday, Caroline," Jim said as Maria walked over and got the cake ready and lit all eighteen candles.

"Rebecca called earlier," Maria said to her daughter as she was finishing up. "She is still tied up with some newsletter pieces she needs to get done for Mr. Taylor, but she is working from home today rather than the El Paso offices. She said she would try to stop by later tonight if it does not get too late."

Caroline smiled as she looked at the wall nearest the telephone where the pictures of Charlotte Cassidy, Mel Porter, and Michael Anderson, the man they knew as David Stephenson, were displayed.

As Maria walked over with the cake they all started singing happy birthday and with tradition, Caroline made a wish and blew out all seventeen candles and the extra one for the upcoming year.

As they cut up the cake to enjoy it, a car pulled into the side parking lot and shut off. Maria walked out toward the side door to open it as the door had been locked because it was after hours.

An older looking gentleman stepped in holding a folder and some paperwork. He reached up and took off his hat.

"Good evening. My name is Adam Owens. I represent Berucci, Samson and McGuire, Attorneys at Law. I have some paperwork for a Caroline Moreno and a Maria Moreno."

"I'm Caroline," Caroline responded as she walked around the counter. "My mother is Maria." Caroline pointed to her mother.

"Thank you. I am here to inform you of the transfer of a trust effective this date and per this information included here," he said as he handed the two large manila envelopes over to each of them. Attached to the front of each was a faded white number ten envelope. "Please review the attached letters first, then the contents in the larger envelopes. I am available to answer all and any questions before I depart."

"Should we go, Maria? Do you need some time to look this over?" Jim asked, as he was prepared to stand up.

"No, please stay and enjoy the birthday cake. I am sure we will be just a few moments," Maria responded as she looked at her daughter.

The two of them walked over to the far end of the customer side of the counter and sat down with the packages.

Maria opened up the small faded white envelope on the exterior marked 'personal' and took the letter out to read as Caroline looked on.

Dear Maria,

I am sending you this letter after your thirty-fifth birthday, as it should arrive on Caroline's seventeenth, along with a letter for her.

It will be many years since I entered and left your lives. I am hopeful that you did, in fact, love me enough to forgive me for leaving. There are undoubtedly many things I should have told you then and perhaps now as well.

It is probably simpler to keep things to just a few core facts.

I never meant to fall in love with you. As I had mentioned, I never meant to stay. I couldn't. When I arrived in Westville, I was already diagnosed as being terminally ill and well past my survival limitation. My time remaining at that point wasn't being measured in months anymore. It was barely weeks and days. All of it was borrowed time.

Despite all of that, I fell in love with you as much as any man loves a woman. I loved Caroline like my own daughter. I know both of these things to be true because I had a wife and daughter, and I lost them both to a horrible accident. I was never the same after that. I never wanted a loss like that for anyone else. Certain things simply happen in life. Losing loved ones is one of those things. I knew I was going to die and I didn't want anyone going through a pain and loss like that because of me.

I realize that it might seem selfish, presumptuous, and perhaps not correctly my decision to make. I hope you'll forgive me for doing so anyway.

Enclosed with this letter are legal documents that transfer the remainder of my estate, whatever I did not need through the end of my days, to you and Caroline.

It is my hope that it will make the remainder of both your lives easier.

"What you have in your heart, what you pass onto others, while you are here and after you are gone, matters more than anything else."

I love you.

David

As they both finished Maria's letter, they looked at one another. Caroline then looked at her letter and opened it.

Dear Caroline,

I write this letter to you when you are still eight years old and just ahead of your ninth birthday.

I see a wonderfully balanced child who is gifted and bright, who thinks about others more than she thinks of herself.

You are to receive this letter on your seventeenth birthday. Despite the fact that you will be becoming a young woman at that time, I would hope your life is not much different than it was when you were a child and I was there in Westville. I would imagine that you are sitting at Charlotte's Place surrounded by family and friends on your birthday.

I am sure you were confused and upset at the time because I left and how I decided to leave. I am confident that your mother took the time to explain it to you as best she could. She didn't have all of the information at the time, but she will have the rest of it provided to her with her letter that she will also receive today. I would expect in the fullness of time, and if it is still of relevance, that she will give those details to you.

What I do want you to know is I felt it was very important for me to go. If I didn't feel it was absolutely necessary, I would have otherwise stayed. I came to love you and your mother very much.

You had such an adult grasp of things as a child without all the adult complications. I hope you were able to keep that. You cannot control life. In most cases, it just happens to you. You can control how it affects you. I am confident you will, as best you can, meet all of your challenges head on and in a positive manner.

There are so many things I would like to say to you. I really feel that, when I walked away, I lost my right to do so. I will take the chance to leave you with one final thought, however.

No one is destined for greatness. That should not deter you from attempting to achieve great things.

I love you, Caroline.

David.

Caroline folded the letter gently and put it back in the envelope.

Maria opened hers up again and read one line aloud. "'What you have in your heart, what you pass onto others, while you are here and after you are gone, matters more than anything else.' He sure knew how to do that, didn't he?"

Caroline smiled at her mother and they both turned and looked at his picture hanging on the wall.

CPSIA information can be obtained at www.ICGtesting.com
Printed in the USA
BVOW09s0017121114

374702BV00001B/1/P